THE STARS WE STEAL

ALSO BY ALEXA DONNE
AND AVAILABLE FROM TITAN BOOKS

Brightly Burning

THE STARS WE STEAL

ALEXA DONNE

TITAN BOOKS

THE STARS WE STEAL
Print edition ISBN: 9781789090185
E-book edition ISBN: 9781789090192

Published by Titan Books
A division of Titan Publishing Group Ltd
144 Southwark Street, London SE1 0UP
www.titanbooks.com

First edition: February 2020
10 9 8 7 6 5 4 3 2 1

Names, places and incidents are either products of the author's imagination or used fictitiously. Any resemblance to actual persons, living or dead (except for satirical purposes), is entirely coincidental.

A CIP catalogue record for this title is available from the British Library.

Printed and bound by CPI Group (UK) Ltd, Croydon, CR0 4YY

For Jane, who always impeccably balanced feeling with wit, and inspired a million real life heroines

1

The extravagance made my teeth hurt.

Fractures of light bounced off diamonds set into tiaras and other baubles that were as impractical as the silk frocks and dress jackets swimming about the room. Champagne flutes and vodka shots flew by on trays lofted high by servants dressed in simple black bodysuits, casting the partygoers into even more ridiculous relief. This wasn't an imperial ballroom in a great royal palace in Sweden—it was just modeled to look like one. The aim was to forget where we were and why. Everyone accomplished that beautifully.

I retreated farther into a gilded archway I'd made my temporary home, shuddering to think about the cold vacuum of space that hung ominously beyond the confines of this cushy spaceship. A woman in an elaborately tiered and poofed ball gown waltzed past me as she let out a high-pitched laugh. Pain shot through my jaw. *Unclench your teeth, Leo,* I scolded myself.

I glanced down at the name tag on my chest and felt everything go tight again. All the champagne and dancing in the world couldn't erase the reason I was here, why I was hiding in the back corner of a ludicrous ballroom in the center of a ludicrous spaceship.

Tonight was the start of the official Valg Season, a barbaric courtship ritual we engaged in every five years so the rich could avoid marrying their cousins.

All the eligible girls and boys wore name tags to the opening ball so that we could better check out the specimens on offer. Mine read: *Princess Leonie Kolburg, 19,* Prinzessin Sofi. Title, name, age, ship of origin—all the relevant details. What it should have said: *Princess of Nowhere because we're in space, not on Earth; Leonie Kolburg, 19, from a ship rapidly falling apart, honestly a bit destitute, seeking a wealthy spouse by order of her father.* But that would have been too wordy.

Cornflower-blue taffeta silk spilled over my hips, the floor-length fabric whispering over the pointed toes of matching heels. My hair was twisted up into a braided crown, my face painted to simulate the flush of sun-kissed health. At least I had refused the tiara my sister had offered up. Despite what my father, my sister, Carina, and my name tag insisted, I was no princess. Old-World royal titles are meaningless in space.

Or should be, I thought. The reality on board was different, and I knew I was a target for any boy looking for his ticket to the upper echelons of power. It made me sick to my stomach. I was a commodity in a pretty dress, on display for all to see.

I drifted back into a shadowy alcove, hoping I could

disappear. As if on cue, I caught the gaze of an absurdly attractive boy with short black hair and deep golden eyes. I stared a beat too long, and he smirked at me. Heat rushed to my cheeks, and I flicked my gaze away.

And there was my father, grabbing another glass of champagne we couldn't afford. I felt tension winding its way back up my spine. I'd crunched the budgets six ways to Sunday, and in no iteration could we afford to supply the party with champagne imported from the *Versailles*. But Father had insisted; it was a way of displaying our nonexistent wealth and would hopefully make me a more attractive candidate for marriage. I inched closer to where Father was sucking up to a count, trying to spin our circumstances in the right light.

"Oh, we've grown bored of our ship, so we figured, why not give some commoners a thrill, rent it out for a few months?" He prattled on, his crown slipping forward on his temple. His clipped consonants, meant to emphasize his high-class accent, were dimmed somewhat by the way he slurred his *s*'s. He had to be at least six drinks in. "It's the perfect excuse to visit our dear cousins here and enjoy the Valg Season in style! And a banner anniversary year, to boot! To our one hundred and seventieth!"

One hundred and seventy years in space. The fleet, not us personally, though sometimes it felt as if I'd been up here that long. I allowed myself a fanciful moment, imagining vampires in space.

Every day was just another one spent in an exquisitely appointed tin can, waiting for our planet to thaw. I grabbed a glass of champagne as a tray went past and took a gulp. The money was spent, so I might as well.

"Leo, darling, why are you sulking on the sidelines?" My cousin Klara appeared before me like magic, a vision in sparkling white-and-silver brocade. The way her lips turned down slightly in rebuke felt familiar. Her hazel eyes always danced with a certain knowing, her lips most frequently quirked into a smile, complementing the perfect symmetry of her face. Only a few years older than I, twenty-one to my only-just nineteen, Klara presided over parties like the princess she was, cool and elegant, with a keen sense of a good time.

"You should dance," she said, nodding at the center of the dance floor. "There are plenty of eligible young men who would happily partner you."

"'Eligible' isn't enough. Hasn't father told you? I'm to be flung in the direction of money, above all else." I took a bracing sip of champagne.

Klara frowned again. "I'm certain several of them have more than enough digicoin to satisfy him. If you would only get to know some of them, you might find someone you like . . ."

A sickening déjà vu came over me: Klara speaking with me in hushed tones at another extravagant party, defending my father's wishes, convincing me I did not know my own heart. I shook away the thought.

"And what about you? You're older than I am. Isn't this your last Valg Season?"

She visibly tensed at the reminder. I should have felt

bad, but she'd kicked things off by rubbing salt in my own, similar wound.

"I'm in no rush to marry, regardless of what my mother thinks. There's time." Klara's voice was tight. "She is in good health, and we have no financial problems."

"What about your apprenticeship? I thought you said a strategic marriage was important. Surely there's some faded prince or duke with political aspirations who might tempt you." Klara's mother was captain, and Klara had been learning the ropes from her for the past two years. Klara remained optimistic that if she worked hard enough, she could step into the role before she was twenty-five. Me, I assumed Klara would acquire the captainship at whatever age her mother finally shuffled off this mortal coil. *From her cold, dead hands* was a phrase that sprang to mind.

"I see the same people all the time. Boys I grew up with bore me." She picked at a perfectly manicured nail. "I should travel outside the Season, perhaps to the *Lady Liberty* or *Nikkei,* but I've heard of filthy rogues attacking people from ships like ours, stealing their credentials for travel visas."

"Nonsense," I said. "The overcrowding can't possibly be that bad. Sounds like a tale told to scare you out of traveling."

"It sounds believable to me."

"Why bother traveling later when everyone's come here now?

The pickings will get slim once the Season is over."

"Pickings are slim in the Season, too," Klara countered. "Lots of man-children with big dreams of stepping over their future wife to grasp at power. I was as wise to it at sixteen as I am at twenty-one. I can't believe my mother made me do it last time. Who marries that young?"

"Carina plans on trying," I said, indicating my baby sister, freshly sixteen and enjoying herself immensely. Her aim seemed to be to dance with every single boy here. She was on her sixth dance partner at least.

"I'm surprised you're letting her take part. Aren't you worried she might steal your best prospects? This is your last-and-best chance, isn't it?"

I ignored the digs, both of them, and bitterly enjoyed the irony of Klara lecturing me on last chances when she was being so nonchalant about the Season. We both knew, despite her protests, that the captain—her mother—was going to make her pick *someone* to marry. This was how we sparred, though, cousins and friends but also often competitors. Captain Lind had the most annoying habit of praising me for my best traits whilst criticizing Klara for lacking them. And my father would, in turn, chastise me for not being as pretty, thin, and socially adept as my cousin. The reality was, we were both participating in the Season whether we liked it or not. And while neither of us seemed to like it much, we were each encouraging the other to chin up and try. How exhausting.

We fell into companionable silence, watching the revelry on the dance floor as we kept court on the side. Carina moved on to her seventh dance partner. And then there was a sound to my left, like someone clearing his throat. I turned to find those deep golden eyes wickedly glinting and the boy attached to them performing a slight bow.

"May I have the honor of a dance?" he asked. I made note of his British accent and his name tag. *Daniel Turan,* it read, and he was from the *Empire.* I looked to my left, to my right, and behind me. Surely he had meant to ask someone else? Finally, I looked across the way, catching a haughty brunette and a ginger boy smirking over at us, whispering to each other. Of course, a little prank—the model asking me to dance so that everyone could laugh at me when I said yes and he suddenly changed his mind. I wasn't born yesterday.

"No, thank you," I said. "But my cousin Klara would love to!" I shoved her at him before either could protest, and I scurried off in the opposite direction.

It was a shame, really, because I did love to dance. Well, screw it. I would dance by myself, far away from the end of the room where Klara was now awkwardly swaying with the British boy. They looked good together, though she towered over him in her heels.

I found my own spot on the dance floor and got into the zone. Much like the rococo ballroom built smack-dab in the middle of a chrome-and-steel spaceship, the music was decidedly anachronistic. I'd seen plenty of movies about royalty and balls, the music supplied by an orchestra, couples perfecting a crisp waltz. But this party was on the *Scandinavian,* and it honored its most recent musical roots with a DJ who spun layered electronic beats with catchy melodies sung on top. I mouthed familiar words as I made my way into the throng of dancers. I lost myself to the music, swaying my hips and bobbing my head in time to the beat, working up a light sweat.

"Princess Leonie!" a recognizable voice interrupted my trance-like focus. I had hoped a stonefaced expression and refusal to meet anyone's eye would keep people from talking to me, but alas. I spun around to face him.

"Lukas," I said through clenched teeth and a forced smile, "you know I hate that name." I meant both the royal moniker and my full name. Most people called me Leo.

"Just showing my respect," he simpered, grabbing my hand with clammy fingers and bowing into a kiss, which he planted across my knuckles. I tolerated it for a beat, then wrested my hand away. I wiped it surreptitiously on the back of my dress. "Will you dance with me?" he asked, unfazed. His eyes kept flicking between my face and my cleavage, so it wasn't like he noticed the whereabouts of my hand, anyway.

I hesitated, catching my father's attention from the sidelines. Eyes with calculating focus bored into mine, his message clear: *Say yes.* Lukas was only a baron, but his family had plenty of digicoin, thanks to some smart business ventures. With a resigned sigh, I nodded, allowing him into my personal dance bubble.

Then he grabbed me by the small of my back, pulling our bodies close, and I immediately regretted everything. I'd give him one song.

I made it to the bridge. That's when I caught sight of Carina entering the ballroom—when had she left?—her eyes searching the crowd until they locked with mine. Furrowed concentration was replaced with her usual easy smile. At least four boys turned to stare, two taking steps to ask her to dance, but she breezed past them, heading for me like a rocket toward its destination.

"Leo, I need you!" she said breezily, throwing Lukas and his closeness to me a look before grabbing my arm and obligingly pulling me free. "The renters have arrived."

"Can't you see to them?" I asked. Carina shook her head. "You're the only one who knows how to use the bio-lock. I let the renters in but can't figure it out." My little sister batted her eyelashes at me, and, as always, I bent too easily. When my father acted like a child, I could fully resent him for it, but Carina's age gave her an excuse for being clueless. Though, I reminded myself, at sixteen I'd been taking care of most of the family affairs for several years. Regardless, I was happy to take a break. We'd been here nearly three hours, and my feet hurt.

"You're the best, Leo!" Carina kissed me on the cheek and moved back into the throng to find a dance partner. I saw her pointedly reject Lukas and chuckled to myself as I made my way toward the exit. At the door, I turned one last time to check that she'd settled well with someone who wasn't a creep.

That's when I saw him. My heart stuttered and stopped in my chest.

Square spectacles half obscuring soft grayish-blue eyes; strong, regal nose; mouth set in a firm line, rendering his expression carefully neutral. He was always neutral until he let a smile light up his face, telling me I was brilliant and that he loved me. I blinked hard, sure I was imagining him. And when I looked up again, he was gone.

I forced myself to take several deep breaths, then used the rhythmic click of my heels as I walked to reset my heart's cadence to normal. Elliot wasn't here. He wouldn't come back. Would he? The security personnel guarding the ballroom doors nodded silently as I passed from the royal quarters to the *Scandinavian*'s public decks, making my way aft and up to where our family ship, the *Prinzessin Sofi*, was docked. We'd been here for years, living off the generous hospitality of our cousins—large ships in the fleet charged private vessels like ours docking fees as a matter of course, but we were family, and thus Captain Lind reluctantly waived them. Otherwise we'd be destitute and would likely have to give up the *Sofi*, our home. We were struggling to keep her up in repairs as it was.

The Valg presented a unique opportunity to earn some extra digicoin. A week ago, I'd received a reply to my advertisement of a ship for rent from a Captain Orlov of the *Saint Petersburg*, traveling with his family and some friends. He hadn't mentioned the Valg Season, and I didn't pry for more details, happy for the money, though I was curious. If he had the title of captain, wasn't he needed on his own ship?

As I rounded the last corner, clipping through the familiar frosted white corridor to our decidedly dingier chrome door, a warm voice boomed. "You must be Miss Kolburg. Maxim Orlov." A large hand engulfed mine in a firm-gripped handshake, while mirthful, pale eyes leveled with mine. He seemed short for a Russian—he was my height, an even five foot eleven. I'd heard they were a ship of giants, not unlike those on the *Scandinavian*. I was one of the shorter ladies. I took in his companions. One was a pretty woman who looked about midtwenties, and the other was an equally handsome dark-haired man the same age as the captain—early thirties?

"Welcome, Captain Orlov," I said, turning to the woman. "This must be your wife?" To my surprise, all three laughed as if I'd told the most hysterical joke.

"Evgenia Orlova," she said. "Maxim is my brother."

My cheeks heated furiously as I stammered out an apology. "An easy mistake," the captain said. "And you may call me Max. This is Ewan Reid, my husband." He indicated the other man.

"Pleased to meet you," Ewan said, a lilt to his tone that was clearly not Russian. He must have caught my puzzlement. "It's Scottish."

"Are you from the *Empire*?" I asked.

"*The Islay,* a private ship, not unlike your own, by way of the *Saint Petersburg.*"

"Thank you for coming so quickly," Captain Max said. "Your sister escorted us here from our transport, but you are apparently the keeper of the keys, so to speak."

I nodded. "I'll get all your bio scans coded in so you can come and go as you please."

"Perfect," Max said. "We're just waiting for one more person. He slipped away to check out the party."

"Eager to mingle with the ladies," Evgenia said with a laugh. "You judge me too harshly, Evy," said a voice I recognized immediately. Soft and firm and infuriatingly calm.

He rounded the corner, and my breath caught. I hadn't imagined him at all. It was the boy whose heart I'd broken and for whom my heart still fluttered.

It was Elliot.

2

I tried to swallow past the lump in my throat as my heart thudded hard in my chest. Everyone else was oblivious. "Wentworth!" Max bellowed. "Excellent timing. Now we can get ourselves settled and finally go to bed."

"But I wanted to go to the party," Evgenia said with an exaggerated pout.

"It'll be going a few hours more, at least," I said, careful to keep my tone even, my eyes locked on anyone except Elliot. I could not betray my panic, nor could I bear to look at him.

"They have champagne," Elliot said, half-breathless beside me. I risked a quick glance, catching his lopsided grin paired with my favorite dimple. Still the perfect mix of awkward and beautiful. "And vodka."

"But no whiskey?" Ewan asked. "Heathens." Everyone laughed at a joke I did not understand.

"So I can get all of you set up on the bio-scan system now." I unlocked the door with my own fingerprints and led them through the loading bay to the aft control room. I stayed in front, throwing my shoulders back, affecting confidence, resisting the urge to check my hair.

"Maybe you're still in the system, El," Evgenia said as we came to a stop beside the control panel. "You two know each other, right?"

Finally I met Elliot's eyes. Carefully controlled fire burned behind his glasses. It caught me off-guard, though it shouldn't have. Of course he hated me now. I stammered out my response. "Uh, yes, of course. I wasn't sure you remembered me," I lied poorly, and for no good reason but for being stupidly blindsided by his disdain, yet Elliot did not betray me. He replied tightly.

"Good to see you again, Princess Leonie."

His words were a dagger jabbed into my rib cage and twisted just so. *Princess Leonie.* Formal, and the name he knew very well I hated. In return, I gave a small curtsy, playing the princess he wished me to be. I could be formal too.

"Unfortunately your bio scan was erased when you left. But setting up a new one is easy. Here." I pressed my index finger and thumb to the bio scan, then keyed in a code set, followed by my admin password. "Now you place your fingers on the scanner." Elliot did so, hovering close. I breathed in the faint scent of smoke and some spice I could not name, a swooping sadness tugging at my insides. He'd left me, and now he even *smelled* different. This was not my Elliot. "There, all done," I said.

"Me next!" Evgenia jumped forward. "So you and I can

THE STARS WE STEAL

go enjoy the party." She nudged Elliot's shoulder and threw him a wink. He smiled, and my insides swirled, champagne threatening its way up my throat.

"Of course," I ground out, repeating the process for her, though I miscoded my admin password twice. Elliot and Evgenia left, leaving me heartsick yet relieved. I took care of Max and Ewan in short order.

"Thank you, Your Highness," Max said as I finished him off. "Oh, please don't call me that," I begged as we moved out into the corridor. "I hate titles. Feel free to use pomp and circumstance with my father. He's a bit . . . old-fashioned. But please call me Leo."

Max nodded. "Good name, Leo. Like the lion."

"I'm more like a kitten," I joked.

"Don't sell yourself short." He patted me on the shoulder.

"So are you guys here for the Valg Season?" I made small talk as they walked me to the exit.

Max and Ewan shared a look that was meaningful only to the two of them. "Yes," Maxim replied with mild hesitance. "Those two are. Ewan and I are here to drum up some new business, I suppose you could say."

"Oh? What is it that you do?" I asked, forcing a bright nonchalance into my tone. Beneath that, my heart wrenched in my chest. Elliot was here to find a spouse.

"Transports," Maxim replied. "Elliot insisted we rent somewhere nicer for the Season, but we've got our usual vessel docked here. Every so often we'll jet off for a few days on a job."

"So that explained the Captain thing. Well, have a good night," I said. "If you need anything, you can ping me anytime. You'll find tab consoles in every room."

"We definitely will," Ewan said with a broad smile, and then finally I was able to extricate myself. Passing back through the loading bay, I estimated how long I'd have to stay at the party before I could turn in for bed. If I left before one in the morning, my father would whine for days about my lack of effort in securing our fortunes, never mind that I was the only family member coming up with concrete solutions. The four weeks' rent from the Orlovs would float us for the rest of the year, at least, with just enough left over that I could invest in our long-term solution: a patent for my water-filtration system.

If I could just sell it to another ship, the license fees would solve all our financial problems. I would still have to marry eventually, but I could put it off until the next Season, and as the one with money, I would have my choice of beaus. But filing the patent would require a trip to the *Olympus,* whose docking fees I could not afford, and then still more fees to file the patent itself.

I reminded myself of the overwhelming practicality of my rental plan as I marched with somber steps toward the exit. Leaving home was never easy.

"We thought we'd wait for you!" a voice chirped as I stepped out into the *Scandinavian*'s corridor. I yelped, startling off-balance, falling right into *him.* Elliot. I blinked past my panic, bringing a smiling Evgenia into focus, and quickly righted

THE STARS WE STEAL

myself, away from Elliot, who brushed a hand down his shoulder as if I'd burned him.

"Oh, you didn't have to do that—"

"Nonsense! You're the closest we have to a friend on board, and this way we can get to know one another!" Evgenia linked arms with me, pulling me into a stroll. "Your dress is exquisite, by the way."

"Thanks," I mumbled. "Yours too."

"Oh, this old thing?" She laughed it off, as if the art deco–inspired number hadn't cost a fortune. It had to be an Old-Earth antique. The silver beading was worn a bit on the cap sleeves and drop waist, but nothing detracted from the delicate handiwork. It hugged in all the right places, the sea-foam-green chiffon underlayer complementing her similarly hued eyes. "Luckily I'm always a bit overdressed for travel," she conceded with a laugh. She'd fit right in among the fading royal families of Europe. New money among old. "I did make Elliot here change, though."

Against my better judgment, I turned to look at him as he followed along behind us, even though I'd already seen what he was wearing. It was standard evening attire, fancier than anything he'd ever owned before, when I knew him. The waistcoat and pants had the look of custom-tailored pieces, and he cut a dashing figure in them. I also noted that his glasses had new, expensive-looking frames. Wealth suited him. Too well.

I turned away to hide the blush of my cheeks. We were in the *Scandinavian* proper now, away from the dingy docking area. Everything was sleek and white, lights always high enough to capture the details. I didn't want him to know how flustered I was. "So what did we miss?" Evgenia asked. "We tried to make it before the opening Valg party but got held up by a very annoying mid-transport visa check."

"What's that?" I asked. Elliot's clipped reply came from behind. "The *Olympus* has taken to stopping free-flying transport ships and demanding their papers. To ensure no one is going where they shouldn't be. Wouldn't want the rabble mixing with the well-to-do, and all that."

"Which is silly." Evgenia's tone was bright, but we were still linked by the arms, and I could feel her tense up. "I simply informed them that we were traveling for the Valg, and that I am twenty-four years old and not getting any younger, and of course they understood."

It was clearly a joke, and accordingly, I managed a small, forced laugh. But the chill coming off Elliot practically set my breath visible in the air before me.

"Well, you've not missed much at all." I tried to recover. "Just a bit of champagne and dancing. Captain Lind always reserves her speeches for a few hours into any party, to capitalize on the most people being there. You're likely right on time."

"Are her speeches particularly good, then?"

"She's rather pedantic and full of herself, actually," I replied.

"But she gives such great advice," Elliot cut in again. I didn't have to look back to see his sneer—it came through in every syllable. He knew my aunt had been one of the main people to talk me out of marrying him.

To my left, I caught Evgenia's brow furrow in confusion. She could tell Elliot was not happy about something, but it was clear she lacked context. So he hadn't told her about us. That we'd been engaged to be married—for twelve hours, at least—until I'd broken it off, upon receiving an earful from my aunt, father, and cousin.

"Anyway," I continued, attempting to brush it off, "tonight is just speeches and a bit of dancing, but things don't really start for a few days, when the parents leave."

"Have you done a Valg Season before?" Evgenia asked. "You seem to know a lot about it."

"Oh, no. I'm only nineteen, so I was too young the last time. I just read a lot about it. I like to be prepared." The more I knew, the better I could avoid the worst of it.

"So you're participating?" Elliot appeared beside us, expression carefully neutral. I schooled my features as well.

"Yes. Father insisted," I said.

"And you listened to him?" Evgenia tittered. "My father has all sorts of ideas about me and whom I should marry, but I simply ignore him."

"Leo's not that kind of girl," Elliot said, his tone cutting like knives. Evgenia barreled on, oblivious.

"This place is incredible." Her head whipped in every which direction. "Everything is so . . . clean."

"The *Saint Petersburg* isn't like this?" I asked, happy for the change of subject. I hurried a few paces ahead, putting distance between Elliot and myself again.

"It's far more weathered," she replied. "And we tend toward a more ... practical build." I felt a tug on my arm as she steered us to the left so she could run her fingers over the wall. "All this façade work makes her prettier, but no stronger. What a waste of money and manpower, no? Your people could have built two ships instead of only one."

"Oh, they weren't my people," I said as we continued along. "We're German." I felt silly even saying it. National affiliations were pretty meaningless now. We associated ourselves with the ships whence we hailed, regardless of our countries of origin. I'd lived attached to the *Scandinavian* for more than a decade now.

"Tell me, Evy." Elliot pulled up level with us, taking her other arm. "Did the Russian oligarchs build a second ship?"

"You know I'm only kidding, El," she said, dropping any pretense of outrage. "We both know they built extravagant private ships too. It was all the rage. And now that we're rich, we get to enjoy the spoils!" She broke off into a light skip as we neared the security checkpoint outside the ballroom doors.

"*Plus ça change, plus c'est la même chose,*" Elliot muttered under his breath.

"When did you learn French?" I asked. He cast me a withering look that hollowed out my stomach like acid and walked ahead. There was no time to dwell on it or pry. We'd reached the two towering security guards, who nodded upon seeing me—I'd attended enough parties to be well-known. All I had to do was tell them Evgenia and Elliot were with me, and they waved us through.

"How did you get through before?" I dared to ask Elliot, who just shrugged, nonchalant.

"Guess I look the part now."

As soon as he said it, I looked again, just for a second, before scolding myself to stop. Elliot strode with a confidence he'd never had before. In three short years, he'd transformed from the sweet, awkward boy of sixteen to a cool and suave nineteen. Had I changed as drastically? I wore the same silly frocks, felt the same resigned exasperation with my father and sister's reckless spending. What did he think of me?

Right now? Clearly nothing.

"Let's mingle," he said as we entered the ballroom, offering his arm to Evgenia and promptly whisking her away. I stood in the door in a daze. They weren't even wearing name tags. I would have introduced them to the Valg social liaison, gotten them set up, if they hadn't been so eager to leave me.

"Was that Elliot Wentworth?" Carina rushed up, cheeks flushed at the hint of scandal, or perhaps it was from dancing. She whipped her head around, craning to see him. "He grew up," she said in apparent positive assessment. I rolled my eyes at the obtuse comment. Of course he'd grown up, as had she. Three years will do that. "What is he doing here?"

"He came with our new renters."

A tray of drinks whizzed by, the server pausing just long enough for me to grab two glasses. Carina went for one, but I shook my head at her, downing one glass in a series of gulps, leaving the second for me to nurse.

"Jeez, Leo, weren't you the one complaining earlier about

Father ordering the stuff? Now you're the lush."

So she *did* notice our financial woes, as well as boys.

"I've eaten my weight in hors d'oeuvres. I can take it." I took another sip as a hole opened up in the crowd, giving me a perfect view to Elliot bowing, kissing the gloved hand of Asta Madsen. "Let's dance." I changed tack, grabbing Carina by the hand and dragging her along behind me. I finished the champagne along the way, depositing the empty glass on a nearby balustrade.

I felt the bassline in my bones, threw my head back and my hands up, letting the music wash through me. Only an hour ago, I'd been right here, my only care Lukas's wandering hands and eyes on me, my father winking from the sidelines. Now it was Elliot standing by, his eyes and hands interested in other girls. I refused to look, spinning, jumping, twirling Carina at intervals, sure to keep my back to wherever he and Evgenia were.

Then, suddenly, the music screeched to a stop. I was mid-spin and stumbled gracelessly to a halt, surprised to find a steady hand on my arm, preventing me from face-planting on the floor. I looked up at my savior. Then down. He was shorter than I was—it was the boy from earlier, the one who had asked me to dance, only to be shunted onto my cousin. I checked his name tag again. Daniel from the *Empire*. Where had he come from? I mumbled a thank-you and turned back to my sister, who looked more than a little put out.

"When will they turn the music back on?" Carina pouted.

Our ears were treated to the muffled tap of someone's fingers on the microphone instead.

"Good evening, ladies and gentlemen," came the precise, crisp voice of Captain Lind. I sighed and turned toward the stage. On a large screen behind my aunt was the Valg logo—a golden rose emblem intertwined with an elaborate V—which shimmered and pulsed in time to a silent beat. She spotted me immediately and gave me a nod, ruling out any chance I had to duck out and skip what was sure to be a long, bombastic speech about the Valg, and marriage, and family.

She did not disappoint.

"Many years ago, it became clear that in order to keep our population healthy and thriving, we needed a solution for finding . . . suitable partners. The *Scandinavian* was happy to host the first of these illustrious matching events, which is how we all got stuck with such a dreary name as the Valg." She paused for the polite smattering of laughter that she clearly had expected.

"Valg means 'choice' in Norwegian and Danish. And, yes, we Swedes did protest, but *Val* just doesn't have quite the same ring to it!"

Another pause, more polite laughter.

"Over the next four weeks, you young people will be faced with many options. Everything will culminate in you making the most important decision of your life: who to marry."

I groaned, seemingly in stereo. I twisted around to find Daniel, still beside me, who apparently agreed with my sentiment.

"I encourage you to cast a wide net and make good *choices*." Captain Lind paused once more, but this time no one got the joke. "Anyway," she recovered smoothly, "thank you so much for being with us, and—"

There was an electric *snap*, and then the entire ballroom was plunged into darkness. Some people screamed; beside me, my sister drew in a sharp breath and dug her fingers into my arm. The blackness lingered ten seconds, then twenty, and the cascade of confused murmurs crescendoed to worried cries.

"Everyone remain calm! Stay where you are so there is no stampede," Captain Lind shouted above the din. Her mic wasn't working.

"The doors are locked!" someone yelled from the ballroom entrance.

"Check the others," the captain commanded, and after a tense moment, the same report echoed back from the four corners of the room.

Then the large digital screen affixed behind the stage blinked on, casting a pale glow across two hundred faces. A hush fell over the room as we read the words splashed across the screen in big, bold letters:

MURDERERS.

3

"Leo, what's happening?" Carina whispered in my ear as my eyes clawed over the word again and again.

Murderers.

It was an accusation. My brain started clicking as I pieced it all together. The screen, the doors—we had been hacked in order for someone to send us a message.

But who?

And then the word faded from the screen and was replaced by a woman with drab, stringy hair and deep, dark circles under her eyes. She looked exhausted, wrung out.

"Now that I have your attention, we need to talk," the woman said.

"Find them now!" I heard my aunt hiss from the stage, though I didn't know how far she expected security to get if they couldn't leave the room. We were a captive audience, with no choice but to focus on the screen.

"My name is Lena," the woman onscreen said, "though

of course you all don't care enough to give me food, so why would you care to know my name? Regardless, my parents taught me to be polite, so you have my name, and my apologies for interrupting your celebration. I wish I could be there, but you all like to restrict visas, so it was impossible to join you. Happily for me, your system was easy to hack."

My eyes flitted over to my aunt, who was now hunched at the back of the stage, fingers flying over a tab unit, clearly trying to put a stop to this. She was brilliant but no match against hackers, so Lena continued on.

"Don't worry, tonight's program will be short. I just want to share with you a little glimpse of how some of the other half of the fleet has been living. Given that a prudent marriage appears to be your foremost concern, I assume none of you are aware of the exact cost of your lifestyle. Allow me to show you."

With that, the video changed, the screen flooding with images of human misery. Packed medical wards and insufficient supplies. Children weeping at a funeral—one could only assume their parents'. Signage forbidding the consumption of fruits and vegetables "reserved exclusively for the *Empire*." A government memo about a series of brownouts on the *Stalwart*. A sweeping shot of an endless line of emaciated people. There were even graphs comparing the population-to-food ratios of several ships. The *Scandinavian* had only three hundred permanent residents compared to the *Saint Petersburg*'s twelve hundred. Both ships received the same amount of food.

Shame seared hot through me. I thought about my dramatics over having meat less often and the occasional blackout because Father and Carina used electricity a little too enthusiastically. It was so easy for me to jaunt over to the *Scandinavian* and enjoy my extended family's finery. People in the fleet were starving while we lived like queens. And pretended we still were.

Lena's face appeared once more.

"Amazing how none of this has appeared in the media. Now you know." She smiled, sickly sweet. "Many of the people in this room play a part in government. If you wanted to, you could change everything. Fairly distribute resources. Allow ships with overcrowded populations to migrate to less crowded ships. But I won't bore you any longer. I'm sure you want to get back to your party. Just know that we know how to get in now. Cheers."

Lena lifted an empty hand, as if to toast us, further driving home the point. I imagined many hands in the room tipping back their champagne flutes, draining them dry.

The screen went black, then sparked orange at the edges. Something sizzled, then cracked, and the giant screen burst into flames. Everything exploded into noise and movement. The crowd behind me retreated, then surged. The doors were locked, but damned if everyone wasn't making a break for them anyway. I felt my knees buckle as bodies behind me pressed in; I was so close to the stage, I could feel the heat from the flames on my skin. Someone behind me—someone strong—held me upright, and I grabbed tightly onto my sister, keeping her with me. Captain Lind had made a mad dash for the nearest bar, grasped a giant pitcher of water, and flung it at the screen, but it only tempered the flames.

Then, suddenly, there was light—the doors were open again.

"Everyone, go back to your rooms. Go! Now!" Captain Lind commanded into the mic, now turned back on. And then she flew from the stage, pushing for the exit herself.

Someone tugged on my arm—Daniel—and he urged me to follow him to safety, but Carina's grip was tighter, and she had other ideas. We fled under the cover of chaos, heading for the back of the ballroom to avoid the bottlenecks at the side doors. My apologies got lost in the shuffle. Then my sister got lost too. I felt her wrenched away from me, a reveler built like a tank pushing his way through our clasped hands. I screamed her name, straining to hear mine in return, but it was too loud; too many people were running in all directions.

I made my way out of the throttle of people, along the back wall, straining up on my very tiptoes to peer over the crowd to try to find my sister. But this was the *Scandinavian,* so Tall and Blond was a calling card for far too many women here. I couldn't spot her.

I had to go on the way we'd been heading. I could catch up with Carina, who was probably just ahead of me, taking our favorite shortcut. Midship was a maze of ballrooms, libraries, galleries, and lounges stacked back-to-back, and cutting through them all was the quickest way to the forward ship corridor, which would take us back to the royal quarters. I jogged as fast as my heels would allow, through a succession of rooms, until I was nearly to the very last receiving room.

I ran straight into Elliot. Coming from the exit. I stopped just short of full-body collision and said the first thing that popped into my mind.

"What are you doing here?"

"I'm free to come and go," Elliot snapped, like I'd accused him of trespassing.

"That's not what I mean," I said, breathless and exasperated. "Something happened."

"What are you talking about?"

I eyed him, looking for a trick, him pulling one over on me. But I didn't think he was playing dumb. He didn't know.

"We were hacked by some protesters. They locked all the doors and broadcast a video. Then they set the screen on fire. You really weren't there? Where did you go?"

Elliot glossed right over my question. "What were they protesting?"

"Overcrowding. Visa denials. Not enough food, medicine," I replied, exasperated. Had he missed the part about the *fire*?

"What, you don't like that they ruined your fun?" Elliot sneered. "I'm so sorry your party is over because people are starving."

I was stunned at his venom. "It's not that at all—"

He didn't let me finish. "I have to go." And he maneuvered past me.

"It's not safe." I tried to stop him, grabbed him by the arm and pulled him my way. Elliot pulled violently from my grasp.

"I have to find Evy. Go, Leo. Run away. It's what you do."

"That's rich, coming from you," I snapped.

We held each other's gaze, the air sizzling with tension. Elliot didn't bother to fight any further. He just left me . . . again.

*

I pressed my fingers to the royal quarters' bio-lock, and with a *whoosh,* the doors opened, spilling the bright hallway lights into the dark foyer.

"Lights on," I commanded, stepping inside as soft light illuminated the entryway and living room beyond. I leaned heavily against the closed door, contorting as best I could in my dress to pry my heels from aching, red-lined feet. It was still a two-minute walk to our temporary apartment within the Linds' quarters, but it would be easier done in bare feet.

"Carina?" I called out gently, in case she'd had a similar idea and come in through the main entrance as I had. Blast it all that we never wore our wrist tabs with party dresses. If we weren't so vain, I could just send her a message to check in. Instead, we were bound by the analog.

"Miss Kolburg, you surprised me!" Nora, Klara's personal maid, emerged from the dark doorway of the dining room into the light. She held a slip of fabric and some thread in her hands. "I was just finishing up some work, about to go home. You're back early."

"So no one else is back yet, then?"

"No. Why would they be? It's not even eleven," Nora replied. I filled her in on everything that had happened in the ballroom, and her eyes went wide. "Oh, those poor people. I'd heard about things elsewhere in the fleet, but I never imagined . . . I hope they won't be punished too badly, the hackers."

"Why do you say that?"

Nora's cheeks spotted bright pink. "Of course they should be punished," she hedged. "Just hopefully they'll be allowed to live. They're only trying to help, is all I mean."

The death penalty for a harmless—if scary—demonstration? She had to be exaggerating. I switched subjects. "And you're here late. You shouldn't have to stay all hours of the night to mend Klara's things."

"She wants to wear this to tomorrow's concert, and the seams need reinforcing." Nora shrugged. My cousin was oblivious when she wanted something. She didn't understand how her demand would mean extra hours of work for poor Nora.

"I wish I'd known," I said. "I would have snuck you some champagne."

"Oh, that's all right, miss. A friend brought me some already."

"Please call me Leo. And you should get back home to your family. I'm sure the whole ship is going into lockdown, and you don't want to get stuck here."

"That's a good idea." Nora considered the sewing in her hands with a frown. "Though I'd better take this with me, so it's done by morning." She curtsied and headed for the door. "Have a good night, then, Miss Kolburg."

I headed back to the foyer, then left, down another corridor to the East Wing. I hoped Carina was there.

The inside corridor was cozy, domestic instead of sterile and white, and dim lights turned on automatically as I moved swiftly along the passage. The royal quarters arced on either side like a horseshoe, and our temporary home was to the very end of the hall, in a sub-apartment that opened with yet another bio-lock. These were Klara's uncle's quarters usually, but he'd taken our need for a place to stay as an excuse to vacation aboard the *Lady Liberty* for the Season.

At last, I came to our apartment and slipped quietly inside, careful not to trip over trunks cluttering the foyer. Father and Carina were slow to unpack, primarily because they were fully expecting a servant to do it. I could ask Nora to help, but I'd never felt entirely comfortable with the upstairs/downstairs dynamic on board this ship. Once you'd loved the valet's son, it was hard to expect people to wait on you. Besides, Nora was my age—that made it awkward.

I called out Carina's name again, then checked every room in the small apartment. I was alone—my father hadn't returned either. I sat down in the living room to wait.

The adrenaline rush of the last twenty minutes slowly ebbed, leaving me to a surreal silence. My world had tilted precariously on its axis in the space of less than an hour. What did it mean that people could hack our systems and set things on fire as they pleased? There were so many electronics on board that making enough of them overheat would spell death for us all. And there I went, being myopically selfish. People in the fleet were dying, starving. I hadn't realized it was this bad. Maybe we *were* the monsters they'd accused us of being, with our parties and champagne and finery.

And then there was Elliot. I had imagined a reunion

between us more times than I cared to admit, the scene always melodramatic and romantic and happy in the end. Reality was altogether different. I wasn't prepared for the sheer force of Elliot's hatred toward me. It knocked me off-center, hollowed me out. And now I'd have to see him nearly every day for a month, while he flirted with other girls, no less.

How had he changed so drastically in only three years? Now he was brusque and cold and secretive, sneaking off to parts unknown during the party, probably with some girl. The old Elliot was steadfast and frankly a little bit boring— just like me. And he liked me, and only me.

I needed to get a grip on myself. Jealousy was not a good look. With a deep sigh, I sank back into the couch cushions, resigned to wait. My mind spiraled from Elliot to my father and sister's safety—what if something terrible had happened to them and that's why they weren't back yet? I hoped it wouldn't be too much longer. Left alone with my thoughts was a dangerous place to be.

4

The smell of bacon, tangy and sweet, woke me.

Was it morning? Time was relative up here, the view from the window always dark, sprawling space. I groaned, rubbing at my sleep-crusted eyes.

Carina had swanned in at two a.m. like it was any other night, explaining breezily that she'd been pulled into an after-party some friends were throwing and lost track of the time. Too tired to yell, I'd simply collapsed onto my bed and fallen asleep in what I had on. And now, as I kicked my legs over the side of the bed and stood, I assessed the damage to my dress. Wrinkled but not ruined.

The bacon, on the other hand, might be. The acrid whiff of burnt meat hit my nostrils, sending me sprinting to the kitchen to find a sheepish Carina, uselessly moving charbroiled strips from the pan to a plate to cool. People were starving in the fleet, and we were burning bacon. Guilt swooped at my insides.

"Whoops," Carina said with a shrug. "It's the thought that counts?"

"I'm still mad," I said. "But apology accepted. At least you tried. Help me out of my dress?"

She undid the eyehook closures and buttons that ran up the back, and I shuffled back to our room, clasping the dress to my front. It was a relief to change into a slick black bodysuit and a casual day dress. By the time I was done and had washed my face clean of last night's makeup, Carina had Breakfast, Take Two, laid out on the dining table. She stuck to toasted rolls and a selection of cheeses and sliced meats. Both that and the bacon must have come from Klara. We'd not been able to afford meats for the past year.

Father shuffled blearily to the table as I prepared an open-faced sandwich. He demanded coffee as he plopped down into the seat of honor. Normally I wouldn't baby him, but today I fetched the coffee as ordered. It was easier not to poke the bear, especially when the bear was tired and hungover.

"What time did you turn in?" I asked, biting into the simultaneously crisp and fluffy bread, buttery cheese, and salty salami. I only just suppressed a satisfied groan. I'd missed this.

"Late," Father grumbled between greedy sips of coffee. "Very late indeed. Had to help Freja sort things out, of course."

I nodded along obediently, even though I was picturing my dad blustering around, pretending usefulness while the other adults did the actual work. Father enjoyed feeling important more than anything. I was sure my aunt had done the lion's share of damage control after last night's incident. I dared to prod a bit further.

"Did you find out anything? About who did it?" I asked.

"Lena Wendt from the *Sternshiff*," Father sniffed. "Styles herself leader of some group called Freiheit. They like to blame everyone else for their problems instead of themselves."

"That's harsh," I said. "People are dying."

"And that's our fault? People die, Leonie."

I took a deep breath rather than say the first thing that came to mind. I would never win with my father, who was always right. Especially when he was very, very wrong.

"And what will happen to the hackers?" I forced a lightness into my tone.

"She and her fellow . . . terrorists will be dealt with on the *Olympus*."

"It was hardly terrorism." I went back on all my best intentions, because I just couldn't let the word *terrorists* stand. "It was a protest. A statement, no?"

"They hacked us and started a fire. How is that not terrorism?"

"I heard they're known to be peaceful protesters," Carina piped up, surprising us both. "Lukas told Klara, who told Asta, who told Evy, who told me."

I perked up at the mention of our renter, but then my father drew my focus, his lips pursed together so tightly, they went white. I could tell he was about to explode into a rant that I was too sleep-deprived to handle.

"I was sad not to see Lukas again last night. I'll have to

speak to him again tonight at the Klaviermeister concert," I said, deflecting and lying all at once. It seemed to work. Father abruptly changed tack.

"Oh, good. That's the worst of it, you know. That the ball ended so abruptly, and you girls lost so much mingling time."

Yes, that was absolutely the worst part about last night, I thought. *Not the locked door, or the panic, or the fire.*

"Besides which, several crates of champagne went missing," he continued. "I had to deal with that unpleasant business, on top of everything else."

"So sorry you had to deal with that. I can handle it today."

But he waved me off. "Oh, no, I managed it. I scolded the catering staff for miscounting. But I do wish you hadn't run off."

"Speaking of the renters," Carina jumped in, seizing on the slightest scrap to steer the conversation where she wanted, "you did an excellent job picking them out, Leo. Evgenia and I became fast friends last night. We're about the same size, and she said she has the latest fashions from the *Saint Petersburg* and *Empire,* and that I could borrow them while they're here. And can you believe the insane luck that they know Elliot and brought him along?"

"Elliot?" Father chimed in, suddenly interested. "Wentworth?"

"Yes, Daddy." Carina nodded vigorously. "Your old valet! Apparently he migrated over to the *Saint Petersburg,* but now he lives somewhere called the *Islay*?"

"Technically he wasn't a valet," I said against my better judgment. I regretted it immediately.

ALEXA DONNE

"Don't be obtuse, Leonie, of course he was my valet,"
Father said, a hawkish warning layered beneath his look of
light censure. "His *father* was your valet," I plowed forward
as calmly as I could manage. "Elliot performed some of his
duties after he died, but he never fully took on the role." We'd
have to have been able to *afford* that, was what I didn't say.
Elliot was far more than an underling my father had ordered
around. He'd left to make something of himself, after I'd
broken off our engagement and refused to go with him.

White-hot embarrassment seared through me, the sip
of coffee I'd just taken turning bitter on my tongue and my
insides seizing as if caught in a vise. I couldn't bear to think of
my actions, even three years later. It was my greatest regret. I
coughed to hide my situation.

Carina didn't notice, anyway. "Valet, valet's son, whatever.
Elliot Wentworth, who we grew up with, back here!
Apparently he's filthy rich now." Father perked up at that, and
I could have thrown myself across the table to strangle him
for it. Carina continued heedlessly. "He certainly behaves like
a gentleman. Kissed my hand and everything."

That got my attention. "You spoke with him?" I asked,
amazed at how measured I sounded. Inside, the vise grip
had seized again, giving way to a swirling in my stomach and
palpitations in my chest.

"Of course! He came to the after-party. He told me all
about the *Saint Petersburg* and how he knows the Orlovs. He
said he had hoped he might see me again and marveled that
he had barely recognized me." Carina preened, checking her

reflection in the silver coffeepot. Indeed, she was dark blond and beautiful, with large, deep brown eyes that had previously overpowered her face but now played perfectly against pouty pink lips and a fuller figure. I shared the figure and the big eyes, mine green to her brown, but only a fraction of the beauty. Father said my seriousness rendered me ordinary, where Carina's carefree disposition transformed her.

Elliot had said he liked my seriousness, that he found me beautiful, but now . . .

"I've just remembered," I said, pushing back from the table, "I promised Klara I'd meet her this morning. Thank you for breakfast, Carina. I'll see you later, before the concert."

Klara, of course, had requested no such meeting, but I hurried to my room regardless, making my face and hair presentable so that I had the excuse to leave. Anything to distract myself from tales of Elliot and Carina, him kissing her hand . . . only her hand, I reassured myself. Like a gentleman, as she said. Still, *kissed* and *Elliot* in relation to my sister turned my stomach. I had no right to hold any claim on him, but my heart refused to be rational.

*

I decided to take a long walk to decompress and channel my pent-up energy in a more productive direction. Last night's interruption had rattled me. I wasn't completely ignorant of the growing problems of the wider fleet—I'd heard whispers about overcrowding and implementation of strict rations on board certain ships. My mother had seen it and argued fruitlessly with my father and her sister to open up our respective ships for families in need. But then she died, and I'd gone back to living in my bubble. Last night, it had burst. Our family was now precariously closer in circumstances to those people, to desperation and death, than were our wealthy cousins on the *Scandinavian*. If my aunt ever decided to withdraw her support, we would be destitute.

I made the walk nice and long, so as to distract myself. There was an entire promenade on the top level for that very purpose, but my favorite thing was to make my way through the royal private public quarters, which were as oxymoronic as they sounded. They were a series of ballrooms, libraries, drawing rooms, and other leisure spaces shared among the elite of the ship, "public" in the sense that anyone with bio-lock access to the forward and upper decks could use them, but essentially private for the same reason.

I wended my way through gallery after gallery, into the royal ballroom (half of it cordoned off due to fire damage), through to the library, one of my favorite spaces on board. No one read real books anymore, but the library kept hundreds of them carefully under glass, in addition to the digital stations where the residents could reload their tabs with more things to read. Plus, it was where the *Scandinavian* housed historical documents, cultural artifacts, and more from Earth's history. I browsed the exhibits I'd looked at a hundred times.

This was where I'd found the idea for my water-filtration system, a home-improvement project I'd undertaken several years ago to help the *Sofi* extend precious resources. A thought slithered up my spine unbidden. If other ships were on rations, water rations especially, my system could offer some relief. It could save lives. And the license fees to use it would save my family.

I hated myself for thinking it, profiting off misery. But this presented a real opportunity. Perhaps I could appeal to other ships, get their buy-in first, then use the startup funds to get my patent. All it would take was one ship saying yes. I wouldn't need to wait out the Valg to get the Orlovs' rent. I wouldn't need the Valg at all. The thought of escaping this barbaric marriage ritual filled me with such relief that it overpowered the guilt for just a moment.

I picked up one of the library's public tab readers and wandered through a maze of glass-encased stacks to an overstuffed chair. I disappeared into the latest Jupiter Morrow mystery for several hours, but then a musical laugh pinged my ears. I rose, creeping through the stacks, following the sound until I spotted the source. Evgenia and Elliot were strolling through. I shot down into a crouch, ducking low behind a display case so they wouldn't see me.

"This is no laughing matter, Evy," I heard Elliot's cutting response to whatever Evgenia had been laughing about. "They might execute her."

"For a little interruption? They're overreacting, don't you think?"

My breath caught in my throat. They were talking about last night.

"You expect them to underreact? Someone crashed their special party and called them on their bullshit. Heads will roll."

There was a long silence, and for a moment I wondered if they'd somehow snuck off without my hearing. I didn't dare pop around the display case to check. But then Evgenia spoke, her voice low.

"Are you worried, then?"

Elliot's response was tight. "I know what I'm doing."

What by the moon was Elliot up to? He couldn't be involved with Freiheit, could he? It was awfully convenient that he was outside the ballroom when everything happened, come to think of it. Father said they had hacked the system from the inside.

"Now, what are you going to wear tonight?" Evgenia abruptly changed tone, light and bright once more, and Elliot returned a low response I couldn't hear. "Elliot Wentworth, I will not allow you to abandon me to those vultures. You are going. We have work to do."

"They seemed to like you well enough. Hardly vultures," Elliot said.

"Please," Evgenia spat. "They're happy enough to drink and laugh with us, but we both know we're nothing to them but crude new money. Once they know how Max makes his fortune, they'll devour us like jackals."

"First vultures, now jackals . . . next you'll be telling me they're wolves."

"Don't tease me. You're the one who wanted to come here. The Valg Season is the perfect opportunity, you said."

"Maybe I was wrong."

I imagined Evgenia's ears steaming, but her next words sounded nothing but amused.

"But what about that girl? Don't you want to see her?" My breath quickened, palms going sweaty.

"Leo?" Elliot replied. I leaned precariously forward, trying to get closer. They had paused momentarily. "We said hello last night."

"Um, yes, I know, I was there," Evgenia said with a laugh. "Anyway, I didn't mean her. I was talking about the other one. Carina."

"Carina?" Elliot parroted back, and my heart froze in my chest. I couldn't decipher his tone. If only I could *see* them properly. "She's so young."

"She's sixteen. You're nineteen. It's nothing."

Evgenia was rapidly falling in my esteem.

"Last time I saw her, she was practically a child . . ."

Exactly! I wanted to scream at them.

"Well, now she's practically a woman. Beautiful. And a bit sweet on you, I think."

Dammit, I couldn't hear Elliot's response—they'd started moving again. All I heard was Evgenia's tinkling laugh, as if Elliot had said the most hilarious thing.

5

For the second time in two days, I let Carina have her way with me. She poked, prodded, and strapped me into a deep-navy tea dress, my least heinously boring dress, according to her. I walked into one of the *Scandinavian*'s larger galleries, wearing my fashion like armor. My shield: hair curled into pretty ringlets, eyes lined with kohl, and lips painted a shocking red. Like the previous evening's party, the concert was being held in the royal private public quarters. The crowd inside the meticulously appointed Andersson Lounge was small, maybe fifty people. They were the most elite of the elite participating in the Valg Season, plus their parents.

My eyes scanned the room, and I feigned calm, despite the way my heart was pounding in my chest. Finally I found Elliot holding court by the canapés. I scolded myself for locking onto him like a heat-seeking missile. He'd been here only twenty-four hours, and I'd lost all sense. My eyes flitted to Evgenia, Max, and Ewan. Yes, I decided, I would be equally interested in the entire rental party, like a good host.

Everyone cut a dashing figure. Max and Ewan had forgone dress whites for dapper suits of deep blue and emerald green. Evgenia sported another stunning vintage dress, a little black French classic.

"Who are you staring at?" Father asked, following my line of vision. "Those outfits are . . . interesting."

"Those are our renters, Father," Carina said, ignoring his comment. "Come, you should meet them." Carina took off with him before I could protest. I forced confidence into my step as I followed them across the room. This was how I would proceed. Bravely, composed. Elliot would not rattle me.

"Max, Ewan, Evgenia," I said, approaching them, taking the lead. Elliot's back was turned to us as he talked to some far-flung royal cousin whose name I couldn't remember. "Allow me to introduce my father. His Royal Highness King Gerhard Kolburg. He is very eager to meet you."

Eager or not, my father performed the part, graciously accepting their bows and curtsy, a benevolent smile turning his lips. "Oh, please don't call me King," he demurred.

"Of course," Max said as my stomach stirred with worry. "Your Highness, we wouldn't dream of it." Father's smile turned genuine. He loved the HRH distinction. I let out a relieved breath. Max was doing perfectly.

"Let me just say that I hope you are enjoying our modest ship while we enjoy our little vacation on board the *Scandinavian*."

"Hardly modest, Your Highness," Ewan jumped in.

"*Prinzessin Sofi* is the finest ship I've been privileged to stay on."

"Surely nothing compared to the grandeur of this ship," Father parried.

"She is lovely, to be sure." Ewan nodded. "But so large. We prefer the intimacy of your *Sofi*."

Color me impressed by our renters' bullshitting talents. Evgenia and I locked eyes, hers reflecting my amusement. She sidled up next to me, opening her mouth to say something, but then Father started calling out.

"Elliot! Elliot Wentworth. Come over here."

Oh, no. I pasted on a smile just in time for Elliot to join our little circle and stand on Evgenia's other side. At least I wouldn't have to look directly at him. We might burn each other to ashes for the power of our glares.

"Good to see you again, Your Highness," Elliot said. I thought I caught a tightness to his voice, though maybe it was my imagination.

"My boy, what brings you here? And in such a fine suit!" Father cast an askew glance at Max and Ewan in comparison.

"Evgenia invited me," Elliot answered as Evgenia linked her arm in his. "I hadn't seen Max and Ewan in ages, and I was keen to see old friends here." His gaze drifted over to Carina. "And the suit? I have only the one." He laughed. "I haven't changed that much."

"I helped him choose it, of course." Evgenia picked an imaginary piece of lint off his shoulder, leaning into him.

"Oh, are you two . . . ?" My father asked the question I

wouldn't dare. He knew what we were before and wanted to ensure Elliot was completely off the table.

"Oh, God, no!" Evgenia laughed. "What is it with your family trying to pair me off with every man they see me with? I am very much single, if you know any eligible young women." She winked. I found her growing on me, even if she was trying to push Elliot toward my sister. But she was bold and bubbly, with a frank sense of humor, and I liked that.

"You might have some trouble finding . . . like-minded individuals in the Valg Season," my father said. I could have smacked him.

"Not everyone is looking for a wealthy husband to whom to attach herself," I snapped without thinking. "Plenty of people marry for love, and don't have trouble finding it."

Six pairs of eyes cut to me. Elliot's in particular I could feel crawling over my skin. He must have been thinking I was the biggest hypocrite. I did not have a history of marrying for love.

"Ooh, I like you," Evgenia cooed.

"Hear, hear!" Max chimed in. "Now, what about you, my dear? I see both you and your sister have on name tags, so you're in the thick of it. What are you two looking for, then?"

"Not girls." Carina chirped a nervous laugh. What was with my family embarrassing me tonight? Then I caught her gaze, which was squarely on Elliot. So that clarification of her dating preferences was for *his* benefit. "I'd like to marry for love, though." She ducked her head as her cheeks flushed pink. This was awful.

"That makes one Kolburg for love, then." Elliot tipped his champagne glass in my direction. "And one for ruthless pragmatism."

"That's right," I said, glaring back at him. "I will be flinging myself at every man with a substantial fortune whilst consuming my body weight in alcohol." Father nodded his approval, while everyone but Evgenia looked at the floor. My new best friend laughed, bless her.

"On that note, we're going to go hunt down some beverages," she said, hooking me by the arm and pulling me out of this conversation from hell. Evgenia swiped two glasses of champagne, handing me one. "That was ghastly. But you're fun."

"I'm sorry my family is so awful. I don't know what's wrong with them."

"Oh, never mind that. I'm used to people being snobby little shits and yammering on about repopulating the fleet. They have trouble grasping that queer people can have children as well, thank you very much. Or, a radical notion, I know, that some people might not want to have children at all!" She pulled me into an alcove so we could observe the room at greater advantage. "So clue me in to who's who. And why are there only twenty, thirty young people, tops? The ball was crawling with hotties last night, but I don't see even a quarter of them here. And why are there so many parents?"

"Welcome to Night Two of the Valg Kickoff, Super-Elite Edition," I intoned wryly. "The concert is invite-only from the captain. It's a chance for the parents to scope out the very best matches of the Season and push their hapless children in the direction they would like. It's the last event the parents get to attend, though."

"Then how the heck did we get invited? I'm under no delusions as to how people like you—no offense—feel about new money."

"My cousin thought you were the 'right kind of people.'" I couldn't help but do air quotes as I recited back Klara's words.

"Who is your cousin?"

"Oh, Klara Lind. She's also the captain's daughter, so—"

"The knockout blonde with the exquisite dress sense! I'm starting to put the pieces together now. Is everyone here related?"

"Now you know why we need the Valg Season to find partners," I quipped.

And as if we had spoken her into being, Klara walked through the lounge doors at that very moment, resplendent in a dark-navy tulle dress overlaid with sparkling gold stars.

"I'm going to go chat with her—you want to come?" Evgenia asked.

I opened my mouth, ready to say yes, when I caught my father's searing gaze. He gestured to my left and widened his eyes for emphasis. "No, that's okay," I told Evgenia. "I see a potential wealthy suitor, and if I don't at least attempt conversation, my father will whine about it all evening."

"Godspeed." She patted me on the arm with encouragement before sashaying off in the direction of my cousin.

Now to suffer the shortest conversation possible with Lukas Hagen.

"Lukas, I didn't think you enjoyed classical music," I said by way of greeting.

"I don't. My mom made me come."

He waved at someone behind my shoulder, and I twisted around to see Baroness Hagen, eyes narrowed in my direction. Her lips turned down into a grimace. Not a fan of me, then. The elevated royal title that would come from a match with me was not enough to override the uncouthness of Father flinging me toward anyone with money, it seemed.

"Well, at least the food is good?" I grabbed a puff pastry from a passing tray, relieved my family wasn't footing the bill for anything this evening. I planned on stuffing myself.

"Should you be eating that?" Lukas eyed me up and down, lingering on my perfectly proportional hips, thank you very much. It took all my strength not to fling the pastry in his face. But then I'd have lost the buttery, flaky pastry and salty cheese that passed my lips as I bit into it with great relish, just for Lukas's benefit. As another tray passed, I snatched up a cucumber sandwich and ate it with equal care. Lukas took the hint.

"I'll see you after the concert, then," he said, though I doubted very much that that was true. He turned and went to find his seats.

Surprised to find her alone, I spotted the captain off to the side and saw an opportunity.

"Captain Lind?" I tapped Klara's mom on the shoulder, allowing myself a deep, steadying breath before she turned around. Talking to Captain Lind required nerves of steel.

"Leonie, darling!" she exclaimed, engulfing me in a stiff, perfunctory hug. This was Freja Lind in a nutshell: all superficial charm with an undercurrent of stiff cool. Klara took after her. "You know to call me Aunt Freja, my dear," she continued. The captain used endearments like weapons.

"Well, I wanted to talk business," I hedged.

"Oh?" Her hostess's veneer slipped. Freja smoothed her hands over the crisp pink sateen bodice of her ball gown, a subconscious gesture I'd seen her make with the fabric edges of her captain's-uniform jacket a million times. "Still." She coughed. "Call me Freja, even for business."

"Okay, Aunt Freja." I followed her instructions but remained on guard nonetheless. "I wanted to talk to you about my water-filtration system again—"

She cut me off. "I just don't think it's the most prudent course of action for us. The retrofit would be costly and time-consuming, and I just can't get past the . . . urine thing." She wrinkled her nose in disdain, as if I'd waved a urine-soaked rag beneath it.

"It's completely clean and safe," I pleaded. "We've been using it on the *Sofi* for over a year, and my father and sister haven't even noticed!"

"You mean they don't know?" The captain literally clutched her pearls. I had to pinch myself in the thigh to stop a giggle. "My dear, that's precisely proving my point. You don't want to reveal to them the source of their water, and I absolutely cannot and will not lie to my people."

I was naked, castigated under her piercing blue-eyed stare.

"Only a small fraction of the potable water supply comes from the wastewater," I mumbled, though I knew my pitch was done. The captain was family. If I couldn't get her to buy into my filtration system, then I was doomed with other ships, wasn't I?

"I'm sorry, Leonie." She gave me a patronizing pat on the arm and a halfhearted smile. "You're so like your mother. A hopeless idealist. May she rest in peace," she seemed to add perfunctorily. Come to think of it, it was the first time she'd mentioned my mom in years.

"What are you sorry about, Mother?" Klara breezed in, sipping at her champagne in lieu of eating. I knew she rarely ate at these things. It was unseemly and would ruin her lipstick, she always said.

"I was saying sorry that she hadn't found a suitor yet," Freja answered smoothly, making things both better and worse. She covered the embarrassment of my failed business venture but opened up a whole other can of worms.

"Ugh, Mother, not everyone is gagging to get married," Klara groaned. I nodded in agreement.

"You'd do well to get comfortable with the idea," Freja scolded her daughter. "I won't live forever. You need a well-positioned spouse if you want to run for captain—at a future time of my choosing, of course. And Leonie has other concerns for marriage," she added. Well, there it was. "I saw you rebuff the young count from the *Sternshiff*." My aunt frowned at me, the spitting image of my father. Parental disappointment was a universal look.

"We don't have very much in common," I said.

"You rarely do." Freja sighed.

A loaded look passed between my cousin and me, both thinking of her father. He'd been a strategic Valg match, and, well, it hadn't ended on the best terms. He'd left when Klara was twelve, off to parts unknown and a pregnant mistress, and my aunt had refused to talk about him ever since. How she didn't understand why her daughter was deeply resistant to marriage was beyond me. Or she understood but didn't care.

"Well, it's time for my speech," the captain said, leaving Klara and me to find our seats.

I groaned. "Another one? Or is it the same from last night, but she wants to get to finish it this time?" Unwillingly I flashed back on the show from last night. I pinched my eyes shut to clear the image.

"No, not the same one," Klara said. "It's her candidate speech. She's all full of vim and vigor, and will be kicking off the election Season early to coincide with the Valg. Aren't you excited?" Sarcasm dripped from every word.

"Seriously?"

Klara nodded. "She's capitalizing on last night's interruption to galvanize everyone for a quick and uncontested reelection. Her words."

"But no one ever runs against her," I said as we made our way forward to take our seats. We found two seats on the aisle in the third row. The plush settees that usually occupied the middle of the room had been pushed to the sides to make room for a sea of chairs. "It's been just the Lind family going up for captain basically our whole lives."

Klara leaned in close, her voice carefully low. "And Mother would like to ensure that doesn't change. Apparently the Madsens were making some bold statements last night after the attack, and she's antsy."

"There aren't enough Danes on board to swing it their way," I reasoned.

"True, but you know their son Theo is participating in the Valg, along with Asta. Mother has forbidden me from considering him. She's afraid they're angling for a political marriage so they can sneak in through me."

"How are you feeling about the election? What does it mean for you?"

Klara sighed back into her chair. "It is what it is. Mother's buying herself a few more years in the position, since elections can't be held less than three years apart. I'll have to be patient."

"Would you run against her?" Anyone directly connected to the royal families on board was eligible to become captain. We had had "elections," of sorts, to determine who held the role going back about a hundred years. Even I could run if I wanted to, since my mother was a Lind. But I had zero desire to go up against my aunt, let alone captain a ship this big.

"Without a political marriage in place? Nope. Which she's headed off at the pass by doing it simultaneous with the Valg. Clever. Anyway, I saw you talking to Elliot back there." She expertly changed the subject.

"Not exactly. It was more of a super-awkward group-chat

kind of thing. Elliot has no interest in talking to me. Yelling at me, yes. Talking, not so much."

Klara raised an eyebrow. "He's still mad about the engagement?"

"Apparently."

"And how are you feeling?"

"Annoyed," I said, for lack of a better word. Klara gestured for me to go on. "It's fine," I hedged. "I'm so over him, I don't even have an issue with him and my sister openly flirting." If I said it out loud, perhaps that would make it true? Klara laughed.

"Carina and Elliot? That's a terrible idea."

She didn't bother to keep her voice low now, and to my mortification, my father, Carina, Elliot, and his friends moved to sit in the row in front of us. Hopefully, they'd heard only the tail end of what she'd said. Elliot and Carina sat directly in front of us. I hunched down in my chair and inched closer to Klara. Then her mother started her speech.

It was long and over-the-top. The words *terrorism* and *security* were used no fewer than five times each. She didn't mention people starving, or really anything that might force us to think about our position in the fleet. How we wined and dined while people were dying.

Then, finally, Captain Lind introduced the Klaviermeister, taking care to remind us that, as our captain, she was responsible for booking such excellent entertainment at regular intervals. *VOTE FOR ME,* she practically screamed.

The Klaviermeister sat down at the piano to play. It was

one of my favorites, a score by Philip Glass, somber and longing and wistful all at the same time. Elliot shifted in front of me, leaning forward in his chair, settling elbows on knees, as if to get closer to the music. He, too, loved this piece, I remembered.

I tried to get lost in the music, closing my eyes to isolate my senses, purposely refraining from leaning forward too. I was my own person, dammit. We weren't *that* alike. Not anymore. But then I heard my sister giggle in front of me and, cracking an eye open, saw her tap Elliot on the shoulder, wresting him back up so she could whisper in his ear. I was unable to pick up the words, but her tone came through. Carina asked him a question, playful, earnest, and I watched with both horror and fascination as he turned, pressing his lips close to her ear, and answered. I caught a few words from his husky baritone. *Favorite. Melancholy.*

I looked past their heads, trying to ignore their whispering, but it went on. Carina was clearly not interested in the concert at all, and Elliot kept indulging her. She probably didn't remember how close Elliot and I had been. I had certainly never told her about the engagement. That explained *her* actions, but not *his*.

A quick check of the time told me it had been ten minutes. I couldn't bear another forty. I needed air. One piece ended, everyone clapped politely, and I took my chance to slip away.

I made my way through a maze of drawing rooms until I hit the outer corridor. While it was cooler out here and Elliot-free, it wasn't enough, so I headed up one deck to the uppermost deck's promenade. The next song from the Klaviermeister played from the sound system, so it was like I wasn't missing it at all. I'd emerged on the Earth side of the ship, and the melancholy Glass score seemed appropriate. I gazed down at our former home planet, reflecting white up into the black vastness of space. I'd learned all about it in Earth History; we'd watched dramatic reenactments of the supervolcano exploding, setting off a chain reaction that led to an ice age. The music swelled, a discordant minor melody filling me with a distinct sadness for all the people who had been left behind. Who had perished.

We were alive only because our ancestors had known the right people, had had enough money. And we continued to let money and status dictate who lived well.

I let out a deep sigh.

"Everything okay?"

I whirled around.

"Elliot, what are you doing here?"

"You ran out like there was something wrong."

"You noticed?"

"It was hard not to." He pointed to my feet—heels. Of course.

The whole audience likely heard me *click-clack*ing out of there.

"Well, I'm surprised you care. Since I'm so ruthlessly pragmatic."

He looked at me askance but appeared anything but contrite.

"Aren't you, though?"

"You know it was more complicated than that."

There it was, the thing between us. I was a bit shocked at myself for having brought it up first, even if obliquely. But, hey, what better time to hash it out? We could say our piece and then avoid each other entirely for the next month.

"I didn't think it was very complicated at all." Elliot shrugged. "Money or love. You chose money."

Half a dozen retorts flashed across my mind, all the nuances and complicated reasons that he was wrong, but all I could force out of my mouth was "And now *you're* rich too. So I guess money isn't important at all, huh?"

My face heated at my own stupidity. What a flaccid argument.

"Of course you wish I'd stayed poor and downtrodden. That's what you all want. The rest of us under your heels, staying out of the way while you stuff yourselves."

"That's a mischaracterization, and you know it. I'm not like them."

"Aren't you? Just 'cause you're maybe not as bad doesn't mean you're absolved. You used to talk a big talk, agreed with all the things I said, about things needing to change. But have you done anything to impact that change since I left? I see the same rigid class system as before. You're complacent and complicit."

There he was, the Elliot who clearly thought I was the very worst kind of person. A spoiled princess hardly worth his time. This Elliot made it easier, and the anger that boiled up from my stomach and turned to acid on my tongue was the very thing I needed to get over him. We would spar, and I would learn to hate him, too.

"And what are you, coming over here to participate in the Valg? Doesn't that make you just as complicit?"

"You don't know me anymore, Leo, or what I want."

"Likewise," I spat back. "Why did you even come up here? You don't care about me. You were just spoiling for a fight."

"Maybe I want to see you suffer a bit."

It was as if he had struck me in the face. My whole body began to shake—with rage, devastation. I clenched my hands into fists, locked my knees, anything to control myself in front of him. And then I let loose.

"Well, congratulations. The universe has taken care of that for you. My ship is falling apart, we're inches from complete financial ruin, my father and sister are useless, and I'll be married off to the highest bidder in a matter of weeks, kicking off a lifetime of unhappiness. Enjoy the show. Now, good night."

Just then, Klara rounded the corner. "I wondered where you two had disappeared to!" Her wide smile promptly faded when she got a proper look at the two of us, stiff as boards and clearly sparring.

"I was just going." I cast Elliot my most saccharine smile. "Enjoy your stay, and the Valg. I hope you get everything you want."

With that, I whipped around and headed for my quarters, having had the last word but leaving with the heaviest of hearts.

6

I translated my anger into action, writing letters to every captain in the fleet about my water-recycling system, begging for a meeting. Every time I flashed back to Elliot's wish to see me suffer, to Captain Lind's disdain, I found someone else to write to. All I needed was one ship to take a chance on my idea.

This way, I was working on three potential scenarios, each increasingly less pleasant. Ideally someone would agree to be the pilot ship for my system, and I could use their startup investment to fly to the *Olympus* and file my patent. Otherwise, I would suffer Elliot's presence for the next month but happily collect the Orlovs' weekly rent, which I would use to take care of the patent then. But that would bring me perilously close to the end of the Valg Season and the worst-case scenario, with Father breathing down my neck to marry to save the family. He just didn't understand that I was trying to do that already, but in a way so that the price wasn't my own happiness.

The Valg kickoff complete, the social-events calendar had been paused while the majority of parents returned to their ships. That meant a forty-eight-hour reprieve before the tug-of-war with my father began in earnest.

I busied myself with unpacking, tidying our temporary apartments, balancing our new and slightly improved budget. Another reason I hoped for some other ship's buy-in was so that I could use the Orlovs' rent to make improvements rather than bank it all for the patent fees.

On the day after this all-too-brief reprieve, my wrist tab and personal tab began to chirp repeatedly and annoyingly in unison. I glanced down at my wrist to see an insistently flashing rose-entangled *V.* I tried swiping it away, but the noise didn't stop. With a huff, I woke up my personal tab and tapped to open the Valg app. Finally, both devices quieted, now that I'd locked eyes with today's scheduled event notification—there was a pool party starting in half an hour.

I ignored the other half-dozen blinking notifications—I needed to fill out my profile, take the dating personality quiz, RSVP for the next event, browse profiles. My fingertip was hovering over the skip button for today's event, but then Carina appeared.

"Don't tell me you're doing budgets again," Carina scolded, pausing at the living room entrance. I looked up from my tab, blinking hard before confirming that, yes, my sister was wearing next to nothing and had a towel slung over one arm.

"I'm not going," I said.

She gave an exasperated sigh. "Leo, you can't hole yourself up in here doing work the whole time. The Valg Season is supposed to be fun."

I bristled. "Maybe I was reading, which is fun."

"Father said you have to go with me to Valg events or I can't go. Please? I want to go swimming. I won't make you socialize or swim, but come. You can read by the side, and maybe some similarly antisocial boy will also be reading, and you can bond."

"Fine." I pulled myself up. "I'll go, but only for a little while."

I swiped away the Valg app and pulled up my favorite book, trudging after Carina. At least this was a daytime activity and not one of the faux-romantic nighttime ones. I would get one event out of the way and limit Father's complaining for a few days.

Carina insisted we travel by lift pod instead of foot, despite my protests. The lift unsettled me more than a little bit. It felt as if we were hanging off the side of the ship, nothing between us and the vastness of space but a bit of glass. It was heavily reinforced, I knew, but logic didn't save my stomach from doing somersaults as we glided parallel the *Scandinavian*'s side. I let out a relieved breath as we came to a stop all the way aft, the lift doors sliding open, spilling us out into an alcove off the promenade.

The pool occupied prime real estate on the uppermost deck where the ship's backside curved in an elegant arc and, as on the promenade and bridge, sprawling windows were prioritized over more practical appointments. We had to key in with our bio-signatures, as the pool was accessible to the general public on board only on Mondays. The rest of the time it was private-access only, to maintain an air of luxury. Crowds would dampen the mood. And everything in the pool area meticulously cultivated a mood.

The large entranceway door slid open at our touch, and we stepped into the oblong-shaped lobby. Immediately I was engulfed in low, sultry lighting and the smell of tropical fruit. I drew a deep breath. Pineapple. They pumped it through the air vents, a different scent every few hours.

Mingling with the seemingly distant echo of lapping water and chatter were mellow chimes, the preferred soundtrack of the spa, located to our left. To the right was the all-gender locker room, where Carina deposited her shoes and shucked off the thin tunic I'd made her put on before we left. She frowned at me.

"You're really only going to read? No bathing suit?"

"I'm not wearing one," I reminded her.

"You can buy one here . . ." I shook my head. She rolled her eyes. "Then at least take off your shoes so you're not totally out of place."

I indulged her, throwing them into a locker with her things.

"Hey, can I ask you something?" Carina glanced around, checking that no one was there. "Uh, yeah?"

"It's about Elliot."

My heart zipped up into my throat. I nodded.

"I know you two used to be really close. Maybe a little

romantic? But that ended when he left, right?"

Again, I nodded. Words failed me.

"Good." She let out a breath. "Last night, I think he was really into me. And he's so cute. You don't mind?"

I shook my head. Carina didn't know about the failed engagement, and now certainly wasn't the time to tell her. Elliot did seem into her, so who was I to stand in the way? I offered her a thin smile.

"Great! Thanks, Leo." She clapped her hands and grabbed her towel.

We stepped back into the lobby, making our way forward down a short corridor. Carina skipped ahead of me, all too eager to show off her cherry-red two-piece.

As the shadowy hallway ended and the pool area came into full view, I marveled, as always. The crescent-shaped swimming pool hugged the floor-to-ceiling windows, so you could literally swim with the stars. The windowed ceiling arced above our heads almost as far as one could crane one's neck, giving a similar feeling to being in the lift pod.

The party was sparsely attended thus far—there were maybe fifteen people at the very far end of the pool, by the bar. I spotted a spread of empty chairs to our left, but Carina had other ideas.

"Evy! Elliot!" Carina called out, heading straight for a semicircle of chairs on our right. Evgenia was treading water at the edge of the pool, chatting with Elliot, who sat poolside. I noticed a reader tab in his hand and inwardly cursed our similar inclinations. I'd found my quiet reader, all right.

Against my instincts, I reversed course and followed my sister, who unceremoniously dumped her towel on the chair next to Elliot and joined Evgenia in the water. I selected a chair as far from Elliot as possible, next to what was likely Evgenia's sheer pink cover-up. It was vintage and incredibly luxe, Evgenia's MO.

"Leo, you're not wearing a suit." Evgenia frowned up at me, and I burned under the stares of the whole party. Elliot looked at me with dispassionate interest, either unsurprised that I was stubbornly wearing my day clothes or approving of a fellow reader; I couldn't tell which. Yet he wore a swimsuit, I noticed. He'd developed a muscular physique in the years since we'd parted. I sat down on my lounge chair and turned away from him before he could notice my attentions.

"I tried to change her mind," Carina piped up. "Leo doesn't like swimming much."

"Why not?" Evgenia asked. I took a steadying breath before replying. Telling someone your mother drowned in this very pool tended to bring down the mood.

"Just a personal preference," I said, as light and airy as I could. As soon as you called something a fear, people tended to try to reason with you, use logic to defeat your objections. Though I thought my fear was perfectly logical—my mother had been a strong swimmer, yet she'd drowned. I was a middling swimmer at best.

Elliot shifted almost imperceptibly. He'd been with me when I'd heard the news, hugged me tight when I cried, held my hand through her funeral.

"Well, at least you have another bookworm to keep you company." She indicated Elliot, who offered a polite nod but did not make eye contact.

I settled into my lounge chair, letting Evgenia and Carina's chatter and the sound of someone swimming laps fade into the background as I dove into my Jasper Fforde book, which kept me occupied for at least an hour before movement to my left snapped me to attention. Elliot stood up, his near nakedness once again capturing my gaze. I wasn't sure how I felt about Elliot with muscles—it seemed to me that he'd become hard in more ways than one. I stared at his torso far longer than was wise.

"See something you like, Leo?" Carina laughed, emerging from the pool like Lady Godiva while I shot daggers at her with my eyes. I could feel Elliot looking at me, and I willed my cheeks not to flush embarrassingly and tellingly red, but to no avail.

"Maybe she likes my money."

I glared at him in response.

"You're so muscular now, Elliot!" Carina went on, slinking up to him and laying a hand on his chest as if he were some alien specimen that had to be felt to be believed.

"The work on the *Saint Petersburg* and then the *Islay* demanded a lot of me. It just happened," Elliot demurred.

"I bet you could pick me up and throw me in the pool, no problem," Carina said, now hanging on to Elliot by the arm, squeezing his now-pronounced bicep. I looked again while he was distracted by her. He was still tall and lean, the new musculature subtle but uncanny in the difference it made. It took him another step away from the boy I'd loved.

"I mean, do you *want* me to throw you in the pool?"

Evgenia, now floating on her back with an ear cocked above water and in our direction, said in a singsong voice, "Don't you dare, my darlings. Not anywhere near me."

"Maybe you could just carry me in," Carina continued. "I am a princess, after all."

Elliot's smile dimmed, Carina clueless to the implications for a valet's son of a royal demanding to be waited on. Evgenia had drifted away, leaving me to save the moment.

"I bet *I* could pick you up and throw you in," I jumped in with the first retort that came to mind. Carina reeled around to me, a lemon-sucking expression on her face.

"Not funny, Leo."

"Just saying. I totally could."

"Well, of course you could; you're, like, eight feet tall and you weigh twice as much as I do."

For several uncomfortable beats, there was nothing but the gentle swish of Evgenia's backstroke and the beating of my own heart thumping loudly in my chest. I was sure Elliot could hear it, the manifestation of my hurt and anger at my stupid sister, who was so careless with her words. Whether she realized it or not, they were exactly the right ones to wound me, at the worst possible moment, in front of the worst possible audience.

"Hello, beautiful party people!" Klara's distinctive sly tone announced her presence before we all turned to see her approach. It was both the ideal distraction and another kick in the stomach. Klara and I were the same height, tall stature being nothing out of the ordinary on a ship like the *Scandinavian*. But where she'd lucked into genes that rendered her long and lean, with perfect, perky boobs that filled out her stunning black bathing suit, I was curvy. And while I would call myself "height-weight appropriate," there was no denying I had . . . more where most other girls my age had a lot less. Usually I didn't care, but Carina weaponizing my body in front of Elliot?

I barely stopped myself from pushing her into the pool.

"Elliot, are you going in? Help me down the steps!" And with that, Elliot was swept over to the pool by Klara, who inadvertently managed my revenge for me. Carina silently fumed while I fought a smirk. It wouldn't be kind to tease her about it. She took a moment to collect herself, like an actress preparing backstage before her cue, then jogged over to join Klara and Elliot in the water.

I watched them, chatting and laughing as they swam, while I battled a wave of feelings. I might as well have been in the pool, its crystal-blue deep threatening to pull me under. I gulped a breath, fighting to steady my racing pulse, the mental image of drowning enough to send me into a mild panic. What had hurt more than my sister's carelessness was Elliot's reaction. He'd had none. We'd gone from open aggression to just . . . nothing. I might as well be a stranger.

I relinquished my book, far too keyed up to read and the noise of the party now too overpowering anyway. Another two dozen people had shown up since our arrival, and they'd all availed themselves of the bar. Lowered inhibitions meant louder voices and a few people performing tricks from the high dive.

I didn't want to give Elliot the satisfaction of leaving, so instead I swung myself up and padded over to the bar. I asked for something sweet and not too strong, and the bartender inspired a full-body flush by handing me something crudely titled a Sex on the Beach.

As I was taking my first sip, a ruckus erupted to my left. I turned to find a gaggle of drunken boys and girls starting to whoop and clap, their gazes pointed up at a boy with light-brown skin, poised on the edge of the high dive. I squinted up at him, shading my eyes with the flat edge of my hand against my forehead, trying to place him. The boy grinned down at his audience. Then it clicked into place—it was Daniel, from the ball.

"Anyone who doesn't think I can make a double half twist will owe me a drink!"

"It's an open bar!" someone shouted in response. He merely winked and took his dive position. Then, for just a second, I thought his gaze snapped to mine. Which was, of course, preposterous. I blinked and broke the spell; he catapulted off the diving board, performing an elaborate twist and tuck before arcing cleanly into the water. The boy's groupies swarmed him as he exited the pool, and I didn't pay him any more mind. My drink, embarrassing name or no, was really quite delicious, and I realized I'd already sucked down most of it. Might as well get another while I was up.

I got in line and finished my previous drink with a noisy slurp. The person in front of me turned, and we blinked at each other. Elliot.

To his credit, he neither turned back around immediately nor called me a money-grubbing alcoholic. He set his bar so low.

"I take it it's good?" He nodded at my drink. "What did you get?"

"Something about a beach," I hedged, feeling my cheeks heat. I would not say the full name to him. "Maybe you'll get lucky and I'll choke on the mini umbrella, and you can watch me suffer."

"Leo," he said my name like a warning. Or maybe an apology? Elliot squinched his eyes shut, adjusted his glasses higher on the bridge of his nose. "Carina shouldn't have said that about you, about your body."

"You're censuring my *sister* for being too mean?"

"I saw the way you reacted."

"And you jumped right to my defense."

"I—"

"What can I get you, sir?" We'd reached the front, and the bartender looked at us expectantly.

"Two of whatever she's having," Elliot said, indicating my empty glass.

"Two Sex on the Beaches, coming up."

And there it was. Elliot snorted a laugh. I punched him lightly on the shoulder, without even thinking. We just fell into old patterns.

"It's not funny," I said.

"It's a little funny. 'Something about beaches,' huh?"

"Who has sex on a beach, anyway? The sand would get everywhere. I hate beaches," I dug in grumpily.

"You've been to the beach, then? In space. And, uh, had sex there?"

"Klara had a beach birthday party on the digi-deck last year. There was manufactured sand and everything."

"Rich people," Elliot grumbled, bringing us right back around to the sticky point.

"You're one of us now. One of *them*," I corrected myself. "You can access the digi-deck anytime you want, go wherever you want." It was a gamble, pointing out his hypocrisy again. But he simply handed me my drink and hummed under his breath as we walked back toward our deck chairs.

"You didn't answer the question about sex. On the beach." I couldn't tell whether he was trying to be funny or genuinely asking.

"I'll leave that to your imagination," I replied. Let him chew on that.

"Leave what to the imagination?" Evgenia asked, pulling herself up and out of the pool.

"Uh, how speed dating on the digi-deck is going to work," I came up with on the fly as I settled back onto my chair. "It's the Valg event tonight."

"Yes, Leo was just telling me how much she's looking forward to going," Elliot parried.

Oh, no.

"Really?" My sister kicked over to the side of the pool, squealing with delight. "Leo, I was so sure you wouldn't go! Father said I couldn't do the nighttime activities without you, so this is perfect!"

Thoroughly stuck, I nodded. Guess I was going to be suffering through some virtual-reality speed dating tonight.

"Who is that?" Evgenia asked as she toweled off and put on her vintage wrap.

"Who?" I whipped around to find Daniel looking our way.

"He likes something over here," she mused. Then Evgenia pointed to herself and shouted loudly. "Lesbian, sorry!"

He cocked his head in confusion, then cracked a lopsided smile.

"That's Daniel Turan," Klara said from the edge of the pool. She was treading water like a sea nymph, hair and makeup dry and perfect. "His mother's from here, and he used to spend summers with us as a child," she continued. "Or so he told me when you pawned him off on me for a dance the other night. I don't remember him at all. And, of course, he's interested in politics." My cousin threw me a hard look.

Evgenia's lesbian disclaimer seemed to work. When I looked back over, he was wrapped up in conversation with a leggy redhead. Evgenia flounced down beside me with a dramatic sigh.

"How am I going to find like-minded ladies at this thing at this rate? I tried mingling earlier, and every girl kept prattling on about finding the perfect husband. And boys like that make me feel like a piece of meat."

I hummed my agreement. I could relate, to the feeling-like-an-object part at least. Just for good measure, I did a quick scan to confirm that Lukas Hagen was not in attendance.

"This name-tag thing is completely useless to me, besides," Evgenia continued on. "I don't need to know where people are from, but where they're going, you know?"

"There won't be name tags at the subsequent events, anyway," I said. "But you can browse profiles in the Valg app."

Evgenia rolled her head dramatically along with her eyes. "I'm so sick of that bloody rose chirping at me ten times a day," she said. "There needs to be an opt-out feature. Besides which, why a rose? We don't even have those up here."

"The *Scandinavian* does," I said. "There's a rose garden in the arboretum on the top level. And they chose the emblem a hundred years ago, apparently as some homage to an Old-World television program about love."

"I think it's romantic," Carina chimed in. She'd pulled herself from the pool as well, and was slowly and strategically drying herself off within Elliot's eyeline. "Like in *Beauty and the Beast*."

"That rose was cursed," I couldn't help pointing out. My sister shushed me.

"Are you coming to speed dating with us?" Carina asked Evgenia.

"Ugh, no, it's going to be a heteronormative snoozefest," Evgenia drawled. "Boys and girls circling each other like prey. I'll stick to the app, noisy flower and all. I've already matched with a few girls."

79

"There's going to be a queer and non-gender binary mixer later this week," Klara piped up. "But I know that regardless, this speed-dating event must feel very exclusionary."

Since when did Klara care about making things more equitable for all? Then I caught her stealing a glance over at Elliot. Seeking his approval? Was every woman I knew interested in him?

"Speaking of the app," Klara went on, "everyone going tonight, don't forget to fill out the dating questionnaire. It's required to participate. Leo, are you going?"

Suddenly all eyes were on me.

"I guess so?"

With a groan, I pulled out my tab, looking for that "bloody rose," as Evgenia called it. When I tried to tap on the dating questionnaire, I was prompted to fill out my personal profile first—which contained a whopping two hundred questions. Taking a long drag of my drink, I settled in to play catch-up. It seemed I would be participating in the Valg, whether I liked it or not.

7

The digi-deck was nearly at the bottom of the ship, two decks down from the royal quarters and located in the same forward section. The back half of the deck was all servants' quarters. Outside the entrance to the digi-deck, the walls were painted with dynamic Earth landscapes and serene sunsets, a preview of the delights on offer. Or perhaps they were a way to keep us calm so we wouldn't remember we were about to enter a giant windowless box. Though, really, weren't we already on a giant box, floating in space? Did the windows make it better? I took a deep breath.

The digi-deck was the *Scandinavian*'s passport to escape, a cavernous space that offered a 360-degree virtual experience of your choice. There were props to sell the lie, like the sand at Klara's beach party, and they even had rigs you'd strap into that jerked you to and fro, aiding the illusion that you were hang-gliding, or mountain climbing, or what have you.

I was not a big fan.

And so of course the speed-dating event was being held here. Two things I didn't care for, rolled into one. I was surrounded on all sides by a sea of smarmy, smug boys who were already scoping out the women—I noticed their eyes skim over and past me, settling on the younger, prettier, wealthier girls on either side. This was going to be a trial in self-control. Already I wanted to leave, and we hadn't even started.

We were corralled inside the digi-deck proper by Captain Lind, who made us line up in front of a series of doors arranged in a horseshoe shape, girls facing boys. Then she explained.

"First off, congratulations on arriving early and making the cut," she began as I cursed under my breath. They'd capped the event at the first twenty-five girls and boys to arrive, and I'd been stupid enough to be on time. "The digi-deck has been partitioned off into individual chambers, into which you ladies will go and sit. A young man will join you, and you'll be whisked away onto his idea of a perfect date."

I raised my hand. "What about *our* ideal dates? We had to answer a ton of questions on the Valg app about that."

"This event is about the men wooing the women. Go with it, Leonie," Captain Lind snapped.

My cheeks burned at her censure. I edged for the exit, imagining I could just slip away and escape this torture, but my sister caught me.

"Oh, no, you don't." She grabbed me by the arm and held me fast to her side while I squirmed. Quite the role-reversal for us.

"Every five minutes, a buzzer will sound and a new gentleman will join you," my aunt continued. "Gentlemen, you move to your right on each rotation."

I glanced across at my first "date," Theo Madsen. Like his sister, Asta, Theo was lanky, with short honey-blond hair and deep blue eyes, which were currently focused to my right, at my sister. Also to my right, next up for me, was Lukas Hagen. This was going to go so well.

"Now, you are each wearing a special sensor on your lapel that will pull up each other's profiles on your Valg app and offer you a yes-or-no option. At the end of the evening, we'll notify you of any mutual matches, and you can see your compatibility score based on your questionnaire. Easy!"

I fussed with my sensor, which I'd pinned awkwardly to my dress, whose unfortunately plunging neckline meant I kept feeling the sensor slip down into my cleavage. I righted it once more and caught Lukas enjoying the view.

"All right, ladies, head inside!" Lind called out, leaving me no time to do anything about it.

I slunk uneasily into a ten-by-ten room that was wall-to-wall screens. A dull purple light illuminated the space, barely. Even the floor was made of glass that would conform to the illusion. I didn't see any props in the room, which made me curious what Theo's ideal date would be. He'd always been a bit wild, so I was just relieved there weren't any rigs indicating an extreme-sport activity.

After about thirty seconds of waiting, the door shuttled open and Theo stepped inside. He offered a little wave, a nod to our having known each other pretty much our whole lives and yet rarely speaking.

"Hey," he said.

"Hey."

And then we fell into silence as we waited for the door to seal and the room to plunge us into Theo's fantasy date.

First the screens went black. Then the room swelled suddenly with loud music—insistent percussion, growling guitar riffs, and men screeching at the top of their voices. The light on the screens came up, just slightly, and we were in the middle of a crowded club. Well, the illusion of one. On one wall was a stage with a band playing its instruments with aggressive feeling, and on all other sides were people swaying, jumping, shoving one another.

"What the hell is this?" I screamed over at Theo, who had his eyes closed as he bounced up and down to the beat.

"PROG METAL!" Theo shouted back with a full-on grin.

"This is your idea of a great date?"

"Don't you like it?"

"Uh." I loved dance music, like EDM, and this had the barest hints of that. But it was just a bit beyond me. "It's fine," I hedged.

For a minute, I tried to dance, let Theo have his fun. But then he remembered that the point of this, theoretically, was to talk to each other. He pulled in close, talking loudly into my ear.

"What are you thinking?"

"Is that a trick question?" I didn't trust too-attractive

people. And Asta was always playing tricks in school. Theo was three years older than we were, so I wasn't sure where he stood.

He shrugged. "Just a conversation starter."

"Okay . . ." I tried to think of something semi-clever and not too personal. "I'm thinking it's very weird that the captain is moderating a speed-dating event. Bit below her pay grade."

"She's your family, so I figured you'd have guessed."

"Dressed?" I shouted back, mightily confused.

He shook his head, leaning in even closer and pitching his voice louder. "She's glad-handing. For elections. At least a quarter of us here are voting age, and another quarter may very well marry the quarter of us who live here. Lots of new voters to woo. I think she wants us all to think she's hip and fun."

"She is neither of those things."

Theo threw back his head and gave a great laugh. And then for a minute we danced. Or, more accurately, leaped around a bit. You couldn't say I didn't try. The song, at least, had levels, and during a slightly quieter bridge section, I took up the conversation again.

"What about you? I hear you're angling to marry a Lind to get a foot in yourself. Maybe my aunt's here to keep an eye on my cousin, make sure you two don't get too close."

Theo eyed me shrewdly. "What if my plan is to woo you, instead? Or your sister?"

"My sister is the least political person you'll ever meet, and we both know you have zero interest in me."

Theo stepped back, sly grin on his face. "You're feistier than I thought you'd be."

"And you're . . . tall," I replied, deadpan. "But seriously, are you interested in my cousin?"

"Should I be?"

"If you're aiming to become captain of this ship someday, yeah, probably. Though, that said, she'd never let you be captain. But you'd still get the political access, if that's what you want."

"It's what my parents want," he said, "and maybe what I want, just a little. I'm not the only one, you know. I've heard at least three other guys here are interested in the Lind ladies for the same reason. A few women, too, if you're so inclined. So watch out."

"How kind of you to look out for my virtue," I said. "I don't get the appeal of political power, anyway."

"It's your family's fault for limiting Scandinavian power in the fleet to the royal family and captainship. Some of us want to protect ourselves, and having a voice in fleet government is the only way to do that. You saw at the opening ball. Things are getting messy out there."

A buzzer sounded, calling time and ending my conversation with Theo on an oddly chilling note. The sounds of the concert faded into nothing, and the screens went dormant.

"See you later, Leo." He gave me a small salute and exited through the now-open door.

My wrist tab buzzed, prompting me to rate him yes or no. Surely I was a no for him, but . . . what if he put yes? Just in case, I picked no—I didn't want to match with him and seem desperate.

I leaned against the far wall, marveling at the sweat pooling at the base of my spine, as if I'd actually been jumping around at a concert. In fact, it was stuffy in here—of course they'd altered the room temperature to suit the illusion. Gross.

A soft chime sounded, and the wall at my back began to buzz.

"Please step back from the wall," a mechanical female voice said.

I jolted forward just in time as the back wall slid up. All I could see beyond was black, but I could hear something shuttling, like a conveyor belt. After a moment, a platform slid in through the opening in the wall, and I had to hop back to avoid it hitting me in the shins.

I didn't even notice the door behind me open and Lukas come in. I was too distracted by the piece of equipment in front of me.

"Awesome!" Lukas crowed, launching himself at the bench press in the middle of the room. He whipped off his shirt and lay down, clasping the weight with both hands. I was left speechless as the screens, all now fully back in place, transported us to a gym.

"Aren't you gonna spot me?" Lukas asked. I felt my jaw clicking.

"Your ideal date is you working out at the gym?" I asked. There was only one piece of equipment. Nothing for me to do but watch him. At least I'd be less sweaty. I could feel cool air now being pumped into the room.

"Don't you like the view?" Lukas waggled his eyebrows, flexing his muscles. "And seriously, I need you to spot me."

I spotted him, all right. And I talked about all the food I enjoyed eating the whole time, just to irk him. Five minutes couldn't be over fast enough, and rating him no was easy.

And on and on it went, a parade of boys from so many ships—the *Versailles, Nikkei, Shanghai, Empire*—and I feared my brain might begin to dribble out my ears, for all the dull small talk I was engaging in. And then there were the "dates." I was subjected to rock climbing, hiking, three instances of "dinner" (sans food), a cheesy sunset walk on the beach, the opera, deep-sea diving—all virtual facsimiles of the real thing that ranged from boring to excruciating. A few of the boys were cute and well-meaning enough, but after fifteen, they all began to blur together and I couldn't remember their names.

Then Elliot walked in.

"Uh, hi," I offered awkwardly, taking a seat on the couch that had shuttled in through the wall seconds earlier. It began to snow. A fireplace crackled to life on the screen across from us. Oh, no, it was quiet and cozy, which meant we'd have to actually talk.

"Hey. How's it been going?" He joined me on the couch, which I realized as he sat down was really more of a love seat. It was definitely built for two and meant to corral us close. Which it did. I could see beads of sweat drying on his temple.

"Been exerting yourself?" I asked.

"Dancing. Why? Do I smell?"

"Oh, no, just you're a bit sweaty."

"So are you. Dancing too?"

"Rock climbing."

Elliot furrowed his brow. "That's weird. You hate outdoor sports."

I hated how well he knew me. And the thrill of happiness that spiked through me at his consideration of what I did or didn't like—I hated that, too. It would be pathetic of me to allow myself even a moment of hope. Elliot had come here to see me suffer; he'd said so himself. That he'd been kind of nice to me at the pool, that he was being kind of okay now, was meaningless. I needed to remind myself of that. I reminded him, as well.

"What are we doing, Elliot? A few days ago you wanted me to suffer, and now that I am, you're concerned."

He looked as if I'd caught him mid–high-priced heist. Red crept into his cheeks.

"I'm really sorry I ever said that. It was in the heat of the moment, and . . . well, I did mean it, before I came here. I entertained wild fantasies of you being miserable, petty, and shallow, that it would be easy to hate you. But it's weird. You're exactly the same but completely different."

That statement was uncannily correct, for both of us.

"Anyway, it seems wrong to kick you when you're down." He grimaced. "Sorry; that came out wrong."

"No, that's pretty accurate." I sighed. "I owe you an apology. For everything that happened. My reasons for not marrying you were right for me at the time. I don't regret that. But I'm sorry for the way it went down. It was cruel to say yes and then change my mind the next day."

There was still so much left unsaid, like how despite the logic of it all, I'd never stopped loving him. That I'd said yes to his proposal and been happy for those fleeting twelve hours because I hadn't wanted to think about the practicalities. I had wanted to be another person, the kind of person who could run off with the person she loved and be poor but happy. A part of me still wondered if I could have been.

"Wow." Elliot sank back into love seat. For a moment, he wouldn't look at me, and panic seized at my insides. It felt like the right thing to say at the time, but what if I'd gone and made things irreparably worse—?

"Thank you, Leo. I didn't realize how much I needed to hear that. I hope this means we can be friends again?"

Friends, yes. We could be friends. I nodded.

"Good! I think you're the only person on board who likes the same things I do."

He indicated the side table, and for the first time, I noticed there was something on it. Two somethings. I picked them up.

"Are these reader tabs?"

"Reading by firelight as it snows outside," Elliot supplied. "A mix of a few things I mentioned on my questionnaire. And you like books. So this is why I'm wondering if the app tries to mesh together the interests of both parties."

"Well, my date with Lukas was him lifting weights and me spotting him, so tell me what part of that aligned with my interests?"

"Oof." Elliot cringed. "Other than that, you meet anyone you like yet?"

Oh, okay, we were launching into this level of friendship straightaway. It wasn't awkward discussing my marriage prospects with my ex-fiancé at all. I forced a laugh. "No, and I have no intention to."

Elliot tilted his head in confusion. "Aren't you trying to find a husband?" I appreciated that he left off the word "wealthy."

"Uh, no, that's my father's plan. I have other ideas for saving my family, thank you very much."

"Like?"

So I explained: about the water-recycling system, the patent, trying to find a pilot ship. Perhaps it wasn't wise to tell him everything, but a part of me wanted to show off. Show him that I wasn't some damsel in distress.

"But what happens if you can't get the patent or the pilot ship before the Valg Season is over? Won't your father make you marry someone?"

"Please don't remind me."

"Well, maybe one of these guys will be a mutual match?"

"I doubt it. I'm sure they all said no."

Elliot grinned and picked up his tablet. "I bet you're wrong." He began to tap and swipe the screen, his smile turning more mischievous than I liked.

I leaned forward with a whisper. "What are you doing?"

"You'll see . . ." He glanced down, then quickly back up. What was he—oh, God, I'd given him a view straight down my cleavage. I shot back up and waited. Finally he thrust the screen at me. "You have three yeses."

"Did you . . . *hack* the speed-dating system?"

Elliot shrugged. "I helped Captain Lind program it, so not exactly. But yes. I can't tamper with the results, but I can see what everyone put."

I'd forgotten he could do that. His father, who had managed the *Sofi*'s security systems, had taught his son everything he knew. Apparently Elliot had sought additional education since leaving us and had progressed to full-on hacking.

"You shouldn't be such a pessimist," he said, taking back the tablet. "Three out of fifteen is pretty good."

"You should check my sister," I said, more than a bit petulantly. "Bet she's gotten fifteen out of fifteen. Surely you gave her a yes."

"Leo—"

Elliot started to speak, but then the buzzer sounded. My wrist tab buzzed, insisting on the rating, but my finger hesitated over the screen. Who was I kidding? Elliot was a yes, always. I couldn't hate him, not really. But there was no way he was marking me a yes, and since he could easily hack the system, that meant I had to rate him no. My pride demanded it; I wouldn't give him the satisfaction of my desperation. Still, hitting no made me itch.

I deflated back into the couch cushions, half tempted to curl up and take a nap. My next few "dates" could watch me sleep! But then came the chiming voice again, telling me to vacate my position. I hopped up just as the couch started moving backward into the wall. It was replaced by a karaoke machine. Oh, no.

I looked up to find Daniel walking inside. Finally, I remembered his name.

"Are you as exhausted as I am?" he asked. "I think I've discussed my hobbies and family at least eight times by now. Uh, not that I don't want to hear about yours."

"I'm boring," I replied. "I like to read, dance . . ."

"And sing, I hope." Daniel picked up one of the mics and handed it to me. With a couple of taps and swipes, he pulled up the song-catalog menu. "We don't have time for any of the classic marathon numbers, but we could do something short and poppy."

"We're seriously going to sing karaoke?"

His laugh was warm. "Only if you want to. But I'm hoping you want to."

I didn't actually hate karaoke, so it wasn't too hard to acquiesce. It beat most of my preceding dates by a mile. I let Daniel pick the song and knew it immediately as it started up. It was an old, cheesy British pop song about the person you loved no longer loving you. And Daniel, sneaky thing, pushed the mic at me when it was time to start singing.

"This one's a bit high for me."

I should have been annoyed, but I liked the way his eyes sparkled and the fact that he was my first suitor who seemed to care whether I was having fun. Even if his song choice was unintentionally a little bit on the nose. And so I belted the hell out of the song, even as inside I cringed at every lyric reminding me of Elliot.

"Don't take this the wrong way," Daniel said, stopping the song as it launched into the third repeat of the chorus, "but you seem miserable."

I felt my face heat as I brought my focus back to Daniel. "Oh, I'm sorry." I stammered out an apology. "It's not you, I promise."

"Oh, it's fine! I like it. It's good to know someone else hates this whole thing as much as I do."

Even as he said it, he was grinning.

"You don't seem like you're miserable."

But he waved me off. "I'm the son of entertainers. It's in my DNA to fake it."

"Who are your parents?" I asked half out of politeness, half from desperate curiosity.

"Turan Entertainment?" he offered sheepishly.

It hit me like a lightning strike. I couldn't believe I hadn't put it together before. "You basically own the Klaviermeisters."

"Uh, just the tours. Not the people," he said with a laugh. "So is it your dad making you do this? Or your mom?"

"Both," he said. "They met during the Valg and swear by it. Mum wants grandkids, and Dad wants to ensure an heir to continue the family business. They act like I'm going to die any day now, but I keep reminding them I'm only twenty."

"Right? My dad acts like I'm a spinster at nineteen!"

Daniel suddenly turned grim. "You're nineteen? Oh, dear, that's it . . . We're done; you're ancient." Then he cracked a grin, and I couldn't help but laugh.

"You are far too good an actor," I said. "I believed you for a second. Although I'm fairly certain half the boys here totally believe that. I'm over the hill, and far too serious."

"Not too serious. You're keeping up with me, and that's quite the feat." He winked.

"You're rather full of yourself, aren't you?" I could say the same of so many people here, but on Daniel, I liked it.

"If only we had time for me to explain myself through song."

"We could have sung a duet, you know."

"Next time. There's a karaoke night in a few weeks. We'll show everyone."

And then the buzzer called time. I waved Daniel goodbye and then turned to the app on my wrist tab. My finger hovered over yes, but then panic spiked through me. What if he said no? What if he said *yes*? A mutual match was the last thing I needed right now. I couldn't conscientiously object to the whole Valg thing, to the idea that marriage was necessary to solve my problems, while also actively participating. No, I needed to focus on my other plans, on getting a meeting with one of the other ship captains. Not dating.

I hit no on Daniel, and the eight boys who followed. Then, finally, the twenty-fifth guy left my room—two marathon hours of social and emotional torture complete. But we weren't done! No, there was a dessert bar and cocktails and forced mingling for another hour. Everyone seemed to be happily conversing with someone—Carina was talking to Theo; Klara to Elliot. I hung back by the dessert table, availing myself of every variety of macaron, while I avoided speaking with Daniel again. It would be too awkward later when he realized I'd rated him no. He was nice, and it seemed cruel to lead him on.

Unfortunately, that left me wide open for Captain Lind to swoop in like a hawk diving for prey.

"Leonie, darling," she began, pressing her lips together tighter than a finger vise, "may I ask you something rather . . . indelicate?"

I braced myself for impact as she leaned in close.

"Did you run any background checks on your renters? What do you know of them?"

It wasn't what I was expecting. "Uh, no, I didn't," I said. "Their business is transports, and they were able to procure the necessary visas, so I didn't question them. Should I have?"

"Don't get so defensive. I'm not interrogating you," my aunt retorted. "But in light of the terrorist attack the other evening, it is my duty to investigate every avenue and every new person on board. As your guests went through you privately to rent your ship and join us on board, it represents a loophole in our security. I've personally vetted all the other Valg participants from off-ship . . ."

She let that hang, a tacit accusation that my renters had to be the missing link. "Don't call it a terrorist attack," I said. "It was a protest. They made a statement."

"Freiheit hacked our system from the inside and started a fire. Locked us in."

"And then let us out."

"Leonie, you are terribly naive."

Normally her condescension would have bothered me, but I was too preoccupied by a thought twisting in the pit of my stomach. The same day that Elliot arrived, we'd been hacked. And he had seriously leveled up his hacking skills since I last saw him. Elliot hated the rich and inequity in the fleet. Oh, no.

"Are you okay, Leonie?" Captain Lind asked in a way that was gentle—for her, at least.

"Leo," I corrected her absent-mindedly. I took a deep breath, schooling my features. "I'm fine. To be honest with you, I didn't think it was necessary to run a background check on my renters, since they came on Elliot's recommendation. He's practically family. And you had him help you with the speed-dating app, he told me? So clearly you trust him . . ." This was me taking a page from Daniel's book, trying my hand at being an actress. I must have done well enough, as my aunt seemed to back down, though I didn't entirely trust that she wasn't acting herself.

"Yes, sure, that makes sense," she said, flashing me a tight smile. "Thought I'd ask." She rapidly changed tacks, tone going brighter than a light bulb. "Now, how did you enjoy speed dating? Do you have your eye on any particular bachelor?"

Keeping up my airy façade for the rest of the hour was tedious, as all I itched to do was get back to my quarters as soon as possible. I needed to do that due diligence I most certainly hadn't done before the Orlovs arrived, or since Elliot's return. I needed to look into my new friends, into who exactly Elliot Wentworth had become. I was scared by what I might find.

"Attention, everyone!" Captain Lind called out, the end of the evening finally upon us. "Check your Valg app in an hour's time to see your results! Anyone you say yes to, tonight or over the course of the Valg, you'll gain access to your compatibility scores with and be able to browse their profile more in-depth. We've made sure to leave tomorrow free of formal Valg activities so you are able to connect one-on-one with any matches. Good luck, everyone, and good night!"

"So, how was it?" Carina bounded up to me, looking so hopeful that I hated to disappoint her. I'd get an earful if she knew I'd rated everyone a no, just in case.

"Great," I pretended, forcing a veneer of cheer into my voice. "How about you? Anyone promising?"

"Oh, yes, everyone was so nice! I had some really fun dates, including rock climbing! Klara! Elliot!" She waved vigorously, calling them over. I braced myself for impact, pasting on a smile.

"How did it go for you guys?" Carina asked.

I felt Elliot fall in next to me as we made our way back to the lift, but I refused to look over.

"Went well enough," he said. Suddenly I heard caginess in every syllable, deceit lingering behind every line. I risked a glance to my left and found a perfect poker face.

"Come on, Elliot, spill about all the girls you wooed. How many did you say yes to and who was your favorite?" Klara cut in, demure. She'd clearly given him an opening to compliment her, and I caught her look of annoyance when he didn't. Wait, was Klara into Elliot now?

"A gentleman never tells."

"Well, we'll find out in an hour who you said yes to, won't we?" Klara clenched her teeth as she said it.

Elliot escaped us at the first possible opportunity, heading aft toward the *Sofi* as soon as we stepped off the lift. By the time we got back to the Linds' quarters, it was nearly eleven—hardly late by any stretch, but after a long day, I was exhausted. First thing in the morning, I'd start digging into Elliot, look for anything that tied him to Freiheit.

"Leo, you can't go to bed yet," Carina scolded when I tried to turn in. "We have to wait for the matches."

I didn't have the heart to tell her I'd have none, but regardless, I humored her. We waited another half-hour, and just as my eyelids were drooping perilously low, both Carina's and my wrist tabs pinged. My sister squealed with delight, rushing to check. I was in no such hurry. She read off each name, and they were as numerous as I suspected—Ludwig, Philip, Min-ho, Oliver, Michel, Kaito, Theo, Elliot.

Elliot. His name repeated, rang in my ears. Elliot said yes to my sister.

My ears rushed with blood, drowning out the sounds of my sister's delight at all her options, at Elliot being one of them, especially.

Finally, I looked down to my own wrist tab and my notifications. I knew there were no matches waiting for me, but it gave me something to do, a distraction.

Even so, I couldn't help but feel hollowed out, disappointed at the message:

You have no matches.

8

I slept poorly and rose early to start my research. I didn't know what my aunt expected me to be able to discover on my own, given that the average resident was very limited in terms of access to fleet records. But still I found the Orlovs' business page and advertisements in the *Fleet Tribune*—they specialized in ferrying people to and from vacation spots, as well as moving food and supplies between the major ships. I found Evgenia in multiple party notices from the fleet's finest, usually arm in arm with Elliot, posing for the camera. Which brought me to my true quarry.

Little of where Elliot had been and done warranted news coverage. I did manage to find a minor note in the society section about his being named heir to the *Islay*, which mentioned that he came from the *Saint Petersburg* by way of *Lady Liberty.* He'd completely erased his history, where he'd truly come from—the *Sofi.* From me. I hadn't even known he'd gone to the *Lady Liberty* after he left us. The prospect loomed large that Elliot was now a stranger who'd gotten himself involved in something huge and dangerous.

What I hated was that in a way, it totally tracked. Growing up, when my mother was still alive and the *Sofi* could afford to fly on her own, though Elliot's father was technically a servant and my father had always been a horrible snob, we'd treated Elliot as an equal. Then both our parents died—his father and my mother—and everything changed. Docking with the *Scandinavian* and entering that world was a wake-up call for us both. Where you were born and into what position in society mattered. I received the best royal education, alongside my cousin and the rich of the fleet. Elliot was left on board *Sofi* to wait on my father part-time—though I fought vigorously against his ever being officially named valet. I didn't want that life for him. *He* didn't want that life for him. Elliot would rant against the trappings of the rich, and I'd agree with him, which was all well and good, until reality came crashing down. He wanted to marry me and escape to a better ship. I had to stay—my family couldn't function without me, and I didn't know anything else. My life was safe, and I was easily persuaded to stick to the status quo.

Even though we'd seemed to have buried the hatchet yesterday, the memory of a shockingly hateful and bitter Elliot clung to me like a film. I could see his hurt feelings, his big opinions about the state of the fleet, festering like a wound over three years. I could see him becoming radicalized. But would he really be complicit in attacking my ship? My home? Did he truly hate us that much?

I wasn't sure. With a groan, I dropped my head into my hands. Then my tab pinged a notification—since I was still logged into the *Tribune* database, it flashed up at me a breaking-news alert. The headline caught my attention.

FAIRFAX PROPOSES CONTROVERSIAL USEFULNESS MEASURE; SEVERAL SHIPS REVOLT

I clicked into the body and found the actual story less incendiary than the word *revolt* would indicate, though it was still a pretty dramatic development. Miranda Fairfax, who owned the largest American ship in the fleet, the *Lady Liberty,* and thus wielded significant power in the government, was proposing that all major ships be required to produce and export a resource that was vitally useful to sustaining the fleet population. Ships that were unable to meet the new standard would be embargoed from receiving the best goods, including and especially food and other luxury items. The *Scandinavian*'s chief industry was luxury accommodation, and it would not meet the new guidelines, should they pass a vote being held on the *Olympus* in four weeks' time. Other ships at risk included the *Empire,* the *Crusader,* the *Wuthering Heights,* and—indeed—the *Lady Liberty.* I was fascinated especially by the article's quote from Fairfax:

"I am not a hypocrite, and in fact it is an examination of my own conscience and the inexcusable drain on fleet resources that my own ship represents that has forced me to look inward and forward. The *Lady Liberty* is fully committed to reassessing our role in the fleet and making changes going forward," said Fairfax at a press conference held this morning.

It gave me a horrifically brilliant idea. My mother had been Miranda Fairfax's godmother, which would hopefully give me an edge—I couldn't believe I hadn't thought of it before. But this news gave me the perfect angle to pitch my water-recycling system. It would make whatever ship took it on very useful to the fleet. As long as they paid me the appropriate license fee, I would let them use their ship as the base of operations for the whole thing. My aunt would regret turning me down. Time to see if Miranda Fairfax wanted to go into business with me.

I switched to the messaging app and quickly searched the directory for her contact information, but it wasn't publicly available. Any contact information my mother had had was lost. So I'd try the general *Lady Liberty* administrative office contact and hope for the best. I made my case for a meeting in a quick message, being sure to drop my mother's name and connection to Miranda, and sent it off. It made me feel productive and softened the blow of the four rejections I'd received from other ships in the past few days. I was running out of major ships to which to appeal.

My wrist tab pinged with an invitation from Klara—in lieu of a formal Valg event, she had arranged a dinner party for that evening. I heard Carina's squeal of delight from the other room, followed by a shriek of "What am I going to wear?"

Forget clothes; how was I going to sit at a dinner table with Elliot for three hours and not explode? I had so many questions and feelings, including but not limited to "Are you part of Freiheit?" and "How could you say yes to my sister?"

Either could lead to my throwing myself across the table and throttling him. There was nothing I could do about my sister, short of telling her about the full extent of Elliot's and my history and admitting to the swirl of feelings I still harbored. And that just wouldn't do—my feelings were sacrosanct and not something my naive baby sister would understand.

But I could do something about my aunt's suspicions, my mounting fear that she was right. Resolved, I marched myself up to the bridge, where I found her crouched over her tab screen, brow furrowed. I knocked on the wall to announce my presence.

"Leonie, what a surprise to see you up here. Do you need something?"

"Yes," I answered, then backtracked. "No. Not exactly. I have an idea."

Her deep sigh communicated her annoyance. "My dear, I already told you that your little water-recycling idea is not a good fit."

"Even with the new usefulness measure being proposed?" It wasn't what I'd come to talk with her about, but I took my opportunity where I saw it. Captain Lind narrowed her eyes at me.

"That measure still has to pass, which I doubt it will, and look at you, keeping up with all the latest news. Regardless, I am not yet that desperate. No one wants to drink, bathe in, or touch dirty water."

"It's not dirty," I groaned. "That's the whole point. I refined the original designs I found, and it's truly seamless—"

"Leonie," she snapped my name like a command.

"That's not what I came here for, anyway," I said. "It's about my renters. The Orlovs and Elliot Wentworth. After we talked, you got me thinking . . . It was really bad form on my part, not requesting that they have background checks. That said, I really don't think they're radicals—"

"Terrorists, dear," Lind cut me off, like semantics were the point.

"Anyway. I'm here because I think you should ask them to submit to a background check. I'm sure they would. We can clear all this up."

"I don't know if that's wise. Tipping them off may inspire them to flee. I've promised my constituents not only an answer, but justice."

I barely suppressed an eyeroll at her politicking. "I'll ask them. Give me whatever I need to get their DNA, and I'll make up some excuse. I'll do it today."

Captain Lind considered me for a beat, tapping her fingers on the tab console. "Fine, you do that, and in the meantime, I'll interview the two transporters, for good measure. Max and Ewan Orlov?"

I nodded and obtained an advanced tab model from her. It had a small indentation at the bottom, the size of an index finger, which collected DNA and then interfaced directly with the highest-level fleet records.

"Don't go poking around on that thing," she scolded. "I'll be checking the search records after you've returned it, and don't think I won't jail my own niece for malfeasance."

Certainly I did not put that past her.

As I left the bridge, relief swooped at my insides—this would get everything sorted out by morning. Elliot and the Orlovs would pass the background check, surely, and I'd have to deal only with my other tormented feelings regarding Elliot, the Valg, and my sister. But then when I actually got to the *Sofi* and faced the deed of asking my new friends to undergo the procedure, I found my body superheating with shame and dread. I might as well march up to them and say, "Hi, I don't trust you." What if they took such great offense that they left?

I hesitated outside the *Sofi*'s aft entrance, pacing the *Scandinavian*'s dark loading bay, rehearsing what I might say to make the request sound less accusatory. Evgenia caught me mid-stride as she was exiting the *Sofi* and I was trying to enter.

"Leo!" she exclaimed, turning a near collision into a hug. Then she pulled me inside and started walking me into the ship, apparently changing her mind about wherever she was going. "I'm assuming you came for something to wear?"

"Uh, no? Why would I need something to wear? Weren't you going somewhere?"

"Oh, it's nothing—I was just going to avail myself of something from the med bay. I have a headache. And I meant for the dinner party tonight! I told Carina to tell you that the invitation was open to both of you, anytime. I have more clothes than I could possibly ever wear."

"We're not exactly the same size," I said, but she waved me off and bustled me past the maintenance hold and security bay, into the main artery of the ship, and into her room. Which was usually Carina's room.

"You're a bit bustier, wide in the hips, but I'm sure we can find something! Ooh, what's that?" She finally noticed the DNA tab in my hand.

"Oh, um, it's for background checks," I said. "I just got an earful from my aunt for not having you guys submit them before you arrived to rent out the ship. Apparently I'm in breach of protocol." A pared-down version of the truth came to me in the moment. Evgenia blinked at me, the smile seeming to fall from her face.

"Are you okay?" Suspicion snaked its way up my spine.

"Yes, yes," she said. "It's just . . . drunk-and-disorderly conduct wouldn't preclude us from being here, would it? I, um, may have had a few incidents in the past where I had a little bit too much, and might have stripped naked and run about a ship or two?"

"It happened more than once?"

"Maybe?"

I was relieved that it was something so minor, and also deeply ashamed at myself. That my first thought had been that, of course, they were guilty.

"Here, let me do it now, and then we'll find the others." Evgenia offered her index finger while I powered up the tab.

"I'm sorry to spring this on you," I said as she inserted her finger and the unit drew her blood. "I would actually love your help with a dress, if the offer still stands. I don't have that many nice dresses."

"Are you trying to impress someone specific? Eh?" She waggled her eyebrows at me comically. Then the tab unit beeped, and she withdrew her finger. I logged her submission and hit the prompt to sterilize the finger scanner, like Captain Lind had shown me.

"Uh, no, I don't even know who else is invited to the dinner party." Was I horribly transparent? That I knew Elliot would be there, and wanted to look my best? Looking good was the best revenge. Hope he enjoyed courting my sister right in front of me.

Evgenia didn't press any further.

"Well, let's go find the boys so they can get scanned," she chirped, and off we went.

Max and Ewan provided their fingers without even a shrug, which lulled me into a false sense of security. Because when we got to Elliot, whom we found reading in the lounge, he did anything but make it easy.

"Why do you need this all of a sudden?" he grilled me.

"Captain Lind insisted. She was reviewing everyone here for the Valg and realized I'd never had you all cleared. She'll have my head if I don't get it sorted."

"It's not so bad; only hurts a little," Evgenia chimed in helpfully.

"You're telling me that every single Valg participant from off-ship had to submit to a background check? Or is it just the rabble?" Elliot growled. And with that, I felt our little truce collapse in on itself. The twenty-four hours in which we were civil to each other had been nice, but now I could see I-want-to-see-you-suffer-a-bit Elliot back in full force.

I stuck to the script. "I'm just going by my aunt's instructions."

"And you always do what she says, right?" His eyes burned with accusation. This was about more than just a request for a background check. Elliot expected to get a rise out of me, but he got none. No, I shrugged and countered.

"I don't know what the big deal is, El. Don't you want to stay for the rest of the Season, take my sister out on dates? She was so excited when you mutually matched."

I heard Evgenia gasp but didn't take my eyes off his. Elliot's nostrils flared as he exhaled a shock of breath. "Leo—" he said, but whether he intended to argue or explain, I didn't wait to find out. I cut him off, delivering my sweetest smile and nudging the DNA tab forward, an innocent offering. Finally, he gave his finger over, and I couldn't help but feel that I had both won and lost something.

9

I delivered the DNA tab to captain lind as promised, and I returned to the *Sofi* several hours later to be made over. If Evgenia had a problem with Elliot's and my sparring, she didn't show it. I found her as bubbly as ever, and a dress was already laid out for me when Carina and I arrived. It was a vintage 1920s magenta-and-silver beaded-silk drop-waist dress that made me think of *The Great Gatsby* or an Agatha Christie story. Evgenia clapped twice, ordering me to spin. I was sure I looked like a disco ball crossed with a sugary French confection.

"Where did you get all of these, Evy?" Carina asked, surveying Evgenia's bursting wardrobe—previously Carina's wardrobe—her fingers wisping over intricate, lustrous beading and silk skirts. She, of course, had had her pick of Evgenia's dresses, and looked stunning in a deep-turquoise ruffled-and-tiered evening gown that showed off her tapered waist and slim hips. I was wearing the one and only dress of hers that would fit me.

"Oh, there are plenty of vintage sales on the *Lady Liberty*, *Versailles*, and *Saint Petersburg*," Evgenia replied breezily. "Whenever someone misspends their digicoin and falls on hard times, the family fashion heirlooms are the first to go. I've scored a lot of pieces from private ships merging with better-off ones, too. There are lots of old private ships going out of commission."

I thought about my mother's beautiful antique ball gowns in storage and who might purchase them when we finally gave up on the *Sofi* and sold everything off in desperation. Our ancestors had kept prize pieces from the twentieth century's most famous designers, though nothing that predated a 1950s Dior. I had to wonder about the fleet citizens who would have been rich and well-to-do enough to rocket off into space with actual 1920s pieces in such good condition.

Now that I thought about it, perhaps these were replicas from the 2020s. Even so, they were nearly two hundred years old and in impeccable condition. And I couldn't help but feel sad for the previous owners, wherever they were in the fleet now. If they had made it.

Following the theme of Old World Meets Pale Imitation, Klara decided to hold her fancy dinner party on the digi-deck. The compartments they'd used for speed dating were gone, and a long and narrow table was set in the middle of the large space. Four dozen candles—real ones—flickered low, sultry light onto a table packed with enough food to feed twenty, though we were only a party of six. And the setting Klara had chosen was a different *style* of ballroom than the one located two decks above. There were gilt wall accents and giant portraits of comely high-class ladies and stern-faced men in uniform on all sides.

"The ballroom is still being restored from the fire," she explained, but really I think she just wanted to show off her access.

So few people meant there was no avoiding awkwardness with Elliot, and indeed, because of Klara's seating arrangements, I ended up in the middle of his and Carina's flirting path.

The table was too large for the six of us, so the ends went unused and we sat three on each side. Klara and I held the middle positions on either side, with Lukas and Elliot flanking her, while I had the girls on either side. I frowned across the table to my left, an elaborate candelabra positioned just so to allow Lukas's appraising gaze to fall squarely on my décolletage. Thankfully, the 1920s were not a decade that favored hoisted cleavage.

And from my right came Elliot's gaze . . . which grazed straight past me to my sister, seated directly to my left. For her part, Carina simpered his way, eating her salad with a level of care that could only be to please him. While my eyes desperately wished to flick Elliot's way to analyze his every look at my sister, I refused to give him the satisfaction of my attention. And Lukas's appraisal made me want to fling myself across the table at him with my butter knife, so it left me to intently focus on my cousin. Or her profile, really. She angled herself toward Elliot and seemed to lean into him.

"Read any good books lately, El?" she asked. "You always had the best recommendations. Like that amazing Romanovs biography. I absolutely devoured that one."

"Really?" Elliot and I said practically in unison. A seven-hundred-page exacting biography of the last tsars of Russia wasn't exactly my cousin's speed. But she nodded emphatically at Elliot. "I adore the bloody and beautiful tsars and tsarinas," she said, while Elliot asked, "And what was your favorite part?"

"It was a bit dry at first," she started slowly, and I caught just a hint of force behind her smile. Aha—I wasn't wrong. No way she'd actually read it. She continued to hedge. "And I read it so long ago . . . but I'd have to go with Catherine the Great. I can't believe she was shipped off to Russia at fourteen and married off to her crazy cousin! It's like something from a dramatic romance novel!"

I'd told her that tidbit about Catherine the Great. *I'd* read the Romanov biography. *I* was the one with so much in common with Elliot. What was my cousin playing at?

"Complete with uprising and coup," I threw in slyly.

"And lesbians!" Evgenia chimed in. Klara looked confused, so she clarified. "Well, bisexuals, technically. Ekaterina had both male and female lovers."

"How gauche." Klara raised a carefully groomed brow. Evgenia scowled at her across the table.

"Hot," Lukas said. Despite his countering my cousin, I threw a dinner roll at his head and thankfully did not miss.

"Oh, aren't you two cute!" Klara's tone was cloying, a

wicked spark in her eyes. "I should have seated you next to each other, shouldn't I?"

"Why would you do that?" I asked through gritted teeth.

"You're courting, aren't you?"

"What an antiquated term," I deflected.

Klara nudged Lukas in the side and play-whispered, "Leo's shy."

"No, she's stubborn," he said. "You didn't say yes to me at speed dating. Playing hard to get, then?"

"I rated everyone no," I said. "I'm not interested in this stupid dating competition."

"But don't you have . . . financial problems?"

His false sympathy made me wish for the nearest airlock so I could throw him out of it. And throw in my cousin, for good measure. She'd fixed onto Elliot like a laser, her intentions more than clear—Klara wanted Elliot, and I was a threat. Meanwhile, I watched my sister deflate next to me, unable to keep up with talk of books and verbal sparring. Bizarrely, I felt bad for her—she had a crush on my Elliot, and he seemed to return the sentiment, which spread white-hot fire through my insides. Jealousy. Despair. Anger, at myself, mostly. And yet she was my baby sister, and I hated seeing her miserable.

"Speaking of playing hard to get, Elliot, you rated me a no as well," Klara segued, batting Elliot playfully on the shoulder.

"Uh . . ." he stammered, squirming in his chair. To my left, Carina unexpectedly bloomed, spine zipping up straight and a brilliant smile spreading her cheeks. She was back in play. I shoved a roll in my mouth, drowning out my groan.

"That's okay, I forgive you," Klara said, razor's edge in her voice. "But anyway! Tell me what you've been up to the last three years," she said. "I feel like I've not been able to properly interrogate you since your arrival, and I want to know everything."

Interrogate was the poorest possible word choice, given the background-check situation, but Elliot responded like a pro.

"There's not much to tell," he started. "I moved to the *Lady Liberty*, then made my way to the *Saint Petersburg*, starting out at the vodka distillery, nothing special. I met Count Korevsky—"

"A family friend," Evgenia interjected.

"The count promoted me and introduced me around—"

"This is where I come in!" It was Evgenia again. "He was too adorable, so I introduced him to my brother, and everyone became fast friends. Then Ewan introduced him to James and, ipso facto, now Elliot is the heir to the *Islay*!"

"Uh, yeah, that's the broad overview." Elliot smiled, taking a sip of wine. Evgenia was like his hype woman.

"What does that mean, exactly?" Carina asked, trying to reclaim Elliot's focus. "And didn't this Islay person have a son or daughter to pass their ship on to?"

"Oh, his name's not Islay," Elliot corrected, latching onto the least pertinent of her questions. "The ship is named after a place, not the family. He's called Thain. James Thain. And, no, he's childless, and he lost his First Officer some years ago to, uh, illness. I just came along at the right time, and he's training me to take over the family business."

"Whiskey's not that popular, is it?" Lukas asked, hiding a self-satisfied smirk behind a sip of his wine.

"No, not as popular as vodka, as far as spirits are concerned," Elliot answered politely, playing the airs-and-graces game like an old pro. "But I have ideas for increasing its profile among the fleet. With all due respect to vodka—" He nodded at Evgenia, who demurred, then looked down the table at Lukas and continued pointedly, "Whiskey requires a bit more appreciation and, in many cases, education."

I nearly choked on my own laughter, trying to play it off as a cough, and found Elliot's eyes on mine, burning with something I couldn't place. Not anger, like before. Relief? No, maybe it was the low light playing tricks.

"Well, you'll have to teach all of us to appreciate it, El," Carina said, stealing his focus once more. At least it wasn't Klara this time.

He grinned, rifling around for something under the table. A few noisy clinks later, and he triumphantly plunked a dusty bottle onto the table. "Great minds think alike, Carina. I brought some prize *Islay* whiskey for everyone to try."

"Blech." Evgenia further expressed her disregard by downing the rest of her champagne and refilling her glass.

"Hey, all the more for us," Elliot teased. But then he frowned. "Do you have glasses?"

Panic crossed Klara's features, the champion hostess challenged at her sport. I scanned the table; Elliot was right—we had champagne flutes, wineglasses, water glasses, elaborately decorated china, real silver utensils, candelabras, centerpieces

. . . a full spread, but no tumblers for the unexpected liquor. Klara snapped her fingers twice, beckoning her maid, Nora, over from the shadows. I'd forgotten she was there.

"We wish to sample some of Captain Wentworth's fine whiskey," she said, and promptly Nora disappeared again.

"I'm technically not a captain yet," he objected.

"You're too modest." Klara's voice tinkled like a bell, melodic and sweet. I'd never properly appreciated her skill at flirting. Did Elliot really like this stuff? He seemed to now.

"When will you become captain, then?" Carina asked, a seemingly innocuous question, but then Elliot blanched.

"When Captain Thain dies, presumably," he replied glumly. The mood of the entire party promptly plummeted through the floor. Then, fortuitously, Nora returned with the glasses.

"Wonderful!" Klara clapped her hands gleefully. I shared the sentiment. *Pour me a stiff one, please.* Elliot filled five tumblers with amber liquid and passed them around.

First I smelled it, tentatively. It did indeed smell earthy, similar to the mossy peat that sustained plant life in the *Scandinavian*'s greenhouse park. I'd forgotten the smell, here mixed with the tang of alcohol, and something else I couldn't quite place. Like a spice whose name I'd never learned.

Then I sipped. *Bitter* and *burns* came to mind as I tried to keep my features carefully neutral. I did not want to appear uncouth, too simple to enjoy such a refined drink. I swallowed it down. More burning. I surveyed the rest of the party, pleased to find Carina grimacing, Lukas confused, and Klara also carefully and suspiciously neutral. Then when she smiled wide and declared it delicious, I knew she was bullshitting. She found most wines too acidic and "like cat piss" to be drunk, and always reached for the fruitiest alcoholic option when presented—there was no way she cared for this spicy, earthy, burning stuff. I myself didn't hate it, but I now got what Elliot meant by it needing education and appreciation.

"It's, um, interesting," I said.

"You don't like it?" I couldn't read Elliot's tone. It didn't exactly sound judgmental. I took another sip. This time the burn was almost pleasant.

"Just interesting," I repeated.

"I think it's"—Carina coughed—"great." Everyone couldn't help but laugh at the ridiculous lie as she sputtered first from the remaining kick of the whiskey and then in indignation at our finding it so amusing.

"Don't worry, it took me a while to get into it," Elliot reassured her. This time, however, I could read him properly. He was lying to spare her feelings. Carina recovered quickly, beaming across the table at him. I returned to my glass of whiskey and took a bracing sip. This time, I just about liked it.

10

I suffered the flirting tug-of-war between Carina, Klara, and Elliot for another hour, becoming so desperate for relief at one point that I willingly talked to Lukas. Finally we moved on to the dessert course, and with each bite of crème brûlée, I counted down to freedom. But then Klara had to go and suggest dancing.

"Nora—" She beckoned her maid to come forward. "I know the servants like to throw parties on off nights. Is there one tonight? Think we could crash?"

"Um, yes," Nora said, voice small, tentative. "I could . . . take you as my guests? I'm sure no one would mind."

"What do you think, everyone? You up for it?"

It was the best idea my cousin had had all evening. Dancing was always a yes from me. I nodded enthusiastically. Carina clapped her hands at the idea. "Below decks? I've never been!"

"Isn't there the Scandi Club we could go to?" Elliot asked, voice strangely tight. "It's much nicer."

"Oh, yes, we haven't been there yet," Evgenia chimed in.

Klara waved him off. "We're already down here. And it'll be fun, partying with the help." She winked at him, and I saw Elliot clench his jaw so hard, the muscles in his neck jumped. Had she completely forgotten where Elliot had come from? She must have, to have her sights set on marrying him. I resolved to pull her aside later tonight, confront her about her newfound ambitions.

We finished our drinks and left our mess on the table for some poor servant to clear up, exiting the digi-deck area over to the other side of the deck. To get there, we had to make our way up one level via a public stairwell, then wend our way around a corner and a back hallway to a set of stairs labeled PRIVATE PERSONNEL ACCESS ONLY.

And then we were back down on the same level but on the other side, and in a different world. The servant-class quarters on board were still pretty nice, all things considered. There was just . . . less of everything down here. Less light, less heat, less food, less water, less space, less leisure. Captain Lind had put them on a rations system for water, food, and heat years ago—but only them. I couldn't help but think of Freiheit and their graphs, showing food supplies, population, and distribution. The *Sofi* had been on rations for years, and I knew how tough it could be. It was strange to realize I had more in common with the servant class than my royal cousins.

Nora led the way down a dim corridor past a row of identical plain doors, which were spaced more closely together than those above decks. I'd been inside one once, when Klara and I visited her childhood nanny. I remembered marveling at how little space one of the most important people in Klara's life got compared to what the royal family had. I wondered how small the bunks would feel now that I was four times the size I'd been at six.

We passed a shared kitchen-and-dining space on the right, but it was empty. A loud thumping sound reverberated down the hall and under our feet, signaling the party ahead. I knew exactly where we were headed. Elliot and I had crashed many a party down here, back when we were flush with love but had to hide it. The servant class was full of good people who didn't give a shit about a princess "slumming it with the help." I shivered despite the heat as my father's words echoed through my mind.

"The decor down here is . . . interesting." I caught Evgenia slowing briefly to squint at the walls.

"The servant decks are ABBA themed," I said, barely suppressing a giggle. It was one of the more bizarre things on board the *Scandinavian,* though I found it oddly charming, too.

"Why?" Evgenia tilted her head like a confused puppy. She was staring at a floor-to-ceiling-size portrait of Benny done in an abstract, Warholian style.

"You have a problem with ABBA?" Klara rounded on her, eyes aflame.

"Uh, no? I like that one song . . ."

Klara rolled her eyes. "'Dancing Queen'? So basic." Okay, sometimes I really loved my cousin. I snorted a laugh, quickly turning it into a cough when Evgenia's eyes flashed with hurt.

"All the words on the walls are lyrics," I launched into an explanation. "ABBA is a huge part of our pop-culture history."

"Miss Kolburg is right," Nora piped in.

"Call me Leo!" I corrected her.

"Uh, yes, I mean Leo's right. The decor is ridiculous, but we do quite like the music. You might hear some at the party tonight."

Evgenia raised her hands in surrender. "Okay, okay, it seems I am outnumbered!" She laughed, clearly not taking it too seriously. She hooked her arm through mine and mock-whispered conspiratorially into my ear, "You'll have to teach me the finer points of ABBA appreciation so I can fit in with the crowd."

We set off again, walking another minute down the long corridor until we arrived at the spot I remembered so well. They'd painted every possible surface black and lit everything with purple, pink, and blue strobes that washed over the central dance floor in alternating patterns. The old stage housed the DJ, who was sporting electric-blue hair and a shiny silver jacket that stood out among the crowd. Everyone was considerably dressed down, certainly compared to us, in sleek black with similar pops of metallic, neon, and bright. We looked ridiculous, like cream puffs and penguins in our finery. Accordingly, Elliot and Lukas shrugged out of their suit jackets, finding a clear table and an arrangement of seats on which to discard them.

I kicked off my shoes with a sigh, hearing a hiss beside me.

Klara frowned at my bare feet, nose wrinkled with disdain. "Gross, Leo." But I only shrugged.

"No one cares down here, and they clean the floors every day." This much I remembered from my adventures with Elliot.

"How bizarre!" Evgenia burst out a laugh, though not one at my expense, I thought. She sounded delighted. Balancing herself with a hand on my shoulder, she stepped out of her shoes as well, losing several inches of height but gaining a more radiant smile. Luckily, she was already dressed for dancing, having chosen a magenta tea dress with a vibrant butterfly-patterned tulle overlay. Then she grabbed me by the hand and dragged me over to the dance floor.

"We'll leave them to cluck about fashion faux pas over champagne while we have fun!" We wove through a sea of bodies to the center of the dance floor. Evgenia finally stopped and spun me around under her arm, like I was her date.

"Actually, they don't serve champagne down here," I shouted over the loud music. "And I'm surprised you're so low-key about fashion, considering!"

She shrugged, though maybe it was just a dance move. "I like dressing up, but what's the point if you can't have fun? It's good luck you chose the drop-waist silk, though, dear Leo. Not too frilly and perfect for dancing!"

I had to agree. Evgenia was earning more than a few looks in her fancy party frock. I glimpsed Klara, Carina, Lukas, and Elliot making their way onto the edges of the dance floor, and I saw many looks of confusion, as well as a choice few of consternation. I craned my neck to find Nora, who blended in easily in her black work clothes, and caught her making plaintive faces at those nearest her. A silent apology for bringing Klara below decks. Poor thing.

Lights strobed over my face, momentarily blinding me; I closed my eyes to feel the bass throbbing up through my feet. It felt good to be back. I'd not dared come back without Elliot in the years since he left. This used to be our place, where we could have fun and be free without fear of censure from my family. He used to kiss me on this very dance floor, and in the dark corners, and in the corridors . . .

My lips tingled from phantom kisses, burned with memories and regrets. I needed to stop thinking about it, about him. I flung my head back and closed my eyes as my body swayed drunkenly to the music.

The night was young, which meant many of the residents of the deck were still on duty. It meant I could never quite lose Elliot on my periphery. I danced, tried to let myself go, jumping up and down like an idiot every time the beat dropped, clasping hands with Evgenia and taking turns with spins and dips. Lukas circled the two of us, sidling up to me whenever I accidentally gave him an opening, pulling up too close, hips drawn to my ass like a stubborn magnet, hands far too grabby for my liking. But Evgenia had the sense of a hawk and would quickly edge him back out from our circle of two every time. She was rapidly becoming my favorite person, not only for this, but because she was currently the only woman I knew who wasn't trying to court Elliot.

. . . Unlike Carina and Klara, who were locked in the

most awkward little dance circle with him, their frustration mounting to the point of palpability. I could feel it across the dance floor, ten feet away. My eyes betrayed my better sense, flicking over to the trio far too often, cataloging the unfolding of events: Klara edging Carina out of the circle, grabbing Elliot by the shoulders, and trying to force him into an intimate slow dance, counter to the beat of the music. Carina smartly used a song transition to grab him by the hand, spin under his arm, and restore the circle. Well, it was more of a triangle, really. Or a cluster.

Nora joined them, welcomed readily by Elliot, who opened up the circle for her and graced her with that smile, those dimples. Rightly distracted by the brilliance of Elliot's affection, Nora missed Klara's contemptuous glare. The music changed, to an ABBA song of all things, and the group dynamic shifted. The song was slower, though by no means a slow-dance kind of song, yet Elliot grabbed Nora by the arm and pulled her into a twosome, leaving Carina and Klara to dance awkwardly with each other.

But I scarcely noticed the drama with the two girls. Instead, I watched Elliot and Nora, rapt. Nora threw her arms up over his shoulders, and his arms whispered over her hips. Elliot leaned down close to her ear, and I watched his lips move like someone from a silent movie. Whatever he was saying was delivered with a half grin. Nora's cheeks flushed, though maybe from the dancing?

My throat went tight. Here I was, forced to watch Elliot flirt with yet another girl, right in front of me. Dance with someone else, hold her the way he used to hold me, in this very place. Every second was torture. I could see them swaying to the music, Nora bouncing up onto her tiptoes to respond in kind, lips to Elliot's ear, a matching smile on her face. What I wouldn't give to hear what they were saying!

I felt someone jostle my side, and I whipped my head around to tell him off. Ugh, Lukas again. Evgenia the saint swooped in, giving him an uncharacteristic ice-cold look, and he finally gave up, going over to join Klara and Carina. Both were dancing halfheartedly, as engrossed in *The Elliot-and-Nora Show* as I was. Lukas was poorly received. It became a pleasure to see him ignored by both my sister and my cousin. I almost felt bad for him.

Almost.

Laughter bubbled up my throat, my brain conjuring a sliver of humor from the depths of my misery. I threw my head back, guffawing, admittedly fueled by many more drinks than just the evening's earlier whiskey, and spun myself around in a giddy circle. And caught Elliot staring at me. I stopped midspin, rendered frustratingly self-conscious. I fussed with my hair, elegant-curls-turned-tangled-mess, and tugged again at my slip, which had ridden up frustratingly high from all the dancing. Elliot's gaze was assessing, of what, I wasn't sure. I didn't see Nora.

"Why did you stop?" Evgenia had to raise her voice high to be heard above the music.

"I'm going to grab another drink," I shouted back, though I did not tear my eyes away from Elliot's. I was a glutton for punishment. But then Elliot flinched, turned his focus back to Carina and Klara. Had I just won something? And where had Nora gone?

"Do you want one?" I asked Evgenia, making good on my story. I could use a break, anyway.

"No, I'm good!"

I made my way over to the bar and ordered water. It was time to reclaim my head and avoid a headache tomorrow morning. I turned, cooling my sweaty back against the ridge of the bar, scanning the room for Elliot's familiar blond head. I scolded myself for my obsession, and again for the swoop of disappointment I felt when I couldn't find him.

"Done dancing?"

Elliot snuck up on my left, startling me off-balance. I swayed drunkenly to my right, but his hand on my left arm steadied me upright. In the process, I lost half my water, which sloshed over my right hand and down my arm. I flipped around to lean front-ward against the bar, gesturing with my hand and half-empty glass at the bartender to top me back up. Then I turned to Elliot.

"Plus ça change, plus c'est la même chose," I said.

"Since when do you speak French?"

"I don't. But you do now," I replied pointedly. "I looked it up."

Elliot laughed. "I don't speak French, Leo. Just that phrase. 'The more things change, the more things stay the same,'" he quoted. "Ewan says it all the time. He's the polyglot, not me. Don't you know that, from your background check?"

It was a dig, but he didn't say it with too much venom. Were we being playful now?

"I told you, the background checks weren't for me. And the results aren't in," I grumbled. I could feel my cheeks reddening, not that Elliot could see it in the low light.

"You really think I've changed that much? You don't trust me?"

"Lind doesn't trust you," I said. "And . . . yes, you've changed. You have your own ship, and money, and can hack apps. You drink whiskey."

Elliot considered me a moment, expression carefully neutral. "I don't think I've changed in the ways that matter," he said.

I found that hard to believe. Even now, standing next to him, I felt stiff, unsure, on guard—things I had never felt with Elliot before. *I* hadn't been the one to change, had I?

"Sprechen Sie noch Deutsch?" I asked, going for a bit of levity. My tongue always went more readily to German when I had been drinking, and I did wonder if he still remembered it.

"Ja, natürlich," Elliot replied. "And why are you using *Sie* with me?" He switched back to English, pointing out my use of the formal *you,* typically used with elders, authority figures, and strangers. But the informal *you* felt wrong with him now. Bless German, with a whole system for putting distance between you and another person.

I shrugged, refusing to put into words the change in our relationship, and hoped he would drop it. I sucked down the rest of my water. Then I got a refill.

"Were you getting a drink too?"

"You've got the right idea, I think." Elliot signaled the bartender and asked for his own water.

"It's fun being back here," I said after a minute of nicely awkward silence as we both sipped our waters.

Elliot grimaced. "Sure. But you, uh, didn't think it was kind of inappropriate to come here?"

"What do you mean? We used to come all the time."

"I brought you as my guest, because we were . . . you know. And they considered me one of them. But now I'm just some rich asshole, and half the royal family has descended on their private space. We're putting Nora in a really uncomfortable position."

"She said it was fine . . ." I offered anemically. Cold realization washed over and through me, the chill converting to acidic heat as it settled in the pit of my stomach. He was right.

"You usually read people better than that, Leo. I was hoping you'd understand, say no when Klara tried to rally us."

"You're saying this is my fault?" Guilt was replaced with indignation. I'd made a mistake, yes, but why was he putting all this on my shoulders? "It was Klara's idea."

"Carina follows your lead, and you could have outvoted Klara. I thought you'd get it when I suggested the Scandi Club."

"I can't read your mind!"

"It's common sense. And asking Nora to call you Leo in front of everyone? You're not her equal, not with the way things work here. Couldn't you see it made her uncomfortable?"

My whole body burned with shame, mingled with the electric tingle of jealousy. Elliot was awfully concerned with Nora's feelings all of a sudden.

"Fine, then I'll leave, since it seems I've fucked up so unimaginably." I pushed myself off from the bar, ready to flounce off in my embarrassment, but Elliot caught my arm.

"Don't be so dramatic." He sighed and rubbed the bridge of his nose, under the frontispiece of his glasses. "We're already here, so leaving is pointless."

I wrenched my arm free. "I'm not being dramatic," I scolded him for scolding me. Even though I was, indeed, being dramatic. But he was being patronizing.

"I should get back to Evgenia," I said, finishing my drink. Really, despite his reassurances, I still wanted to leave. But I felt duty bound to ensure that Carina got home without incident. I'd let her drink tonight only because I was supervising, which in hindsight was a huge mistake, given her apparent goal of making Elliot notice her. Dangerous when young and drunk.

He gave me a parting salute as I careened back onto the dance floor, keen to lose myself again to dancing and waste away the hours until I could leave. My bed called to me, but I pushed myself on. I found Evgenia dancing close with a gorgeous redhead and couldn't bear to interrupt. Like a shark sensing blood in the water, Lukas appeared.

"Hey, Princess!" he shouted into my ear.

"Don't call me that!" I shouted back.

"Okay, okay." His hands went up in a defensive position in front of his chest, as if I'd brandished a weapon. Then he balled his hands into fists, doing a little maraca shake with them and rolling his shoulders along to the music, clearly blitzed and dancing like an idiot without care. It almost endeared him to me. Then Lukas offered his hand and actually waited for me to take it, like a gentleman. After a moment's hesitation, I did, letting him spin me under his arm, then back out, and in, ending up flush against his chest. But his free hand didn't grab my waist or hips or butt as I had expected him to. Had I misjudged him?

Lukas sidled close, nudging his nose close to my ear. "Imma kish you, 'kay?" he slurred, and with that, I was officially done.

"No, thanks!" I pushed back hard against his chest, and he stumbled back into two girls who toppled over in their too-high heels, who then shoved him back in my direction. He deflated like a punctured tent, flopping himself against me and leaning into my side for support.

"Leo, don't be such a tease!" I could smell the alcohol on his breath, his face uncomfortably close to mine. If he went in for a kiss, I could elbow him in the ribs. Or knee him in the groin? Before I could decide, he jerked away as if from an invisible force. "Frex you!" he shouted, but not at me, I realized. At Elliot. Who had pulled him off me.

The scene came to me in flashes as the strobe lights fanned down over the crowd. Lukas struggling against Elliot's grip on his arms. Elliot shouting something at him as he pulled him farther away from me. Lukas breaking free, slamming his fists into Elliot's chest, barely moving El an inch. He was taller and stronger.

The crowd fell back, putting us in the middle of a circle none of us cared to be in. Electricity crackled in the air with the anticipation of a fight. But even though Lukas squared off, fists raised to chest level, feet bouncing like a boxer, Elliot refused to take that bait. I held my breath as he gave Lukas one last appraising look, shook his head, and turned to leave.

I inched back, equal parts glad they didn't come to blows and crestfallen that Elliot had left me with Lukas. What had *that* been? If the point was saving me, why not finish the job properly? Whisk me away, like a knight in shining armor, and make sure I was okay?

Because he didn't care about me anymore, not like that, I realized. I craned my neck above the crowd, falling back into their messy dance clusters, seeing Elliot go over to Carina, duck his head to say something close to her ear. He must have come over at Carina's urging. It was my sister who had watched out for me. I felt a surge of sisterly love, replacing the sour tinge of bitter disappointment.

"Leo, what just happened?" Evgenia appeared beside me, eyeing Lukas accusingly. He was still standing several feet away, pouting like a five-year-old, but not coming any closer. I allowed myself to be led off the dance floor, Evgenia going into mother-hen mode. "I'm sorry. I was caught up with a . . . new friend, and I heard the commotion . . ."

Once we made our way to the sidelines, I took note of her smudged lipstick. Good for her. I leaned against the wall and craned my neck back, letting a cool stream of air from the vents wash over me.

"It's nothing," I said. "Lukas was too drunk and tried to kiss me. Well, wanted to. I shut it down." Now I was feeling a bit defensive. Had I really needed saving? I'd been doing just fine. "Elliot misunderstood."

"Did he? Lukas has been pretty pushy with you all night," she said. "I should have been there." Then she enveloped me in a hug, which at first I found confusing but then melted into. It was exactly what I needed.

"I think I just need to go to bed, but I don't want to leave Carina."

"Carina? I don't want to leave *you!* We need to decompress a bit, I think. Hold on."

Evgenia disappeared into the crowd, which had grown considerably since we'd arrived, and I hung back in the shadows to wait for her. Then Klara clopped by in her heels, probably on her way back from the bathroom. Remembering that I needed to talk to her, I called her over.

"What's gotten into you?" I asked the question that had been bugging me all evening. "You went from zero to sixty with Elliot. It's a little weird."

"Why is it weird?" Her words were a little too loud and enunciated. She'd had too much to drink.

"Well, he's my ex, for one," I continued against my better judgment. "And you didn't even want to go to the Valg a week ago, and now you're all in and gunning for him, of all people. Not being subtle about it, either."

She gave an exasperated sigh, like I was such a bother

to her. "Leo, he doesn't even like you anymore. You said so yourself to me."

I stammered incoherently, rendered speechless by her throwing my own words back at me.

"You know how hard it is to find a guy who's nice, pretty solid all around. Not trying to use me for my family name. I need this."

"But why Elliot? And who's to say he wouldn't use you? He's pretty political."

"He runs his own business. We'd be on equal footing."

"I cannot believe you."

My cousin merely shrugged. "Would you rather have him land with your sister? I saw you losing your mind at dinner." Klara was sharper than I'd given her credit for.

"I—" There was no good way to follow on that.

Evgenia picked that moment to return, her satisfied look melting into one of concern at the sight of us. "What's wrong?"

"Nothing!" Klara chirped, promptly swanning off and leaving me wholly unsatisfied.

"I'll tell you about it later," I mumbled under my breath.

"Well, I've got it all sorted," she said, forging on. "I'm taking you home with me, and Nora will make sure Carina gets back to your place safe and snug and a bit more sober. I instructed Elliot to start feeding her water, and scolded him soundly for not yet having done so."

"Wait, what do you mean by 'taking me home with you'?" I asked.

"We're going to have a sleepover. Girls' night. You and me."

"Aren't we too old for that?"

"Never!" Evgenia hooked her arm through mine and started pulling me toward the door before I could protest further.

11

The club was located aft near the docking area, so it took only a few minutes to get home. Proper home, the one I almost missed; *Sofi* welcomed us with her aging chrome and dim lighting.

"Now, I think *you* actually would know the best sleeping arrangements in this case," Evgenia said as we got to her room. Well, Carina's room. "Are there spare linens so you can kip on the floor? Do you want to crash in a spare room? Are there any?"

There were the staff quarters, which I had no desire to revisit, let alone sleep in. My choices there were limited to Elliot's old room, his father's quarters, or a couch in the crew mess. No, thank you. And the Orlovs, plus Elliot, were using all the viable bedrooms. While there were additional quarters tucked away from when the Kolburg family was a bit more generous, allowing a cousin or three on board, I'd decommissioned them years ago to save energy resources.

Opening them up, making the beds, heating them . . . it wasn't worth the hassle, and I wasn't in the right state to manage it, anyway. The floor looked great.

"I'll grab a spare duvet and pillow," I said, leaving Evgenia and heading on instinct down the hall from Carina's room to mine, where I kept extra bedding.

I crammed my fingers against the bio-lock, fumbling the first time and missing a finger—I clearly was still a bit tipsy—and then autopilot carried me across the room, past my inviting bed, to my closet. Another bio-lock there—an extra layer of security I added to keep Father and Carina out—and I walked inside. I stopped short, frowning at the space that used to hold my dresses now full of trousers, shirts, and waistcoats. A fresh wave of mortification rolled over me that Elliot was sleeping in my room, had access to my things. I checked my underwear drawer, just for good measure. Empty. I was being silly. I shook it off, turning and going a few more steps in to the back shelf where I kept the linens.

On my way out, I had a thought. There was no way Evgenia had any sleepwear that would fit me, the dress tonight a fluke of generous draping. I chucked the bedding out into the bedroom proper and pulled a simple sleep dress from a drawer. Now to get out of *this* dress . . .

I never felt better removing the stupid slip, dumping it on top of the silk dress, and standing still a minute to let the cool air dry the sweat that had pooled around my chest and lower-back areas. Then I stepped out of my low heels and went to unhook my bustier.

"Scheisse!"

I whipped around at the voice behind me.

Elliot stood at the door, his mouth agape.

"What are you doing here?" I screeched, holding the sleep dress over the front of my body, though it covered very little. He'd certainly gotten an eyeful of me in my underwear. Elliot's back was turned now, anyway.

"What are *you* doing here?" he shot back accusingly. "I'm sleeping in Evgenia's room. I came to get sheets."

"And undress?"

"It *is* my room," I sniped back.

"You're not supposed to be here," Elliot insisted. I looked down at the crumpled slip and dress. No way was I putting them back on. Fine, we'd do this the annoying way.

"Don't turn around," I instructed with a huff, turning my own back for good measure while I contorted my arms around to unhook my bustier. Once I had it off, I threw it on top of everything else and pulled my nightie on as fast as I could. I hated how skimpy it was, but my modest pajamas were with the rest of my things on the *Scandinavian.* It was as if fate had manufactured this moment to be as embarrassing as possible.

Gathering up the discarded clothes in my arms, shoes hanging from my thumbs, I moved back out into the room, stepping around Elliot. He stood still as a statue but swiveled his head around to me, then darted his eyes down at the floor.

"You've, uh, grown a bit since you last wore that, I think," he said, his tone holding a hint of amusement.

"It's the only one left here," I grumbled, pulling awkwardly at the tight fabric catching on my too-wide hips. There was nothing to be done for the strain in the bust area. Nudging the fabric in any direction would be disastrous. "Teasing me isn't very nice."

"It's better than yelling?"

I remembered the duvet, sheets, and pillows, pooled near his feet. Utterly gracelessly I bent down, holding everything tight against my body like a shield.

"It's safe to look now," I informed him, and finally he pulled his focus from the floor. Then he laughed at me again.

"You know it's kind of ridiculous, considering I've seen everything before."

I suffered a full-body flush at the implication. "Yeah, well, those privileges have been revoked. And on that note, I don't need you to defend my honor. Lukas didn't even do anything."

"It didn't look that way to me."

"I had it handled," I huffed. "And now everyone is going to talk about how you got into a fistfight with him over me."

"Does that bother you?"

"Does what bother me?"

"That people might talk about us." Elliot dropped his voice low and took a step toward me.

I might as well have chucked the duvet and stripped off the ill-fitting nightie—I felt naked anyway. I writhed under his stare. "You're still drunk," I blurted. "I think you have me confused for the wrong sister. Good night."

And then I left.

*

"You look as if you've seen a ghost," Evgenia remarked when I returned. She tilted her head and squinted in assessment. "And you're . . . really pissed off about it? What did I miss?"

"I'm mad at myself for being completely useless," I said, too keyed up to lie. "Elliot walked in on me practically naked, and then I think we were flirting with each other, but then I reminded him how he's interested in my sister." I worked consciously to stop scowling. It took several tries to unclench my jaw.

Head righted, now Evgenia's perfectly groomed brow disappeared up into her fringe. "And why were you practically naked?"

I dropped the duvet, sheets, and pillow to the floor.

"Ah, I see. Cute nightie." She hopped up from the bed, grabbing her dress and slip from me to hang them back up in the wardrobe. Then she took both hands and pulled me over to the bed. She patted beside her, directive clear: *Sit.* So I did.

"Spill," she said. "You and El have been acting incredibly odd, hostile one minute and sneaking glances at each other the next. Don't think I haven't noticed."

"It's . . . complicated," I hedged, trying to buy myself a bit of time. It was, after all, true. I opened my mouth to speak, but the answer didn't come tripping off my tongue. My tongue was weighted like a slug in my mouth, stubbornly staying put.

Evgenia eyed me circumspectly, then said, "Let me guess: You're utterly and terribly in love with me, right?" The joke broke the tension, and I laughed.

"Listen, it's—"

"Don't say 'complicated' again."

At this point, I'd danced around it too long and too awkwardly not to just come clean. But I'd also kept it in so long, so used to not telling anyone. Exposing myself and my pain did not come easily, but neither did new friends. Evgenia was the closest I'd had to a true, equal companionship since, well, Elliot. I took a deep breath. Finally, it tumbled out.

"We were engaged. Technically only for twelve hours," I quickly corrected. Eight of those hours I'd been sleeping, on cloud nine. It took only four from the moment Father found out for him to dismantle everything, with an assist from Klara and Aunt Freja.

"Engaged! Wow, that is serious." Evgenia frowned. "You know, that does make sense, now that I think about it. I knew he was bitter about his past here, and weird about you . . . and then there's the whole Valg thing." I didn't miss the way Evgenia cringed, as if in self-censure from saying too much.

"What do you mean?" I asked. She suddenly found her fingernails incredibly interesting. "Evy, please."

"It's just that he may have mentioned to me that his plan was to hurt his ex a little, make her jealous, by participating in the Valg. I just never put it all together, that it was you. I thought Klara might be the one—"

"Klara and Elliot?" I exploded. "No way. He was way too poor for her . . ." My mouth soured at the realization that that was no longer the case. Klara and Elliot could very well now be a union that came to fruition. He had money, and apparently she'd changed her mind about the whole marriage thing.

"Now that I know it's you, I'll be smacking him fully upside the head for his idiocy. You're amazing. And . . . wait. Wasn't he flirting with your sister tonight?" Her mouth twisted. "Oh, Elliot, you colossal moron."

I barked a laugh. "Right?" Then I fully processed the implications of Evgenia's confession. The Valg had been his plan to make me suffer. Well, he'd succeeded admirably.

"And if I'm half as good at reading people as I know I am, you're in no way over him. You still care."

I groaned. "Yes, because I'm a glutton for punishment. But . . ."

"But?"

"I don't trust him. With the Freiheit hack the very night he arrived, it all seems too coincidental. He's a pretty good hacker, and he was outside the ballroom when it happened." I let it all out against my better judgment, realizing as I rattled on that I was too intoxicated to be having this conversation, and with Evgenia of all people. I slapped a hand over my mouth, as if to take it back. "I'm sorry. I shouldn't have . . . I know you're his friend." *Friend, and possible accomplice,* I realized. None of them had passed the background checks yet. Evgenia remembered too.

"So that's why there was the whole thing with the checks," she said. "We're not involved with that faction. Elliot didn't help them. None of us did; I promise you that." Evgenia worried her bottom lip with her teeth. "Leo, you're really nice, and I—" She sighed. "I had no idea you were Elliot's target, I promise. I'm going to talk to him. He needs to stop this charade; it's gone too far."

"Oh, God, no, don't do that." Panic shot through me. "I'd be mortified if he knew, if he thought that I was still desperately in love with him or something, and that I needed you to go to bat for me."

"*Are* you desperately in love with him?"

She stopped me short with her question. I took a breath, ready to reply, then deflated back into the pillows for a moment to think. "I don't know," I said finally. It was as close as I could get to the truth that I was willing to admit to myself. My feelings for Elliot were complicated. He'd turned into a bit of a dick, but the worst parts of me loved his fire, regardless. I could give as good as he gave; as ever, we were stubbornly well-matched. I hadn't been my best self either since his return.

"Fine, I won't talk to him about that," Evgenia said, clearly not happy about it. "However, you need to talk to your sister. Or does she know that you two were engaged and you still have feelings for him, and she's throwing herself at him, regardless?"

"Carina knows about the relationship, not the engagement. And she thinks I'm over it. I told her I was over it," I said. "And it's not entirely her fault. He matched with her at speed dating. He said yes."

Evgenia furrowed her brow. She had no ready reply, some explanation that would excuse Elliot. "Well, you need to talk to your sister anyway. If she doesn't back off to spare your feelings, then she's a horrible person. Your suffering in silence is a terrible idea, and their getting married is out of the question. It'll torture you."

"Okay, I'll talk to her. But there's the bigger problem of Klara," I said, feeling my jaw lock and fighting to keep my teeth from grinding together. "She's gunning for him too."

Evgenia snorted. "I could tell. She has the subtlety of a speeding meteor. You'll have to talk to her, too, then."

I shook my head. "I did talk to her tonight. She said it's really obvious he doesn't like me anymore, so I should back off."

"I kind of hate her. Is that okay to say? Since she's your cousin?"

"Right now, I kind of hate her too," I had to admit. "I don't understand what's gotten into her, to be honest. She wants to get married less than I do. Or wanted." I exhaled heavily through my nose. "I don't even want Elliot for myself. I've resigned myself to it being over. But I can't bear her having him."

I ducked my head to avoid Evgenia's piercing stare. She was calling bullshit.

"We're going to fix this," Evgenia said, clapping her hands. "I will be your wing-woman. Elliot's my friend, and you're my friend, and frankly I am kicking myself for not seeing all of this before, because only thinking about it for two seconds, it's supremely obvious how perfect you are for each other. Of course you were in love."

Were. I flinched at her use of the past tense. She noticed.

"Oh, Leo," she said, and then she pulled me into another well-needed hug. "Don't worry. We'll figure it out. I'll do everything short of talking to Elliot. It'll work out. You'll see."

The warm circle of her arms seeped into my weary bones, and a spark of hope ignited somewhere deep inside me. Maybe this was just what I needed. Someone to talk to, be honest with, who didn't blame me and wasn't trying to win Elliot for herself. I hugged her back and allowed my hope to burst into a raging flame.

12

Breakfast was awkward.

I'd pretended I hadn't known what Elliot meant—did it bother me that people might think we had something between us? The deflection about my sister was a jab at him, a sidestep of my true feelings. But I would not expose myself, be vulnerable, especially not in light of Evgenia revealing his plans. How could I trust that his revenge scheme was over, that everything Elliot had been doing wasn't a part of that long game? His apologies, coming to my defense, teasing me about old times. I couldn't trust any of it.

Elliot stared at a point just past my head, though I didn't miss the way his eyes flicked down to my chest every so often. Each time, he would flinch, catching himself and immediately going back to looking anywhere but at me.

It was Evgenia's fault. She'd insisted I come to breakfast in my too-small nightie.

"He won't know you have a change of clothes from

yesterday," she'd said with a sly smile, and so here I was, feeling half naked and exposed at the dining room table.

I became very interested in my food, examining each piece of soy bacon before putting it in my mouth. I spent a full minute carefully buttering my toast. Anything to avoid conversation.

Meanwhile, Evgenia prattled on, trying to facilitate a successful social interaction.

"The DJ was quite good last night, don't you think?"

I nodded. Elliot grunted in the affirmative.

Evgenia let out a belabored sigh.

"I'm glad we turned in early. Good thinking, Leo," she said. "I loathe hangovers, and I'm always drinking far past my expiration date. You turned in early too, El."

"Um, yes, I was very tired," he said, forced to engage in actual conversation. Evgenia nodded enthusiastically.

"Well, you almost got into a fistfight, so I can only imagine."

"It was a mistake," he mumbled. His eyes darted up to mine. I nearly choked on my tea. He looked away.

"I'm sure Leo doesn't see it that way."

Maybe I should have told Evgenia about our fight. Elliot merely raised an eyebrow and let the subject drop.

"Where are Max and Ewan?" I asked, looking to fill the void with safe small talk.

"Oh, they're off-ship. On a cargo run that came up and paid too well to pass on," Evgenia said breezily. "Should be back tomorrow."

My wrist tab pinged with a message from my aunt. *Background checks on all guests cleared,* it said. I must have blanched, because Elliot asked if everything was okay. I met his gaze, finding worry there, which I promptly torpedoed.

"My aunt says you all passed your background checks," I said, not even thinking to lie.

"Don't look so surprised," Elliot said, a decided chill descending.

"I'm not surprised," I said, even though I kind of was. But I didn't appreciate his assumption regarding my assumptions. "I think it's great. Now my aunt will leave you alone. She's been on the rampage about those protesters, and I don't want any of you to be inconvenienced."

"We had nothing to do with that," he snapped.

"I didn't say you did."

"Lighten up, El," Evgenia jumped in. "Captain Lind made her do it. It wasn't a value judgment."

While Elliot didn't look convinced, he let it drop. I disappeared back into my toast, Elliot into his eggs, and Evgenia into mounting consternation at the both of us. Then their wrist tabs went off simultaneously. Mine remained silent.

"'Meet me on the bridge if you want to have fun tonight. Twenty hundred hours,'" Evgenia read aloud. "It's from Klara. Any clue what it might be, Leo?"

"My guess is that it's spacewalking," I said. It was usually her go-to to impress guests, and now that she had her focus on Elliot, of course this was her plan.

"Do you mean what I think you mean? Literally walking . . . out in space?" Evgenia's eyes went wide.

"Yep. They have special spacesuits tethered to the ship.

Technically they're for maintenance, but since Klara's mom is captain, we get a special exception."

"Ooh, then we have to go!" Evgenia looked right at me as she said it.

"I wasn't invited," I said in my smallest voice.

"Who cares? You're going with us." When she pointed at Elliot on the "us," he groaned.

"I'd give my right arm for a night in."

Him and me both. It was another reminder of how similar we were.

"Nope." Evgenia shook her head emphatically. "You're going. Because I want to go for a space walk, and I want to do so with my friends. Both of you."

Evgenia ordered, and we followed.

"Fine, fine," Elliot acquiesced. I nodded my agreement as well.

Evgenia was already proving adept at wing-womaning.

Now I had approximately ten hours to figure out exactly how I felt about the whole thing.

*

The afternoon nap I indulged in didn't help clear my head any. I awoke groggy and conflicted.

I'd pored over every interaction I'd had with Elliot in the last forty-eight hours. I wanted to believe that his overtures were sincere, but I just couldn't reconcile the part where he said yes to my sister at speed dating. It was too cruel, to both her and me, if he wasn't interested.

And my sister was so eager to be fallen in love with. Evgenia was right. I needed to nudge her in the direction of someone, anyone, else. Regardless of my feelings for Elliot, she was sparring with Klara now, who played dirty, and she was going to get hurt.

Carina made it easy. We finished getting ready for the space walk with ten minutes to spare, and she flopped down onto the couch with a dramatic sigh.

"Leo, do you think he likes me? Do you think he likes Klara? Do you think compatibility scores really matter? Because Klara told me theirs last night and it's way higher than his and mine, and what if he cares about that sort of thing?"

"Hold on, slow down," I said, my head spinning. I sat down next to her. "What do you mean, compatibility scores?"

Carina dragged her head up to look at me. "In the Valg app. Have you not used it at all?" She grabbed her tab from the coffee table and pulled up the app. "When you say yes to someone, it shows you your compatibility rating." Carina tapped into her matches and handed the tab over to me to look.

She had twenty-two matches, with compatibility scores ranging from thirty-eight percent to ninety-two. Carina's compatibility with Elliot was sixty-four percent.

"What's his score match with Klara?" I asked as nonchalantly as I could manage. Inside, I burned with the fear that it would be an impossibly high number.

"Seventy-two." Carina pouted. "Much higher than mine."

"But not that high." I let out a sigh of relief. "What about this guy you have a ninety-two-percent match with?" I checked the name. "Paul from the *Versailles*."

"He's five foot four." Carina wrinkled her nose. "I said yes before seeing him in person. Does that make me shallow?"

"A little bit," I conceded.

"What about you? Have you really not said yes to anyone? Does Daddy know?"

I rolled my eyes. "I don't care what he thinks. He knows I hate this whole thing."

"Still. Where's your tab? You should say yes to *someone*. At least try."

I decided on an experiment. "I'll log in to the app, and I'll say yes to some people. But only if you promise to give a few of your eighty-percent-and-up matches a shot."

"You *do* think Elliot prefers Klara, then!"

"No, I most definitely do not," I said quite honestly. "It's just a good idea to broaden your options. Plus, you're only sixteen. You don't have to match with anyone this Valg. There will be another one."

"When I'm twenty-one! I'm not waiting that long."

It took me a minute to grab my tab from our room and open the Valg app.

"Fine, then let's make a deal. *I* will try if *you* do." I pulled up the match index. All the ones from speed dating were switched to no. All it would take was a swipe to undo any of them. My finger hovered over Elliot's name. What was our compatibility rating?

"Let's switch." Carina didn't give me time to protest before swapping our tabs. "You pick out two guys for me—not the short one, please—and I'll pick out some for you."

"Not Lukas!" I screeched. I imagined him getting a notification that I'd changed my mind about him. Really, I didn't want anyone to get that ping. I couldn't believe I was doing this.

"Don't worry, I'm a good sister," Carina said, tapping her finger several times on the screen. Her eyes widened. "Oh, wow, you've got a ninety-three percent with this one," she said.

"Who?"

"Daniel Turan. And Theo is eighty-four percent. Higher than I thought he would be."

"Carina, no, you did not make Theo Madsen a yes for me!"

She shrugged. "I was curious about your rating. I picked a few other random ones who looked cute, but the scores are really low." I wrested the tab back from her and scanned the results. I didn't recognize most of the ones she'd picked, and she was right. Most of them were under fifty percent. Elliot was still a no. My finger itched, but I resisted.

A knock sounded at the door, and there he was in front of me, next to Evgenia. I seemed to have interrupted a tense conversation between them, almost an argument—about me? They cut themselves off as soon as I flung open the door. Without thinking, my hands flew to my torso, smoothing down the bodice of my dress. Elliot's eyes seemed to pass through me, anyway.

Carina burst through the door, angling past me.

"Evy! El!" She hugged each of them in turn, as if after a long separation and not a mere twenty-four hours. Less than, in fact. Evgenia cast me a look as Carina held Elliot for a beat longer than was strictly friendly, and I tried to appear contrite. I'd tried, but apparently Carina wasn't giving up on Elliot just yet. She monopolized his attentions all the way up to the top deck, asking him questions about his travels and whiskey, and responding to everything he said with "That's so interesting!"

Distracted by them, I almost forgot I wasn't actually invited to the evening's activities, but my cousin's face was a quick reminder as she greeted us.

"Leo . . . hi?" I offered a tepid wave. She didn't say anything else or turn me away, instead ushering us all inside to the bridge. We found her mother at the console. The ship mostly ran itself, so I knew she wasn't piloting us, and the silence told me the captain wasn't fielding communication from other ships. Freja looked up, blinking at us in confusion.

"Klara? What is the meaning of this? You know I use Sunday evenings to catch up on paperwork."

"We'd like to go for a space walk." From Klara, it was a statement, not a question.

"When I said I wanted you to take an interest in the ship, this isn't what I had in mind," Captain Lind said, rising from her chair and removing her spectacles. But she also didn't say no. "I'm surprised to see you here, Leonie."

I was the resident wuss, called out. Or maybe Klara had told her mother how strained things were between us. The captain eyed our large party. "Only two of you can go out at a time."

Finally, I did the math. Klara, Evgenia, Elliot, Carina . . . and me. Five. That's why Klara hadn't invited me. I was the fifth wheel.

"Thank you, Mummy," Klara said, seemingly oblivious.

"Language," Captain Lind scolded. She could serve terms of endearment like a pro but didn't like Klara being so informal with her in public.

Freja returned to the console, tapping and swiping for a minute. "All right, I've given Leonie temporary bio-scan access to the maintenance airlock and storage room. It will expire at midnight."

"Leo?" Klara parroted back, incredulous. "Why would you give *her* access? *I'm* your apprentice."

"Because you're always swanning off, indulging your fancy, and Leonie is unfailingly reliable."

Klara glared but did not protest further. Captain Lind was not a woman with whom you argued. We left the bridge and walked the short distance to our destination, Klara fuming all the way. The captain had now made me essential to the evening's activities. Bully for me.

"The suits are in here." Klara grabbed Elliot by the hand and pulled him to the storage room, stopping at the bio-lock and waiting for me to open it. I found myself so close to the two of them that I could smell Klara's perfume, so sweet it tickled my nose hairs. Underneath was Elliot, the new musky scent fast becoming familiar to me. I took a deep inhale. Hastily, I mashed my fingers against the bio-lock.

Dunk-dunk.

Attempt failed. Klara huffed noisily, and my eyes flicked over to catch Elliot's reaction. He dug his incisor into his bottom lip, eyes laser-focused at the door. Avoiding my gaze. I thought about kissing him, how long it had been. I wiped my sweaty hand against my dress and tried again. This time, the door whooshed open.

We all filed inside, availing ourselves of a bench that ran along the far wall.

"Guests first," Klara said, standing before us like a drill sergeant with her brigade. "Evgenia and Carina, I insist you go."

The way Carina's face fell, opportunity lost to go out with Elliot, made my heart ache a little. Yet I felt the slightest swell of happiness for my own agenda, then promptly became filled with self-loathing. Carina dutifully rose and started climbing into one of the twin spacesuits.

"Leo, help me, would you?" Evgenia called me over to her side, then pulled me close as I held her arms so she could step in.

"So Elliot will go out with Klara, obviously, but that's your window," Evgenia husked into my ear. "Ask him to go again, with you, for your turn."

"Oh, no, I couldn't—"

"Yes"—Evgenia cut me off, then turned so I could zip her up—"you can."

"Carina, you want zipper help, too?" I asked, to which she halfheartedly nodded. I followed her eyeline to Elliot and Klara having a lively chat in the corner. Oh, boy.

After I'd zipped her up, I gave her shoulder a squeeze, though

I wasn't sure she could feel it through the layers of insulation. And, feeling a misplaced sense of obligation for the future heartbreak I would be dealing her once I told her the full truth, I hefted her helmet underneath one arm, as if playing valet. In that spirit, plus as the so-called keeper of the keys, I escorted the fully suited-up ladies to the maintenance airlock, a sharp right turn and ten-foot walk from the storage room. Hands dry this time, my fingers unlocked the door on the first try.

"I'll tether you in, since I've done this before," I explained as we entered the forward airlock, where the controls were. Evgenia and Carina moved past a bulkhead, which would soon separate us, to the outer door, beyond which lay wide-open space.

"Here." I handed Carina her helmet and moved to either side, unhooking a springy tether wire, which I wound through loops at their waists and then pressure-sealed into a twist opening on each of their backs.

"You're sure this is safe?" Carina asked nervously, in a strange reversal of position. Usually I was the worrywart, second-guessing the safety and prudence of a situation. But I'd done this enough times to speak with confidence.

"The maintenance crews do this all the time. You'll be tethered to the ship, and I can pull you back if you get scared."

"I'm not scared," she bristled. *There* was the little sister I knew.

"How long do we get out there?" Evgenia jumped in, voice thrumming with excitement. She bounced up and down as best she could in her heavy suit.

There were no set rules, so it seemed it was up to me. "Ten minutes?"

It seemed like enough time for a thrill but not so much that Klara and Elliot, the next pair to go, would have extra time to bond. Was that terrible? I put it out of my mind.

"Yes, ten minutes," I repeated, surer this time.

I snapped a small can of compressed air into their suits, then showed them where the release buttons were located on either arm to use it.

"Use this to direct yourselves, but use it conservatively. Small can, and all that."

They both nodded, and with that, I retreated behind the separating bulkhead, depressing a button to shuttle a quadruple-paned glass partition that would keep me safe from space's harsh clime while they were outside.

I counted them down from ten while I fiddled with the control panel, which, like the door, was keyed to my bio-signature. So I'd definitely have to oversee Klara and Elliot's turn, too. I released the outer doors.

The girls didn't actually need me to keep watch—it was a fully automated system, and they could pull themselves back anytime, should they wish. But watch them I did, for a solid three minutes before they drifted from view. With the press of a button on the control console, I could hear them, too, but I listened for only a minute. Just enough time to hear their twin squeals of delight and Evgenia dare Carina to do a backflip.

Then I allowed myself to drift into fantasy, imagining

myself asking Elliot to accompany me on my turn. He'd say yes, mouth turning up into the slightest smile, setting off the dimples I loved so much. Klara would fume, but I wouldn't care. I'd be floating long before we left the airlock. He'd take my hand, never leaving my side as we cartwheeled, weightless among the stars.

Ahem.

A loud cough behind me broke me from my reverie. I flipped around to find Klara and Elliot standing in the door frame.

"Are they done yet?" Klara asked testily.

I checked the automatic timer I'd set. They had three minutes left. The look on Klara's face told me that, regardless, their time was up. Oh, well. I pressed the communication button, opening up the channel so they could hear me.

"Sorry, I have to pull you back now," I said, manually overriding the system. I took care to leave the communication channel open and on speaker so Klara would hear Evgenia and Carina's sullen protests.

Once they were back and the airlock doors closed, I released the glass safety partition separating us. No sooner had the girls started zipping out of their suits than Klara was dragging Elliot by the hand over to them, and they went ahead and got into the suits right there. I noticed Evgenia sway on her feet. Lightning-fast, Elliot offered his arm to steady her; then I saw him pull close to whisper something in her ear, which only made Evgenia look queasier. I performed the same ritual as before, tethering and snapping them in, instructing Elliot on the compressed air, then moving behind the partition and back to the control panel.

"Leo, give us fifteen minutes," Klara said breezily, helmet under her arm, looking more glamorous in a spacesuit than was fair. "We want to really take it all in."

Carina let out the faintest chirp of outrage but held her tongue, so far as calling Klara out on the inequity. I also knew better than to argue with her, so I dutifully programmed fifteen minutes into the system as Carina and Evgenia fell back behind me. Evgenia was resting against the wall, looking a bit flushed.

My eyes remained glued to the console as I keyed in the final commands to close the safety partition and open the airlock. My complete focus was required if I wanted to avoid the way Klara and Elliot were linking arms as the doors shuttled open.

Nope, I did not see that at all.

"All right, how are we going to kill fifteen minutes?" I asked, spinning around to face the girls.

And then Evgenia fainted.

13

"Evgenia!"

I rushed to catch her before she cracked her head on the floor, my heart practically jumping into my throat as I realized I was too far away. It happened both faster than a blink and as if the world had switched to slow motion. Thankfully Carina reacted to my reaction, grabbing Evgenia by the arm just in time.

"What's wrong with her?" Carina shrieked. Evgenia's dead weight pulled her down and back, despite Carina's wrenching her up by the armpits. My sister wilted back against the wall, and I rushed to help them both.

"I don't know!" Together, we lowered Evgenia to the floor. I tried fanning her with my hand, but it did nothing to stop the beads of sweat crowding her brow. Something was very wrong.

Then, suddenly, her eyelids fluttered open.

"What happened?" she asked groggily. "Why am I on the floor?"

"You fainted," I said. She groaned, clutching one hand to her head and the other to her stomach.

"I don't feel so good, come to think of it. I should maybe lie down." Evgenia grimaced. "Not on the floor, though. I'd prefer a bed. Beautiful woman optional."

If she was joking, she had to be half okay, I figured. I laid a hand on her forehead—she was warm, but not burning hot. But then she kept clutching her stomach.

"Do you feel like you're going to vomit?" I asked, fishing for a diagnosis. I was no medical professional, but I'd seen food poisoning before.

"Definitely maybe a lot," she replied, clinching it.

I lowered my voice, ducking my head so only Carina could hear. "There's no time to take her all the way back to the *Sofi*. She's probably going to start vomiting, among other things, very soon."

Carina wrinkled her nose in clear disgust but jumped into action, nevertheless. "We'll take you downstairs to our quarters," she said, and we helped Evgenia back on her feet. With the two of us supporting Evgenia's weight, we managed to half walk/half carry her to the lift, but Evgenia rallied at the doors, pushing me back out into the hallway with her limited but not insubstantial strength.

"No, you have to take your turn with Elliot. Carina can take me."

Still lucid enough to wing-woman. Amazing. Even so, I was reluctant.

"No, I should go with you," I said, trying to cross the

threshold. But Evgenia slammed her hand against the lift hold button.

"You have to operate the console, remember?" Evgenia insisted. "Please, stay for me."

Unfortunately she was right—the system would automatically bring Klara and Elliot back into the airlock, but I was the only one who could open the safety partition and shut everything down. Still, I lingered until the door closed, then stood there a minute, contemplating following along after them anyway. I should have enough time to get them settled—fifteen minutes, right? Or, I reasoned with myself, I could go down as soon as they got back, forgoing my turn. Elliot probably wouldn't say yes to accompanying me, anyway.

The lift zipped away, and I found myself alone in the near darkness. The night settings were on, the usually stark-white ship interiors a flat almost-gray with the brightness turned all the way down. It was eerie. Sterile and ghostly.

A loud sound, a snap like flesh against metal, made me jump. I turned, seeking out the source of the sound, but it did not repeat itself. I crept back the way we'd come, toward the bridge. And there, when I closed my eyes and concentrated on listening, I could hear the muffled rise and fall of someone speaking. Clearly we'd been too swept up in our own crisis to hear the captain, still holed up on deck, and she did not sound happy about something. I hovered outside the open doorway, wondering at the fact that she'd not engaged the automatic close function. Guess she wasn't used to having company up here this time of night and didn't expect anyone to be listening in.

"I don't care what you think. That solution is untenable."

There was silence for a minute, Captain Lind clearly listening to a response. Then: "I'll not succumb to idle threats. This is *my* ship."

That certainly piqued my interest. Who was threatening Captain Lind? And about what?

"Well, you are entitled to that opinion. Good evening."

The captain cut short the obviously tense conversation, and I suspected that whoever had been on the other line might not have been quite done with it themselves. Captain Lind was a conversations-end-when-she-wants-them-to type of woman, however.

I was left with silence and a sudden foreboding. With her no longer distracted by her off-ship communication, there was no way for me to make my way past the bridge without her noticing me. While she might have thought me faultlessly reliable on the best of days, Captain Lind would not take kindly to my eavesdropping. I had to be careful.

With great care, I craned my neck around the bridge door to see if the coast was clear. She had her back to me. But then she spoke.

"I'm afraid my patience has worn thin. You'll need to be more forthcoming with me."

I jumped back, heart stuttering in my rib cage, even though it was impossible for her to have seen me, been addressing me. The captain had hailed someone else. I used the opportunity of her new distraction to dart past the doorway. Once on the other side, I couldn't help but continue to listen in.

"I've tried being nice, but now the *Olympus* is breathing down my neck, and—"

A loaded pause.

"*Blackmail* is a strong word. Think of it as a business opportunity. We can discuss more in person. I'm nearly done here."

The conversation was clearly wrapping up, so I made haste to slip away. I knew my aunt could be stone cold, but I never imagined she'd resort to petty blackmail. If she caught me, who knew what she'd do? Returning to the maintenance hold, I found my heart beating unnaturally fast. Between the emergency with Evgenia and my aunt's suspicious calls, I was on edge. Then it got worse. The communications channel was still open and on speaker, so I got a full stream of Elliot and Klara's conversation.

"You did not!" Klara shrieked with laughter.

"I absolutely did! Stripped off right there and jumped into the freezing water."

Elliot naked *where* and *how*? Now there was no way I could turn off the comms.

"Totally sober?"

"One hundred percent," Elliot confirmed.

"Why would any ship want to simulate snow, ice, freezing water? We came all the way up here just to avoid that."

I could hear Elliot shrug in his suit, mic picking up everything, even the way his glasses clinked against his helmet. "They say it's a way of staying connected to their roots. It's a tradition. When you come of age, you jump into the freezing water naked. Everyone does it."

"But I'd wager most of them do it full of vodka. You just enjoy getting naked; admit it."

I could practically hear the wink in her tone. Klara was flirting with him, hard.

"I wonder how much time we have left." That was Elliot again.

Klara's reply came a moment later.

"I can't believe I never took you out here with me before. You were here the whole time, but we never really hung out, socially."

"I don't expect princesses to hang out with the help."

"You weren't the help," Klara was quick to correct him, and now the flame of rage warmed my insides. Just a few weeks ago, she was stubbornly referring to him as the valet! "Besides, you've changed a lot since then. We all have."

"You haven't."

"Is that a compliment or an insult?"

I wanted to know as well. Elliot remained coy.

"I hear you're looking for a husband. That's new."

"I have my eye out, but I'm not looking too seriously. I have high standards."

"That I knew," Elliot said, tone annoyingly neutral. Was that about her advice to me? Idle flirting?

"And what about you?" Klara volleyed back. "Tell me what you're looking for. Maybe I can help."

There was a long pause, some heavy breathing that I thought was Elliot.

"Doing pirouettes to escape my line of questioning, huh?" Klara laughed.

"Just enjoying our time out here."

"Hmm," Klara hummed, then grunted. Whatever she did impressed Elliot.

"Showoff."

"I'll start you off!" Klara said breathlessly. "You want someone tall."

"Or short," Elliot countered. "No preference."

"Blond?"

"No preference."

I hated that I couldn't see them, couldn't read his body language. Also, was it just me or was Klara describing herself? The next adjective did nothing to dissuade me of that notion.

"Beautiful, of course—and don't you dare say 'No preference,' you liar."

"I'm not that shallow," Elliot defended himself. "I care more about who someone is. Their personality. I want someone practical and kind and smart and funny and loyal—"

"You want someone like Leo."

My heart shot up into my throat. Elliot said nothing. Klara let him hang. I checked the timer. They had less than a minute before the automated system would pull them back.

"If you think I want Leo, then why are you flirting with me? You're her cousin; doesn't that violate some kind of code?"

It was maddening how he didn't actually answer her question, but I pumped the air with my fist at how Elliot threw her flirtation back in her face. He saw it as well as I did—the hypocrisy.

Klara didn't respond right away, and I could only imagine her sour expression. But then she hit back. "You said yes to her sister at speed dating; isn't *that* violating some kind of code?"

The system started to beep, cutting off whatever reply Elliot might have had. It was pulling them back in. Hastily, I switched off the comms speaker so they wouldn't know I'd been eavesdropping.

I plastered on a smile as twin spacesuits came into view of the airlock.

"Have fun?" I chirped once they'd touched down on the deck and the airlock had closed.

"Oh, yes," Klara said, shaking her long hair loose from her helmet.

"Where's Evgenia and Carina?" Elliot asked.

"Evgenia got sick," I said, moving over to them to help them out of their suits. "Carina took her down to our quarters."

"She didn't vomit in here, right?" Klara wrinkled her nose.

"Uh, no."

"We should go check on her," Klara said, suddenly curiously concerned with Evgenia's well-being. Elliot paused, brow wrinkling.

"Wait, someone needs to go out with Leo. It's her turn."

He spoke to Klara about me like I wasn't standing right there.

"I'm fine," I interjected. "You can go. Don't worry about me."

"See? She's fine." Klara grabbed Elliot by the arm and tugged him toward the door.

Yep, I was totally fine. With the way Elliot allowed himself to be led away, with how he'd utterly failed to read the disappointment on my face. He used to be so good at reading me, and now . . .

I was left to silence.

My feet carried me, up from the console, through the open safety partition, and over to the window. I stared out into space, black and sparkling. I wanted to scream into the vacuum, feel my lungs burn, the sound dying before it left my throat.

But, no, I wasn't going to wallow in self-pity. I came up here to space walk, and so that's what I would do. I didn't need anyone to go with me, let alone Elliot. With that, I programmed the system for ten minutes to start once I manually triggered the outer airlock, then went inside the bay to get ready.

I did find one benefit to tandem spacewalking—having someone else to help you into your spacesuit was a boon. It took me ages to climb into the bulky costume, contorting myself to find the zipper to close myself in, struggling to bend over to retrieve the helmet. And as I was half bent over, I realized I'd left the second suit in the middle of the floor. I'd have to secure it to the wall before I could go anywhere. Just as I was trying to gain purchase with my awkwardly gloved fingers, there came a rapid *tap, tap, tap* on the glass behind me.

I whipped around to find Elliot on the other side of the partition, mouthing something I couldn't quite hear. He was gesturing at me and the other suit. He must have left something behind.

With an annoyed huff, I signaled to him to hold his horses. The external comms were off, so he couldn't hear me. It would take a moment to unscrew my gloves so I could unlock the door with my bio-signature. Finally I managed it, and as the door whooshed open, I addressed him, not without significant annoyance in my voice.

"What did you forget?"

"Forget?"

"Yeah, in here. You must have forgotten something."

I turned around and tromped back over to the second suit. Might as well secure it more easily now that my hands were free.

"Leo."

"Come on in. Not like I was almost dressed and ready to go."

"Leo."

The force in Elliot's voice, the bemused consternation, made me turn. What did he want?

"I came back for you," he said.

And it was like all the air had been sucked out of the room.

14

"Sorry, what?" I blinked at Elliot, a bit dazed. I would have pinched myself, if I had had any available skin I could reach.

"I came back?" he repeated. "I felt bad leaving you like that. Came to my senses once we reached the lift."

"It's not a big deal." I played it off casually, like my heart wasn't thumping so hard in my chest that I could hear it in my ears. "Didn't even bother me. As you see, I was going to go out on my own."

"Isn't that dangerous?"

"No, the maintenance crew does it all the time. Solo missions, and all that."

"Yeah, but that's during the day, when there are people around. I really don't mind," Elliot insisted. He made a move to grab the second spacesuit, but I yanked it back.

"Elliot, I don't need your pity. Go have fun."

"I'm trying to. Out there." He gestured beyond the airlock window. "I want to go. Leo, it's not a big deal. Stop

170

being a martyr."

And just like that, any pretense of romantic intention evaporated. This was Elliot ribbing me like an old friend. He knew me too well.

"Fine." I gave in, handing over the suit. "You can help me with my air canister."

Soon we were both suited up, the crackle of the active comms in my ear as we floated out the open airlock and into the glittering black. The sight of unfiltered space took my breath away; I reached out my hand, as if I could collect stardust in my palm. It had been too long since I'd done this, years since Klara had called for a space-walk party and deigned to invite me. Well, she hadn't invited me to this one either, technically. It made my dance with the stars all the sweeter.

"How long did you program it for?" Elliot asked, launching right into a somersault.

"Ten minutes," I said, doing not much more than a twirl. I never liked going head over heels. One turn felt like the beginning of something uncontrollable, like if I weren't careful, I would spin endlessly and be lost to the stars.

"Too bad. I could stay out here forever."

"You always had that wanderlust," I remarked. I paddled with my arms, swimming out as far as my tether would take me. The gentle tug of pressure as I reached my outer limits was reassuring. I wouldn't float away. "Did you really jump in a freezing lake naked? You would never have done that here," I mused without thinking.

"Were you listening in on my conversation with Klara?"

On instinct, I turned, seeking Elliot out, even though he remained loud and clear in my helmet. He'd ceased all gymnastics and had his arms crossed over his chest, a good fifty feet away from me. Were it not for the pale gray of his suit, he'd have been swallowed up by the vastness all around. We were tiny, compared to the endless expanse.

"It wasn't on purpose," I said. I deployed some compressed air, pushing me closer to him. I was too far out, tether or no.

"Uh-huh." He did another somersault. "And there are a lot of things I've done since you last saw me that I would never have done before. Jumping into a freezing body of water without any clothes on is just the tip of the iceberg."

"Was that supposed to be a pun?"

"A bad one."

"Okay, so you jumped in a lake. What happened next?" I floated close enough to see Elliot's face behind the thick glass of his helmet. His breath had partially fogged up his lenses.

"I proved myself cool enough for the Russians. Evgenia swooped in, took me under her wing. I became one of them. Honestly I'm amazed the *Scandinavian* doesn't have a weather room like the *Saint Petersburg*. I've heard the *Lady Liberty* has a rain room."

"The Swedish aren't as metal as the Russians," I said dryly. "Maybe the Finns, though."

Elliot laughed, the deep timbre triggering a sense memory. Tucked up warm in his bed, some wry comment I made setting him off. The rumble of his laughter tickling my cheek against his bare chest. I experienced a full-body flush, suddenly wishing I had a frigid pool of water to jump into.

"How desperately do you want to clean your glasses right now?" I asked instead, deflecting. Only it made him laugh again, which didn't help much at all. This was getting perilously close to feeling romantic, even though I knew it wasn't. Elliot was mending our friendship. I was chasing dreams like starlight.

"You know me too well," he said. "I'm so close to ripping off my helmet." Then he grabbed me by the hands, shocking my heart up into my throat. "Let's make the most of our time. Just floating out here is boring."

It was like dancing. Elliot pushed against my hands, sending each of us flying back, him into an easy spin, me fighting the momentum so I wouldn't end up ass over elbow. And he laughed at me every time for my stubbornness. Then we found our way back to each other and started over.

There was a metaphor for our relationship somewhere in there.

I tried not to think about it.

"Listen, Leo," Elliot started, tone somber and serious. I'd floated away from him, testing the limits of my tether again. I turned, pumped my arms and legs to swim back closer. But he spun away, allowed himself to drift. "It's easier to say this if, uh, we're not looking at each other," he said. "It's about Carina."

For a moment, there was just the sound of our breathing coming scratchily through the comms.

"Saying yes to her at speed dating was a mistake. A

remnant of my stupid, horrible plan to make you jealous. I was in her room before yours, and then you apologized . . . You knocked me sideways, Leo. And, well, you were big enough to apologize to me then, and I'm apologizing to you now. So if you could stop bringing it up constantly, that would be great."

"Maybe I wanted to make you suffer a bit," I quipped. I played it light and easy, but his confession pinched and pulled at my insides. It felt so real, and I wanted it to be. No long game, just Elliot being himself with me. I wanted a chance with Elliot again. I did a pinwheel flip, let myself go around a few times. Head over heels. And then I got a grip on myself.

"I'm not the only one you need to apologize to," I said breathlessly. "Carina's been twisting herself into pretzels over you. And you were flirting with her as recently as last night. If you're not interested, she deserves to know. Gently."

Elliot sucked in air through his teeth. "Is she really that smitten?"

"Elliot," I responded sternly, "listen, I'm trying to get her interested in someone else, but she's stubborn."

"Family trait," he said. "And you're trying to get her interested in someone else, huh?"

"With Klara vying for your attention and Carina in her cross hairs? Absolutely." He was fishing again for my feelings, and I refused to lay everything out for him.

"Being rich and eligible is exhausting."

"If only you could see how hard I'm rolling my eyes right now."

The timer began to beep in our earpieces and the tethers pulled taut, the ship already reeling us in.

"Goodbye, terrifying yet beautiful vacuum of space," I said with one last turn toward the stars before we crossed the airlock threshold.

"You are nothing if not a contradiction," Elliot mused as we bobbed up toward the ceiling. I hooked an arm around a protruding handlebar, managing to drag myself closer to the floor so that when the outer airlock door finally shuttled closed and gravity returned to the room, the shock of impact wasn't too bad. Elliot, however, wasn't quick enough, and he fell to the floor with an undignified grunt.

"Why a contradiction?" I asked breezily, suppressing a laugh. My helmet came off with a twist, and I sucked in several pulls of fresh air. Well, fresh*er* inside our spaceship than inside the spacesuit. Not a complete monster, I offered Elliot a hand to get to his feet.

"Why did you go on a space walk if it terrifies you?"

I knew that "Spite" wasn't a great answer, so I shrugged. "It was too beautiful to miss."

Several contortions, and I still couldn't quite grasp the end of the suit zipper. I swiveled once, twice, like a wavering top, until on my third go-round I caught Elliot staring at me. "What?"

He snapped out of his reverie. "Let me help you with that. Then you can do me. Help me out of my suit, I mean."

I nodded, because of course, yes, we should help each other; that was normal. Elliot and I were normal. Except that we most decidedly were not. Suddenly the air was thick with the awareness of each other's bodies as we shed our spacesuits one at a time, moving slowly, like an awkward pair of lovers. Which we were, once. Though I was fully clothed, I felt naked. Elliot refused to look me in the eyes. What had gotten into him?

"We should return these to the maintenance hold," I said once we'd fully unsuited ourselves. Elliot nodded and followed without a word as I led us out of the airlock and back to the storage room. We stowed the suits where we'd found them and made our way back to the lift. The bridge was empty as we passed, I noted. Captain Lind, whatever she was up to, had retired for the night.

"I hope Evgenia's all right," I said, attempting neutral conversation as we walked.

"Evgenia?"

"Yeah, she's sick?"

"Oh, right. Maybe take her to the med bay?"

We drifted into opposite corners of the lift once it arrived. After thirty seconds of going nowhere, it became obvious that neither of us had hit the button. Nervous laugher bubbled between us, and we each deferred to the other to do the honors. Finally, I gave up on awkward politeness and did it myself. What was wrong with us?

The silent but happily short lift ride didn't provide any answers—Elliot pointedly studied the floor, then the walls as we walked the rest of the way to the royal quarters. As soon as we went inside, Elliot was back on form, placating a snippy

Klara, who pouted at him for abandoning her. My cousin waved me in the direction of my family's apartment when I inquired as to Evgenia's status, so I left them behind. Elliot didn't seem very worried about her, oddly.

I found our quarters quiet but for the sound of retching coming from the en suite bathroom my sister and I shared. I popped my head into the bedroom to find Carina sitting on her bed, staring worriedly at the closed bathroom door.

"She didn't want me in there," Carina explained. "And I told her she could have your bed . . ."

"Yes, good thinking," I said, wanting to be annoyed. But I had to applaud her thoughtfulness—my bed was nearest the bathroom door. "I'll kip on the couch."

"You're leaving me with her?"

"I'll be in the next room, twenty feet away."

Carina worried her bottom lip. "What if she gets worse?"

"Then wake me, and I'll take her to the med bay."

"Klara said they were closed," Evgenia croaked, appearing in the bathroom door. Her usually porcelain-perfect skin was red and blotchy. "She said we could go in the morning."

I rolled my eyes. "Klara knows as well as I do that the doctor can be reached at any and all hours for emergencies. Dr. Jensen just loathes being woken up in the middle of the night. It's not even that late yet. I can call him and have him come here."

"No, no." Evgenia shuffled over to my bed with a hand clutching her stomach. "I'm okay for now. I'll ride it out tonight, and we can go to the med bay in the morning. I don't want to make a fuss." She collapsed onto my bed but stopped herself short of lying down. "Wait. I can't take your bed. Sorry." Her attempts to heave herself back up onto her feet were sad, to say the least.

"I insist. Just last night, you hosted me. It's my turn."

"Yeah, but I made you sleep on the floor."

We both laughed, hers quickly turning into a groan. Then Evgenia curled into a ball on top of the covers. I threw a duvet over her and grabbed a spare for myself, plus a pillow, from the closet.

I considered heading back out to the royal quarters, to disrupt Klara and Elliot's flirting time, but caught myself. After how awkwardly the space walk with Elliot had ended, I would be a masochist to subject myself to being the third wheel, the interloper, in whatever conversation they were having. At this point, I wasn't sure if it would ever be okay between Elliot and me again. Every time I thought we'd fallen back into an old, familiar rhythm, something would knock us off-track.

No, I would sleep, recharge my body and my mind from an emotionally exhausting twenty-four hours. I needed to get up early anyway to check on Evgenia. Med bay opened at seven, and despite the flicker of responsibility Carina had displayed, I knew that if anyone would be sacrificing a lie-in tomorrow morning for the sake of our friend, it would be me.

I closed my eyes and thought of stars. Swimming in them, pushing aside the terror to find the calm. Recalled floating, the steady pressure of the tether. The calm that came from knowing Elliot was there by my side. Try as I might to banish him from my mind while awake, now I was on the edge of dreams. And in my dreams, Elliot could stay.

15

My traitorous body dutifully awoke me at six a.m. I rubbed the sleep from my eyes and padded over to my bedroom to peek inside. Evgenia was still curled up under the covers. I hadn't heard any retching in the night. Maybe she was better.

I veered over to the recess kitchen, where I discovered our coffee stores frustratingly bare. I had given my father one job—to keep us stocked in his precious coffee—and he couldn't even manage it. I'd have to venture out into the greater royal quarters to snag some from their kitchen. Briefly I debated getting dressed, but at six a.m., who would I possibly run into? Maybe one of the servants, but I didn't think they would judge me in my pajamas. At least I was in proper clothes this morning. A simple pants-and-top set, it covered all my essential bits.

"You're up early."

I startled, swinging around in a circle to identify the source's location. I found Elliot sitting to my right.

"What are you doing here?"

"Sleeping. Or I was."

"On Klara's couch?"

"Technically I think this is Captain Lind's couch," he said. "I wanted to stay close for Evy. How is she doing?"

"Last I saw her, she was sleeping. And it's not like you checked on her last night." I frowned. Elliot might have disavowed any feelings for Carina last night during the space walk, but he'd cracked a joke when I'd mentioned Klara. My stomach turned at the thought of the two of them together.

"And what are you doing out here?"

"I need coffee. We're out."

"Good thing the Linds have more than enough of everything."

I raised a brow at the unusually cutting remark but didn't respond.

"Elliot, I think I figured out—Oh." Nora stopped short of the doorway that led to the dining room, two cups of coffee in hand. One for her, one for Elliot? "Hi, Leo."

"Leo was looking for coffee," Elliot filled in.

"Here, you can have this one." Nora closed the distance between us, offering me one of the cups. She kept her gaze angled toward the floor.

"No, I couldn't. That's yours. Besides, I was going to grab a bag, replenish our stock."

"But—" Nora shoved the cup my way again, shooting a glance over at Elliot, as if he could help.

"I'll just go do that, leave you two to it." I was already on my way to the door before I was done speaking. If I stayed any longer, I'd blurt something unkind. Questions. Accusations.

Suddenly I remembered something Nora had said to me the night of the opening ball and the terrorist attack. A "friend" had brought her champagne. Elliot had come back into the royal private public quarters from this direction. And Father had been fussing about champagne going missing. And then just the other night, Elliot had paid extra attention to Nora at the below-decks party, dancing with her.

I rushed into the darkness of the Linds' supply cupboard, which was actually its own room, for all the supplies they kept. But that was neither here nor there. I hated the way my blood thrummed faster, how upset the prospect of Elliot and Nora made me. Elliot and anyone. I was a mess.

I needed to get back on mission. Scanning the shelves, I finally found the coffee supply, which wasn't in its usual spot. They were down to only three canisters, and I felt bad taking one, but needs must. Odd, given that they usually had at least ten stocked at all times.

Ding-ding.

My wrist tab pinged with an incoming message. I pulled it up. It was an infuriatingly dry form response from the office of Miranda Fairfax, full of *Thank you for your inquiries* and *Ms. Fairfax offers select walk-in hours*. No indication that an actual human had read my words or given a shit. I almost fired off a snippy response but just stopped myself. I'd have to dig more, ask around, and try to get Miranda's personal-message details. Going via her office just wasn't getting me anywhere.

Then came a message from Carina.

Where are you? Evgenia's throwing up again. Need to take her to med bay.

I pushed aside my questions—and dreams of a hot cup of coffee anytime soon—and sprang into action as I always did. As my aunt had said, I was reliable to a fault.

After rallying a grumpy doctor to work, I dropped Evgenia off at the med bay to rehydrate, at her insistence. I had tried to stay with her, entertain her through the boredom of being hooked up to an IV drip, but her want won out over mine. Evgenia was quite someone to engage in a battle of wills with. Besides, I was uncaffeinated and thus not at my best.

By the time I returned to our apartment, Father was up and had brewed coffee. Nothing was said about where the new canister might have magically appeared from. I didn't press it, just poured myself a generous cup.

"What's on the Valg agenda for today?" His tone was suspiciously light, too pointedly neutral.

"I don't know," I said with a protracted sigh. "Despite two days without anything on the official roster, I've been out with Klara and the gang the past two nights. I'm exhausted." I could play the passive-aggressive game too, show him I'd been trying.

Father frowned. "That group hardly counts. No one there for you, is there?"

"Lukas was there the other night," I snapped defensively, immediately regretting it as Father lit up with interest.

"Oh, the Hagens are a fine family. Very wealthy." He always

got to the heart of the matter. "Still, you mustn't put all your eggs in one basket. Check today's schedule. Go ahead."

Too tired to adequately protest, I pulled up my tab and dutifully did so. "There is a wine-and-painting event this afternoon," I read off. "I'll pass."

"No, no, go. Take Carina. Cultured boys will be there."

"Dad," I ground out.

"Don't try me, Leonie. You need to make an effort. No resting on laurels. You have less than three weeks left, and that's not a lot of time for you."

"What do you mean, *for me?*"

"Don't read into it—"

"What, you mean that I need more time to get some hapless fool to agree to marry me because I'm so difficult to like?"

"We both know you're prickly."

"Dad!"

"Your mother was just the same. Very passionate. Chatty. An acquired taste."

I rolled my eyes. How dare a woman speak her mind? And Carina prattled on just as much as I did, just about innocuous things, like parties and people in our social circles.

"Speaking of your mother," he continued, "I didn't see you bring on board her prize dress collection. You girls will be needing those for the Valg Ball. Everyone will be there, and I want my girls looking their best. To be perfectly frank, I'm a bit shocked you left them on the *Sofi* for those renters of yours to get their hands on. My crown jewels, too. What if they steal them?"

"They're not going to steal them," I scolded. "I couldn't possibly realistically bring every single one of our possessions over here for just a four-week stay. The jewels are in the safe, and Mom's gowns are in storage. I'll get them this week, though, if you're really worried."

Father nodded, frowning seriously. Then he handed me his tab. "Read that, from today's *Tribune*. So you understand how serious this is."

As my eyes scanned the words on the screen, I felt the blood drain from my face. There had been an amendment to the proposed usefulness measure. Private ships were to meet a wealth threshold or else be decommissioned and used for scrap. It was a preemptive measure as our fleet neared its two-hundredth year and several ships were beginning to seriously wear. The vote would be held next month, just in time for the Valg Season's end. So now there was a real expiration date—I needed to either patent and license my filtration system and thus become useful, or marry rich.

"So you and Carina will be attending the sip-and-paint event?" Father asked innocently, and I just nodded.

*

I daubed my paintbrush until it was heavy with blinding yellow, then worked it on top of the inky black-and-blue swirling sky. It was strange to represent the stars from such a foreign perspective. I wondered at how the Earthbound masters once gazed up at the night sky, contrasting mountains and cathedrals with dazzling brilliance on their canvases. We were recreating a Van Gogh, our too-tipsy instructor going off on long tangents about texture and ears and proper Dutch pronunciation.

I wasn't sure how we were meant to romantically connect to anyone during this activity—everyone sat hunched over their respective canvases, trying to mimic the style of a master. Plus, we'd been left to choose our own stations, which meant I was in a cluster with my friends, and so the few conversations we could get in edgewise were hardly in service of the Season. Which suited me just fine, of course. It was all ladies, besides, as Elliot was pointedly absent. My stomach twisted with worry that it might be because of me. When Klara had asked, Evgenia had offered an excuse of his needing to run some errands. As for Evgenia, when I inquired about her fast recovery and rallying for the painting event, she'd waved me off, citing her robust Russian immune system.

"I don't know how we are supposed to meet people, glued to a canvas," Evgenia said, voicing my very thoughts. She craned her neck around the arboretum at the crowd. "It's an awful turnout, too. Hardly any interesting women."

"Or men," Klara huffed. "It's my stupid mother's fault. Holding her political luncheon at the same bloody time. She invited all the most interesting boys, trying to win them over for votes."

"I don't understand the point of campaigning if she is unopposed," Evgenia mused. "It's a strange practice. Is it a Swedish thing, like the ABBA decor?"

"It's all pomp and circumstance," I said. "Gives the appearance of democracy without any of the messiness. And my aunt doesn't need an excuse to throw a party."

"But you were not invited?" Evy indicated Klara, Carina, and me.

"Bor-ing," Carina singsonged, lost in her painting. Hers was not even remotely faithful to the original, but I found her neon- pink-and-purple swirls charming, nonetheless.

"I was not invited." Klara took a heavy draw of her wine.

"And I'm the unfortunate niece," I explained. "When I go to those things, anyone old enough to remember my mom asks me all sorts of questions, how I felt about her ideas, if I would want to run myself. Aunt Freja hates it."

"Oh? Was your mom a politician, then?" Evgenia asked.

"Kind of," I said. "Her dad was captain, so she grew up around it. She was really into social welfare, improving conditions on the ship and in the fleet. But she never ran for captainship. Aunt Freja was better suited to it."

Klara made a lemon-sucking expression. "What does that mean?"

"Nothing. Just that my mom didn't like all the red tape and the glad-handing." It seemed to satisfy her. She returned to her starry night.

"So when is this sham election being held?" Evy banged on.

"The day after the Valg Ball," I said. "Once engagements are announced, new partners moving to the *Scandinavian* will be eligible to vote. Everyone will be so happy and hungover, she'll win in a landslide."

"But of course she will. She's unopposed, remember?" Evgenia threw back her head and laughed. "You lot are as bad as we Russians used to be."

Her wrist tab pinged, and she put down her paintbrush to check the message. First she furrowed her brow, then worried her lip and read with intense concentration.

"Everything okay?" I asked, and immediately she brightened. "Oh, yes, of course. It's just Elliot and his grand ideas. He wants to get away from the Valg, go visit an old friend on board the *Lady Liberty*. We're leaving tonight, apparently."

I was confused. "You're taking a vacation from a vacation?"

"Something like that. But it's only for a few days. A minibreak," Evgenia said breezily.

An idea began to crystallize. "Can I go with you?"

Evgenia blinked at me with surprise. "Why would you want to do that?" she squeaked.

"I have to meet with someone." I felt out my plan as I said it. Yes, this might work. "Miranda Fairfax. If you're going anyway, I can hang a ride with you." The opportunity was too perfect. They would pay the expensive docking fees I could never afford, and I could talk my way in front of Miranda. Messages weren't getting me anywhere.

"Ooh, can I come too?" Carina chimed in, clapping her hands with glee. "We haven't been in ages, and I've heard it's too much fun!"

"I'd have to ask Elliot," Evgenia stammered.

"I'm sure he won't mind. He's a peach," Klara tittered. Wait, was she doing what I thought she was? "It's been too long since I visited the *Lady Liberty* too," she continued. "Almost six months. Besides which, Mum is in a tizzy about missing supplies, and I just cannot deal with her. I need a break. We'll make a girls' trip of it!"

"Okay, but we weren't going to be gone for long—"

"Perfect! We can't miss too much of the Valg, anyway," Klara chirped, suddenly playing the part of the ringleader. "Let's meet at five. We can get there in time for dinner!"

Suddenly this was Klara's mini-break, and we were just going along for the ride.

"The more, the merrier," Evgenia said tightly. "I'm sure Elliot won't mind."

From her reaction, I wondered if he did mind. Was this mini-break to get away from me?

Now that I'd gone and invited myself along, it had started a chain reaction that led to my sister and cousin crashing the party. But I couldn't pull out now. I wasn't going to miss my opportunity to pitch myself in person. Screw Elliot being uncomfortable. I was going to do this for me. It was about time something good came from his disastrous return.

16

"Be sure to bring back beer," was all my father had said to me when I told him we were leaving for a few days, his mind one-track and his concern for what I did with my time hovering just above zero. Carina he pressed into a tight, lasting hug and demanded she return as soon as possible.

Klara and Nora met us in the main foyer, a large trunk sitting beside them.

"You call that an overnight bag?" I asked, eyebrows wrenching up.

"Yes," Klara replied matter-of-factly, and I knew better than to argue. We set off for the very back end of the ship, where transports like ours docked, Nora trudging along behind us, dragging the bulky trunk, rendered unwieldy by ancient wheels.

"I loathe coming down here," Klara said as we rounded the final corner and the *Sofi*'s aft door came into view. While she wrinkled her nose in disdain, I breathed a happy sigh. This was home. It was dingy and kind of falling apart, but it was mine.

Quietly I keyed some commands into my wrist tab to turn on the heating in additional rooms—any Klara might make use of—in order to avoid her complaining about that as well. I groaned at the realization that this trip would use up a lot of resources with her on board. And Nora, too, it seemed. I noticed, for the first time, that she had a small rucksack tucked under her arm. Klara apparently could not travel for even a few days without someone to wait on her.

We made our way past the maintenance hold and my workshop to the living quarters. I called out, announcing our arrival, and Evgenia popped out of her bedroom, blinking red-rimmed eyes at us.

"You're early!" she chirped, sweeping each of us into a warm hug. "Forgive my face. This place gives me the most terrible allergies."

"I truly do wish you'd come stay on the *Scandinavian* proper," Klara said. "This place is dusty and awful. No offense, Leo."

I smiled thinly as I always did.

"Elliot!" Evgenia shouted out. "Our guests have arrived."

He popped out from the adjacent lounge, shrewd eyes sweeping over our party. With his mouth pressed into a firm disapproving line, he nodded politely at each of us. I could feel discomfort radiating from him. Elliot was clearly not happy that I was here, crashing his mini-break. Then his eyes fell on Nora, to whom he offered a flash of smile.

"We'll be a full house, then," he said. "Sleeping arrangements may be tough."

I hadn't thought about that.

"I'll stay in the guest quarters, like usual," Klara immediately sang out, claiming the last remaining available above-decks rooms. They were a small but standalone apartment, with a master bedroom, bathroom, small living room, and servant's room, perfect for Nora. With Elliot in my room, Evgenia in Carina's, and Max and Ewan—absent though they were—in my father's apartment, that left the only option for Carina and me: the old below-deck servant's quarters. Elliot's old room. I swallowed hard.

Carina looked equally put out, having done the mental calculations herself and come to the same conclusion. But she bore it well. "Let's go, Leo," she said. "We should drop off our bags downstairs." My heart swelled to see my baby sister slowly but surely growing up. Immediately Elliot put her to another test.

"Could you take your sister's bag down too?" he asked. "I need to talk to her about something."

I was sure the surprise on Carina's face reflected my own. But my sister nodded, accepting my bag without protest, and headed in the direction of the kitchen and back staircase. I turned to find Klara and Nora already gone, having doubled back behind us to the guest apartment. Evgenia popped back into her room, too, leaving me and Elliot alone.

"What is it?" I asked as neutrally as possible. Inside, my body was thrumming with near panic. Was he going to ask me to leave? No, he couldn't—Carina had just taken my things downstairs. Was he going to address why things had gotten awkward last night? Or, worst of all, could it be to confide in me his secret romance with Nora, to get my congratulations or endorsement?

"Follow me," he said more than a little cryptically. But I did, too curious for my own good. He led me all the way forward and upstairs to the bridge. We emerged into the half-moon space, and I flinched to see the control panels and screens gray from dust. My poor disused ship.

"What is it, El?" I forced a nonchalance into my voice, leaning casually on the back of the captain's chair.

"Do you still know how to fly this thing?" he asked.

"Of course. I haven't in years, but I can. Why?"

"It turns out it's actually a good thing you invited yourself along, because I think we need you to pilot."

"So you *are* annoyed that we're here!"

He bristled. "Evy and I had our own plans, so yes."

"Listen, it got out of control, with Carina and Klara inviting themselves along and then Nora coming along too." I paused, looking for a reaction out of Elliot at the mention of his maybe-girlfriend. Nothing. "I'm sorry to put you out, but I need this trip to the *Lady Liberty*. You have the money for docking fees, and I don't. I need to see Miranda Fairfax, and her office is ignoring my messages."

Elliot seemed to soften at that. "Is it about your water-filtration system?"

I nodded. "Did you see the latest news on the usefulness measure? It may impact the private ships as well."

"I did see that. And the latest on visa regulations as well. We don't have one for the *Lady Liberty*. Which is why we need you. People of a . . . certain class are exempted from preapproval to dock."

"So I'm like your Trojan horse?"

"You get us to dock; I'll pay the docking fees." He extended a hand, as if to shake on it. Touching him was out of the question, even for something as casual as a handshake. Any contact, and he'd feel my thready pulse, catch on to how frazzled he made me.

"I'll do it," I said, playing it cool. "Obviously. But what was your plan before I showed up?"

"Honestly? I was going to pretend to be your dad."

"Like he'd ever deign to pilot! Let alone beg customs to let us dock." I laughed.

"Yep, I realized that too. So I probably would have invited you anyway."

"Isn't the point of this whole trip to get away from me? Escape me and the Valg for a few days to visit old friends?" I repeated Evgenia's reasoning, tacking avoidance of myself on for good measure.

"I'm not trying to get away from you, Leo," Elliot said quietly. Then he coughed, and ducked his head. "But I do wish you hadn't brought Klara along."

"Have you *met* Klara? She brought *herself* along." I didn't mean to be funny, but it made Elliot crack a smile.

"And, uh, you brought Carina, too. I can take a hint. I'll talk to her tonight. Any luck trying to get her onto someone else?"

Oh, wow, this wasn't awkward at all. I took a bracing deep breath. "I haven't checked in with her, but I can tonight. She was supposed to reach out to a few guys she matched eighty percent or higher with."

"Yeah, we were a sixty-four percent, which is a bit of a stretch."

"She was very worried about Klara's seventy-two."

Elliot's eyebrows quirked up. "You know, if *someone* had said yes to me at speed dating, we might know *our* percent match."

"I said no to everyone," I defended, feeling my cheeks heat. "And why would we want to match with each other? We're just friends now."

The statement hung between us. I watched Elliot, and he watched me, both of us carefully neutral. Yes, then, we were friends now.

"I checked; you said yes to a bunch of guys the other day," he said. "One of them was a ninety-three percent."

"Are you stalking me?" I was half joking, half willing my heart to return from my throat back to my rib cage.

"I was curious."

I took a moment to make my way over to the main console, to wake *Sofi* up. I needed the space to breathe, figure out the next thing to say. We'd been docked with the *Scandinavian* for years at this point. I hoped she could still fly. She turned on, at least. With a slow, grinding whir, the black-under-gray console lit up dim blue, the screens flickering to life.

"Carina changed my answers in the app," I said, searching for a scrap of something I could use to dust the console. "It was quid pro quo to get her to consider new guys. She picked a bunch of them at random."

I settled on the edge of my skirt as a dustcloth, but just as I was about to swipe at the desk keyboard, a white square of fabric whipped in front of my face. A handkerchief. I swiveled, raising an eyebrow at Elliot.

"I'm a gentleman now," was all he said. And I was some lady, forgetting to line my own pockets with a similar tool.

The cloth kicked up a tempest of dust motes, and we both jumped back, coughing.

"You haven't flown anywhere lately, I see," Elliot said.

"I've needed every scrap of solar power for basic ship functions and, well, the docking fees. So no joy riding for me, or grand vacations."

I turned back to the console, taking a seat and pulling up the fly controls. I could feel Elliot hovering behind me. I waited a beat, leaving him space to say something. The moment lingered, heavy with intent.

"Are you going to ask Mr. Ninety-Three Percent out?" he asked finally. His voice was soft, edging on playful. "That's practically love-match levels."

"There's not going to be a love match," I said matter-of-factly. I would never love anyone but Elliot, I'd realized. Any iteration of him was one I would love to the edges of the universe. Not that I could *say* that to him. "This is why I have to speak to Miranda Fairfax, get this license agreement. If I can make my own money, I won't have to marry anyone."

Elliot didn't respond. I felt only the breeze at my back that signaled his departure. I was left to the stars, winking at me from the window, and the warm console under my hands as I nudged *Sofi* back out into the black skies.

*

It was a short trip to the *Lady Liberty*, since we were on the same side of the orbit roster. What ate up the better part of two hours was all the red tape to secure a flight path and landing dock for us, which required my best diplomacy skills and a little name-dropping. We hadn't seen the Fairfaxes since my mother was alive, but you can bet I mentioned Miranda Fairfax no fewer than six times in the course of my conversation with Brent, the terse logistics manager for the famous American ship.

I was as vague as possible when it came to the occupants of my ship, save for also mentioning Her Royal Highness Klara Lind at least three times. If they knew about Evgenia and Elliot, we'd get into sticky territory in terms of visas. Still, eventually I got it settled, and so we found ourselves docked by evening, just in time for dinner. Bully for Klara.

We made for an awkward boarding party. I led the way, seeing as the *Sofi* was registered under my name (Father having transferred it to me to avoid subsequent paperwork), and it would be my rank—and ship—that garnered us easy entry at customs. Klara trailed behind me, silently fuming that in this case her name and higher rank were unimportant.

She made me pay at dinner, metaphorically and literally. Not only did Klara choose the most expensive restaurant in the New York Ward, but she spent the entire meal flirting with Elliot like it was her job. But Elliot politely rebuffed her at every turn, which should have made my heart soar but instead was like watching a slowly escalating horror show.

Every time Elliot countered one of Klara's jokes, softly chided her for an ill-formed thought, Carina bloomed a bit more in her chair. She radiated hope. In turn, Elliot squirmed with every smile my sister threw his way. With every contrite or miserable look that he and I shared, I settled farther into the sticky bog of my own feelings. Anger boiled in my veins that Elliot expected me to be sympathetic toward this mess of his own making. But elation buoyed me up toward the ceiling with each reminder that he was interested in neither my sister nor my cousin. Self-loathing quickly followed, that I would find joy in my sister's misery.

When the meal was done, Elliot insisted on picking up the whole tab.

"We absolutely must go swimming," Klara gushed as we exited the restaurant. "I've already called ahead to get us special access to the pool, and I've arranged for a bit of shopping."

She dragged us to a fancy swim boutique where a timid shopkeeper nodded us inside without a word.

"Everyone pick out a suit. Even you, Leo. It's on me."

So it seemed this was her revenge. Night swimming. Bathing suits mandatory.

Carina didn't need to be told twice to shop; she was already rifling through the racks, Klara by her side. Elliot was off somewhere too.

"Let's knock their socks off." Evgenia grabbed me by the arm and steered me toward a display of vintage pieces. "This one has underwire!" She handed me a magenta one-piece with a sweetheart neckline and ruching on the bodice, then picked out a similar one in emerald for herself.

Evgenia lowered her voice as we made our way to the fitting rooms. "So, dinner was interesting. Elliot's stopped flirting with your family members, so that's progress. Now all you have to do is admit your feelings. I'm sure he feels the same way."

"No, we're just friends. We've talked about it."

"You have?"

"Not directly. It's obvious."

Evgenia exhaled a deep sigh, then muttered something in Russian.

The suit was perfect, hugging my curves while hoisting up that which needed to be hoisted. I kind of looked hot, if I did say so myself. Still, I wanted Evgenia's opinion, so I stepped out of the changing room and into the foyer.

"Klara, I think these are too small—"

And there was Elliot mere feet in front of me, in nothing but a pair of formfitting black shorts. My hands flew to my chest in a futile attempt to cover myself up.

"She picked out your suit?" I asked, trying but failing to avoid scanning the length of his body again. I caught Elliot doing the same with me.

"Yeah, I uh, prefer looser swim shorts. These are a bit tight."

"I think they're fine." I coughed.

"Your suit is really nice too. The color's great."

We both nodded. A sense of déjà vu washed over me, like the other night in my bedroom, only this time, Elliot was nearly as naked as I was. But bathing suits weren't nudity, I reminded myself. This was normal. We were normal.

"What was that, El?" Klara emerged from her dressing room in a sophisticated cream-colored suit with a plunging neckline. Not a bikini, as I'd expected. "Oh, you're definitely getting those," she said, pointing at Elliot's shorts. Then her assessing eye turned to me. "Leo, you look amazing. Definitely get that one."

The weirdest thing was that I think she actually meant it.

At my cousin's insistence, we wore our suits out of the boutique, making the far trek from the New York Ward to California. Apparently, California had been the land of swimming pools and beaches, and each of the state-themed wards on the *Lady Liberty* was meticulously on-brand. The ship also specialized in excess, so we discovered both a pool *and* a beach from which to choose. Well, it was one long and large pool of water, but with two access points—one a white-sand beach at which the shallow, crystal-blue water gently lapped; the other, shallow descending stone stairs.

Ignoring either entrance, I found a quiet deck chair on which to plant myself. I made it only halfway before Evgenia appeared.

"Oh, no, you don't! You don't have to swim, but at least dangle your legs in the water, since you're in your adorable bathing suit. I want you close to all of us." She inclined her head in Elliot's direction. I'd have to tell her later that the wing-womaning was off. For now, I didn't argue. I could sit on the edge of a pool. It was the deeper parts that stressed me out, though logic told me that if there was a freak gravity failure in here, as there had been the night my mom died, it wouldn't matter which part of the pool I was in.

Pool accessories had appeared from somewhere. My sister drifted by on a floatie, her head tilted back and eyes closed, as if she were sunning herself. It was probably to show off the lines of her body in her blue bikini.

Klara and Elliot drifted to the deeper middle of the pool, each clutching a pool noodle and softly kicking. Evgenia stood between them and me, bridging the gap.

"So what did you think of my mother's political luncheon? I hear you crashed it," Klara asked Elliot, her voice reverberating so it was like we were all in on the conversation.

"I'm not one to pass up free food." Elliot shrugged.

"What did she talk about? Tell me everything."

"She had a lot to say about the usefulness measure, promising she was already at work on a solution. And then she went on and on about the liars in Freiheit."

"Why did she call them liars?" Klara asked at the same time I jumped in with "What did she say she was doing about the usefulness measure?"

I wondered what my aunt was going to do after turning down my water-filtration idea. The *Scandinavian* served no real purpose other than providing luxury-vacation accommodations.

Elliot looked between us both, then locked on me. He

paddled closer as he spoke. "She was vague in the way only politicians can be. Just said she was having tough conversations with key people and that she'd have a solution by the vote." Then he answered Klara, who'd followed him like an obedient puppy. "And she claims Freiheit faked all those images. That they're lying about starvation and death in the fleet."

"Wow, your mom is ice-cold," Evgenia said. "It's definitely real. Elliot and I have seen it. Allowing the rich to continue their delusion isn't helping anyone."

It was the most political thing I had ever heard Evgenia utter. She and Elliot exchanged a loaded glance. Carina had sat up on her floatie and was now watching the rest of us, feigning interest.

"I wouldn't call her ice-cold." Klara jumped to her mother's defense. "She's trying to prevent panic."

"This is why I don't trust politicians," Evgenia said with a sniff, wading away from them and over toward me.

"If she were smart, she'd acknowledge Freiheit, what they showed us, and offer to help. Put the *Scandinavian* on rations. Allow open immigration," I said. "We should be ashamed of the way we live while others suffer." My voice rang out, echoed against silence. Elliot's eyes bored into me like lasers; he assessed me, studied me for bullshit. He found none. I meant it, every single word.

"Maybe *you* should run." Evgenia joined me on the side of the pool, nudging me in the shoulder as she sat down.

"Leo's not political." My sister puffed up her chest proudly that she finally could contribute.

"Not usually," Elliot said quietly. I squirmed under his heady gaze.

"Those ideas are well and good, but not at all practical," Klara snapped, breaking the spell. "This is why my side of the family is in charge. You and yours are hopeless dreamers. My mother and I understand reality."

"Really? Then why hasn't she come to me about my water-filtration system since the usefulness measure was announced? I could save you all, but she's too snobby and stubborn to even consider it."

"No one wants your pee device, Leo. And she doesn't need it. Mother has other plans." Perhaps subconsciously, Klara's eyes flitted over to Elliot, just for a second. Of course. Klara was gunning for Elliot, to marry him for his whiskey ship. If the *Scandinavian* produced alcohol, we'd be useful.

For an awkward moment, no one spoke. There was just the sound of water lapping gently at the pool's edges. Then came the loud splash of Carina sliding off her floatie.

"I'm bored. Let's play Marco Polo!"

If only my sister could have seen the death glare I threw at her back.

"Ooh, yes! I call 'it' first!" Klara trilled, already swimming to the middle of the pool to take position.

Evgenia jumped in, signaling her participation, while Elliot shrugged tacit approval. Fine, I would play—I waded in slowly and clung close to the wall while Klara closed her eyes and counted to twenty. Everyone else made a mad splash-and-dash for other parts of the pool. I stayed put.

Klara shouted a musical "Marco!" to which everyone else responded with "Polo!" With her eyes squinched firmly shut, my cousin tilted her head in my direction.

"Leo, you have to play! I didn't hear you. Marco!"

With a groan, I joined in on the chorus of "Polos." My cousin waded in my direction. I moved along the wall, closer to Evgenia. Elliot and Carina were in the deep end, playing smart. It took only a few more calls and responses before Klara caught me with a laugh.

"You're so easy because you never leave the shallow end! You're it."

I gritted my teeth and threw a false smile before walking with baby steps closer to the middle of the pool. I wouldn't give my cousin the satisfaction of my flouncing out of the pool, swearing off the stupid game. I wrenched my eyes closed and started a loud countdown, splashing roaring in my ears.

The first "Polo" rang in my ears, the musical cacophony bouncing off tile and glass. I called out again, parsing the sound to pinpoint the higher register coming from the right, the lower from my left. The girls in the deep end, and Elliot in the shallows. There was no point bothering with the girls. No way was I swimming into the deep end with my eyes closed. Elliot had to be my quarry.

I called out again, warm reassurance spreading through me when his voice position did not change. Was he staying put for me? I moved toward the sound of his voice, swallowing past the lump that had suddenly formed in my throat.

A few more "Marco Polos" and I had to be within feet of him.

I zombie-walked with my arms floating in front of me, fingers feeling for his arm. I held my breath in anticipation of the catch, reminded that games like this could be fun. I could have fun.

It had gone quiet, too quiet. All I could pick out was the low burble of water and Elliot's breathing somewhere near.

"Marco?" I called out feebly.

"Polo." His voice was low, husky. And right in front of me. I didn't move, so he must have. My fingers grazed skin, Elliot's heartbeat thumping against my fingertips.

"You're it," I said softly. I didn't dare open my eyes, break the spell. I flattened my palm against his chest. My breath caught in my throat as I felt his fingers whisper against my hip under the water. I opened my eyes to drown in his.

"Elliot's turn!" Klara shouted, followed by a splash and the sound of strenuous swimming. Elliot flinched away, and then it was over.

Elliot counted from the middle of the pool while everyone swam into position. I noted that the others chose to congregate in the shallow end this turn. I retreated over to the stairs, needing very much to sit for a while. To my surprise, Evgenia joined me, keeping her voice nice and low between calls and responses.

"Are you afraid of the deep end or something?"

I nodded. Evgenia cursed under her breath.

"Klara told us all to go into the deep end, make it hard for you. I didn't know . . . I'm sorry, Leo."

Well, that explained a lot. Elliot had deliberately saved me from embarrassment. A gesture of friendship, surely. Not that that explained the hand on the hip. It was probably a mistake.

Evgenia swam away on the next "Polo," though by then it was pretty much guaranteed Elliot would be catching Carina. My sister played without subtlety, moving in whatever direction Elliot did on each turn, putting herself closer and closer to him. I watched Klara watching Carina, my cousin's frustration mounting until her nostrils flared and eyes blazed with rage.

At last, Elliot had no choice but to catch my sister, who giggled loudly and threw her arms around his shoulders. "You got me!"

Elliot squirmed, wriggling his shoulder to try to dislodge her embrace. And then he leaned in close to her ear, said something in hushed tones.

"What?" my sister responded, her eyes going wide.

Oh, no, was he doing what I thought he was doing?

He said something else I couldn't hear, and then my sister went limp, finally releasing him and falling backwards into the water up to her chin. The chin started to wobble. But my sister did not cry. Carina stood up, walked over to the stairs, and got out of the pool.

"I'm sick of playing," she said. Now the wobble was in her voice. And then she ran out of the room.

I threw Elliot a look that could have boiled the pool in two seconds. Then I got out, grabbed two towels and our bag of clothes, and rushed after my sister.

17

I followed the wet slapping of Carina's feet until I caught up with her at the lift bank. Her red-rimmed eyes told me there had been tears, though it seemed they were brief. Now she was just hiccupping sporadically. Without words, I handed her a towel, then her shoes, and we made our way back to the *Sofi*.

To add insult to my sister's injury, we were staying in Elliot's old room. There was no escaping him. She threw herself down on one of the beds, coincidentally the one where he and I used to sleep.

"I feel so stupid," she groaned into the pillow.

"You shouldn't," I said. "Elliot led you on. And when I told him to let you down gently, I did *not* mean in public—"

Carina whipped around. "Wait, you *told* him to do that to me?"

"No! Well, yes. Kind of. It's really complicated."

My sister sat up and leveled me with a stare. "Explain."

ALEXA DONNE

I sat down on the bottom bunk opposite her, buying myself time to work up my courage. I wanted to tell her everything, but I was used to telling her nothing, so it was hard. Unnatural.

"Elliot and I used to have a thing, as you know."

"You told me it was over," she said.

"I know. It is. But things were a bit more . . . serious between us than you knew. And it ended dramatically."

"What does that mean? Leo, just tell me."

I took a deep breath and let it tumble out. "We were engaged, back when. But then we weren't. I'm sorry I never told you. Anyway, Elliot was kind of bitter about it, so when he came back here, he was trying to make me miserable, and one of the ways he did that was by saying yes to you at speed dating. I scolded him soundly for it, for toying with your feelings, and told him to let you down gently—"

"Whoa, whoa, Leo." Carina held out her arms, as if to brace herself against the onslaught of information. "You were *engaged to Elliot?*"

"Uh, yeah. Surprise?"

Carina furrowed her brow. "Did you lie to me? When you said you were over Elliot? You let me throw myself at him, with speed dating and everything else?"

"That was before I knew Elliot's agenda, though. I know I should have told you about the engagement, been honest, but I want you to be happy and—"

Next thing I knew, I was engulfed in a tight hug, Carina having thrown herself practically on top of me.

"You're such a good sister," she said into my hair. "But you're also a huge idiot." She pulled back with a disapproving look. "You should have told me. I would never hurt you, not on purpose. Unlike some people." She frowned. "Our cousin is such a witch. She knew, right? And she's been throwing herself at him too."

I nodded. "Witch, though?"

"Well, she *is* family," Carina reasoned. "Now you're going to tell me the full story of you and Elliot. I need to know exactly what I was stepping in the middle of."

So I filled my little sister in on all the sordid details, watching as her brow inched farther and farther up, until it fully disappeared into her fringe.

"Dad, Aunt Freja, and Klara staged an intervention? Wow." She looked down at her hands in her lap, then laced one of them through mine. "You know I never would have been into him, gone after him, if I had known, right? You're my sister."

"I know." I drew her into a hug, this one of mutual comfort. This felt far more natural, being her big sister, offering myself.

"He's gorgeous, of course, and definitely kind of flirty?" She looked to me for affirmation, which I had to give. Elliot wasn't innocent in all this. "But if I'm honest, he and I have basically nothing in common."

Laughter shot through me. Never had there been a truer statement to tumble from my baby sister's lips.

"We'll find you someone perfectly suited to you," I promised. "You're wonderful, and I'm really happy that you're my sister."

"Ugh." She smacked me playfully on the shoulder, poorly suppressing a smile. "So sappy. And what about you? Do you still love him?"

My face must have said it all.

"Leo! You should tell him! He either hates you or loves you back, with the way he's been acting. I noticed him flirting, but like I said, he flirts with everyone, and I thought you weren't interested."

"We're just friends. We buried the hatchet," I said.

"Uh-huh."

"It's true!"

"I'll ask you again tomorrow, after you've spent the night in his bed." She pointed across the way. "So you two, like . . . you know. In that bed?"

"Conversation's over. Let's go to bed." I left her giggling after me as I went to shower. Carina would be just fine.

*

I rose to find the ship eerily quiet. It seemed I was on a new sleeping schedule, and waking before everyone else was my new normal. I crept into the hall and listened up the stairs, but I heard no sign of another early-morning coffee tryst between Elliot and Nora. My pleasure at the realization was far too acute. I didn't want to run into him, anyway. I'd be too tempted to give him a piece of my mind about how atrociously he'd handled the Carina situation.

I took the opportunity to do some housekeeping and retrieve my mother's dresses. We'd sealed them up years ago after Father complained they were taking up too much space in his closet. I hadn't wanted them in mine. The daily reminder that she was gone would have been too much.

I padded in bare feet out of the servants' wing to the mid-deck storage unit. It was dark inside and musty, only one of which was helped by my turning on the lights. The room was full to the brim with old furniture, dusty boxes, and a graveyard of fashion. Too many of my ancestors had been too proud to recycle fraying and faded clothing, so they ended up here, crammed into a series of wire racks someone had fashioned from scrap. I'd started upcycling pieces as best I could, which went for the furniture, too, but so many of the pieces were too fine to cut up. My mother's dresses especially, which I kept carefully wrapped and stored so that one day Carina and I could actually wear them. That day was coming soon. The Valg Ball was too close for my liking.

I maneuvered around stacks of boxes and decaying furniture to my mother's trunk, kneeling on the floor and prising open the lid. I blinked hard, deliberately, as if to clear my vision. Then I did it again. Nothing changed—the trunk was half empty. My mother's dresses were gone. Tightness seized my chest.

There had to be a logical explanation. Carina or Father must have moved the dresses when the Valg Season started, to air them out. Yes, that was it, surely. First I searched all the racks behind me, but I didn't find them.

I left the storage room, drawing deep breaths to calm myself. Panicking was silly. I'd let my father's paranoia get to me, as if someone would have stolen them. There was nowhere for them to go, so they must be on board. My money was on Carina to have messed with them and forgotten to tell me. The door to the cargo bay appeared on my periphery. Yes, very likely she would have taken them down there. There was more room, better air.

I pressed fingers to the cargo-room bio-lock, anticipating the *click-whoosh* of the doors. Instead I ended up checking the door with my shoulder as I charged forward. *Ow.* I rubbed the sore spot with one hand and tried the bio-lock again. No *click-whoosh.* I was locked out.

Instinctively, my fingers flew to my wrist tab, but then I remembered. I could access security protocols only from the tab unit in the maintenance hold. I'd have to go up there, see who changed the security permissions on the cargo hold. Then I could figure out why.

I ignored the cold that slithered up my back as I made my way upstairs and flew through the kitchen, past the family rooms, and toward the aft end. Nothing looked out of place in the maintenance hold, least of all the tab unit, screen black from sleep. I touched the screen, bringing her awake, and chewed my lower lip nervously as my fingers dangled over the keyboard to input my administrator password. With a deep inhale of breath, I quickly keyed in the code and hit enter. I held my breath until the home screen winked open in front of me. A laugh escaped as I rapidly exhaled.

Almost everything was in order, including and especially resource management—lights, heating, water, electricity—all still under my master control. But someone had tampered with the kitchen-pantry bio-lock (*What?*), as well as the cargo hold. I opened the permissions console for the pantry first, typing in a short string of code. *Dink-dink,* the tab chirped with dissent. Someone far more sophisticated at computer code than I was had locked me out.

Elliot. The question was why? Were Elliot and the Orlovs really so worried that I might violate their privacy, rifle through their private belongings? The cargo hold I could maybe understand, but surely nothing in the pantry could be so private. Preserved food, powdered milk, coffee. Basic necessities of life.

I needed to talk to Elliot, just ask him straight why he'd changed the security permissions, and on those rooms in particular. I reminded myself that he'd passed his background check. They all had. The explanation was surely a reasonable one.

And then there was the matter of the dresses. I was not looking forward to searching the ship for them. I imagined it would involve a lot of sweat and muscle strain.

I checked the time. People would be stirring by now. I headed back out into the ship, my feet carrying me on instinct to the kitchen. Coffee called me. I quickened my step, practically tasting the blessed sharp bitterness on my tongue already.

"Oh, good, Leo, you're up." Klara appeared from the study, cutting me off in the corridor, steps away from my caffeine hit. "We're all ready to go over to the *Lady Liberty*. You should get dressed." Her eyes scanned my PJs and bare feet with apparent disdain.

"Isn't it a bit early?" I asked, craning my neck around her toward the kitchen. I was so close.

"Elliot woke us all up, said it's important to make our way over early. I assume he's keen to get breakfast on board, as am I."

"I just need coffee—"

"There's no time. The best breakfast spots will already have a line by nine a.m. You can get coffee there."

No, I couldn't, since my plan was to head up to Miranda Fairfax's office and sit outside until she saw me. There was no arguing with Klara, who walked off shouting to Nora to grab her jacket. Downstairs, I found Carina lacing up her boots. When she saw me, her eyes went wide with horror at my sleep-mussed hair, unwashed face, and slouchy sleep set. She leaped into makeover mode, getting me presentable in ten minutes flat.

It was another awkward boarding, as it seemed each of us wasn't speaking to another member of the party. Carina marched along in front to avoid Elliot, I followed close behind to avoid blowing up at said-same boy, Evgenia wasn't speaking to Klara ("for her deep-end stunt," she said to me), and Klara didn't deign to speak to Nora, even on a good day. She was coming along to carry Klara's bags, as she planned on shopping.

The *Lady Liberty* was among the largest and most populous ships in the fleet, housing about two thousand people across six luxury decks. Each level, named for a notable American from the Old World, was circular, like a planet's rings, rotating around a central lift column. We had docked and come through security on the very bottom level, and we exited the customs sector and moved into the central lift bank.

"Our friend lives on the Roosevelt Level," Evgenia said, pressing the lift button. "Elliot and I would like to go see him first thing, but you ladies can go have breakfast, do some shopping while we—"

"No, I want to meet your friend!" Klara trilled, flashing her widest grin at Elliot. "And the Roosevelt Level . . . how colorful."

That was her code for "plebeian," but she didn't let her smile drop, even if it became a bit strained.

"And you mustn't skip breakfast. It's the most important meal of the day. It's on me, since Elliot got us dinner last night."

"Uh, sure, yes, you're right," Elliot said, exchanging a portentous glance with Evgenia. Maybe an apology?

Klara clapped her hands. "Excellent. We absolutely must go to the Left Coast in the California Ward. Their huevos rancheros are to die for." The lift dinged, signaling its arrival. Klara breezed in first, snapping at Nora to follow close behind. Then Evgenia went, and Carina.

"The space in here is tight. You take the next one, Leo," Klara singsonged, sweet as sugar. Just when I was bemoaning Klara winning another point in our little war, Elliot, who had been stepping over the threshold, hopped back out.

"I'll go with her," he said. Klara's protest was cut off by the doors promptly closing. I thought I saw Carina jamming her thumb into the close-door button.

"You didn't have to do that," I said, hitting the call button once their lift had shuttled off. I fought the flutter in my stomach at his choosing to come with me, reminding myself that he'd messed with my ship behind my back. "I was going to take my own lift anyway, to the Gates Level. It's above Oprah, so now you'll have to backtrack."

"Why are you going to the Gates Level?"

"To meet with Miranda Fairfax, remember?" The next lift arrived and we stepped inside, drifting to opposite ends of the too-small space, facing off as the lift rose rapidly. My ears became tight with pressure, and I swallowed hard. The *Lady Liberty* was massive, so even at speed, this would be at least a two-minute trip. Plenty of time.

"So when I said to let my sister down gently, I didn't mean in front of everyone," I said.

Elliot ducked his head down as spots of color rose on his cheeks. "Is she okay? I didn't mean to do it that way; it just sort of happened."

"You're lucky my sister is so resilient. She'll be fine. But I'm still mad at you. About you fiddling with my security protocols, too." I threw him a loaded look.

"How—"

"I was looking for something," I answered. "If you needed privacy, you could have asked me."

"We, uh, weren't exactly speaking for a while there." Elliot laughed awkwardly. "Max and Ewan needed to store some valuables, and they felt more comfortable with the bio-locks changed . . ."

"So, what, you guys have some extra-fancy food in the pantry you don't want me to steal?"

"It wasn't about you stealing," he said after a moment of consideration. "It's hard to explain. I made sure it was only those two places, though, and I didn't think—"

"I'd find out?"

Elliot grimaced.

The explanation was reasonable enough, but he was holding back. I wanted to press him, shout, make him confess whatever it was he was keeping from me, but Elliot and I were still on tenuous ground. We'd been on somewhat friendly speaking terms for, what, forty-eight hours?

We fell into silence. I felt with my fingers for the bar at my back, to feel myself anchored to the wall. I was suddenly lightheaded. I dared a glance in Elliot's direction and caught his head jerking ever so slightly away. Had he been watching me?

Now we were both watching the lift console flash the names of the levels as we passed them—Roosevelt, Bly, Hamilton, Lincoln.

Elliot took a deep breath. "Leo, listen, I have to tell you—"

Ding! The lift signaled our arrival, cutting him off midsentence. Elliot stepped out with me, I assumed to finish what he'd been saying. My stomach was twisted into knots. We hovered awkwardly in the lift bank, both looking at the floor.

"Were you going to say something?" I asked finally, unable to bear it any longer.

"Oh, it's nothing," he said, waving me off. "We can talk about it later."

"Don't you need to go back down, then? They're waiting for you on Oprah."

He shrugged. "I don't really care about breakfast. Hold on." He tapped his wrist tab several times, brought it to his mouth. "Evy, we're skipping breakfast. Leo has an errand to run, and I'm gonna keep her company."

"What about Ben?" Evgenia's voice was tinny coming through the wrist-tab speaker.

"I trust you to take care of it, send me updates. Either way, we'll do dinner on the *Sofi* tonight; invite him over."

"Okay."

Elliot tapped off his wrist tab and turned back to me. "There, all settled. Let's head over to the office, shall we?"

I nodded numbly, too stunned not to follow.

"What's Evgenia supposed to take care of with Ben?" I asked as we took a pair of seats in the waiting room of the Fairfax office. Her administrative assistant disappeared back into the inner office, leaving us to wait in the small antechamber.

"Take care of? Nothing, just saying hi."

I wasn't sure I believed him, but I simply shrugged. Then I retrieved my portable tab from my purse and settled in to wait.

"We're not going to talk?" Elliot pouted.

"I had planned on reading," I responded breezily, teasing him a little.

"That's not fair. I didn't bring anything."

"You chose to come," I reminded him. "But okay, we'll

talk." I put away the tab. "What were you going to say to me in the lift?"

Elliot squinted, as if trying to remember. "Oh, just that I really appreciated what you said last night. About Freiheit, and how the *Scandinavian* should do the right thing. It really is getting bad out there. I've seen a lot of things that can't be unseen. If you hadn't said something, I might have knocked Klara off her noodle, just to mess with her. But you put her in her place."

"And then she promptly put me back in mine," I said. "I'm a useless dreamer, not fit for politics."

"I don't think that's true," Elliot responded earnestly. "It wasn't true about your mom, either. I think she would have run if she could, and won. The *Scandinavian* under her captainship would be a very different ship. And you could still challenge your aunt, if you wanted. I'd help you."

"I'm overwhelmed enough as it is, running my own tiny ship," I deflected.

"I think you've done a great job. I see your handiwork all over it. Generators, energy-saving switches, and the water system. You're practical and self-sacrificing. You were smart enough to bring on the Orlovs as renters, and you have this plan to get the license and patent. You're a born leader. I mean, it's why you, uh, couldn't come with me. You had to stay, be responsible."

It was both flattering and devastating to have Elliot throw the reasons for my rejection back at me as a compliment. I shrugged.

"Thanks, El, but I really don't want to go into politics. You know me well enough to know that, surely?"

"I can tell you meant what you said last night. You want to help."

"I'm just a uselessly titled princess with no way to do anything. I'm nobody."

"You're not nobody, Leo." Elliot's voice was soft, barely above a whisper.

I had no response to that, so I gave none. I couldn't even bear to look at him, afraid of what I might find if I did. Perfect neutral or burning passion—either possibility washed cold fear straight through me.

I was relieved when we fell into perfectly pleasant silence and were able to pass the next few hours without any hard-hitting conversation. As we moved into hour three of waiting, Elliot's wrist tab beeped.

"It's from Evy," he said, a frown overtaking his face.

"Bad news?"

"What? No, it's fine. I was just hoping Ben would have something for me, but he doesn't. Evy says they're heading back to Oprah so Klara can get in her shopping, then Ben is coming over tonight for dinner. I think you'll like him."

"Who is he? You keep saying 'old friend.' How do you know each other?"

"I stayed with his family for a while, after I'd left the *Sofi*. The *Lady Liberty* was my first stop as part of a work-rotation program. After that, I moved to the *Saint Petersburg*."

"Oh," I said. There wasn't much else to say. This was part of Elliot's post-Leo life. It didn't belong to me.

We waited another hour. Miranda Fairfax, it turned out,

had either the worst administrative assistant in the fleet or the best. He informed us eventually that she wasn't even on board. Was he lying or just incompetent? I couldn't tell. If she was here, he'd done a bang-up job protecting her from me.

"I feel bad that you wasted all this time with me for nothing," I said to Elliot as we headed back to the lift bank.

"It wasn't a waste," he said, once again teetering on the edge of innuendo. Was he being kind or flirting? "I'm sure they're done shopping by now, so we can head back to the *Sofi*."

He didn't have to tell me twice. I desperately needed a nap. We walked back toward the lift bank as I tried not to be swallowed up by despair. There was no way we could stay the whole week, waiting for Miranda's return, and I didn't think I could finagle a trip to the *Olympus* to catch her there. I chewed on self-misery the whole lift ride.

"Leo, it'll be okay," Elliot said as we exited. "I was thinking. You can pitch Ben, tonight at dinner. He works in sanitation. Not at the very top, but high enough that he sees Miranda Fairfax every once in a while. Maybe he could help?"

"Thanks, El." I offered him a half-smile. "I'm kind of on the clock, though. The Valg ends in less than three weeks. Either this works out, or I get hitched."

"Enter Mr. Ninety-Three Percent."

"It's not funny," I snapped.

"No, I guess it isn't."

I wanted to apologize, but prodding further would prompt a frank conversation about Elliot, me, and the Valg that I wasn't ready to have. We didn't speak the rest of the way back.

18

"What are you *wearing*?" from Carina's tone, you would have thought I was decked out in a dirty potato sack. I checked myself, finding the same simple tea dress I'd had on all day. It had even survived my nap.

"Clothes?" I replied.

"*Leo*." Carina's tone was chiding. She jumped up from the vanity and crossed the room over to where I stood by the door. "Klara has been getting ready for three hours. You need to bring your A-game." She fussed with my hair, then brushed an imaginary speck of dirt from my shoulder.

"For what?" I was purposely obtuse, just to get a rise out of her.

"LEO!"

"Calm down; I'm only kidding." I made my way over to my suitcase to retrieve a special dress I'd been saving for just such a night as this. "But I'm going to wear it because I want to, not to engage in some bizarre competition with

Klara for Elliot's affection, for the record."

I pulled out the dress to show her, and my sister's eyebrows rose with approval. It was sleeveless and black, with a stiff bodice that streamlined into a full but sleek skirt, black chiffon transitioning into magenta, ultraviolet, and apricot streaks of color before fading into the palest off-white at the bottom of the skirt. It was the darkest point of night blooming into a brilliant sunrise, in dress form.

"Why have I not seen that before?"

"I was saving it for the Valg Ball," I said.

"So you *do* care!"

I groaned. "Only a little. Anyway, Father reminded me about Mom's dresses. He wants us to wear them instead. Did you take them out of storage to air them out?"

"Me? No. Why?"

"It's nothing." I didn't want to pull her into my mounting alarm. I'd checked everywhere this afternoon and hadn't found them. Pasting on a smile, I surveyed Carina's outfit and shifted the subject. "And talking of new dresses." She was in a champagne-and-silver silk-brocade tea dress, not only a muted color palette for her, but a more mature style. I cocked an eyebrow, aiming a wordless question.

"Evgenia lent it to me," she clarified, explaining everything.

"You look beautiful," I said, liking the new look on her. She typically erred on the side of bright blues, purples, and pinks, favoring tiered chiffon and the aptly titled princess-dress style. "Are you dressed up for any particular reason? Not that you need an excuse."

Carina ducked her chin down to hide a blush. "So it turns out Ben is really cute, and super nice."

I swatted her on the arm. "Carina!"

"What? You wanted me to move on!"

She had me there. But still. Were all sixteen-year-olds this changeable? I hadn't been. And there I went, reminding myself of Elliot again.

"I don't know what to do with my hair."

"I do," I said, grabbing a few supplies from my bag and pulling her over to my bed. I scooted back against the wall, spreading my legs and patting the space between them. We transformed into younger versions of ourselves, her sitting cross-legged in front of me, my patient and more dexterous fingers weaving patterns into her thick hair. But instead of a single braid falling down the center of her back, I wove two on either side, twisting them up into a makeshift crown. Finally, I pinned everything to her head with our mother's diamond-and-ruby flower pins. Carina touched tentative fingers to her hair.

"Are these . . ." She let the question hang.

"You're old enough now that I should share them with you," I said. "Just don't get drunk and lose them."

"You're going to let me drink, too? Like, actually drink?"

"Everything in moderation."

We scooted off the bed, and while Carina put the finishing touches on her makeup, I poured myself into my most robust bustier and stepped into my dress. Carina helped me fasten it in the back and held my hand so I could step into a pair of wildly impractical heels.

Evgenia pinged us via the wall tab, letting us know that Ben had arrived and dinner was nearly ready. We would start with drinks in the study. I didn't miss how my sister lit up at the mention of Ben's name.

I hadn't set foot in my father's study in ages, it seemed like. This was one of the rooms I'd left to the Orlovs and we'd not used during our few occasions on board since their arrival. It was as I remembered it, but somehow it was made warmer by the company and by the fact that I wasn't sitting in my usual chair, worrying over sums while my father and sister schemed up ways to spend money we didn't have.

Row after row of antique books, untouched by my family for decades, crowded the towering wooden bookshelves that lined the walls. Their smell always brought me comfort, the light musk of the binding and paper, my nerves soothed by the color-coded and alphabetized arrangement one of my ancestors had long ago decided on. My practical side knew that if I touched them, I'd hasten their demise, so I read exclusively on a tab, but I remained thankful that our family had valued books enough to bring them with us all those years ago.

As Carina and I waltzed in, Elliot and someone I assumed to be Ben halted their conversation immediately—it looked serious, tense. They stood up from the bottle-green overstuffed leather couch that was my favorite and offered both of us the slightest bow. They played the role of gentlemen, an antiquated gesture I found both flattering and jarring. We curtsied, elevating the whole thing to ridiculous levels.

"Should I call you two Your Royal Highnesses, like

the other one?" Ben joked, offering a wink. I understood Carina's rapidly developed crush. Ben was tall, gorgeous, and charming. I guessed he was twenty, maybe twenty-one. Warm brown eyes peered out from behind rectangular spectacles, his skin medium dark, hair curly but close-cropped. When he smiled, my eyes were drawn to his strong jawline and high cheekbones. I could stare at him all day.

And he was staring at my sister.

"I'm Leo," I offered, along with my best and firmest handshake—a point of family pride. "No royal titles required." I moved off to the sideboard to pour my sister and me each a glass of wine. I checked the bottle—not one of ours, thankfully. This was a premium brand from the *Versailles,* more than we could afford.

"And of course I'm just Carina," my sister said. "Royal titles are so stuffy, and silly, given we don't rule over anything anymore."

Now my sister just sounded like *me.* I snorted a laugh, but they didn't notice with my back to them. I turned to walk the glasses over to the love seat, where Carina had taken up residency across from Ben. I wondered if the reason for her sudden practical turn was to impress our guest, who hailed from an egalitarian American ship and was second-in-command in the sanitation department. Regardless, I was pleased.

The sound of someone loudly clearing her throat came from behind me. I turned to find Klara, decked out in a glittering floor-length silver-and-white number, one of her many tiaras sitting upon her golden head; she paused on the threshold as if she expected a trumpet to announce her arrival. Nora did it instead.

"Her Royal Highness, Princess Klara Lind." Nora's soft voice barely carried as far as the love seat, not even ten feet from the door, but it was enough. The gentlemen jumped to their feet again, bowing and simpering a greeting, and both of them took Klara's gloved hand in turn and kissed the back of it.

Elliot caught my eye as he rose from his bow, comically widening his eyes, and I suppressed a giggle behind my cousin's back.

During all this pomp and circumstance, Nora scurried over to the sideboard and poured a glass of wine for Klara, which she pressed into her hand before retreating from the room. She had likely been instructed by Klara to take over things in the kitchen and serve us at dinner. Shame shot through me as I observed Ben watching her retreat. For all my posturing about royal titles, equality, and inequities in the fleet, I allowed my cousin to treat another human being like an accessory in my own home.

I resolved to invite Nora to join us for dinner, damn the consequences. And I didn't have to wait long—after a few minutes of painful small talk, Evgenia arrived, breathless and beautiful as always, announcing that dinner was ready and we'd best move off to the dining room before it grew cold. Nora hovered on the sidelines, ready to spring into action.

"Tonight, I bring you a taste of Mother Russia," Evgenia said with a flourish over the spread. "A variety of *pelmeni,* or 'dumplings' to the uninitiated, as well as stuffed cabbage—a bunch of dishes with cabbage, really—and everything drowning in butter."

"Nora, please join us. We'll serve ourselves," I said, biting the bullet quickly. Klara didn't dare counter me in front of our guest, though I felt her glare on the back of my neck. But it was worth Ben's look of relief. Oddly, from Elliot I caught a flicker of doubt. Uncertainty swooped at my insides—did he think I was doing it for brownie points?

We settled into our places, and I found myself at the head of the table, flanked by Ben and Nora, opposite Klara on the other end, who was next to Elliot and Evgenia. Nora made one person too many for the six-person arrangement, but Carina didn't seem to mind at all squeezing in between Elliot and Ben on the left side of the table.

"I want to hear more about how you met, Elliot and Ben," Klara said, throwing the first volley my way. As the highest-ranking person here, she saw herself as the hostess for this gathering. I didn't mind—I was curious too and didn't want Elliot to think I was overly interested in him or his time away from me.

"When I left the *Sofi* three years ago, I was accepted onto the *Lady Liberty* on a work-vacation visa," Elliot started. "Which meant I could work for six months and enjoy the ship's amenities, and I was provided free housing with a family who had room to spare."

"My dad was fascinated to have a displaced Brit, who grew up on a German ship and spent a lot of time on the *Scandinavian*, living with us. He loved asking questions about life on other ships," Ben chimed in. He and Elliot shared a grin, a brotherly affection bouncing unspoken between them. Did Elliot really identify as a displaced Brit? That had never come up with us. He'd been born on the *Sofi,* so it seemed strange.

"I started busing tables; then I waited on them, and eventually I became a line cook."

"How did you end up in whiskey, then?" Klara asked.

Elliot shrugged. "An opportunity came up with the beverage industry, and I pivoted."

"Elliot is good at everything he tries." Ben laughed. "I think my dad preferred him to me."

"Sounds about right." Elliot played along.

"Where is your dad now?" Carina asked.

"Oh, he died last year," Ben said. "There was an accident. Old ships, and all that."

The mood turned unexpectedly somber. Soon, we broke off into our own little chat clusters, Klara conversing primarily with Elliot and Evgenia, while Ben held court with the rest of us. Carina, Nora, and I were rapt as he regaled us with jokes, ghost stories, and what had to be tall tales about the richest residents of the *Lady Liberty.* At least I hoped.

I did my best to wing-woman my sister, turning fully to Nora to engage her in conversation as we served ourselves dessert. I hoped it would leave Ben and Carina to have some one-on-one time, which I could sense she craved.

"Tell me more about yourself, Nora," I said, attempting to sound casual. She shot me a skeptical look. I lowered my voice. "I wanted to give them a moment to themselves. So,

just making conversation." I indicated my sister and Ben, and
Nora nodded knowingly.

"Love is in the air, it would seem." Her words dripped with
sarcasm as she shot a look at Klara batting her eyelashes at
Elliot while he regaled her with some story. My eyes darted
down the table, but I didn't allow myself to linger. I wanted to
watch Nora and her reaction.

"I don't think she even likes him that much," she said,
keeping her voice conspiratorially low. No hint of jealousy.
"But her mother has turned up the heat on the marriage
conversation, and he stands to inherit a very useful ship."

"And he's a good match politically, as well," I added. "Has
she mentioned anything about challenging her mother for
captainship?"

"If anyone should be marrying Elliot and challenging the
captain, it's not your cousin."

"Excuse me?"

Nora raised an eyebrow in judgment. "The thing about
being invisible to most people is you observe a lot." Then she
frowned, leaned in very close, and husked into my ear. "But
that said, do not under any circumstances challenge your
aunt. She'll cut you down where you stand. I've given your
cousin the same advice, gentle as I could. Same with him. You
do not want to get involved in what Elliot's got going on."

"What do you mean?"

But Nora was done speaking on the subject. She asked Ben
an innocuous question, opening us up to group conversation
again, and the moment passed. I, however, was stuck.

Unsettled. What did she know about my family that I didn't? What did Nora know about Elliot? The sweet cake I'd been chewing suddenly tasted like ash; the *Versailles* red was bitter as I washed it down.

"None of us are drunk enough!" Evgenia proclaimed, toasting us with an empty glass. Come to think of it, she'd been drinking a lot during dinner. "Shall we adjourn to the study for more drinks and deeper conversation? We came all the way here for nothing, so we might as well have fun."

Elliot shot her a look the meaning of which I couldn't decipher, but then he rose from his seat. We followed him to the study, where in very short order a bottle of whiskey appeared and music was put on. An artificial fire roared in the decorative fireplace, and I calculated the energy cost. Then I chided myself for it, taking a hearty sip of my drink. This whole trip was beyond our means. I would never make the sums square.

The other girls started to dance, but I declined. With Carina vacating her spot on the couch, I plopped down next to Ben, who was the fun kind of drunk, chatty and easy. He fell into conversation with Elliot while I laid my head against the back curve of the couch, angling it toward them. At first they prattled on about silly things, like some movie Ben had seen recently that he thought Elliot would enjoy. Something with dancing and street gangs and star-crossed lovers. But then they shifted to far more interesting topics.

"How long have they been gone?" Ben lowered his voice so the dance party wouldn't hear, but he didn't consider my closeness.

"Three days now," Elliot replied. "They were supposed to come here to pick up the shipment, then on to the *Saint Petersburg*. I messaged Dmitri. They aren't there, either."

"There aren't many more possibilities." Ben left something unspoken, something bleak and awful.

"I know," Elliot said darkly.

"They" had to be Max and Ewan, who were supposed to be on a transport run, according to Evgenia. But it seemed they were missing, and that's why we'd come here. It explained a lot—Evgenia's nihilistic behavior, so unlike her, and both of them being cagey about the reason for this mini-break. This had been a missing-persons mission. Why hadn't he just told me?

More importantly, what business were Max and Ewan involved in, exactly? People transporting normal cargo and passengers didn't just disappear.

"Up, Elliot, now!" Klara appeared like a white witch, snapping her fingers until Elliot hopped to, like a puppet on a string. "I like this one," she said. "But I need a proper dance partner."

And with that, I was left with Ben on the couch. He made no move to join the revelers. Instead, I caught him watching me. I inched up to a proper sitting posture, considering him considering me.

"You're not at all what I expected," he said finally. The subject turning to me caught me off-guard. I'd been so wrapped up in Elliot and Max and Ewan.

"What does that mean?" I tried to keep the defensiveness in my tone to a minimum. It was hard. I imagined the worst.

"I don't know." He shrugged, eyes drifting over in the

direction of Klara and Elliot, dancing. "If you hadn't told me who was who, I would've pegged Klara for you. The illustrious Leo, the haughty princess."

I bristled, opening my mouth to defend myself, but Ben was too quick.

"Either you've mellowed, or Elliot exaggerated. I suspect the latter."

"Was it that bad?" I asked, voice small.

"He was pretty hurt," was all Ben would offer. "But I like you. You're tough, and smart, I can tell."

"Can you, then?" Sarcasm crept back in, as it was wont to do, my vulnerability safely tucked back into my rib cage.

"I know you're pretending to be drunker than you are. That's only your third glass of wine."

"You were counting?"

He took a drag of whiskey, smacking his lips wetly at the end, grimacing only slightly. "I like to pay attention to people, and things. I'm resourceful, and so are you."

Here it came. He knew I'd been eavesdropping on their conversation. I readied my denials, but then Ben surprised me yet again.

"Elliot told me about your special water system. I checked out the bathroom, kitchen. I'm impressed."

"Uh, thank you?"

"You're welcome. He said you're trying to sell your system to the *Lady Liberty*, but you're having trouble getting hold of Miranda Fairfax."

That perked me up. "Not 'sell,'" I said. "But license. Like a business partnership. I want to be able to license it to other ships as well, but I need one large ship to be the guinea pig."

"See? Resourceful and tough, like I said. I'll talk to Miranda next week when she's back, if you'd like. We have a standing quarterly meeting, so your timing is good."

"Thank you. That would be amazing." I couldn't believe my luck, that it would be Elliot's old friend—the person who replaced me, in a way—who would come to my family's rescue. Ben was good people.

"So let's talk about you and your intentions." My gaze flitted over to my sister, and Ben's eyes followed.

He ducked his head, as if embarrassed. "It's a little too soon to be discussing intentions. We just met. Besides, I don't think the likes of her would go for the likes of me."

I shrugged. "The royalty thing is meaningless. We're barely holding on to our ship by the skin of our teeth. And talk about fast. We have the Valg, where the results of a five-minute speed-dating conversation often determine who one will marry."

"What about your father?"

"My father is an idiot." I took a hard swig of wine. Then another, emptying my glass.

"On to glass number four!" Ben laughed.

I hauled myself up and breezed over to the sideboard to get a refill. When I turned back, Ben was on his feet, inching toward the dancers. I leaned against the fireplace and took another long drag of drink, watching the scene.

"Can't we change the music?" he shouted above the

current selection, some up-tempo synth-pop number. "Put on something more modern? Surely one of you has a playlist on your tab?"

I shook my head. "That thing's a digital relic, the dongle reader many generations outdated. None of our tabs are compatible. That's why it's all power ballads and classical music. Whoever loaded it way back when had particular tastes. Mozart and Roxette. Very German." I had a sense of humor about our family, at least.

"I don't care what the music is. Dance with me, Ben!" Carina grabbed his hand, clearly delighted to finally get him in her clutches, and he obliged.

"I should put Her Royal Highness to bed," Nora said, retrieving a near-catatonic Klara from the love seat, where she had collapsed and sprawled out, taking an impromptu nap. The girl demonstrated impressive strength, pulling Klara up by the arms, but she nearly toppled when Klara's full weight came down on her.

"I'll help you," Evgenia offered with a giggle.

With their departure, instantly the mood in the room changed. The lights seemed to dim, the fire crackling lower, though I knew no one had changed the illumination settings, and the fire wasn't real. Ben and Carina were half dancing, half carrying on deep conversation, alternating whispering something in the other's ear and smiling wide at every shared intimacy. It was cute, but it felt private, like I shouldn't be here.

And then there was Elliot. He was without a dance partner now, which left him shuffling awkwardly to the side, taking frequent sips of his whiskey. I noticed a flush creeping up his collar, his skin telegraphing his drunkenness. He was adorable. *No*, I scolded myself. That kind of thinking was dangerous.

Elliot was keeping secrets and had been since he reentered my life. Every time I thought we had cleared the air, that I had pinned him down, I discovered another thing he'd kept from me. The purpose of this trip was one thing, and then I couldn't forget the security permissions. He'd given me a neat answer, but could I trust he'd told me the truth?

He caught me watching him. His eyes locked with mine, and we played stare-down chicken, neither of us willing to break eye contact first. The room narrowed and blurred, my breathing suddenly heavy in my own ears, the seconds seeming to slow. There wasn't a particular, easy emotion I could pin to his stare, like malice or desire. I studied him, sweat beginning to run down my brow.

Intensity. There it was, the best approximation of an emotion I could come up with. Elliot was thinking something that made his eyes burn like cold fire. Then, finally, he blinked and looked away, and I felt a surge of triumph. But then Elliot was moving, taking quick, confident strides across the room and heading straight for me.

"Dance with me," he commanded, coming to a stop in front of me, offering me his hand.

"What?" I stammered out, sure I'd misheard him.

"I know you love to dance, so no excuses." He struggled on the last word, replete with sibilant sounds that proved difficult to his drink-loosened tongue. But Elliot's grip was strong as his fingers encircled my wrist, though he didn't pull. No, he always let me take the lead, set the pace. And against my better judgment, I felt my feet move.

I longed for my glass of wine, left behind on the sideboard, as downing the rest of it might have inured me against my current panic.

Thankfully the music was upbeat enough that it didn't warrant too much close contact. Elliot was doing an awkward yet endearing step-shuffle thing, while I was gently bobbing up and down to the beat. I would not allow my hips to loosen, my arms to flail. I was stiff with unease. I sent desperate pleas to the music player not to turn to a slow song and beg the question of a slow dance, though I glanced over at my sister and Ben, who were wrapped up in each other's arms in spite of the tempo.

But then Elliot grabbed me by the hand and pulled me almost flush against his chest, only to push me back out again. Right, we were dancing, I reminded myself. He wasn't trying to cop a feel or initiate an intimate encounter. I forced myself to loosen up enough to be spun under his arm, let him lead. It was just like the space walk, only without the comforting barrier of full-body spacesuits.

The song changed. Still up-tempo. I smiled in relief, but Elliot must have thought it was for him. He grinned back, shuffled closer. Suddenly my head was spinning as Elliot's hand found the small of my back. I had forgotten that one could easily dance very close—too close—to up-tempo music, too. I never danced like this. I loathed the intimacy with strangers, the way boys in the club and at parties felt entitled to my body, used dancing as an excuse for a cheap thrill. Usually, at this point I would wrench violently away, barbs springing from my lips; I'd dress them down and put them in their place.

But I didn't pull away from Elliot. He wasn't a stranger. I could feel the heat of his body against mine, but not the hard edges. Elliot was respectful to a goddamn fault. It made me want to inch closer, close the gap, take the plunge.

"Your sister is practically asleep on my shoulder," a voice broke through the haze. I jumped back from Elliot and turned toward the voice. There was Ben, expression sheepish, with a sleepy—or perhaps just drunk—Carina lolling against his side. "I'm going to help her get to bed." I must have made a face, incredulous, I was sure, because he quickly continued. "No funny business, I promise. I will be a perfect gentleman."

"And I'm a lady!" Carina giggled, then hiccupped.

"We're bunking below decks. Stairs are behind the kitchen," I instructed Ben, and then they stumbled off, leaving Elliot and me conspicuously alone.

The music changed. Slow this time, the beat languid. Elliot smiled sheepishly, offering his hand once more. "Shall we? For old times' sake?"

I looked to his proffered hand, then the door. I could leave right now, escape before I did something I would regret, like spill out all my pent-up feelings that he surely couldn't return. We were caught up in the artificial mood of the room—the fireplace, the music. That was it. This wasn't alarmingly close to being romantic, no.

"You think too much." Elliot's voice was soft, bemused . . . close. My head snapped up, and there he was, having closed the distance between us quietly and with purpose. He settled one hand on my hip and joined the fingers of his right hand with mine. Instinctively I placed my hand on his side, lightly gripping the fabric of his shirt. There it was. We were dancing—swaying, really—everything simultaneously terrifyingly intimate and frustratingly chaste.

"You invited Nora to dinner," he said. "I did."

"Klara's going to give you hell for it later."

I shrugged, my arm moving his arm. "Let her try."

He led me into a little spin, then cleared his throat nervously.

"I have to tell you something. It's hard for me to say, and I just hope you'll be happy for me . . ."

My heart sank into my shoes. His prelude was prompted by asking about Nora. The song we were swaying to crystallized in my ears.

Must have been love. But it's over now.

"Do you have to tell me now?" I wanted him to wait. Break my heart any other time. Let today be perfect.

"I guess not. We can just dance."

So we danced. There was just enough space between our torsos to avoid impropriety, but his face was so close to mine that I could count the individual eyelashes framing his at-last-unguarded gray-blue eyes. He was staring at my lips, and I wondered if they were stained purple from the wine. The hand that held mine gripped a fraction tighter, making me suddenly painfully aware of his body, and of mine.

"Leo . . ." he started, like he'd changed his mind about talking, but then he trailed off. He licked his lips, and I was mesmerized, pulled back in time, to when this was my normal. To when Elliot was my world. When kissing him was everything. I leaned forward a fraction of an inch.

I could feel the heat of his breath on my face, smell the sweet, earthy musk from the whiskey. Wait, how drunk was he? My eyes darted up to his eyes—there was a wink to them, but they were clear enough. This wasn't a mistake. Or I prayed it wasn't. I needed this. A perfect day. I parted my lips, went to close the gap, and—Elliot's head whipped back like he'd been shot through with electricity.

"I . . ." He frowned. "I, um, need to go find Ben." And then he left.

I blinked at the space where he had just been, stunned. I waited a minute, then two. Elliot didn't come back, nor did anyone else. I deflated down onto the bottle-green couch, spread my arms and legs out like a drunk starfish.

Elliot had been going in for a kiss, right? Or was it all me? If he'd been about to confess his love for Nora to me, did that make me a horrible person? That I still loved him and wanted him for myself? I wasn't sure of anything anymore.

My wrist tab chirped a notification. I swiped into the Valg app and checked to find a mysterious message.

You are over ninety percent compatible with someone! Say yes to more participants to find out who.

Oh, that was just evil—forcing us to randomly accept people until we found out who had also picked us? I picked up a nearby tablet and signed into my account, opened the Valg app, and scrolled to the participant master list. The already-yeses were on the first screen, sorted by percentage. I swiped over to everyone else. The noes from speed dating were on top—I guess any engagement, even negative engagement, was weighted heavily in the app. My finger lingered on Elliot's line, drifted over to the no button. All it would take was a quick swipe to reverse my earlier decision. See if he was the one who had matched with me over ninety percent. Had he run off to check? Say yes to me and see if I'd reversed my decision?

Yes, no, yes, no, yes.

Yes.

Elliot was a yes, and I bloody knew it.

I shut my eyes, slashed my finger across the screen. There, it was done. Carefully, I opened one eye and looked down at the screen, ready to accept my fate.

We had a percentage score, which meant he'd said yes to me, too. It was ninety-six percent.

19

Ninety-six freaking percent. Elliot and I were nearly a perfect match.

And this meant I was a yes. *We* were a yes. Is that what he'd been trying to tell me? Had I shut down a romantic confession? Of course, I was precisely that stubborn, wasn't I?

I had to find him.

I flew from the study, through the dining room and kitchen and to the back stairs. Ben had been putting Carina to bed, so Elliot must have come down here to find him. A sound from the opposite end of the corridor stopped me short. Raised voices. Urgent, but not angry, and definitely male. Ben and Elliot. I didn't even have to think about it before my body was heading toward the sound.

My heart fluttered in my chest at the sound of Elliot's voice echoing out from the open cargo-bay door, but then Ben said something that stopped it cold.

"You can't keep this from her anymore. This is her ship.

And you brought her here. Now she's involved."

"She gave me no choice."

"Did she, now?" Ben's tone was wry, like he clearly didn't believe him. "This is a good start, but you know it's not enough," he continued. "She might help you, if you ask her."

"I'm concerned that our position on board the *Scandinavian* has been compromised," Elliot said. "This is all I have right now. And I want to ask her; I do. I'm just not sure."

I inched closer to the door, aware that now I was in the awkward position of basically eavesdropping—I'd lost my chance to barge in naturally and honestly. Now I'd have to listen and wait, even though I was desperate to shout out questions. What was Elliot keeping from me, wanting to tell me, wanting me to help with?

"Max and Ewan going missing is a huge problem," Ben said darkly.

"I'll find them," Elliot said. "I have to."

"Do it quickly. I'll need more coffee, dehydrated dairy, and grains if we're going to make a real run of it here. Find them, or work her."

"You're not in a position to give me orders, Ben. You're like a brother to me, but this is my operation."

Operation. My blood froze, and I turned Ben's list over in my head again: coffee, dry milk, and grains. Supplies. I thought about the Linds' coffee stores running low. The missing crate of champagne. The locked pantry. I closed my eyes and inhaled a deep breath through my nose.

Gingerly I turned myself around, hugging the door

frame and angling my head back and around to peer inside.

"Yes, and you've pulled me into it," Ben said, the conversation skipping along. "The Orlovs, too. I'm not going to recruit operatives if you can't guarantee their safety."

My eyes confirmed my worst fears. Crates and crates of supplies—more than my family could hope to have.

Fury washed through me, cold and black and uncompromising like merciless space. I stepped into the door frame, caring not one whit that I had been spying on them, that they might be dangerous. My vision narrowed to a single line, straight from me to Elliot. I drew another deep breath, and then I unleashed my fire.

"How could you?"

My voice rang out, and it was foreign to my own ears. Sharp, and hard, like ice.

Elliot and Ben snapped to attention, both sputtering excuses, which I didn't listen to. I charged inside, taking in the full scope of the room. Our family supplies had been shunted into a dusty corner, and the rest of the space was filled with so many boxes. Boxes stamped *Property of the Scandinavian*. Plus a few with the *Lady Liberty*'s emblem. And the *Versailles*. The *Nikkei*. My stomach roiled.

"You're stealing from us?"

"It's not what you think," Elliot stammered.

"I think you're smuggling goods from the *Scandinavian* to other ships," I said, indicating the boxes. "You're involved in the black market."

"I told you she was clever." Ben's tone was just one degree

away from a quip.

"And you're hiding contraband on my ship," I hissed. "If you're caught, we'll be implicated. They'll take the *Sofi*, and we'll go to prison! Or worse, they'll kill us."

"I wouldn't let that happen to you," Elliot said.

"That's not something you can control! All they'll see is my ship and your contraband." My eyes raked over Elliot. The changes I'd observed in him took on a sinister bend. "So, what? You left me and became a criminal?"

I shamed Elliot into silence and Ben into action.

"I should go," he said, slinking past me to the door. I didn't take my eyes off Elliot. From behind me, I heard Ben's parting words. "Nice to meet you, Leo. Bye, El. Good luck."

Finally Elliot and I were alone. His hands were balled into fists at his side, chest rising and falling rapidly. I could practically see the words tripping from his tongue. And then finally he burst.

"I'm not a criminal, Leo. This is justice. People are suffering on other ships for no reason other than that people like you are too selfish to stomach a change in circumstance. You want to pretend we're not running out of time and food up here. If other people die, fine, as long as nothing changes for you, and you can delude yourself a little longer as to our circumstances."

"I am not the *Scandinavian*, Elliot," I said. "You know I care about more than just myself, my own comfort."

"Then help me." He grabbed ahold of my hands. "I was going to tell you everything upstairs, but then you said to wait. I've been dying to tell you. I thought you'd understand."

"Did you miss the part where the fleet will kill us if we're caught? I can't involve my family in this." I wrenched my hands from his. He recoiled as if I'd slapped him.

"You'll always choose them over me, won't you?"

"Oh, no, you don't get to do that," I hissed, taking a step forward. Elliot took a step back. Good. I hoped he was a little scared of me. "You don't get to bring that up. Not wanting to involve my family or myself in a criminal enterprise is not something you get to make me feel guilty about."

"It's not like that. It's not shady. Come on, Leo, you're smart. I'm no more a criminal than Freiheit are terrorists. I'm fighting the good fight, trying to help people. It's worth the risk."

I wanted to believe in his Robin Hood scheme, as he clearly did, but I could only shake my head. The logic didn't hold. "I know things are bad, but the black market isn't the solution," I pleaded. "It creates more problems instead of solving them. Price gouging, and the rich benefiting more than the poor."

"It's not like that. I won't let that happen. We provide fairly priced goods to the people who need them. We take from the rich, for the poor."

"You can't possibly control that," I argued. "Don't you know anything about black markets historically? I know you do. You grew up reading the same books I did. It never works out for the little guy, not really."

"I can control it," he said. "It's my operation. I set the rules."

"What does that mean?"

"The *Islay* is the black market. I'm the heir to the *Islay*.

Thain's been letting me run things for the last year. It's mine."

"Yours," I said, rolling the word around in my mouth, testing the concept in my brain. Elliot's face was quirked with earnestness; he leaned in closer to me, reached out his hands again. Did he think this was romantic? I stepped back, and his face fell.

"How are the Orlovs involved in this?" I finally asked. Elliot flinched, just slightly.

"They're my friends. And my associates," he said. "Max's expertise is transport, and Evgenia's an ace at infiltrating social circles."

Something pinched in my throat. "How exactly does that work, then? The business." Had Evgenia's friendship all been a ruse? Was I just a mark to them?

Elliot studied my face. I clenched my hands into fists to stop myself from squirming under his gaze. Then, finally, he spoke. "We operate twofold. Ally ourselves with the servant and working classes to scope out the best marks, develop a pipeline, and get supplies off-ship. It's amazing what you can accomplish with the lowest of the low on your side."

So that's what his relationship with Nora was all about—he was using her. She was his key to the *Scandinavian*'s servant class. I almost wished my suspicions had been true, that they'd been in a romantic relationship. It would have been less disappointing.

Elliot went on. "We work the higher rungs of the social strata—the families and individuals who won't miss a crate here and there. And we build connections for later. Crunch time will come, and eventually I expect some of these families, and ships, to come to me for what they need."

"So that line was bullshit," I cut in. "About helping the poor. You understand exactly how the black market works. I knew it."

"I meant what I said. I have no problem gouging the rich, but I'll never do that to the poor."

"How magnanimous of you," I snapped. "The noble criminal."

"I did what I had to do to survive." Elliot took several steps toward me. We were within spitting distance now. He lowered his voice, despite the fact that we were alone. "Don't judge me, Leo. You're frexing royalty."

"You know perfectly well how meaningless that is, and frankly I resent the implication." I hated how my voice shook, how my whole body was beginning to shake. I was furious, but also equally on the verge of crying.

"That's easy for you to say. We're born into our stations, and we die in them. I was nothing. You have everything. Your worst day was better than my best." His words were laced with venom. The Elliot from a few weeks ago was back, any of the ground we'd gained now lost. He seemed to hate me again.

"That's unfair," I said, voice just above a whisper.

"Ben wanted to be a communications officer, you know," he continued, oblivious to my pain. "But he came from the wrong deck."

"That's awful," I acknowledged. "But do you really think I can be or do anything I want? You know that's not true."

"I am playing the world's tiniest violin right now. The princess is sad."

"Frex you, Elliot." I took a step forward, jabbing at the air in front of him with my fist. Would that I could connect my hand with his shoulder. I longed to hit him, hurt him, push him back. But I was afraid.

"I see right through you, Leo." Elliot dropped his voice down, losing none of the menace for lack of volume. If anything, it sounded worse when he was saying things quietly. He moved close again, gaining back the ground he'd lost from my retreat. "Interested now that I'm dripping in money and you're desperate."

We were only feet apart now, so I could see every emotion cross his face. None of them were good.

I took a deep breath. "What's the use of being wealthy if the money is dirty, El?" My voice was quiet, but surely he heard the undertone of hurt and concern radiating with every syllable.

"Said like a rich person," he snapped back.

I swallowed thickly, refusing to cry. Desperate for distraction and time to come up with some moderately clever retort, I let my eyes flit around the room. They stuck fast on a pile of clothing in the corner. Draped over the boxes of contraband, the side of the room clearly denoted for Elliot's black-market finds, were my mother's dresses. Her heirloom ball gowns that I had been saving. Her wedding dress.

Elliot followed my gaze, and I saw him blanch. Then he sputtered, but my rage was fast as a bullet, cutting off his excuses.

"Is that how Evgenia finds herself exquisitely outfitted in vintage? You steal family heirlooms?"

No answer. Only the slightest flicker of something approximating guilt. But it wasn't enough. I no longer recognized the person standing in front of me. My Elliot was gone.

"How could you? You know what they mean to me." I marched over to the dresses and took them up in my arms, pressing them to my chest like a shield. At the door, I turned, making sure to meet his eyes with mine. I hoped they burned like fire.

"I don't know you at all anymore. And I don't care to." And with my parting shot, I turned around and left him where he stood before tears spilled down my cheeks.

20

Sleep was fitful, my dreamscape haunted by a series of Elliots. Kind Elliot, Funny Elliot, Secretive Elliot, and finally Hateful Elliot—each version of him was there, smiling, laughing, glaring, yelling at me. Each time I awoke, words like *desperate* ringing in my ears, I hoped he would leave me, but Elliot always came back. I was reeling from the betrayal, my subconscious attempting to process what my waking mind could not. Elliot was a stranger and a criminal. And I loved him. But it didn't matter now.

I woke with the artificial echo of dawn, dressing myself in all-black, a shroud to match my mood. I didn't know what to do next, but I knew I had to do something.

Should I turn Elliot in? Could I even do so without implicating myself, my ship? And what about Evgenia, Max, and Ewan? Would we all go to prison, or worse?

Maybe it was all over already. I reminded myself that Max and Ewan were missing. Now I finally understood the

251

urgency. If they had been caught, it was possible they were being tortured right now to give up the whole operation, to give up Elliot and Evgenia and the *Sofi*'s part in everything. The thought doubled me over just as I reached the kitchen. I sat on the top step and forced myself to breathe. No, I couldn't assume the worst. There had to be a logical explanation for where they had gone. And now I was involved, inextricably, and so I had to help Elliot solve it. I'd figure out how to hurt him later.

And there it was: I wanted to hurt him. I hated myself for it. But this was who I was now. This was who he had made me. He'd taken my heart, my ship, my trust.

I made my way up to the bridge, forgoing coffee, because of course the pantry was still locked to me. At least now I knew why. I allowed myself a string of colorful expletives as I sat down in the captain's chair, all variations on what Elliot could do with his black market and his lies and his stupid, pretty face. And then I quietly piloted us from the *Lady Liberty* back to the *Scandinavian,* docking with her before anyone else was even awake.

I still hadn't decided what I was going to do, but at least I was back where I knew I had somewhere to go. All I had to do was rally Carina and Klara and Nora, and we could escape back to the royal quarters, where I wouldn't have to see Elliot for a while. I wasn't sure I ever wanted to see him again.

I wandered downstairs to the study to wait for the ship to stir and found it eerily trapped in time. The artificial fireplace still crackled, the music was still looping, and the wine was uncorked and abandoned on the sideboard, slowly turning sour. I thought bitterly how much money had been wasted, everything going on all night, and I resolved to simply charge Elliot double the rent. He could afford it now that he was a criminal.

At long last, I heard the clink of coffee cups and silverware coming from the dining room. I powered down everything in the study and emerged, informing everyone of our return.

"I'll be having a serious conversation with Elliot about what constitutes a vacation," Klara grumbled.

Carina's brows knitted with confusion, but then she scarfed down the last of her toast. "I'll go pack, Leo. Meet you downstairs?"

I nodded to her, noting that Elliot was not at the table. Hiding from me, I bet. But Evgenia was there. I tried meeting her gaze, but she kept her focus squarely on the center of her coffee cup. She was wearing another fine dress, probably stolen from some other poor sap she'd pretended to be friends with. Heat prickled behind my eyes. I drew deep breaths to stop myself from crying. Elliot's betrayal was bad, but Evgenia's was a very close second. I hadn't ever really had friends before. Apparently I still didn't.

I followed my sister downstairs to help with the luggage. It didn't take very long to pack. The most challenging thing was finding room for my mother's dresses in my much-too-small suitcase.

"Why are you taking those?" Carina asked.

"Just want to keep them safe for the Valg Ball," I said.

"Do you think I could invite Ben?"

I didn't miss the real question my sister was asking, and it broke my heart. Even twelve hours ago, I would have said yes. Would have borne whatever marriage I had to to save our family so Carina could marry for love, not status. I still wanted that for her. But Ben was involved with Elliot now, and there was just no way. But I wasn't ready to break that awful news.

"We'll see," I hedged, finally giving up and resolving to carry the last two dresses slung over my arm.

As I was doing one last check of the room to be sure we hadn't missed anything, my eyes caught on something lying on top of my pillow. I leaned close. It was an envelope with my name written on it in careful script. Elliot's handwriting. Surely a letter begging my forgiveness, making excuses. Or lobbing more insults. I tasted something sour in my mouth. Screw him, with his antiquated stationery, showing off his new, incredible wealth, and whatever pitiful words he'd put to paper.

I left it behind, and I didn't look back.

*

My father's first words upon my return were "You forgot the beer." Always good to know that I was missed. And then he hit me with his second punch.

"We need to talk about the Valg Ball."

Carina smartly scurried off into the bedroom, leaving Father and me to stand off in the living room. An argument was the last thing I needed after everything that had happened with Elliot. I was afraid I might snap, so I tried begging off.

"This really isn't a good time; I didn't sleep well, and I need a nap—"

"Sit down, Leonie," he said, his voice surprisingly gentle. Apologetic. He took a seat himself in his preferred armchair, leaving me the couch. Warily, I sat.

"The Valg Ball is in two and a half weeks, as you know. And, correct me if I'm wrong, but you still don't have any real prospects."

Instinct told me to protest, tell him off for selling me off like chattel, but instead I squirmed under his sad gaze. "There's just Lukas so far, but I loathe him," I said. "I'm trying to find another way to save the *Sofi*, I swear to you."

As I said it, a lead weight dropped in my stomach. That had been true twelve hours ago. Now it wasn't. My connection to Ben and thus to Miranda was gone. It made what my father said next drop the anchor straight down to my toes.

He shook his head sadly. "It's not enough. This is your last good Season. Who knows where we'll be in five years? And you'll be twenty-four."

"I won't be dead, Dad," I quipped. He shot me a Look.

"We're still a good bargain for someone. We have a ship, a royal title. They just have to have money. Two and a half weeks, Leo. Please tell me you'll try. For us."

"I will, I promise." I couldn't say anything else, not with him looking at me like he needed me. Not needed me to do something *for* him. That he needed *me*. It was the closest I had felt in years to a genuine connection between us.

"Here, there's an event tomorrow night at the arboretum." He handed me my tab unit, the Valg app calendar winking up at me. "See who you meet."

I nodded along, despite my misgivings. I dreaded going to an event by myself for the first time. Surely everyone had paired off by now. Who showed up to a picnic by herself?

It gave me one day to process everything that had happened with Elliot. To wallow in my own misery and make a decision. Would I turn Elliot in? A sinking stone in my gut told me the answer was no. I couldn't turn him in without implicating my family. Perhaps that had been his plan all along, to make me complicit, just in case I found out. Elliot's revenge for a heart broken, pride crushed, all those years ago.

A surge of anger, of my own pride, filled me. I was going to go to that stupid picnic the next day, looking damn good while I was at it, and I was going to make a connection with someone. Elliot was my past. Someone else was going to be my future.

21

Something I vastly underestimated about an evening spent inside the arboretum was how strongly the smell of pungent, mossy earth would bring to mind Elliot's new scent. And how that subconscious reminder would have me fighting a persistent scowl. There were, indeed, a handful of single men at the picnic, but none of them dared approach me. I caught myself every ten minutes or so with a jaw so tight that my temples started to throb, and, with a hiss under my breath to get control of myself, I would once again have to reset my face and try to appear approachable, pleasant.

Thus far, I was fifty pages into my new book and partway through the second course. Because naturally on the *Scandinavian,* "picnic" took on a liberal meaning, and our meal did not skimp on the pomp and circumstance, or finery. Bitterly, I reflected that maybe Elliot was right about us.

"Is there room for one more?"

A voice from high above my head startled me so badly that I spilled champagne onto my tab screen.

"Shoot!" I exclaimed, making a mad dash to balance my glass on the uneven ground while grasping for a napkin to quickly wipe the screen dry.

"The hazards of drinking and reading." Now the voice was lower, level to my face, and he was laughing at me. I looked up, finally, and blinked at a handsome, smiling face. Daniel, from speed dating.

"I'm the professional showoff from the *Empire*," he supplied cheerfully.

"Yes, I remember. Nice to meet you again," I stammered out, feeling my cheeks heat. I noticed he had sat down, despite my never actually responding to his inquiry about space. Guess it was rhetorical.

"Are you sure you mean to sit with me?" I asked. "There are plenty of other available ladies, or gentlemen."

"Don't sell yourself short, Princess Leonie. I've heard great tales of your social graces and sparkling wit. And experienced it once or twice, too."

"Don't call me that," I groaned.

He squinted at me, cocked his head confusedly. "You *are* Princess Leonie? I know there's a sister, but she's . . ."

"Thinner," I supplied. Instead of being rightly cowed, he laughed.

"There's that wit."

"I don't like the royal-title nonsense," I said finally.

"Good, good." He nodded enthusiastically, and then helped

himself to one of my raspberries. I watched, both confused and enthralled by the way he first sucked on it, then chewed, moaning like it was the most fantastic thing. "Your cousin doesn't feel that way at all. We used to visit here when I was a kid—I played with you and your cousin, though I don't think you remember. Anyway, I once called her Klare-Bear, and she punched me in the face."

"She did not!" I exclaimed, pretending to be scandalized. "At best, she punched you on the shoulder."

"Perhaps I'm remembering it wrong," he allowed. "And your cousin has nothing on you. You right punched me in the gut, voting me no at speed dating."

"Don't take it personally," I tried to explain. "I said no to everyone. I was still in my protest stage."

"But you're not anymore. You switched me to a yes four days ago."

"My father has implored me to take it more seriously," I said, not even covering the half of it. "And so here I am," I finished with a flourish.

"So that's why I haven't seen you at any events in the past week!"

I raised an eyebrow at that. "You're keeping a record?"

"Not in a creepy way. I promise." He coughed and averted his gaze, with comic effect. "But I did notice you stopped attending things."

"That's not entirely accurate," I said. "I was at the wine-and-painting event just a few days ago." It was true; that had been only seventy-two hours ago, but with everything that had happened on the trip to the *Lady Liberty* with Elliot, it felt an age ago.

"I missed that one for a political luncheon. It was very dry, but the food was good."

"Oh, my aunt invited you to that?"

He nodded. "I took it as a message to marry a nice Scandinavian girl. Half suspected my mother had arranged it. She's lobbying hard for a fellow Norwegian."

I relaxed back into my drink, setting my tab back inside my bag. I suspected I wouldn't be returning to my book again this evening. A waiter passed with a tray of champagne, so Daniel was able to avail himself as well.

"And your dad?"

"Doesn't care as long as she's titled."

And there it was. A week ago I would have been insulted, written him off immediately, but things had changed. My repeated efforts to save my family the honest way had come to nothing. Renting our ship to pay for my patent had entangled us with criminals. My stomach lurched at my own generalization. Elliot was the criminal. He'd betrayed me.

And then all the major ships had rejected my proposal. Miranda Fairfax was impossible to reach. Marrying for money was my best option. And my title was my best asset in this economy.

I found Daniel studying me, searching my face for a green light. I offered him a firm yellow.

"I can assure you that I am quite wealthy," he added. "I understand how this works."

I narrowed my eyes at him, not unkindly. This felt like a business arrangement, and I needed all the cards on the table. "Why choose me? My sister's out as well, and she has a far more pleasant personality. Klara's apprenticed to her mom, making it all but certain she'll be inheriting her political power. I don't know if you've heard, but I'm hardly the most popular girl on board."

"I remember you from when we were younger. Still devastated to be forgotten, by the way."

I threw a raspberry at him.

"You're smart, practical, resourceful . . . and titled. So am I. The first three, not the last one. I'm not looking for a love match, and I don't think you are either. I sensed a kinship in you, an honesty. That's what I want. I knew when I came here that none of these other girls could give me what I want."

"Then what have you been doing at these things for the past week and a half?" I asked.

Daniel grinned. "Waiting for you to pay attention to me."

*

"Shall I walk you back to your quarters?"

Hours passed as if in the blink of an eye. Now Daniel stood over me, offering a hand to help me up, which I took. Slapping my hands against my backside to clear any stray dirt, I surveyed the arboretum, now empty, save for us and a few scurrying wait staff clearing debris. We'd managed to shut the place down, losing ourselves in hours of lively conversation.

"I'll gladly take the company," I said, easing into a light

stroll beside him. But then I veered right and he veered left.

"I thought you had a ship." He pointed aft. I shook my head. "I do, but we're staying in the Swedish royal quarters. I'm currently renting out my ship."

Daniel jogged to catch up with me. I'd never stopped moving. We exited the shade of the arboretum out onto the top deck, where even the after-ten-p.m. lighting hurt our eyes a little.

"So why rent your ship?"

"We had a standing invitation to visit my aunt on board the *Scandinavian,* and with the Season happening, it just made sense to come. And I figured why have our ship go to waste?" I played it all off like a brilliant business idea, half believing myself as I said it. "You know how much they charge for a vacation suite on board. I'm charging a fraction of that, so it's just a bit of easy money."

Daniel was a perfect gentleman, nodding along, though I could sense his skepticism. He was sharper than I gave him credit for.

"So are you playing host to one of the eligible bachelors? Is that where you've been disappearing off to?"

Pain shot through me at the thought of Elliot, and for a brief moment, my happy-go-lucky act fell apart. Daniel's playful expression rapidly shifted to one of concern.

"I'm sorry; I was trying to be funny. But I guess it's more creepy than anything."

"Oh, no, it's not you," I said. "I've been helping my sister to find a match, and she's met someone, but I'm afraid he's not suitable? Anyway, that's where I've been, so . . ." I rattled off a half-truth, which Daniel seemed to buy. I forced a lightness back into my expression, banishing Elliot from my thoughts for the rest of the evening. This had gone surprisingly well. I wouldn't let my past ruin my future.

I pressed my back against the cool wall, smiling at him, half inviting him to kiss me. I had maybe drunk a little bit too much champagne. He didn't, anyway. Perfect gentleman.

We continued on our stroll toward the forward lift, and I was struck with déjà vu. A few days ago I'd been here with Elliot, and we'd just finished up our space walk, romantic possibilities stretching before us. Now here I was with a new beau, new possibilities.

We rounded the corner smack-dab into another pair.

"Oh, I'm sorry—"

"Pardon us—"

Both parties made rapid excuses, and it wasn't until I'd taken a step back, and reassured a fussing Daniel that I was fine, that I glanced up at who exactly we'd run aground of. I blinked down, hard, to be sure I wasn't hallucinating.

"Max? Ewan? Where have you been? Evgenia and Elliot have been looking for you."

Not only was it them, but they looked awful. Unkempt and broken down, and I smelled them most acutely. It was as if they'd not showered in days.

"It's all very stupid," Max said. "We went for a short trip to the *Versailles* and forgot to tell them where we were going. But now we're back. No big deal."

Ewan nodded along unconvincingly. Lies. They'd been gone four days. I reminded myself that these were smugglers, working alongside Elliot to run his black market. Not friends. And I wasn't stupid. We'd run into them in the forward part of the ship, not the aft, where their shuttle would have docked. It was clear they were heading to the *Sofi* now, from wherever they'd been at the front part of the ship.

I opened my mouth to ask the most pointed of questions, but then I felt Daniel's hand on my elbow.

"Are they your friends, Leo?"

"Oh, yes, these are my renters," I said, too brightly. Daniel didn't notice. Max and Ewan did. They knew I knew about them.

"Nice to meet you. I'm Daniel Turan." Daniel offered his hand, which both men limply shook.

"Nice to meet you, but we must be getting back," Max said tightly. "Good evening, Your Royal Highness."

They were already ambling off before I could protest.

"Sorry to jump in there," Daniel said. "But they seemed off, and I wanted to ensure you were safe. They obviously don't know you well, since they used the honorific." I nodded numbly, watching Max and Ewan retreat. I was left with a creeping suspicion: that Max and Ewan had been on the *Scandinavian* the whole time, and something was very, very wrong.

I tried to put it out of my mind as we made the rest of the way to the royal quarters. Elliot and his friends weren't my problem anymore.

"I had a really good time tonight," Daniel said as we reached my door.

"Me too," I said, surprised that for once, I didn't have to pander. Tonight had been entirely unexpected, in more ways than one. The image of a shell-shocked Max and Ewan resurfaced in my mind, and I shook my head to clear it. Instead, I focused on Daniel's golden-brown eyes, which twinkled like stars.

"I hope you'll see me again? Soon?"

"I'd like that," I stammered out. "Want to sync wrist tabs so you can ping me?"

Daniel nodded enthusiastically and pushed up his sleeve. My eyes went wide. I'd never seen a wrist tab quite like it, far larger and more elegant than any model anyone on the *Scandinavian* had, let alone mine.

"It's the latest from the *Nikkei,*" Daniel said, answering the question before I asked it. I watched, fascinated, as he depressed both sides of the tab face with his thumb and index finger. With that pressure, all four edges sprang back, the screen ballooning to twice its size. The graphics whizzed onto the screen, crisp and full-color, as Daniel pulled up the contacts app. I did the same with mine, my tab face suddenly minute and lackluster in comparison to his, and touched our two units together so they could sync. After a moment, each device let out a pleasant little *plink* to let us know it was done.

"I'll ping you tomorrow, then."

"Okay!" I barely suppressed a high-pitched giggle, hiding it behind a cough. "I'll see you later."

Daniel graced me with one last smile before slinking off, leaving me dazed and giddy. The strange encounter with Max and Ewan now pushed to the back of my mind, I entered our quarters with a stupid grin plastered on my face. The lights were off, save for one lamp, which illuminated my sister and where she sat on the couch.

"What happened to you?" Carina inquired, rising from her perch.

"Were you waiting up for me?" I asked, approaching cautiously.

"Yep."

I narrowed my eyes at her. "Why?"

"Because we came back here very abruptly, you've avoided me since yesterday, and then Father tells me you went to one of the social events, alone and willingly? Are you sure you're my sister?"

I was abuzz from the evening but weary from the whole *Lady Liberty* trip, and not at all ready to share the particulars about Elliot, the black market, and the worry that niggled at me. Carina picked up on my reticence and sighed. "You owe me an explanation. It doesn't have to be tonight. But I do want to know why you looked so happy when you walked in."

"I met a boy," I said, grin bubbling up once again. I caught my sister frowning.

"What about Elliot?"

"I don't want to talk about him." I plunked down onto the couch with a sigh.

"Not even twenty-four hours ago, you were lovesick and

smitten," she said, aghast. "What changed?"

I picked at some imaginary lint on my skirt, pointedly refusing to answer.

"Is that why we left the *Lady Liberty* so abruptly and came back here? I was really bonding with Ben, and all you could think about was your own issues—"

"It has to be over with Ben," I snapped.

"What?" Carina's legs seemed to give out from under her, and she plopped down onto the sofa beside me, face pale, lip quavering.

"He's not suitable," I said. Ugh, here I went, diving into this awful conversation when I'd said I wouldn't; not tonight.

"'Not suitable.'" Carina drew a deep breath, her features now alight with quiet fury. "Because he's poor? Because he works in sanitation? Leo, you massive hypocrite."

"It's complicated," I hedged. "And besides, you knew him for a grand total of twenty-four hours. Not even. Don't be so dramatic," I bit out harshly. I couldn't tell her about Elliot's business, about the danger our family was in because of it. Carina had come a long way, grown up so much lately, but I didn't trust her not to tell someone, or do something stupid like try to fix it.

"Well, I'm glad you met someone *suitable*, Leo. I hope you marry him and he takes you far, far away from here, and from me."

She slammed our bedroom door so hard, I felt it from the couch. Then I heard the click of the door locking. I collapsed back into the couch cushions with a groan and closed my eyes.

That was not the way I had wanted that to go. But I was proud of myself for keeping the truth to myself, for protecting her. Better she hate me than get caught up in the black-market business. She would forgive me eventually, I hoped.

For now, I was locked out of our room, and thus sleeping in my bed would not be an option. Guess I'd be kipping on the couch. With a sigh, I pulled a throw from the back of the couch and settled in to sleep.

As I closed my eyes, I tried to focus on pleasant thoughts to lull me into sleep—Daniel's glittering eyes and half-wicked smile, raspberries and champagne and stars. But then Daniel's visage morphed into Elliot's, his eyes hard and the line of his mouth firm, calling me desperate and sad and awful. Worst of all was how my stomach fluttered at the thought of him still, my heart aching for his touch, despite everything. I gave up, finally sinking into sleep as a replay of our last dance, our almost-kiss, played through my mind. Tomorrow I would work on hating him, but tonight, I let myself have this.

22

I rose early, my back stiff from contorting myself on the couch cushions. I rolled my neck, and it gave a satisfying crack. I needed coffee.

As I opened the canister, taking a deep whiff and then setting to work brewing a pot, I couldn't help thinking on what had set all this in motion—the hunt for more coffee, Elliot and Nora conspiring in the living room, an escape to the *Sofi*, and discovering that Max and Ewan were missing. Was that truly only a few days ago?

No one had come to arrest me, which hopefully meant that things were fine for now. I could simply avoid Elliot and the Orlovs for the next few weeks, the Valg would end, and then it would be over. Goose bumps crawled over my arms and legs as I shivered, not from the cold, but from disgust at myself that I could be so complicit in a criminal enterprise. Because clearly my answer was to avoid them and do nothing. I would keep it all a secret, it seemed, to protect my own hide.

Well, to protect my family, and our home. It was both noble and revolting.

"Ah, good, you've already made coffee," came my father's groggy voice from behind me. "Make some toast with jam, too, while you're at it? You can tell me all about your evening while we eat."

I did so without complaining, for once fine with the prospect of sharing news of my romantic pursuits.

"His name is Daniel, he comes from the *Empire,* and he is fabulously wealthy," I started, tone wry. Father sputtered into his coffee.

"Are you being serious?"

I nodded. "We made a good connection, and he'd like to see me again." Then Father wrinkled his nose.

"British, though?"

"He's British Iranian Norwegian, actually," I offered. "Didn't tell me his mother's family name, come to think of it, but he used to come here as a child. Said he played with Klara, so they must be of some consequence."

"That is the best possible news, Leonie! I'm so proud of you." He meant it. I felt a warmth run through me at winning my father's pride and approval, finally, but then hid the sadness of my smile behind my coffee cup. Why couldn't he be proud of me for my wits, or charm, or business acumen, instead of my ability to net a wealthy husband? I should have been used to my parent disappointing me by now, yet I retained a stubborn, foolish hope that he would value me for who I was.

"When are you seeing him again?"

"He said he'd ping me today." I checked my wrist tab. No missed messages. It was early, though.

"Yes, good, wait for him to contact you. Let him lead. Be careful of being yourself. But be sure to lock him down soon. Two weeks to go until the Valg Ball, and you don't want him to switch his interest to someone else."

As if he were psychic, Daniel chose that very moment to send me a message. Father nearly jumped out of his chair when my wrist tab pinged.

Tonight? the message read, and with my father watching, before I could second-guess myself, I replied, *Sure!*

Then I checked the app to see what tonight's activity was, and groaned. Hiking on the digi-deck. Perhaps I had replied too hastily. Too late now. I would put on pants, and I would walk at a steep incline, and I would try my best to look winning and be warm and clever and marriage material. I had two weeks to convince Daniel he wanted to marry me. Who cared if I hated myself for doing it?

*

The next few days were a whirlwind of perfectly pleasant dates coupled with acute emotional torture. After a pool event came karaoke, and after that came a movie night, where it was as if the film had been selected to remind me of Elliot. In it, a detective showed up in Austria, only to find out his friend had been murdered . . . except that he was actually alive and well and secretly a dastardly criminal. By the time they

ALEXA DONNE

started talking about cuckoo clocks, I was squirming in my chair, and poor Daniel was apologizing for my being bored. I spent the rest of the evening trying to convince him how much I'd liked the movie and that I was having a good time.

I *did* have a good time with Daniel, and whenever I actually allowed myself to be distracted, I almost forgot about Elliot and the Orlovs and their bad business. Almost.

Carina, Klara, Evgenia, Elliot—none of them came to anything for days. The absence of everyone from the Valg events was just a reminder that everything had imploded and no one wanted to see me. Suddenly the people I loved were ghosts. Even in my own home, I barely saw my sister. She fell into bed late and rose early, losing sleep in order to avoid talking to me.

I began to wonder if I'd imagined it all. The last few weeks seemed unreal as the Valg events and dating Daniel settled into a rhythm and started to feel normal. Who needed friends?

Me. I did. So when Evgenia swanned into the next Valg event with Asta Madsen on her arm, my breath seized in my chest. We locked eyes, hers going wide with panic. I felt a twinge in my gut, an ache that my friend was uncomfortable. Promptly my icy veneer melted, and I couldn't help but offer her a half-smile. *Let's talk?* I projected. Evgenia got the message and nodded.

The event of the day was a team cooking challenge where we had to get together in groups of four to produce an entrée and a dessert. Recipes were provided, and the best meal won its team a private evening on the digi-deck. We were left to choose teammates, so it was easy enough to pull Daniel over in Evgenia and Asta's direction.

"So nice to meet one of Leo's friends!" Daniel beamed, shaking Evgenia's hand enthusiastically. "I was worried I'd stolen her away and you all hated me."

"Not at all." Evgenia was too good an actress to betray her surprise.

"Daniel and I matched ninety-three percent in the Valg app," I blurted, suddenly filled with the urge to explain myself to Evgenia. She raised a single, perfectly tweezed brow.

"Higher than my brother," Asta said. "He'll be happy to know he was beat fair and square, then."

"Was it a competition?" I asked. Asta shrugged.

"Evy, come with me to get the ingredients," I said, grabbing the instructions for the first dish and heading for the pantry. I sensed Evgenia at my heels, and silently she picked up a shopping basket while I searched the shelves for an onion. Other couples dashed around us, grabbing ingredients, but we took our time, waiting for the others to filter out, leaving us alone.

I tossed the first volley. "My mother's dresses, Evy?"

She appeared rightly cowed. "I didn't know how much they meant to you. I tucked them away the first few days we were here, before I really got to know you, and I just forgot. I'm sorry."

"Are you, then? For lying to me, or the criminal enterprise?" I couldn't help the chill in my tone.

"Both," she said. I'd never seen her so serious. "It's . . .

complicated. And it got a bit too big for me, all the lies, and layers to it."

"Was I always just a mark to you? Elliot said your specialty is ingratiating yourself with high-class ladies."

"Indeed, that is what I'm good at." Evgenia laughed darkly, half to herself. Then she deposited a bag of sugar into the basket. "But, no, I didn't consider you a mark," she continued with a sigh. "You became a friend, truly. And you have to believe me, I tried to put a stop to it all, almost as soon as we arrived and I got to know you. I told Elliot to quit his stupid jealous revenge mission, begged him to tell you everything. He said he tried?"

"Don't make excuses for him. He knew what he was doing."

She looked at me sadly but didn't contradict me. "You have every right to be mad. And I'll leave Elliot to clean up his own mess. But I hope you and I can try to mend our friendship? You're one of my only girlfriends. I'm surrounded by impulsive, impetuous men. I really like you, Leo. Genuinely. Nutmeg."

"What?"

She pointed behind my head. "The nutmeg is behind you. Last thing we need. Oh, and an egg." We each grabbed our respective final ingredients.

"I . . ." I trailed off, unsure of how to respond. It seemed too easy to just say it was all water under the bridge and move on. But she didn't seem to be lying to me now. Maybe I owed it to myself to try to parse out how much of my friend Evgenia had been real. Good friends, especially girlfriends, were a rare and valuable find. "We can try to be friends again."

Evgenia lit up, her features returning to their natural state. Then, at the door to the pantry, she hesitated, and dropped her voice low.

"Are you going to report us? I'd understand if you did, but of course I'm hoping you won't."

I barked a bitter laugh. "I have no choice. You're using my ship. Elliot set it up perfectly so that our destruction would be mutually assured. I'll keep your secret. It's mine now too."

Evgenia frowned. "This is all a fine mess."

"And we haven't even started cooking." I attempted levity. We headed back to our station, where Daniel and Asta awaited us. We launched into our main dish, exchanging polite small talk as we worked. I counted down the minutes until the break into the dessert, waiting for the next chance to talk with Evgenia more. My mind was only half on the cooking. I kept coming up with more questions for her. To keep them from popping out of my mouth, I stuffed it with the gravy and meatballs we'd made. We were permitted to eat our entrées, I was delighted to learn. Dessert was to be saved for a special event, the instructor, Bjorn, told us. He came around when we were done and tasted our dishes, betraying nothing as he chewed. After Bjorn had made his way around the room, he returned to the front.

"Now for the dessert course! This one will be strictly timed, to make it a bit more challenging. May the best cake win!"

My eyes went wide as I scanned the ingredient list. This cake would require half the pantry. I saw my chance to get a long stretch of alone time with Evgenia without arousing suspicion.

"Daniel and Asta, why don't you go to the pantry this time?" As soon as they left, I pounced. I leaned in close to Evgenia so no one else would hear. "How did you guys pass your background checks? It's been bothering me."

Evgenia's mouth formed an O of surprise, but quickly she composed herself. "Well, Elliot and I did. The business doesn't work unless he and I come out clean, since we hobnob with the well-to-do." Her eyes darted left and right, and she lowered her voice. "Max and Ewan didn't. We knew they wouldn't. They've been in trouble a few times for being caught with contraband. But usually it's not a big deal, because they play all sides. The *Olympus* dings their record, but they make up for it by running a few missions for them free of charge. No one in transport is clean." It meant my aunt had lied to me, and shortly thereafter Max and Ewan had gone missing. Only I was half certain they'd never gone anywhere at all. They played all sides, Evgenia said—were they playing some side with my aunt now?

"There's one more thing I have to tell you. It's been eating me alive with guilt."

I snapped back to attention. "What?"

"The night of the space walk, I wasn't really sick. I was faking it to get into the med bay." Her cheeks burned red with shame. "I hated doing it, fooling you like that—making you take care of me! But it was one of the tasks Elliot had assigned me, and I saw my window. I feel horrible about it."

"What did you steal?" I fought to keep the hard edge out of my voice. At least she was coming clean.

"Some vaccines," she replied. "They're becoming scarce throughout the fleet, and Elliot wants to shore up our own supplies, in case there's an outbreak on one of the poorer ships."

"What, so he can charge them an arm and a leg for protection?" I hissed.

"No, no—he'd give it to them for free," she insisted. "Elliot's not what you think he is. Not as bad, I mean. You have every right to be mad, though."

I took a moment to cool down, turning over this new information. Was Elliot really some Robin Hood figure? Or was he lying to Evgenia, too?

"And where is Elliot?" I tried to sound casual, but we both knew I failed. Evgenia was kind enough to pretend.

"He said he's done with Valg events," she said. "Doesn't see the point anymore." She grimaced. "So, um, you don't have to worry about running into him."

"Running into who?" Daniel asked, he and Asta returning with a basket full to the brim.

"Lukas," Evgenia chirped. "One of Leo's early suitors."

"Ugh, that twerp," Asta groaned. "Very handsy. Good on you, Leo, for ditching him. Daniel here is a gentleman."

I noticed he was carrying the sagging basket. Promptly I relieved him of it and started sorting the ingredients by the order in which we'd need to use them. The dessert task was an elaborate Swedish princess cake composed of many layers of sponge, jam, and pastry cream. More than half the class appeared stunned at the enormity of the task before us, but Asta appeared nonplussed. "My mother made sure I knew how to make an immaculate princess cake," she said. Each of her knuckles gave a satisfying crack as she worked over them. Then she rolled her shoulders, like a boxer in the ring. "We've got this in the bag. Evy, when we win, I want to go skiing."

We set to work under Asta's tutelage, the small talk a little less small this round. It was almost like old times with Evgenia, who brought her trademark wit and charm to the party. Daniel seemed to love her. More than once he nudged me in the ribs and told me the very same. A few times, I caught Evy observing us astutely. Her expression never gave away more than pointed interest, but I couldn't help but wonder if she was cataloging every moment to report back to Elliot. Would he be jealous? No, that thinking was dangerous. *Elliot* was dangerous, I reminded myself.

All the teams put the finishing touches on their cakes, topping them with whipped cream and carefully moving each one into an industrial-size cooler. Bjorn disappeared for a moment and returned a minute later, frowning.

"Captain Lind has requested the prettiest cakes for tomorrow's election dinner," he said. "I, uh, forgot to factor in that I wouldn't be able to taste any of the cakes. So based on watching you work and overall presentation, I am pleased to declare the winners Miss Asta Madsen and Leonie Kolburg's team! See me to coordinate your digi-deck time."

Asta whooped with delight, and we all high-fived.

"The election dinner's going to be a terrible bore, so we should go to the digi-deck during that," Asta suggested.

"Actually, I've been invited to that dinner and I was going to ask Leo to go with me," Daniel said, turning to me. "If you want to go? We can suffer together for a few hours and then mercilessly mock the whole thing with after-dinner drinks. On me, of course."

"I don't know if I can take a six-course meal centered around my aunt giving speeches," I joked. "But I couldn't leave you to the wolves like that. Also, I loathe skiing, so it's best Asta and Evgenia go to the digi-deck on their own." It was a gesture of renewed friendship now that I was in a position to help out Evgenia romantically. Both she and Asta appeared relieved.

Daniel broke into a grin. "I'll pick you up at six thirty."

23

Daniel arrived the following evening at six and spent the extra half-hour buttering up my father with a lively conversation about the theater, about which my father pretended to be an expert. Then at precisely six thirty, Daniel made our excuses and we headed out.

The ballroom was littered with familiar faces, making all the more egregious the fact that I'd not been invited. I recognized nearly everyone participating in the Valg, plus many *Scandinavian* residents I'd grown up with. I harrumphed under my breath as Daniel led me through a clutch of people.

"Don't worry, I'll get you a drink," Daniel said, mistaking the source of my grumbling, but I was grateful for the offer nonetheless. Especially as I spotted Elliot across the room. A shot of ice clutched my heart, but I breathed through my panic, inhaling and exhaling purposefully. This was bound to happen eventually. I had to keep my cool. So I pretended I hadn't seen him at all. The picture of maturity.

We moved over to the check-in table to retrieve our name tags. There wasn't one for me, so I had to make one. I felt so welcome. My aunt clapped eyes on us and really drove home the point with her greeting.

"Leonie, what are you doing here? I didn't think you cared for politics."

"I'm here with Daniel Turan. My date."

He bowed graciously. "A pleasure as always, Captain." Then he kissed the back of her hand. My aunt's lips curled into a smile that almost seemed genuine. Daniel could charm the dead.

She turned her attention back to me. "Look at you, actually making an effort with a boy. Well, a new one."

I could have killed her as she topped off her leading statement with a very pointed glance over at Elliot, who was fifteen feet to her left and currently chatting with Klara. This time, he didn't miss my gaze, which followed my aunt's on instinct. Elliot offered me an awkward wave. I ignored it.

"We should find our seats," Daniel said, linking our arms and already starting to pull me away. "Good luck with your speeches."

Seating wasn't assigned, thankfully, as, knowing my aunt, she'd have been cruel and sat me next to Elliot for good measure. Three long tables with chairs and settings limited to one side were arranged in neat rows. Everyone was to face forward so we could not just listen to but also watch my aunt as she performed. We found a pair of seats at the farthest table at the back, next to Theo Madsen. At least now Daniel would have someone else to talk to. He couldn't have missed my aunt pointing out my ex, and I was sure my pink cheeks had betrayed my feelings on the matter. Surely, after that, Daniel's interest in me was shot.

Before we sat down, Daniel grabbed two puff pastries from a passing tray and handed me one.

"For the girl with the viper of an aunt, and a poncy-looking ex." We pretended our hors d'oeuvres were glasses and clinked them together. I devoured mine in one bite.

And with that, I was struck with the overwhelming sense that I would be an idiot not to marry Daniel. He was exactly what I needed—fun, light, honest, and kind. His wealth was a bonus—the only thing that mattered to my dad, of course— and his business was a legitimate one. Daniel even pulled out my chair for me.

The realization settled in the pit of my stomach like an anvil, the reality and heft of our courtship suddenly real in a way our last few dates hadn't quite driven home. Could I really do it?

There was little time to dwell on such questions as my aunt rose to the stage and started her pontificating. We were to enjoy four courses, not the usual six, happily, but the catch was that, after a speech made to the assembly while we ate our salads, the captain would be joining each of our tables for the subsequent courses so she could answer our questions one-on-one.

I powered through my pea soup with such speed that I ran out of food with which to busy myself, leaving me to actually listen to my aunt's speech. She was just getting to

THE STARS WE STEAL

the good part, it seemed.

"We are entering an age of scarcity," she she starkly. "Of the haves and the have-nots. Where our future and our prosperity are determined by archaic concepts such as *usefulness*," she spat the word like it was dirty, and a grumble moved through the crowd.

"The bigwigs on the *Olympus* talk a big game, but we all know where they spend their vacations. Usefulness is relative." Her tone turned sickly sweet with the jibe, and several people knocked their glasses against the tables to show their approval.

"But listen . . . I am a practical woman. Of course I am. I'm Swedish."

The Danes, Finns, and Norwegians hissed through their teeth, but the captain knew what she was doing. She waited a beat and then continued. "But we are all cut from the same cloth, we Scandinavians. Resilient, resourceful. And so it is my promise that while I will fight tooth and nail against these ridiculous measures that would compromise our way of life, I can also assure you that I have other things up my sleeve. Elect Lind once again, as you have these past twenty years, and I will protect this ship at all costs."

I marveled as people began to cheer and clap and whoop, apparently truly moved by my aunt's bullshit. With no competition, she could say whatever she pleased, make any promises she wanted. I reached across the table for a bread roll, which I buttered heavily and shoved into my mouth. If I was chewing, I wouldn't turn to Daniel and mutter about how ridiculous this all was.

But the public speech was over, and the captain spent
the appetizer and main courses with the two tables in front
of us. We were spared an entire evening of political chatter,
though my table didn't make it easy. Theo and Daniel did
indeed hit it off. Talk turned to visas and population control,
and never was I more grateful for having rejected Theo. He
toed a hard line on both subjects, displaying an appalling lack
of empathy for his fellow human beings that unfortunately
I suspected my aunt would agree with. But Daniel held his
own, smiling while he debated as if they were engaged in
friendly banter, even though he repeatedly eviscerated Theo
with compassionate but well-reasoned arguments. At least I
felt Daniel won the day.

As it happened, Elliot and Klara were seated directly in
front of us at the next table, and throughout the conversation,
Elliot kept leaning back in his chair as if he were keenly
listening. Every time I caught myself watching him listening
to us, I pinched myself in the thigh. I ended up with a very
sore thigh.

Finally, our princess cakes from cooking class appeared,
signaling the dessert course and our table's turn to have the
captain join us. My aunt sat down on the other side of the
table, facing us all. Daniel and I had the misfortune to sit near
the center, which put us just to the captain's immediate left.
She looked over expectantly at us, then right to Theo. Daniel
jumped in before Theo had the chance.

"So, Captain Lind, what's your plan b? If your strenuous
objections don't work and the usefulness measure passes?"

Daniel had gone straight for the jugular, but he was so charming that the captain's first response was to laugh.

"You're tenacious, Mr. Turan, aren't you?" She tittered. Then her razor-sharp eyes flicked to me as if to blame me for my guest's cheek, even though I was the plus-one in this instance. She recovered quickly, and no one else seemed to notice her moment with me.

"Unfortunately I can't disclose what I have in the works to you, nor to anyone else here. It's above your pay grades, so to speak." The captain laughed, forcing the joke, so everyone else followed suit. "But I promise everything will be revealed in good time. I'm hoping to have something I can announce by the Valg Ball. Just in time for the election the next day." She gave an exaggerated wink, and again everyone laughed.

I shoved a forkful of cake into my mouth to stop myself from saying something uncouth. I wondered if Max and Ewan were a part of her secret plan. I bet they were. Though she could hardly announce the black market at the Valg Ball, could she? It was a silver lining to coming tonight. Maybe I could needle information out of her about what had happened with the Orlovs.

Once dessert ended, we were left to casual mingling before the bar shut down, which was basically my aunt's chance to glad-hand some more with everyone here. Daniel had stuck by my side all evening, which was a boon until now. I needed to get her alone, which meant distracting him with conversation. As Klara and Elliot passed on our right, I found myself doing the unthinkable.

"Klara!" I called out to her, flagging them down. "You say hello to Daniel. He hasn't seen you in years!" I dragged Daniel over by the arm, putting him face-to-face with my cousin, who was looking down her nose at me as if I'd suggested we go on a casual murder spree. Elliot hung awkwardly off to the side, eyes darting from Daniel to me and back again.

"Uh, hello," she said, the etiquette that had been drilled her into her as a kid taking over. She offered him her hand, and that gave me my window.

"Oh, I see my aunt. I have to ask her a question!" And I zipped away before they could stop me.

I hadn't actually seen her, but she was easy enough to find. I just followed the sound of disingenuous laughter and terms of endearment.

"Captain Lind," I addressed her formally, and she was talking to a high-ranking Norwegian, so she couldn't ignore me. "Can we have a moment?"

"Oh, of course," she replied with false brightness. I led her off into the shadowy recesses of the ballroom, affording us a modicum of privacy.

"Why did you tell me that the Orlovs had passed their background checks?" I asked before she could shut me down. Surprise, confusion, then smug satisfaction masked by innocence worked their way across her features.

"I don't know what you're talking about."

"Max and Ewan didn't pass. Evgenia told me. You lied to me."

"I'm sure I didn't." She dug in her heels. "I told you that Mr. Wentworth and Miss Orlova passed. I'm sure I didn't mention the two gentlemen. Anyway, Leonie, it's not a big deal. Most transporters don't have a clean record."

It was the second time I'd heard that in as many days.

"Anyway, I heard you went over to the *Lady Liberty* to see Miranda Fairfax. Any luck?"

"Why?"

"Just checking in on my favorite niece!"

I didn't trust my aunt on a good day, let alone now. The trick was, it would be stupid to lie—she'd find out the truth eventually.

"I didn't manage to see her, no," I said carefully.

"Oh, what a shame. Anyway, it was so good to see you tonight. Good luck with Mr. Turan. He's a real catch."

And with that, she left me, retort dying on my tongue. "I know he is," I muttered to myself instead as I made my way back over to him. Just my poor fortune, he was still locked in conversation with Elliot and Klara. From ten feet away, it seemed fine. Klara was nodding, smiling, and talking at intervals, while Elliot remained stoic by her side. His mouth formed a tight line, and every so often his eyebrow jerked a fraction of an inch, only to steady seconds later. Elliot didn't want to be amused or entertained by Daniel, I could see.

"There you guys are!" I plastered on a smile and linked my arm with Daniel's, joining the chat circle. "Aunt Freja had to go kiss some more babies."

"Or kiss something," Klara quipped.

"It's good that she finally invited you to one of these," I said, "since you are apprenticed under her." I meant it genuinely, no

287

hint of sarcasm in my tone, but found myself on the receiving end of an epic glare from my cousin.

"Actually I'm Elliot's plus-one," she ground out.

"Oh. Well." I stumbled over my response. "I wasn't invited either."

"Elliot, what do you do? For a living," Daniel cut in, saving me.

"Whiskey," Elliot replied with a near-perfect poker face. Only I noticed the microscopic wince at the lie. "I'm the heir to the *Islay*. Still learning the ropes a bit."

"I thought you knew everything there was to know about whiskey. All the nuances of how it works, and will always work." I covered my veiled accusations with a syrupy sweetness, throwing in a smile for good measure. Elliot's brow shot up. Satisfaction swooped through me at having broken his cool.

"I'm confident in my skills, the things I believe in. About whiskey," he added hastily.

"Hmm. You don't worry about how it hurts people?"

"Leo, what are you on about?" Klara snapped before I could have the pleasure of Elliot's reply.

"Personally, I don't care for whiskey. Too strong for my tastes." There was Daniel again, saving the day twofold. A waiter zipped by with a tray of wineglasses, and Daniel grabbed two, handing me one. Elliot quirked his head in examination of Daniel, surely wondering if he was in on our code and making a statement about the black market. I enjoyed seeing Elliot squirm.

"You two are too cute," Klara simpered. "I hear you're a ninety-three-percent match. That's practically kismet!"

Heat flared across my cheeks, and now I was the one to squirm. I couldn't help but flick a glance at Elliot. Had he checked his app and seen our ninety-six percent? He betrayed nothing. Elliot was blank. The swell of feeling that had been pushing up my throat drained away swiftly. I took a swig of wine and sidled closer to Daniel.

"Where did you hear that?" I asked my cousin, tone light as whipped cream.

"Carina told me, of course. We've been spending a lot of time together lately."

"Of course! She's always fiddling with my app, saying yes to people to try to nudge me in all sorts of directions."

"I still need to meet her," Daniel jumped in. "If she's the one who switched me to a yes, I owe her my thanks."

"If we leave now, perhaps we can catch her before she goes to bed," I said, even though I knew it was a lie, but I'd just have to explain to Daniel once we'd escaped. I couldn't bear this social torture any longer. Daniel read my signals perfectly.

"Brilliant idea. So nice to chat with you all. Night!"

As we wended our way toward the ballroom doors, Daniel leaned into my ear. "I won't ask you about your ex and what that bizarre whiskey conversation is about, but can you fill me in on your sister?"

So I explained the whole sad saga as he walked me back to my apartment, and I once again thanked my lucky stars that he had found me. For all my talk of needing friends,

Daniel was proving to be a very good one. Now if only I could convince myself to fall in love with him.

24

Love did not sprout and bloom over the next week, though not for lack of trying. Most formal Valg events ceased in the run-up to the engagement ball, likely on the assumption that most people had already paired off and were fine to plan their own private dates. Daniel and I went on our own fair share of them, from a night of dancing at the Scandi Club to a romantic stroll on the upper-deck promenade, a private concert where he showed off his cellist chops, even a day at the library, poring over historical artifacts together. I liked his taste, and we always had a good time together.

My sister, too, seemed to have a full social calendar, not that she shared it or any details with me. I got that she was upset with me, but her persistent silent treatment was frustrating. Most of all, I missed her. I tried not to dwell on it, focusing instead on manufacturing my own enthusiasm for my whirlwind romance with Daniel. If you could call it that. I felt like we were building this amazing friendship, but despite yelling at my traitorous heart to skip a beat when he smiled at me, to thump heavy in my chest when he took my hand, it didn't. I grasped for the memory of what it had been like to fall in love with Elliot. Had it happened this slowly? I simply couldn't remember a time when I didn't swoon for him.

Then again, I reminded myself that most Valg matches weren't based on love. So it was fine that I didn't love Daniel. Right?

My father was pleased as punch, regardless. I grew in his esteem with every date, the condition of his affection finally met. I was less than half a week away from securing a wealthy husband and would be saving our family from ruin. Yet I burned with the feeling of failure. Again and again my thoughts returned to my filtration system, the too-expensive patent left unfiled, my chance to save my family through my own ingenuity dashed. After everything that had happened with Elliot and Ben, I wasn't surprised at all not to hear from the *Lady Liberty* about their licensing my design. Ben likely never even told them about it. I was left to be nothing but a sparkling doily, festooned in silly gowns and laughing on cue to win a man's favor. Though that was being unfair to Daniel, who never treated me like anything other than an equal.

Finally, with four nights until the ball, Daniel had planned a romantic candlelit dinner for two in his vacation suite. He'd ordered in catering, as finally I discovered his sole weakness: he couldn't cook. Still, he banished the wait staff and insisted on serving me himself. I had a horrible feeling I knew what this was leading up to. Was I ready?

THE STARS WE STEAL

I lost myself to the question as the dessert course rolled around, swirling my spoon idly around the rim of my ice cream bowl. Daniel missed nothing.

"Are you okay?"

I stopped, blinking him into focus as I grasped for a good excuse. My questioning the whole progression of our relationship didn't seem like a good dinner topic. I settled on something real, even if not the most immediately true.

"My sister still isn't speaking to me. I'm wondering how long this is going to last."

"As long as first-love heartache can last, I suppose."

So, years? No, Carina wasn't like me, and she barely knew Ben. Elliot and I were a terrible blueprint for young love. I caught Daniel peering at me with some consideration. I sensed he knew exactly what I was thinking about.

"Was it the guy at the political dinner? For you, I mean."

I nodded. "But I knew him far longer than Carina knew this guy. She didn't love him. Couldn't have."

"I've never been in love," he said matter-of-factly. No teasing to his tone, no twinkle in his eye. He was completely serious.

"Is this the part where you quip 'until now,' and I'm supposed to swoon?"

"No. I like you too much to lie to you. That's not what this is."

His candor shocked me into silence. Daniel went on, hardly missing a beat.

"I like you a lot, and I think that we're friends, no? You need to marry me for my wealth, and I need to marry you for

. . ." He hesitated. "I've never actually told anyone about this before. It's hard to get the words out."

"You want my title," I supplied with a slight edge of bitterness.

He laughed.

"Your title, and your access to political power . . . yes. That's what my parents want, especially. And, well, grandchildren."

"I don't have any political power," I said. "You'd have to marry Klara for that."

Daniel shook his head. "No, you could run for captain of this ship if you wanted to. You'd be better suited to it than your aunt, certainly. You have a heart."

"Thanks?"

"This is all coming out wrong." He blew out a long, steady breath. "I don't mean for this to sound like a business arrangement, but I thought we were on the same page—we talked about your title and my wealth at the picnic. Cards on the table. I knew you needed to marry for money, which I have, and I want to get into politics, which you can help with. It's how things are done in our circles."

"I did know," I said quietly, hating myself for feeling disappointed. What a hypocrite I was.

"That was the reason I approached you initially, Leo. But it's not the reason I stayed, the reason I finally messaged my parents the good news. I want to marry you, you have to know. I know this is the world's worst and least romantic proposal. I don't want to marry you because of your title, or my political ambitions. Those are bugs, not features."

"What do you mean?"

Nervous laugher bubbled out of him, and he avoided looking me in the eyes. "God, why is it so hard to say? This is why all my relationships end, quickly and messily. I'm a coward. But you're so perfect, Leo. You're in love with someone else, and so you won't be upset that I won't fall in love with you."

I moved to deny it, but he shot me a look.

"It's okay; I don't mind. I'm—" He took a huge breath, screwed his eyes shut, and then said, rapidly and rushed together. "Imasexual."

"You're . . . asexual?" I repeated back, breaking up the words. Then relief flooded me. I had worried he found me hideous, or too intense and forward to ever love. Then I blurted: "But you're such a spectacular flirt!"

"Asexual people can be flirts," Daniel shot back, as playfully as ever. "And they can be charming, witty. A fantastic catch, if I do say so myself."

He was joking again, so he had to be fine.

"Daniel, why didn't you just tell me sooner?"

"Did you miss the whole 'literally never said this out loud before' thing?"

"Well, I'm honored to be the first person to hear it, then." I mulled everything over in this new context. "Is that why you're such a perfect gentleman, and you've never tried to kiss me?"

"Kissing is kind of awful," he said, making me laugh. With anyone but Elliot, yes, I had to agree.

"So, um, is that a yes? That you'll marry me?"

Oh, God, this was actually real. My second marriage proposal, and I felt . . . numb. And relieved. And disappointed. Everything a girl dreams of. A laugh bubbled up from my chest, and Daniel reeled back as if struck.

"No, no, I'm not laughing at you!" I jumped to reassure him. "I'm laughing at me." With one giant gulp, I finished my wine, then promptly poured myself another. I wiggled the bottle at Daniel, and he accepted a top-off himself. "So let's talk this through. You get my title and political positioning, I get your money, and we're friends."

"If you're okay with that, yes. There are all kinds of ace partnerships, so we can play it by ear. This fleet is pretty myopic when it comes to relationships, marriage, and children, so there will need to be grandchildren, and we'll have to keep a lot of this to ourselves. We can figure that out later." Daniel took a deep drag of wine. "Did you know that back in the day on Earth, tons of people were childless by choice? Sounds amazing."

"You don't have to have kids," I said. "I would never make you . . . you know. With me."

"But you want kids, don't you?"

I did want children. With Elliot. I barely suppressed a groan and instead took a drink. I was too sober for this question.

"I'm the heir to the Kolburg title," I said. "As you said, having babies is compulsory."

"Some days, I hate this place," Daniel muttered, idly drawing patterns on the tablecloth with his fingers. While he wallowed, I considered him seriously.

Daniel was kind, clever, funny. He could keep up with me, never made me feel uncomfortable. And he was totally honest. Had been from the beginning, really. I could trust him. I'd lost that trust, that faith, in the last person I loved. Daniel would never do that to me, I was certain.

"You were right, Daniel," I said, coming to a decision. "We do make a good pair, and if I'm honest, I'm glad you singled me out. I have to get married to save my family. And you're a good person. So yes, I will marry you."

I finished my wine and hoped I wouldn't regret the decision.

25

For the second time, I was secretly engaged to be married. This time, however, I kept my father in horrible suspense for a laugh rather than out of fear. Daniel flew back to the *Empire* to tell his parents the news and make some arrangements, and each successive day he didn't come back to take me on a date, Father unraveled just a bit more.

"What did you *do*, Leo?" he whined on the third consecutive day without Daniel, one day before the Valg Ball was to take place. "Were you yourself with him? Did you scare him off?"

"Don't be silly." I waved him off. "He's running a few errands and will be back tomorrow. We'll see what happens."

"But then he *is* your date for the ball?" Father perked up.

"As far as I know," I managed with careful nonchalance. Father stress-ate a pain au chocolat. Captain Lind had specially shipped in a bevy of pastries from the *Versailles* for the occasion of the Valg Ball, and Father had insisted I secret away half a dozen of them for our personal enjoyment. The act brought me closer to Elliot than I liked, but I did it to avoid my father's petulance. Besides, technically I was allowed access to the royal stores; it wasn't stealing, not really.

I delighted in watching my father stew. I was going to make him wait until the formal announcement ceremony. It was my little line in the sand.

Looking distinctly as though he regretted the pastry, Father frowned in the direction of Carina's empty seat. "Now, what about Carina?"

"What about her?"

"Does she have a date for the Valg Ball?"

"You'll have to ask her."

"She's never home anymore," Father sniffed.

I sighed. "She's still only sixteen. She'll have another Season. Twenty-one isn't quite as spinsterly as twenty-four, after all." I couldn't help the sarcasm that dripped from my tone. Father didn't scold me for it, nevertheless. He was oddly contemplative.

"I just want her to be happy," he said, and I could have wrung his neck. Carina got to be happy. I got to be useful.

No, that wasn't fair, not the way things had shaken out. Daniel was a really good option for me. I would be happy with him. And it was funny how I missed him with just a few days of separation. It was lonely with him gone, given that my social world had narrowed considerably to essentially just him and Evgenia, without my sister and cousin to spend time with. Maybe that's where Carina had disappeared to these past weeks, holding court in the We Hate Leo Club, though

Klara's reasons to hold a grudge were essentially nil. Having cut myself off from Elliot completely, I'd left Klara to him. She should be throwing me a parade.

The thought turned my taste sour, putting me off breakfast completely.

"I'm going for a walk," I announced.

"Are you going to see if Daniel is back?" Father perked up.

I did not dignify the question with an answer. I left him sputtering into his coffee and headed out, hesitating briefly before the stairs. The top-deck promenade was the natural place to take a walk, but it meant risking running into Klara on her morning jaunt. Instead, I pressed my finger to the bio-lock access panel for the royal private public quarters. No sooner had I ducked through a shadowy door into the Andersson Lounge than I was almost mowed down by a pair of servants carrying a chaise longue past.

"Oh, sorry!" I exclaimed, burning under their chastising glares. Indeed, the whole salon was abustle with activity, servants moving furniture, dusting curtains, setting up tables that soon would overflow with food. Setup for the Valg Ball was in full swing. Though surely unwelcome, I pressed on, now curious to see the place in transformation. We'd not hosted a Valg Ball as long as I'd been alive and living on the *Scandinavian*. Our ship, the *Empire*, the *Lady Liberty*, the *Nikkei*, the *Shanghai*, and the *Versailles* traded off the auspicious honor, which meant this was the first Valg Ball held here in thirty years. I assumed my aunt would pull out all the stops. Nervous as I was for the big reveal of my engagement to Daniel and as much as I loathed silly society parties, I was looking forward to this one. The grandeur would likely be unmatched in my lifetime.

I passed through another lounge and then a small library, finally reaching the grand ballroom. Had it really been only four weeks since this all started? I remembered that night, when apparently Elliot had been working his connections, scheming his plot. It looked the same, but I felt so different.

Well, correction—it did not look exactly the same. With the lights all the way up and the room devoid of decor, food, and people, it was stark and eerie. My footsteps echoed loudly, parquet flooring and high, vaulted ceilings seeming to multiply my presence. Or, wait—my head snapped up to the opposite end of the room, where a pair of elaborately carved doors swung open, admitting the forward-charging form of my aunt as well as another woman and, oddly, a small child. The child, a boy, careened out of his mother's grasp and started simulating flight around the edges of the room. I stopped short, glancing back the way I had come, calculating whether I could slip out quietly before she noticed—

"Leonie? What are you doing here?" My aunt's tone remained bright, but I did not miss the strain underneath. She and her guest continued to close the distance between us, and I found myself taking slow but direct steps to meet them in the center of the room.

"Just going for a stroll," I said.

"It's not like we have a promenade deck or anything." Captain Lind laughed, certainly more for her guest's benefit than mine. The guest, for her part, did not laugh at my expense, which I appreciated. I took her in. She was young—certainly no more than midtwenties—and strikingly beautiful, with thick wavy dark hair and bright blue eyes, like an old movie star. She was also clearly someone very important, as best I could tell from the cut of her suit and the deference my aunt showed her. I was given no such deference, however, as my aunt pointedly declined to introduce me. Was I supposed to simply scuttle off like a naughty child?

Finally, the woman cleared her throat and offered me her hand. "I'm Miranda Fairfax, from the *Lady Liberty*," she introduced herself. I tried to contain a shriek as she shook my hand—I'd finally found her! I had to say, I liked the firmness of her handshake and that she offered it in the first place. So many Americans favored hugs.

"Leonie Kolburg, of the *Princessin Sofi*," I returned giddily, offering a small curtsy, besides. Old habit.

"Oh! You're Gerhard and Celine's girl!"

I hadn't heard my mother's name spoken in so long. I leaned into it, toward Miranda, wanting to feel closer to someone who had known her. "Yes!"

"They used to visit all the time, when I was much younger," she went on. "My mother was in your parents' Season. At first, your dad went hard for her, but, well, in my family, we always marry for love." Immediately her cheeks went pink and she glanced down at her feet. She needn't have been embarrassed, though. I knew my parents had entered into a marriage of smart alliances and good sense. Most people did. She wasn't insulting me with talk of love. If anything, it made me like her more.

"Is that your son?" I indicated the boy, who had tuckered himself out and was now sitting in a corner, examining a piece of molding.

"Yes, that's Phillip. I do hate to bring him along on a business trip, but his father is away on the *Marie Curie* at present."

"Well, it's so great that you're here. See, I've been trying to get in touch with you, and was wondering—"

"Dear God, Leonie, don't interrogate our guest!" my aunt cut me off with an exasperated and entirely pasted-on smile. "My niece is quite chatty," she went on to explain to Miranda, as if I required such excuses.

"I don't mind at all," Miranda said, and I couldn't tell where she landed in terms of my aunt scolding me. She was a politician, after all, so part of her job was to keep an even keel.

"I assume I'll see you at the ball tomorrow night?" she asked me, lucky to have my aunt behind her so she couldn't see the way the captain tensed her jaw as she spoke.

"Yes! I have some business I'd like to discuss with you, actually." Miranda quirked a brow, clearly curious what business I could have with her. Proof that that assistant of hers hadn't passed on a single message. But now I had her here in person! "I'll look forward to it, Leonie."

"Oh, you can call me Leo."

"How delightful! Like the constellation, then? I hadn't put that together before."

I nodded. "My sister is Carina. My mother liked naming on a theme."

"I'll confess to merely liking the sound of Phillip, myself."

The boy perked up at the sound of his name and came running over.

"Mommy, I want to go in the lift again." He tugged on Miranda's pant leg. I credited a four-year-old for being more adventurous than I was.

"We will, sweetie; Mommy just has to talk business for a bit longer." The boy's eyes got a bit wide, and for a moment I worried he might cry, but after a beat he gave the tiniest of nods and stood beside his mother obediently. "Anyway, Leo, it was lovely to meet you, and I'll see you tomorrow!"

I took my cue to leave, the better to do so before the captain bored a hole through my forehead with her glare. I wondered if she was nervous about Klara and the Valg Ball. She'd been gunning so hard for Elliot these past weeks, and I knew my aunt wanted them to match, but there was no way he'd marry her. That would leave Klara twenty-one and still single. Her waiting until twenty-six to do another Season was unlikely. After this, Klara would probably be forced to marry whatever boy her mother found for her and deemed suitable, with slim pickings left after the Valg Season ended. I pushed on, weaving my way through airy galleries and byways, thankful once more for Daniel and his welcome offer of friendship and partnership. The fleet was so unkind to those who didn't follow tradition.

Relief mingled with mounting unease as the day wore on.

THE STARS WE STEAL

With each hour that slipped lazily by, one click tighter turned the invisible screw embedded in my back, which seemed to connect to every nerve ending in my body. Everyone would be there.

Elliot would be there. Watching. Judging. And hurting, just a bit, I hoped.

The thought, like a sliver of poison slipping into my bloodstream, made me hate myself a little.

26

I awoke to find my stomach in knots. I plunged my head under the down comforter, cocooning myself into its pillowy warmth. If I just stayed in bed, stayed here forever, would anyone notice?

"Today isn't the day to have a lie-in."

The voice was muffled but distinct. My sister was actually here. I uncovered my head and turned it toward her voice to find her sitting on her bed, assessing me coolly. She was still in her pajamas, but her hair was in curlers.

"I don't know where you put Mother's gowns. And you need me to do your hair and makeup, surely."

I sat up, squinted at her. "Hello to you, too," I said.

"You slept in." Carina sidestepped my volley. "We have six hours to get ready."

"I hardly think it's going to take us six hours to put on a dress and style our hair and makeup."

"Your hair requires at least two. I'll curl it for you the way you like."

This did nothing to alleviate the queasy feeling in my gut or my reluctance to get up. I knew that eventually Carina would have to talk to me again, yet I hadn't imagined this would be the circumstance. Or that she would be so eerily calm and accommodating. I didn't want to ruin it by asking questions or pressing the issue, but I was also desperate to have a heart-to-heart.

"I'll get you coffee," Carina said, getting up and heading for the door. There went my opportunity, lost. "You should shower."

I knew she was right, yet for another minute I lay there, savoring the warmth from the down. A part of me just wasn't ready to become tomorrow's Leo. Engaged Leo. Saving-her-family Leo. I wanted to remain this version of myself a little bit longer.

My wrist tab pinged from the side table. I grabbed it, swiping at the face and squinting at the message from Daniel.

Back with two very happy parents in tow. Can't wait to see you tonight and dance our asses off. And, you know, get engaged and all that. Hugs but NO KISSES! —Daniel

His sign-off made me giggle, and the surge of warmth I felt inside, buoying my spirit and renewing my excitement for the evening, spurred me out of bed, finally. With a dramatic groan performed for no one but myself, I dragged myself out from under the covers and shuffled over to the bathroom.

When I emerged from my shower, I found a mug of coffee waiting for me on my bedside table, along with my sister sitting on the bed again.

ALEXA DONNE

"Dresses?" she asked.

"Oh, yes, of course." I hopped to, like a maid, making my way out into the living room and front hallway, unlocking the front closet with my bio-lock. My mother's dresses always took my breath away. I ran reverent fingers over the fabric, leaning in just so, breathing in their smell. My mother's scent was long gone, yet I swore I caught hints of lavender, mint, and black tea. I closed my eyes and exhaled. I missed her so much still.

"You bio-locked the front closet?" came Carina's voice from behind me. I turned to find her leaning against the doorway to our room, arms crossed and expression sly. "Afraid we'll steal something?"

I rolled my eyes at her, easily falling back into our old sisterly rapport. "Do you trust our father with the valuables?"

"Touché."

"Come help me," I said, grabbing two of the voluminous dresses myself, leaving Carina to the other two. We shuffled back to our bedroom and laid them out on my bed, surveying the spread.

Mom had, of course, owned many more dresses than four, but these were the finest in her collection—the ones she'd set aside for our Seasons and weddings. Which dress she had intended for each of us and for which occasion I could never be sure. Father had known only of her hope for the dresses, not the particulars, which left the choice up to us. Mom thought white for weddings was Old-World patriarchal BS, and all of her dresses were as vibrant as she was. Before us lay

308

gowns of deep azure, brilliant magenta, crisp emerald, and bold crimson, made from the finest silks, satins, chiffon, lace.

"Do you want the red?" I guessed.

"And you're going for the blue, right?"

We shared a laugh. Nearly two weeks of the silent treatment didn't change the fact that we were sisters and knew each other too well.

I ran loving fingers over the crisp taffeta of the blue gown, which sported a plunging V-neckline that made me blush. But, yes, tonight I would be bold and show off the slope of my shoulders, the tuck of my waist, my ample hips and long legs. The dress would complement everything—my body, my eyes, my hair. I'd be a knockout.

My mental image wobbled, however. I was missing jewelry. And the Valg Ball demanded all our finery. We'd be judged, mocked if Carina and I didn't turn up in our royal family heirlooms. That meant tiaras, earrings, necklaces, bracelets, and other baubles. I groaned out loud.

"What?" Carina looked at me quizzically.

"I forgot the jewels are on the *Sofi*. I'll need to go get them."

How stupid could I have been? I'd left everything back on our ship all these weeks, even after discovering Elliot's endeavor! We'd had no need of them on the *Scandinavian*, and honestly I'd forgotten all about them. They only came out every few years. *Scheisse* and frex it all.

"Oh." Carina's expression turned dark. "You haven't been back there since . . ."

"You noticed?"

"I'm not stupid, Leo." She glared, and I frowned, a loaded moment passing between us. But she didn't go farther, so neither did I. Then she sighed. "I'll go and get them so you don't have to."

"No, unfortunately, I do. It's bio-locked to just me."

"You're going to have to learn to trust other people at some point. Especially me." I let her accusation hang.

"I need to get dressed," I said.

"Fine, but I'm going with you." I started to protest, but Carina was too quick. "You need me to run interference with Elliot. You know you do. And don't forget to put curl cream in your hair before we leave."

And so I did, filing away the dread at the conversation we so desperately needed to have. Later. In the meantime, we'd walk to the *Sofi* and continue to limit our conversation strictly to hair, makeup, and dresses.

Outside the royal quarters, the ship was alive with activity. We passed half a dozen wait staff as they hurried through the corridors with garment bags flung over their arms, lugging steaming equipment and makeup cases. I did not envy them their work. Nor I my mission. As we made our way aft with brisk steps, I rehearsed how to get in and out of *Sofi* quickly and quietly, hopefully without being seen. Though, just in case, I'd put on a clean dress. I didn't bother with any makeup—Carina scolded me to leave her a bare canvas to work from.

The trick was, the family jewels were kept in a safe in the study, which would force us to sneak through the main artery of the ship to get there. But then, that's why Carina was with me—to run interference, as she had said. Her thoughtfulness gave me hope that we could mend things between us.

"Let me go first," Carina said as we crossed the threshold through the aft hold. "If I see someone, I'll greet them really loudly so you'll know to keep back, and I'll find a way to get them away from the study."

I put about ten feet of distance between us as Carina led the way, her steps oddly tentative, like she was scared of someone popping around the corner or out of a closed room. I suppose I appreciated her caution, though it was a bit overzealous. Unsurprisingly, the aft corridor was clear. I held back in the shadowy recesses where the corridor curved, just enough that I wouldn't be seen if someone exited a bedroom. I kept tight to the rough wall, feeling safe with my workshop and maintenance hold so close. Carina passed her room, mine, then the door to father's quarters, and then I lost her where the hall ended in a T. Left was the dining room and kitchens, and to the right, the study. She turned left.

I zipped forward, dipping low, like I was on some spy mission, hugging the left side of the hall. Pressing myself flush against the wall, I craned my ear in the direction Carina had turned, and I heard her talking to someone.

"They don't have my favorite tea on the *Scandinavian*, so we should go into the kitchen. Make a cup. You like tea, don't you? My sister prefers coffee . . ." She emphasized "sister," surely code. Trying to tell me it wasn't safe. She had to be talking to Elliot. He didn't respond, but I heard two pairs of feet moving away. *Good job, baby sister!*

Quickly and quietly, I went to the study door, pressed my finger to the bio-lock, and cursed the low beep it made upon opening. Before it had even shuttled completely open, I'd jumped inside and turned to the inner release, pressing it shut behind me. Then, finally, I allowed myself to breathe for what felt like the first time in the last minute. A shaky laugh escaped me. I'd made it! I turned, surveying the room, pressing my back to the wall to stop the beads of sweat running uncomfortably down my spine and traveling rapidly south toward my underwear. My poor dress.

Someone coughed, and I literally squeaked. My eyes searched for the source, sound rushing in my ears and my body instantly going cold. Then I flushed warm all over as I locked eyes with Elliot. He rose from the couch he'd somehow expertly camouflaged with—who wore so much green?—his eyebrow quirked in a frustratingly attractive fashion.

"What are you doing here?" I demanded. It was the first thing that came to mind; the thing I very much wished to ask my sister. Who had she been talking to, if not Elliot?

"I could ask you the same thing," he replied, still with that arch, and now I noticed how his hair was damp from a shower, the green "clothing" actually a large, fluffy bathrobe. I might overheat. I pressed myself hard against the wall, desperate for more space between us, more air.

"I came for the jewels," I croaked.

"Am I being robbed?" He stuck his hands up and laughed,

the sound rich and warm.

"The, um, crown jewels?" I pointed stupidly to the safe behind him.

"I'm surprised you left them here with me." Elliot's tone was light, but, oh, there was an edge. We were still dancing around each other like we had the last time I was in this room with him.

"Me too." I played it cool, finally pushing off the wall and waltzing over to the wall safe. He wasn't making moves to leave, so I would do this with him here. My fingerprint opened the case, and as always, the family heirlooms dazzled me. Diamonds, emeralds, and sapphires set into gold and silver glittered up at me, their splendor a concrete reminder of my family legacy, incongruous with everyday reality but beautiful nonetheless.

"I'm surprised you didn't reprogram the bio-lock, like you did the pantry and the below-decks hold," I said, making quick work of grabbing sapphire pieces to match my dress and diamond ones to complement Carina's. I placed them carefully into a small carrying case.

"I only limited access to those two spaces out of necessity," Elliot replied softly.

"To keep secrets from me." I rounded on him.

"To protect my business."

"A criminal enterprise is not a business," I snapped, breezing back over to the door, eager to leave.

"Leo, please." Elliot grabbed my arm as I passed, not hard, but with my momentum, I was wrenched to a stop. He

313

dropped his hand immediately. "I'm sorry if I hurt you. Your arm, I mean."

"It's fine." I rubbed the spot absent-mindedly.

"I was . . . disappointed you kept away. I honestly thought you'd come back, after—"

"You don't know me very well, then, if you thought that."

He flinched, and bile rose in my throat. Hurting him was painful to me, but he'd hurt me first. That's what I told myself.

"I'll see you tonight, at the ball, then?" I said, casual as could be. My voice wobbled only a little.

Elliot nodded but wouldn't meet my eyes. The floor suddenly became very interesting, and I could take a hint. With a huff I hoped did not sound undignified, I pushed the door-open button and exited. And from one frustration to another, there was Carina, waiting for me.

"Success?" she asked innocuously.

"I got the jewels, if that's what you mean," I said. "But they came with a side of conversation with Elliot."

Carina blanched. "Oh, no, I'm so sorry. I was busy distracting, um, Ewan in the kitchen . . . I didn't think to actually check the study." She cursed softly to herself, calling herself stupid, and my anger melted.

"Don't beat yourself up. I survived." I linked our arms together and pulled her along. "Come on, let's go and get ready."

And we made our way back the *Scandinavian*, where I would ready myself to become tomorrow's Leo. Today's Leo was done.

27

I thought my father might hyperventilate when a knock sounded at the door and he flung it open to find Daniel standing there in his finery.

"I'm so glad you're here!" he exclaimed, pulling Daniel into a messy hug. Father might have been a little bit drunk already. Daniel handled it like a pro, extracting himself gracefully and breezing inside.

"As am I," he said, making a beeline for me. "Leo, I think you may be the most beautiful woman in the universe tonight." He bowed and took my gloved hand as I offered it, lightly kissing the tips of my fingers. We'd decided ahead of time to be as affectionate and sappy as we dared, putting on a grand show for everyone so that later no one would ever question us. Daniel agreed to do everything but kiss, which both of us agreed we probably couldn't pull off convincingly. Besides, we'd hardly be the only couple not quite at the kissing stage yet. A lot of business arrangements disguised as marriages would be going down tonight.

"She looks just like her mother." Father sniffed, moisture gleaming in his eyes. "That was her Valg gown too, though of course she wore it again, many times."

My breath caught, and I drew solemn fingers over the gilt rose embellishments that spidered up my torso. I'd picked this dress for my favorite color, not the rose motif that I found ironic, given my attitude toward the Valg. Of course it had been her engagement dress too.

"And look at you two, so in sync!" Father beamed at the pair of us, indicating Daniel's gold-adorned waistcoat. I didn't have the heart to tell him we'd coordinated over message earlier, Daniel assuring me he had waistcoats in every feasible color, so I need only specify whether I wanted him to match or complement.

"You look fetching yourself, Your Highness," Daniel simpered, indicating my dad's tuxedo. It was the perfect thing to say to Father, who was still put out that I'd not brought his crown for him to wear. I'd purposely left it behind but played it off as a mistake. His crown was ridiculous and far too precious for how drunk he would be getting tonight. I couldn't risk him losing it or breaking it.

"Shall we head over, then?" I asked.

"Where is Carina?" Father craned his head in the direction of our bedroom.

"She left about thirty minutes ago. Said she wanted to make her own entrance." I attempted to hide my hurt. We'd helped each other get ready, even cracked a few jokes between us, but then she'd disappeared again.

"I'm starting to believe that your sister doesn't exist and is merely a figment of your imagination," Daniel teased, tone light, but concern for me reflected in his eyes. It was a reminder that, indeed, with Carina's avoiding me all these weeks, she'd also avoided properly meeting Daniel. Speed dating didn't count.

"We'll see her there," I said, taking Daniel's arm. "And I'm nervous to meet your parents." I leaned in close to Daniel, dropping my voice, but Father heard me regardless.

"Your *parents* are here? Does that mean what I think it does?" he said to Daniel.

"Don't you want to be surprised?" I deflected as we made our way into the corridor. Far off, I heard a high-pitched screech followed by a fit of giggles. Were people at the drunk-and-cavorting stage already? I went to check my wrist tab for the time, but for once, I wasn't wearing it. We were fashionably late, but not *that* late, I was sure.

Having taken my reply for the yes that it was, Father moved quickly ahead of us, clearly in a rush to get to more alcohol and maybe, generously, the food. He took the nearest entrance to the royal private public quarters, but I led Daniel around the long way so we could arrive at the ballroom through the main doors without cutting through side galleries. It would give us more time to talk, as well as the opportunity to make an entrance. We both looked amazing, and I wanted everyone to see. Leo wasn't hopeless after all. And she could really wear a dress. And land an amazing boy.

"Did I miss anything important while I was away?" Daniel asked.

"Not really," I said. "Just my father slowly unraveling. And then my sister did actually speak to me today, so there's that."

"I take it from your expression and her disappearing again that you did not hash things out and become best friends once more?"

"Nope." I sighed. "She did curl my hair, though."

"It's gorgeous," he said, lightly fingering a loose curl, which Carina had artfully left free of the pins holding the rest of my hair to the nape of my neck. "The tiara's not half bad, either," he quipped.

"Get ready to see a lot of them. All the faded and useless royals will be sporting the family jewels."

"And here I am with just my sparkling wit."

We reached the main ballroom entrance, the doors thrown open and two security personnel standing watch, like they had for the opening party. Daniel and I pulled off to the side, watching as a dozen other couples formed a cluster by the door, creating a bottleneck. Definitely not late, then. I smoothed nervous hands down the bodice of the dress, ensuring my cleavage was taped expertly in place, that the lines were smooth. My hands caught on something where my torso turned to hip. This dress had pockets! They were cleverly hidden underneath twin juts of fabric. I slid my hands inside. They were shallow but enough to fit up to my palms. I found it oddly soothing, hiding a part of me in plain sight, pulling myself inward and holding it all in. The fingers of my right hand caught on something solid and flat. Drawing it out and examining it, I was perplexed to find a folded piece of paper. Paper was wildly impractical. What note had my mother stored in this pocket and then forgotten, all those years ago? I unfolded it and read.

Celine,

I've given you unlimited, all-hours bio-scan access to the pool on board.

Happy swimming.

Freja

A shiver skittered down my spine to read the message that inadvertently had led to her death. It hadn't occurred to me that she would have required special nighttime access to the pool, but of course she had. And my aunt Freja, as their father's apprentice at the time, would have had the ability to grant it to her.

"What's that?" Daniel asked.

"Nothing." I shoved the note back into my pocket. I switched my focus to spot-checking him. I fussed with the alignment of his waistcoat and dusted nonexistent fluff off his shoulders. We felt like a real couple. Something inside me twisted.

"Let's go in, then, shall we?" I suggested as soon as the crowd thinned. I grabbed two glasses from the first tray I saw. "Champagne?" Daniel took one, chuckling at me.

"Nervous? I don't see why. You look gorgeous, and my parents are more than primed to adore you."

"What did you tell them about me?" I initiated a stroll

around the room. I wanted to assess the landscape and everyone in it.

"I told them you were smart, funny, beautiful, kind . . ."

"Really? Not that I was titled and had my own ship?"

"I might have led with that, but the rest was my big finish!" He pulled me to a stop in a shallow archway, where we were half obscured by an elaborate column. "Now, they're over there."

Daniel pointed to a couple about twenty feet away. Oh, wow, no wonder Daniel was so attractive. Exquisite bone structure was a gift passed down from both parents, as were the large, expressive eyes, though from there, they differed greatly. His mother was tall and spindly, with elegant, sloping shoulders and a long neck, like a swan. A black swan, though— her hair was long and wavy and deep lustrous brown. Her floor-length black gown was adorned with feathers, which helped the comparison. Daniel's father was a tick shorter than his wife, though hardly short, with a broad chest and what looked like muscular arms hidden underneath his tux. He sported a bit of scruff, which served only to complement his thick, dark eyebrows and, again, that bone structure. I'd have to recommend that Daniel grow some facial hair.

"Now that you've seen they are human, and how you've got at least two inches on them—three on my father—maybe you're a little less scared?" Daniel said.

"If anything, I'm more intimidated. They're even more attractive than you are, and if they're even half as charming, they'll run circles around me," I joked.

"Just flash your tiara at them; you'll be fine." And with that, Daniel swept me over to meet them.

"Mum, Dad, this is Leo," he said by way of introduction. I gave my best curtsy.

"Shouldn't we be curtsying to you?" His mother laughed, and did so. Her husband bowed.

"Your Royal Highness, it is an honor," he addressed me, and luckily Daniel was quick to jump in.

"Oh, she hates that. Just call her Leo. And this is my mum, Jenny, and dad, Jaspar."

"Yes, we know the matching *J*s are a bit ridiculous," Jenny said. "Pure coincidence, I assure you. And 'Leo and Daniel' has a lovely ring to it, doesn't it?" She beamed at the two of us. "And you're quite handsome together. The children will be just adorable!"

"Ugh, Mum," Daniel groaned, shooting me an apologetic look.

"Oh, come on, I'm allowed to be excited that you're finally settling down. We were worried for a bit there." Jenny exchanged a look with her husband.

"Now, Leo, do you have any talents, hobbies?" Jaspar asked, moving the subject along. Though I had no clue how to respond.

"Not particularly," I said.

"Dad is trying to suss out whether you can join the family business," Daniel mock-whispered to me. "If I hadn't found a talent for cello, I would have had to learn to sing or act. Something to make myself useful!"

"He makes it sound like torture," Jaspar quipped. "Like he doesn't love playing. You begged me to learn an instrument! Four years old, pulling on my pant leg while I played the piano, asking for your turn. And you took to the strings like a duck to water!"

I could just picture a young Daniel, concentrating fiercely with a child-size bow in his hands, cello screeching out a tune. And suddenly I could picture a child of our own, begging their grandfather for music lessons, performing on stage. My stomach twisted again.

"Anyway, Leo's a pretty good singer," Daniel threw in, much to my embarrassment.

"Karaoke, at best," I deflected.

"We've had no fewer than two karaoke nights over the course of this thing," Daniel told his parents, who were rapt. They clearly adored him. "Leo's good. Don't let her say otherwise."

Okay, I adored him a lot, too.

"And she can dance, at least recreationally. Which we should go do." Daniel hugged both his parents, who in turn hugged me. I tried not to tense up too much but knew that I did, anyway. Then a warmth prickled at my neck, and my body went tight at the feeling that I was being observed. I swung around, and there was Elliot watching me. No, watching me and Daniel and his parents, with the most perplexing expression on his face. Censure? I couldn't exactly tell; a glare bounced off Elliot's glasses as he shifted away, so I could no longer see his eyes. And then Daniel took me by the hand and pulled me toward the dance floor.

Tonight, the music was fully traditional, which meant classical and instrumental versions of old pop songs. I was less adept at waltzing than bopping up and down to a pulsing beat, but Daniel's steps were sure, his arms high and tight. I let him lead, and with him guiding me, I was sure I almost looked elegant. After twenty minutes, I was short of breath and giddy. We rushed over to the sidelines to catch our breath, and I took in the party anew. The fashionably late had finally arrived, the room now packed. Surely the engagement announcements would start soon. Again, my stomach flipped.

"I'm starving!" I exclaimed, determined to settle my nerves. We swept over to the food table, where heaps of delicacies lay mostly untouched.

"I think you may be the only young woman eating," Daniel husked into my ear. His hand found the small of my back as he hovered close. I reminded myself that Daniel and I were friends and he wasn't interested in more. He was right. The food table seemed to be the domain of mostly the adults present, which I was fine with, as it left more for me. I quickly wolfed down an avocado toast, then helped myself to cheese and crackers.

"They are drinking, though." I nodded over at a cluster of girls and boys across the way, champagne in every hand and a sour expression on more than a few faces. Perhaps the ones who hadn't found a partner.

"Speaking of—" Daniel grabbed two flutes from a passing tray, handing me one. I took a gulp, a poor choice, as bubbles overwhelmed me and I started coughing.

"You okay?" he asked, cracking me on the back a few times until I caught my breath.

"I'm a little too eager to get drunk," I joked.

"It'll be fine. The announcement, I mean. I'll be there with you."

I nodded tightly, eyes catching on Elliot again, because of course they did. I had a habit of finding him, like a compass aligning itself. He was my true north.

This time he didn't see me, though. He was fully immersed in talking to Klara, who was breathtaking in sea-foam chiffon and a full complement of diamonds. Her smile was sly as she whispered something into his ear; Elliot chuckled, though to my eye, the reaction seemed forced. He must have been talking to her out of necessity, having not exactly mingled much with the Valg participants, leaving him with few conversation partners.

Someone tapped me on the shoulder, and I turned. It was Miranda Fairfax.

"That dress is exquisite, Leo," she said, and I returned the compliment—her little black dress was effortlessly elegant.

"Is Phillip here?" I inquired politely. Small talk before business. She shook her head.

"Oh, no, there's no way I could keep track of a four-year-old, and there's business to attend to and all."

"Right, yes, so the thing I wanted to talk to you about—"

"And who is your dashing companion?" Miranda asked at the same time as I tried to start my pitch.

"Oh, sorry, Miranda Fairfax from the *Lady Liberty*—" I pointed to her, then to Daniel. "And this is Daniel Turan, from the *Empire*."

He offered his hand for a shake. "I'm Leo's . . . um." We exchanged an awkward look.

"It's a strange feeling, right?" Miranda said. "Going from maybe to definitely. Are you excited to announce?"

We both nodded. Sure, *excited*. That was the word for it. I gulped down more champagne. A flash of red caught my eye from across the room. Finally, Carina was here! Where had she disappeared to? My gaze shifted to the left, to the man on her arm. Wait, was that—

Suddenly the music stopped, and my aunt's voice came over the speakers. I turned back to Miranda, but she was gone. Drat. I'd have to catch her after the engagements were announced.

"Couples, are you ready for the main event? I have your engagement announcements right here." She lofted a tab unit high for all to see. "So come forward, and we'll get started!"

Excitement crescendoed through the crowd, the couples who had been dancing coming to a stop, everyone pushing closer to the stage, eager to see. The clear delineation between dance floor and sidelines disappeared, and I lost my sister and her companion in the shift. Had I imagined seeing her with who I thought I did?

"Leo?" Daniel touched my arm gently. "Are you ready?"

Was I? I went to gulp down more champagne but found the glass empty. There was nothing left to hide behind. This was it.

"Yes." I let him take my hand.

28

"I'm going to do these in no particular order," Captain Lind said. "When I call your names, come up to the stage so everyone can see you."

Daniel and I left the food table behind, moving closer to the stage, though still sticking to the sidelines. We found an alcove by the bar, and I switched to vodka and juice. Once we'd settled, Daniel's hand at the small of my back again, steady and sure, I shifted up onto my tiptoes, craning my neck to find my sister again, with no luck. I did locate my father, leaning drunkenly against a column and smartly making no moves to join the crowd. If he did, he'd surely topple over without the architectural support. He beamed back at me and offered two thumbs up, then pointed to Daniel. Instead of the warm wash of fatherly approval, I felt queasy.

The captain launched into the announcements, and after a half-hour and a dozen couples, I began to shift restlessly, the soles of my feet beginning to throb.

"Maybe we shouldn't have left the food," Daniel said into my ear as another couple was called that wasn't us or anyone we knew. How many people were getting engaged?

"There can't be that many more engagements. We have to be coming up." At this point, I just wanted to get it over with.

"Next is my very own beloved niece," the captain said finally. I put down my glass and started for the stage.

"Carina Kolburg, come up here!"

Oh, no. I froze, Daniel running into my back with a grunt. I turned my face up to the stage with horror.

There was my baby sister, resplendent in red in the middle of the stage, a tight, nervous smile on her face. My aunt squinted down at the tab in her hand, head quirking to the right. She was confused. Of course she was—she didn't recognize the name. I knew exactly what it was, too. I had to do something, stop this, surely. But what could I do? Storm the stage? That would beg an explanation that I wasn't willing to trigger with an outrageous public display.

"Carina is pleased to announce her engagement to Benjamin Carmichael of the *Lady Liberty*!" the captain said to a smattering of applause. No one else knew who he was either. From the back of the room came a slurred curse in German. That would be my father, thoroughly soused and very confused. Ben joined her on stage, undeniably handsome in a surely borrowed suit, and clearly so happy to take my sister's hand.

The few weeks of my sister's avoidance came into clear focus. All that time, she'd continued a secret relationship with

Ben, first a covert correspondence and then a plan for him to come here for the Valg Ball to announce an engagement. My heart sank at Carina's lack of trust in me, even though I'd done nothing to earn it. I would have tried to talk her out of this, forbade it, even, which was exactly why she hadn't told me. Hadn't been able to see me for all these weeks. Carina had always been terrible at keeping secrets. She wore her heart on her sleeve.

"Who is that?" Daniel said low into my ear.

"The reason my sister stopped talking to me," I answered, watching them bow to the audience, Ben turning to Carina and kissing her gloved hand. They looked so happy. I was happy for them, abstractly. But I was also terrified. Carina was now inextricably a part of Elliot's scheme. I had failed her.

"Now for another Kolburg," my aunt transitioned seamlessly. "Leonie?"

There was my cue. Daniel squeezed my hand one last time before letting go. "See you in a minute," he said.

The crowd before me stood tightly packed, shoulder to shoulder, and my shaky requests for access went unheard.

"Excuse me," I said loudly and forcefully as my vision blurred on the edges. The crowd allowed me a small window through which I dodged, and I wobbled up the stairs, counting out each step carefully so I wouldn't face-plant. Wouldn't that just make this all the more perfect, falling on my face? My focus narrowed to my aunt's plastered-on smile and the ridiculous purple plumage blooming up from her shoulder. She looked like a peacock. Wait, now she was

staring at me. Why was she doing that? Oh, I was supposed
to face the audience.

A sea of faces blinked up at me. I gulped, throat suddenly
dry, palms frustratingly wet. I gripped the sides of my skirt to
dry them and steady myself. I was shaking. And my traitorous
inner compass found my true north. Elliot stood off to my
right, expression locked into neutral. Our eyes met, but Elliot
quickly looked away, as if he couldn't bear to look at me.
Grief washed over and through me, my knees threatening to
buckle. I locked them, forcing myself to stand tall. No more
of that. Tonight, I was moving forward and on with my life.

"Leonie is pleased to announce her engagement to—" My
aunt paused, her eyebrow lifting just a tick. She was impressed.
A first. "Daniel Turan of the *Empire*," she finished. As the
crowd applauded, she pulled close to my ear. "Wealthy and
exceedingly attractive. Better than I'd expected of you, my dear."
I ground my teeth together so hard, my temples throbbed.

But then there was Daniel at my side. He bowed for
the crowd, then grabbed my hand and twirled me into his
embrace. He knew how to put on a show, and I was happy to
be in his arms. I felt safer, less unmoored by the sea of sorrow
that threatened to swallow me up.

And then quickly we were done, the applause having died
out, with only my father's drunken whoops left to embarrass
me.

"That's a very happy father out there somewhere," my aunt
quipped. "Thank you, Leonie and Daniel."

"Okay, now let's go drink some more," Daniel said low in

my ear. We tried to go back the way we'd come, but my aunt shooed us off in the other direction. As we descended the stairs, I looked for Elliot again but instead ran smack-dab into Klara.

"Sorry!" I said. She smiled tightly.

"Congratulations, Leo. I'm impressed." She looked Daniel up and down and turned back toward the stage.

"Now before I announce the final and, in my completely biased opinion, most important engagement . . ." the captain continued from the stage, beaming down at Klara, who shifted uncomfortably under her gaze. It seemed that my aunt had finally managed the impossible and pinned my poor cousin down. But to whom? I caught Lukas standing off to the side behind her, looking smug. And his eyes were directed squarely on my chest. He would never change. Poor Klara. She'd wanted Elliot and ended up with that. I couldn't bear to watch her suffer her big moment on stage. Mine had been bad enough, and I went through it willingly.

"I need some air." I made excuses to leave. "Daniel, if you'll grab me a drink, I'll be back shortly." I kissed him on the cheek and careened toward the exit. A few minutes away from the crowd would do wonders.

The security personnel didn't even look at me as I streamed past; their attention was glued to something farther down the hall—an argument happening about ten feet away. I squinted, drawing near, interest turning to mild panic as I recognized the pair locked in tense conversation and the girl standing by, nervously worrying her fingers against her crimson skirts. Elliot, Ben, and Carina. My limbs froze me in place, reason telling me I should turn tail and run in the opposite direction, but my traitorous ears latched onto snippets of the conversation and were desperate to drink in every word.

"Don't you understand the agonizing position this puts me in?" Elliot pleaded with Ben, who merely shrugged.

"I love her."

"And I love *her*."

Elliot's reply stopped my heart. He loved *her*? My sister? That was surely who Ben meant, but certainly Elliot didn't—

"Leo!" Carina clapped eyes on me, rushing to close the short distance between us. Immediately the boys stopped talking, though there was no chance to see any reaction to my intrusion. I found myself fully engulfed by my sister, who threw her arms around me and clutched me desperately tight. "Please don't be mad at me. It's done, and I'm sorry, but I'm not sorry, and I just couldn't tell you before. You'd have stopped us."

"How could you, you silly girl?" was all I could manage. I sighed into her shoulder. I would have to tell her, warn her about Ben and Elliot's business. The life she was choosing. "Carina, I—" I broke up as I came out of the hug, finding both Ben and Elliot watching me with nervous anticipation. Without another word, I grabbed my sister by the hand and pulled her along, back toward the ballroom, away from the boys so we could speak with better privacy.

"What are you doing?" She tugged against my grip, but I held fast. I spun us into an alcove.

"I just need you to understand," I said.

"Understand what?" She snatched her hand from mine finally, holding it to her torso as if wounded. I stole a glance back at Elliot, who looked away.

"How much do you know about what Ben does for a living?" I hedged.

"He's in the sanitation department; you know that. There's no shame in it."

"No, there's no shame in *that*."

"I don't like the way you said that."

Everything felt wrong. The moment, the words coming out of my mouth, that we were standing in the middle of a bright hallway with the chatter of hundreds of people a dozen feet away. That, and my head starting to fuzz, drinks catching up with me. I sighed, pressing fingers to my temple.

"I'll tell you later," I settled on finally, but Carina was not having it.

"Whatever it is, tell me now, Leo!"

Her voice as it called my name came in stereo, pitched simultaneously high and low. How did she do that?

"Leo!" a decidedly male voice repeated. Wait, it was Daniel, calling to me from the ballroom doors. I turned, blinking him into focus. "Get back here now," he hissed urgently. He looked half sick with worry. Klara appeared beside him, ducking her head out and craning in Elliot's direction. She snapped her fingers at him, calling his name, and he hopped to like a good little soldier. I beat him to the door, letting Daniel grab me by the hand and usher me back inside. Miranda Fairfax was mid-speech.

"—proud to partner with the *Scandinavian* on this exciting new endeavor, which will go a long way toward conserving resources throughout the fleet. Thank you, Freja, for bringing this to me! I know you all must have been concerned by the rumors that every ship in the fleet would have to contribute a concrete resource to the fleet ecosystem, but with this invention, the *Scandinavian* will move forward on sound footing!"

I leaned into Daniel's ear. "What is she talking about?"

"The *Scandinavian*'s new water-conservation system," he answered tightly, shooting me a look.

"Wh-what?" I stammered, all my vital organs dropping into my shoes.

"Thank you, Miranda," my aunt simpered into the microphone, taking over emcee duties again. "The *Scandinavian* is proud to lead the way in water-recycling technology."

They were? Not on my last count. Captain Lind had rejected my proposal out of hand! I waited with bated breath for her to go on, thanking her beloved niece for her brilliant invention, but she did not. Had she been secretly developing her own version all this time? Either way, I felt thoroughly scuppered.

I felt a gentle touch on my elbow and swiveled to find Elliot peering at me with concern. "Why aren't you up there?"

"I—" My mouth hung open, wobbling like a dying fish. My aunt started speaking again. I whipped around to the stage, horror creeping slowly but surely up my spine.

"And now, following this happy news with more happy news, the final engagement of the night, and the one that means the most to me. Klara, darling, come up here."

I watched my cousin ascend the stage as I turned over the facts in my mind. My aunt had made some deal with Miranda Fairfax of the *Lady Liberty*, brokering the use of my invention, or something terribly similar to it. She'd not spoken to me about it, nor said my name. Had she stolen it from me? How? My breath came in short pants, my body flushing hot.

"Leo." Daniel was there again, steady hands on my back and arm. "It has to be a mistake. An oversight. We'll fix it. It's okay."

No, no, no, it *wasn't*. Tears sprang hot into my eyes, blurring my vision. Why was this happening?

"I am thrilled to announce that my daughter, Her Royal Highness Klara Lind, is engaged to . . ." Captain Lind trailed off for dramatic effect, building up suspense. I looked over at Lukas, but he was gone from the sidelines. My eyes flicked to the stairs leading up to the stage, but it wasn't Lukas making his way up them. It was—

My aunt went for the big finish, confirming the suspicion that washed cold over me.

"Elliot Wentworth of the *Islay*!"

And I broke.

29

Tears began to flow hot and freely down my cheeks, my vision blotting out white. My mind screamed out *No!* and my knees threatened to buckle, but Daniel held me fast upright. I was conscious of him whispering something in my ear, something about everything being okay, but as my vision cleared, I became acutely aware of silence. Then a low hum, the murmur of scandal. Everyone had swiveled to face me and Daniel, staring at us. No, no, at *me*. Elliot, Klara, Captain Lind—everyone's eyes were on me, judging, worrying.

Scheisse. I must have shouted "No!" out loud.

So I did the only thing I could think to do. I ran.

"Hey! Stop!" the security men yelled as I dodged past them, hanging a sharp right at the ballroom doors. The champagne and the vodka dulled the painful throb from my too-tight shoes as I sprinted away. To where, I didn't know; all that mattered was that it was away. Away from the horror show of the ballroom, where everything I loved and held dear, all my hopes and dreams, had been crushed right in front of me. Elliot was marrying Klara. My Elliot. And my invention had been stolen. I didn't care that Daniel's wealth meant I no longer needed the water-filtration system to save my family. That wasn't the point. It had been *mine*. Something dear and precious to me, and my aunt had taken that.

Elliot, too.

I slowed to a stop, gasping for air through a sob. I leaned my back against the nearest wall, doubling over and imploring myself to breathe.

Oh, God, what had I done? How could I marry anyone else? I would love him forever and always, until the day I died. That I knew, better than I could ever know anything. And he would love Klara? Marry her, have children with her, while I watched? This was a nightmare. I was in my nightmare.

"Leo!"

I heard Elliot call my name, then saw him as he rounded the corner and jogged to a stop before me. I swiped at my eyes with the back of my hand, black smudges of mascara and liner coming away with it. Great, now I would look like someone had punched me in the face. Well, it felt like it.

"Why weren't you on the stage, Leo?" Elliot demanded.

"What, did you want me to jump up there and fight my cousin? Is this all some sick game?" I teetered from grief to rage.

"What? No! I mean with your aunt. When she announced the partnership with the *Lady Liberty,* for the water-filtration system. Why weren't you up there?"

"Why would I be up there? I had nothing to do with this. I don't know what's happening."

Elliot went quiet, stared at me; then his eyes went wide, as if with revelation.

"You didn't open the letter."

I cocked my head to the side. What was he talking about?

"Leo, why didn't you open the letter? *Verdammt noch mal!*"

Elliot was cursing in German, so this was serious.

"Was für einen verdammten Brief?" I replied in kind. German always came to me more readily when I'd been drinking, so the shift felt natural.

"The one I left on your pillow weeks ago. I haven't been in there since, and I didn't think—" Elliot shook his head. "Dammit, Leo, why are you so stubborn? Go now. Read my letter. Look at the attachment."

"Me? Are you telling me you wrote something crucial in a letter? And now you're blaming me for not opening it?"

"Yes, I'm an idiot, but argue with me later. Go to the *Sofi* now and read it. Please."

I didn't understand what was happening, didn't like his tone at all, but still I pushed back from the wall, though not before removing my heels. I'd go the rest of the way barefoot and worry about how gross that was later. It didn't take me very long at all to reach my ship—subconsciously, I think I'd been heading there already. Why else turn right from the ballroom, away from the royal quarters? This was home.

The *Sofi* was dark and eerily quiet when I boarded. Adrenaline and alcohol warred for my senses, one sharpening my focus and the other fuzzing everything at the edges. I oscillated from the middle of the hall to the left, back to the middle, then to the right as I made my way quickly toward the kitchen and front stairs. Wanting my wits about me when I read whatever this infamous letter was, I stopped in the kitchen to chug down a glass of water. Then, with much steadier footing, I headed below decks, following the familiar pathway to Elliot's room. The door cracked open, the stale air of a disused room washing over me, and I commanded the lights on. There, on Elliot's bed, right where I had left it, was an envelope with my name in his tidy scrawl. I had been so angry at him, at his betrayal, I'd had no interest in whatever feeble words he might have had to offer.

Now I picked up the envelope with trembling fingers and sat down on the edge of the bed to read. I tore at the edge of the flap with my fingernail, enough to wedge my index finger underneath and tear it the rest of the way open. Not pretty, but it did the job. More carefully, I slid out the folded sheaf of paper. The envelope slipped from my grasp, sluicing to the floor like a graceless bird. I spread open the pages, eyes focusing on the handwritten text.

Dear Leo,

I know exactly what you must be thinking: "How antiquated of him to write me a letter, and a bit showy, too, flaunting his wealth—that he can afford paper!" And you'd be right, and wrong at the same time, like always. I am old-fashioned, yes, but above all, practical. If I sent *you a regular message, you could delete it before reading. I want my words immortalized in ink and parchment, something you can hold concrete in your hands and hopefully believe. Besides which, part of this had to be delivered on paper. But I'll get to that.*

I know you in my bones, Leo, as I think you know me. So you must know that I didn't mean to hurt you, but the fact is that I have, and that truth is causing me indescribable agony.

Agony. That is the perfect word to describe how I have felt over the past few weeks, seeing you nearly every day but with you feeling so distant to me. Unreachable. Unknowable. It's how I've felt the past three years, if I'm being honest. I've hated you. And missed you. And I—

Something there was crossed out, scratched out roughly in black, the paper nearly torn. No use trying to decipher it. I kept reading.

Now I write to you, half agony, half hope.

Last night I wanted to kiss you so desperately. I think you wanted to kiss me, too. And then everything fell so spectacularly apart. But despite everything, now I have hope. Hope that you still love me as I still love you. I have always loved you, I love you still, and I will always love you. Three years ago, you crushed my spirit and my hope. That love was enough. It was more than where we came from, how much money we had. I have money now, and power, and position, everything I didn't have before. The spiteful part of me wanted you to love me, to want me again, and I had fantasies of saying no, of crushing you this time. I both revel in and loathe that I have become precisely what your father, and aunt, and cousin found me to be wanting of three years ago. But I was lying to myself. I don't want revenge on you, Leo. I understand why you did what you did. You couldn't leave, and I couldn't stay. All I want, what I desperately wish for, is for you to love me still. Love me back. Take me as I am, and I will love you best, and forever.

If you do not, I ask that you remain my friend. I cannot foresee a future for myself without you in it. I have missed you too much these past three years to miss you forever.

Regardless of how you feel, I leave you with this: I have filed the patent in your name for your water-filtration system with the Olympus, I took care of the fee, and you'll find the papers enclosed. All you need do is sign them. You deserve every happiness.

Love,

Elliot

His words left me speechless, and with quaking fingers, I thumbed to the additional pages, eyes skimming the official jargon. He'd really done it—filed my patent for me. It was dated three weeks ago, and there was the blank signature field winking up at me. It was mine. I had proof. I could use this to prove that the water-filtration system was my invention, if indeed my aunt had stolen it.

And Elliot loved me. Still. Always. Forever!

Then why had he gotten engaged to Klara not even twenty minutes ago?

Because I hadn't read the letter, and he thought that I had. I'd acted cold and indifferent toward him and flung myself into the Season. Latched onto Daniel.

Oh, God, I had ruined everything. Brought this upon myself. The letter and patent slipped from my slack fingers, fluttering noisily to the floor. I flung myself back onto the bed and curled onto my side. I clutched Elliot's pillow to my face and let the tears come again.

30

A knock at the door startled me out of my mood. I rose from the bed, tentatively moving toward the door. "Leo?"

His voice was muffled through the metal, but there was no mistaking that it was Elliot.

I rushed to the mirror to check my complexion. Blotches of pink stained my cheeks, and my mascara had run, smudging streaks of black below my eyes. A bit of spit applied to my finger didn't quite do the job, but I managed to clear away the worst of the mascara damage. My cheeks were a lost cause—there would be no hiding the fact that I'd been messily crying.

Elliot knocked again.

"Maybe you're not in there, and I'm the idiot talking to an empty room, but if you are in there, can we talk? I'll give up in, um, two minutes."

I wasn't cruel, so I didn't make him wait that long. I smoothed a hand over my hair, then my skirt, and took a steadying breath before approaching the door. When I opened it, there he was in all his glory: sophisticated in his suit, face creased with worry. His eyes darted down to the floor, where the pages of the letter were still scattered. I scurried to collect them all, the patent papers especially. While I was doing that, Elliot took the opportunity to come in, shutting the door behind him.

"You read it, then?" He sat down on the lower bunk across from mine. Well, his. But also mine.

I know you in my bones, Leo, as I think you know me.

Suddenly I felt flushed all over. I nodded, taking a seat across from him. I didn't know what to say.

Elliot didn't either. He looked at me expectantly.

"So?" finally he prodded.

"You love me," I offered stupidly. Not a question. A statement of apparent fact. Elliot let out a breath, lips quirking into a smile. "Yes, I do. Do you . . . ?" He let the question hang, as if he could finish the statement with any number of things, such as " . . . like coffee?" But his meaning was clear.

"Yes." There was no use lying, though I didn't see the point in any of this now. We were both engaged to other people. My brow furrowed, the fact washing over me afresh. "Klara, El? How could you?"

"Me? You're engaged to some guy you just met!"

"Daniel's a good person," I said. "And at least he's firmly neutral as far as you're concerned. Klara is family. You had to know what that would do to me."

Elliot's lips were pursed together so tightly, they went

white in the middle. His jaw clicked, like he desperately wanted to say something.

"Well?"

"I had no choice," he ground out. "You cannot possibly understand everything I have done for you. Because I love you."

"What does that mean? Elliot, there's no use being cryptic with me, not after all this; just lay it all out. You owe me the truth."

Elliot chewed on his lower lip, then sighed. "She's black-mailing me."

"Who, Klara?" For all her faults, that didn't seem like my cousin at all. Blackmail was beneath her.

"No, her mother," Elliot said. "The captain."

"How? Why?" I was flabbergasted.

Elliot narrowed his eyes at me, tilting his head. "I run the black market, Leo. Remember? She found out and has been holding it over me ever since. She wants a piece of it. No, she wants it all. If I marry Klara, my empire becomes her empire too. And the *Scandinavian's* position is ensured."

"Didn't she already do that by stealing my invention?" Bitterness sparked in the back of my throat.

"That . . . I think that fell into her lap, and she ran with it. Ben ran your idea up the chain on the *Lady Liberty,* but your name must not have made it to the top, only your host ship—the *Scandinavian.* Miranda Fairfax contacted Captain Lind, and here we are. Ben and I really thought, I swear, that you were involved. We didn't know she'd stolen it from you. It's how I knew you couldn't have read the letter. You didn't have the patent."

"How did she do that, though?" I asked. "I have the blueprints bio-locked on board the *Sofi*. She couldn't have."

Suddenly Elliot found the floor fascinating, and my stomach churned with sick.

"Elliot, no. You couldn't have. You said you didn't."

"I didn't know. I wouldn't lie to you. But I think this is my fault. When I messed with your security protocols, I took a peek at your files in the workshop—I was so curious how much progress you'd made since I left. And I was so proud of you! But now I realize I must have left the security window open, and Max and Ewan got in. They were asking about your workshop after they got back, but I didn't even think about it."

"You think she blackmailed them, too?"

"I know she did. How do you think she found out about the business?"

"She kidnapped them and held them on the *Scandinavian*. I suspected, afterward."

"You did?"

"I'm not stupid, Elliot." My lips turned down into a frown. "Except apparently I am. I knew my aunt was unscrupulous enough to kidnap someone, yet I never considered she might steal from me. I don't understand. Why wouldn't she just ask me? If the *Scandinavian* needed the business to save us, I would have helped."

Elliot shook his head. "She couldn't have you involved, not willingly. That would have scuppered her leverage on me. She wanted everything all at once—the public front of respectability from the water-filtration deal, and then the real long-term insurance policy of my running the black market from her ship."

"That's her deal? That you run it from the *Scandinavian*?"

Elliot nodded. "Yep. I'm to dock the *Islay* with the *Scandinavian,* giving her the whiskey business and the spoils of my real business. In return, she'll keep my secret and protect me from the authorities."

I turned everything over in my brain, connecting all the dots, finally. But I came up short on one thing.

"How would my aunt's coming to me about the water-filtration-system venture have damaged her leverage on you? That has nothing to do with the black market. I don't see the connection."

Elliot let out a bitter laugh. "That wasn't her leverage. Not really. It was you, Leo. She threatened to turn you out. Charge you exorbitant docking fees and ruin your reputation among the other ships, ensure that you were left destitute. She knew I would agree to anything to protect you."

My throat clenched tight as feelings too overwhelming to contain bubbled up from my very core. Though only ten feet of floor separated us, suddenly Elliot was too far away, the space between us cavernous and cold and wrong. I launched at him, my full-body tackle sending him tumbling backwards onto the bed, what started as a hug quickly transforming into something more intimate by virtue of the location. But I didn't care if it was too forward or sudden. I needed him, clutched to me so tight that our heartbeats muddled together.

"You're so stupid." I laughed into his ear, nuzzling the shell of it with my nose, then moving to kiss the edge of his jaw, up to his temple.

"Me? Why?" His hand found my waist, and he crept sure fingers around to the small of my back, pulling me in closer. Then he ducked down to kiss the skin of my exposed shoulder, making his way up the line of my neck, paying reverent attention to every inch of skin. I shivered under his touch.

"I don't know. You just are. For not saying anything sooner, I suppose."

"Pot, kettle."

I wrenched back, stopping him mid-pucker. He looked like a crestfallen duck. A giggle escaped me.

"You acted like you hated me," I said. "Then you tried to be my friend. Then you ran away. Your signals were beyond mixed."

Elliot groaned, flopping onto his back and too far away from my lips for my liking. "Why couldn't you have just read the letter when I gave it to you? You're so stubborn, Leo! Now everything is . . ."

"Royally frexed?" I offered, pulling him by the collar of his shirt back toward me. Our lips hovered an inch apart. Then he frowned. Wait, no, that was all wrong. I needed him to kiss me now.

"You need to talk to Miranda Fairfax," he said, then wrenched his shirt from my grasp and extricated himself from my embrace, sitting up. With a sigh, I followed suit. He clearly wanted to talk.

"No, I need to talk to my aunt," I said. "She's a champion liar who can spin anything. It's no use talking to Miranda or anyone if I can't prove it." My mind clicked through a number of scenarios and options. "Do you think I could record her? Get her to confess?"

Elliot seemed to think it over. "You can record via wrist tab. The feature is disabled automatically for privacy reasons, but I hacked mine ages ago. Here." He removed his and placed it gently into my open hands. "But you have to do it tonight. Miranda could leave at any moment." He paused, brow furrowing deeply. "Even if you can get her to confess, I think I'm stuck. She knows about the black-market business. She can take me down."

"Give up that business, then," I said, running my fingers lightly against his cheek, cupping his face with my hand. Elliot's eyes fluttered closed as he leaned into my touch. "Go legit. The *Islay* is actually a whiskey ship, right? Just manufacture booze, and we'll get married, and everything will be perfect."

Like I'd shocked him with electricity via my fingertips, he shot back and free of my touch. "I like what I'm doing, Leo. I've found my purpose. Something I'm really good at."

"Stealing?" I countered.

"It's not petty theft. You didn't give me a chance to explain that night. Why I'm doing this. How it works."

"Evgenia explained it to me," I said. "You think you're Robin Hood."

"Robin Hood was the hero of the story. And it worked. I'm doing what I can to even the playing field."

"By stealing from people like me."

"Don't you see that they're not on your side?" he pleaded. "You're closer to my end of things than you've ever been. When your ship fails, you'll be at the mercy of whichever ship will grant you a visa and whatever work you can get. The fleet is merciless. Wealth and utility trump all. I want to protect people like you. Redistribute wealth, resources. Help."

I felt myself soften, just so. Elliot had nicked the skin, a sliver of his reasoning invading my bloodstream. My head began to swell with the traitorous rush of mixed feeling. I'd always loathed the extravagance here, the pomp and circumstance of titles and private public quarters and rations for the lower decks while my friends and family swam in champagne and decadent meats. My family had felt the slow crush of dwindling wealth, creeping closer every day to desperation.

And Elliot. My Elliot. Good and loyal Elliot. I couldn't see him as a villain. We'd been apart three years, and no one truly changes so drastically in that period of time. Elliot was ever eager and warm and kind, and I wanted to believe his every word, because he believed it. Or, at least, I would believe it tonight. Let us sort out the messy business in the cold light of day.

"I . . . I think I need time," I said, telling the truth. "I'm not convinced you can control this, but I know your heart is in the right place."

Elliot lit up, then grabbed me by both hands and dragged me up and into his embrace.

"I'm so relieved to hear you say that. I like who I am now, what I do, but I love you, too."

I drew back, observing him. "I thought you had changed so much. That I didn't know you now." I brushed a stray lock of hair away from the frame of his glasses. "It was your confidence that threw me. You didn't have that before. It's sexy."

"I wasn't sexy before?" He grinned a crooked smile, setting off his dimples.

"No comment."

"You're no fun."

"That's what they tell me," I quipped. Then frowned. I could practically hear my cousin's voice echoing in my head. "What are you going to do about Klara?"

Elliot's expression darkened. "I'll talk to her. I don't think she actually wants to marry me. At least, I hope not. She's hard to read. And what about you?"

"Me?"

"You're engaged? To the irritatingly attractive guy."

"Daniel," I corrected him. My stomach swooped uncomfortably. I let myself drift back, out of Elliot's arms. I needed the space to think. *Scheisse.*

"What?"

"We have an arrangement. I made a promise, I . . ." I cursed thrice more, under my breath.

"You don't want to break it off?" Elliot's voice choked with emotion. "Do you—do you love him?"

"What? No! It's not like that at all." I pressed thumb and forefinger to my temple, as if to ward off my impending headache. "He needs a marriage of a certain convenience as badly as I needed a wealthy husband, and he's a really nice guy. We're friends. I hate to hurt him."

"He has to understand that we love each other, though?"

I groaned. "Daniel will understand perfectly, and I'm going to hate myself for doing this to him for that, of all reasons." There was no way to explain everything to Elliot, and now wasn't the time. Nor was it my place to share Daniel's private business with him. Thankfully, Elliot didn't press me for an explanation.

Elliot's wrist tab pinged, three times in quick succession. I glanced down at it, now on my wrist.

"It's Klara," I said, reading the messages. "And she's very cross with your disappearance. Her mother is asking questions."

"So she's still there. Good. You should message the captain now, saying you need to talk. Get her to meet you somewhere quiet and private."

I used the native messaging system on the *Sofi* to contact my aunt, and then we waited.

"I'll talk to Klara," Elliot said. "But I'll leave Daniel and the timing to your discretion."

"Wait, are we really doing this?" I asked, thinking it through properly, now that I was clear of the nonstop feelings train of the last half-hour. "Did you even ask me to marry you? Because I don't think you did."

"Technically, you asked me. Or told me," Elliot said. "Frankly, I was going to scold you on how thoroughly unromantic your proposal was, but I figured I should let you off the hook. You've had a rough night. And I love you, so I don't really mind." A mischievous smile played at his lips as he inched closer to me, extending his hand, as if asking me to dance. I took it, tentative excitement bubbling up from my spine, and I gasped with delight as he yanked me to his chest. His hand came up to cup my cheek, thumb brushing tantalizingly over my bottom lip. I shivered. He pulled closer, lips hovering a breath away from mine; my eyes were glued to them, my breath coming in short puffs.

Then, finally, bliss.

Elliot kissed me hard and deep, meeting me with a near desperation that I matched in kind. We channeled three years of pent-up feelings, of longing and missing and wanting, into the press of our lips, into the way we clutched at each other. I grabbed fistfuls of his shirt to anchor myself to him. Or maybe to burrow myself closer. We couldn't be close enough, after so many years apart, and Elliot seemed to agree; he slipped his hand to the small of my back and pressed me tighter to him. My fists were in the way, so instead I slithered them up his chest and over his shoulders, clasping them together at the base of his neck.

I melted into him, and he walked us backwards until my back hit the bunk frame. His and my movements began to blur; whose knee slid between whose legs first was unclear, several of Elliot's shirt buttons seeming to come undone of their own accord. Just as the kiss started to transform into something more, a metallic ping sounded. My aunt had replied.

Meet me at the pool in twenty minutes, her message said.

"I have to go," I panted as I righted my dress and careened over toward the mirror. I did my best to smooth my hair and unsmudge my lipstick, but I soon gave up, knowing I'd have to rely on the good five minutes it would take to get back up to the pool for my kiss-swollen lips to go down a bit.

"Do you want me to come with you?" Elliot sidled up behind me. He pressed a kiss to the exposed skin where my shoulder met the nape of my neck and slid his arms around my waist, curling into my back. "The pool is a weird place to meet."

"No, go talk to Klara. I can handle my aunt. She probably knows what I'm there to talk about and wants to put me on edge. I hate it up there."

"I'm going to miss you," he mused.

"It's only an hour. You'll live." I twisted out of his grasp and strode toward the door, hoping he couldn't see the stupid grin splashed across my face.

31

The scent of the day was cherry. All the lights in the spa were dimmed down low, and the piquant fruit note made me long for pie. What a mood to go with a bit of espionage. I checked Elliot's wrist tab for the fourth time, ensuring that it was recording. Although I wasn't entirely sure what I would say to my aunt to get her to confess, I was secure in the knowledge that the wrist tab would record every word.

The door had been open when I arrived, signaling my aunt's presence. I crept down the corridor past the locker room, stomach screwing into knots with every step. This was definitely why she'd chosen to meet here. This place made me feel on edge and trapped and desperately unhappy. She wanted to put me off my game.

The pool came into view. There was no light except for those illuminating the water from underneath, casting the whole place with an eerie mood that sent further shivers down my spine. I inhaled deeply through my nose, then slowly exhaled through my mouth, once, twice, thrice, finding my center. Now was the time to polish my acting chops. I couldn't let her see how much I was rattled. I stepped forward, my head and shoulders thrown back, a smile plastered on.

"Aunt Freja!" I greeted her, my voice bouncing and duplicating as it echoed throughout the largely tiled space. I had to squint to find her. She was all the way at the far end of the pool, near the diving platform. I bounded over, feigning delight.

"Uh, Leonie, hi." My enthusiasm seemed to throw her, as I'd hoped. I even hugged her for good measure. She was stiff and cold as always.

"It's so strange that you suggested we meet here! I just wanted to say congratulations, and thank you."

"You said you wanted to meet privately." She gestured around us. "It seemed to be the best location."

"Yes, yes, that's true. Well, it's just so funny, after all that, that Klara is marrying Elliot and you've solved the ship's usefulness problem! What a night."

She tilted her head at me. "Honestly, Leonie, you are a terrible liar, so let's not pretend you're happy."

Any buoyancy I'd felt, false or not, immediately evaporated. I fingered the edge of Elliot's wrist tab nervously.

"Fine," I said. "I think you owe me an explanation."

"I don't know what you're talking about." The captain picked at a nail and leaned casually against the diving platform.

"I think you do." I had to be careful. I didn't want to mention Elliot and the black market and get it on the recording too. I had to get my aunt to confess to what she did on the face of it, stealing my blueprints and passing off my idea as her own.

She narrowed her eyes at me in careful assessment. I may have been a terrible liar, but I was honestly and genuinely stubborn. I held her stare. A minute ticked by, the soft gurgle of the water filters accompanying the syncopated rhythm of our breathing.

"I don't see what the big deal is," she said flippantly. "You've landed yourself a gorgeous and wealthy husband. You don't even need the money anymore. What does it matter?"

Ugh, no, she was being purposefully vague, not admitting to anything. Did she suspect I was recording this, trying to catch her out?

"It's not about the money," I said. "The water-filtration system is mine. I'm the one who discovered the concept in the archives and adapted the Earth-bound version to make it work on our ships. I salvaged the materials, built it, tested it. I've been trying to license it for months, and you stole it out from under me."

"Did I? That sounds so far-fetched, Leo. Why would I steal from my own niece? And how would you even prove that?"

"I have the patent. It was filed weeks before you met with Miranda Fairfax. You pitched her just the other day, right? That's why you were being so cagey when I ran into you two in the ballroom. You kept cutting me off and wouldn't let me speak."

"You were boring her, my dear. I was saving you the embarrassment. Are you feeling okay? I think you might be drunk."

I sputtered incoherently. "No, I'm not drunk. I want you to admit that you stole my invention from me!" I'd gone shrill, and I could feel my blood pumping hotly. My vision started to fuzz with anger.

"You were drinking a lot earlier. I was worried you'd fall off the stage! Do you think that might be where this fantasy is coming from? I'm family, so you don't have to pretend with me. I'm certain Elliot's getting engaged to my daughter was a massive blow. You did make a scene, after all. You're looking to blame me for something."

"I'm looking for the truth," I ground out. "You stole my design and pretended it was yours. That deal with the *Lady Liberty* should be mine. It was my idea."

"Leo, you're so hopelessly idealistic!" My aunt's slick veneer slipped, contempt bleeding through her every word and expression. She pointed to my wrist. "And, what, you're going to record my confession on that thing? Child's play." With violent speed, she snatched the wrist tab from my wrist and held it aloft. Angry red scratch marks appeared at my pulse point.

"I won. Go get married, Leo. Try to be happy."

"You didn't win," I spat. "Elliot's breaking up with Klara right now. He loves me, and I love him."

The captain rolled her eyes at me. "As long as that boy has a hand in the black market, he'll do what I say, including marrying my daughter." She grinned like a cat that had trapped a mouse, shaking the wrist tab teasingly in my direction.

"And now his precious secret is recorded for all to hear. Your entrapment is useless. So even if I fully admit to screwing you over, taking your blueprints from your very own ship and passing them off as my own, it doesn't matter. Because you love your Elliot and couldn't bear to have any harm befall him. So he'll be fine, as long as you don't cross me."

I was trapped. The stupidity of this plan crystallized into a low-grade panic, like acid radiating slowly from my core and into my extremities. I'd come up here by myself, where my aunt unequivocally had the upper hand, to try to get her to admit to a crime that was inextricably tied to Elliot's. And now I'd tipped my hand to someone ruthless enough to steal from her own niece.

My hands felt their way into my pockets as I steeled my expression. I wouldn't give my aunt the satisfaction of my fear. I just needed a moment to collect myself and think. Then my fingers grazed that folded piece of paper I'd stowed away earlier. I remembered the note, written in my aunt's hand, that she'd given to my mother some night many years ago.

Celine,

I've given you unlimited, all-hours bio-scan access to the pool on board.

Happy swimming.

Freja

Unease bubbled up within me. The woman standing across from me was ruthless enough to *threaten her family* in order to remain in power. Why did the note to my mother feel so oddly specific, and significant?

"You gave my mom special all-hours access to the pool," I said slowly.

"What?"

"That's how she got in here at night to swim," I continued, swishing the facts around like a fine wine, reaching for every note and nuance. "You arranged it. So you knew she'd be here."

"Uh, yes, your mother preferred to swim away from a crowd. What's the point, Leonie?"

I wasn't sure of my point, but it was niggling at me. The happenstance of it all. The only gravity failure in the *Scandinavian*'s history happening only in the pool area, at night, after my aunt had given my mother special permission to swim. It was a terrible accident.

Right?

"She told me things were about to change for us, that we might have to leave the *Sofi*. Was she going to challenge you for captain?"

"Who?" My aunt played dumb. I indulged her.

"My mother. There was a power vacuum after Granddad died. Two daughters eligible to run. One an idealist, the other ruthlessly pragmatic." I let it hang, hoping I was wrong, that I was spinning an elaborate fiction. Because anything else was too horrific. Champagne and vodka burned up my throat, and I tasted bile on my tongue.

We watched each other. My aunt's brow was furrowed, her face creased with worry.

"I'm afraid you're not well, my dear Leonie," she said, sickly sweet. False. Everything about my aunt was just a bit off, I realized. I was more comfortable calling her Captain Lind than Aunt Freja, always had been. There was a lingering

359

coldness in every interaction, buried beneath a veneer of charm. Most people didn't see it, but I always had.

"You killed her."

I'd barely whispered it, but it was as if I had shouted. My aunt flinched, and her mask melted away.

"Don't be so dramatic. It was an unfortunate accident." She chewed on the word "unfortunate," like it was funny.

"What did you do?"

She narrowed her eyes to slits. "You really want to know?"

"Yes." My voice was hoarse, throat tight as I choked back tears.

"I simply pushed a button. Let fate decide. If my sister was swimming when the gravity failed . . . I hadn't really done anything. Just pushed a button."

"You're a monster."

The shrug she gave was infuriatingly nonchalant. "I'm a survivor. I take care of myself, and my ship."

"I'm going to tell everyone," I said, barely restrained fury vibrating through me.

"Will you?" She held my gaze as she flicked her wrist, sending Elliot's wrist tab flying into the pool. "Technology is so fragile."

"I still have the note."

"That note doesn't prove anything. You're grasping at straws. You have nothing. And I have everything."

"Aunt Freja—"

"Call me Captain," she snapped coldly. The force of it set me off-balance; I fell back a step, then two. She came closer a step, then two. Her gray-blue eyes were flat and uncaring. "Tell me, are you still afraid of the pool?"

"Wh-why?" I stammered, inching back. She inched forward.

"You should never have come here. You could have just let me have what I wanted." She sighed heavily, as if the weight of the world rested on her shoulders. "Leo, I'm sorry."

"About wh—"

And then she pushed me into the pool.

32

My voluminous ball gown weighed me down like an anchor. I sank down, down, down into the deep, dark water, terror thumping through every inch of my body. I screamed, choking against the chlorinated water. My legs kicked fruitlessly against the twisting, heavy folds of my gown as I furiously pumped my arms up and out, trying to synchronize between arms, legs, everything to pull myself back up. I knew how to swim, God dammit, but my dress was a vise. I couldn't get up. I couldn't breathe. I opened my eyes, blinking against the burn of the chlorine, desperate to orient myself, but I couldn't see the walls or a ladder. Just watery blue dimpled with the yellowed haze of the pool lights.

I kicked harder, tried holding half my skirt up and away from my legs while I used the other arm to paddle up. I managed only to spin in place, tipping forward like an upset top. I was useless in this dress and running out of oxygen.

I was going to die.

My lungs burned, and then I gasped, inhaling more water. I couldn't help it; my body desperately wished to breathe. Pain radiated through me. My vision went black.

. . . And then, suddenly, white. I was coughing up water, retching onto my side, and someone was speaking a litany of "Leo"s into my ear, telling me he loved me and I wasn't allowed to die. Elliot. I pawed weakly at his chest.

"Aunt—" I croaked, trying to get up but barely making it an inch off the ground. I felt as if concrete had been poured throughout my body. I was one with the ground now.

"Klara got her. She's impressively strong, and has a mean right hook."

I rolled over, squinting to focus on the near distance. Ten feet away, my cousin had her mom pinned, arms behind her back. It looked like she'd tied her up with towels?

"Klara, honey, this is ridiculous. Your cousin tripped and fell in. Let me go," Captain Lind pleaded with her daughter, squirming against her restraints. As the shock of near drowning faded, my brain clicked back to something vital.

"The wrist tab, El. She threw it in the pool. The recording's gone."

"Shhh, it's fine. I was recording a live backup. Ben should be here any moment with Miranda Fairfax. It's all going to be okay."

I heard the captain curse under her breath at the mention of "live backup." But then she laughed. "Mutually assured destruction," she singsonged in my direction.

"Help me up," I ordered, using his arms to leverage myself

363

to sitting. Elliot slung a towel over my shoulders and another around my torso, then hugged me close, surely soaking himself in the process. He rubbed warm circles on my back, and I exhaled into his embrace. Elliot had a copy of the recording, so my aunt's dual-pronged confession was immortalized. Every part of it.

"Elliot, did you listen to it? She talked about you and the black market. We can't turn in that recording without compromising you."

He blanched but remained resolute. "We'll cross that bridge then. You got her on stealing your invention, though?"

I nodded. "And confessing to killing my mother. She triggered the gravity failure in the pool. It wasn't an accident." Elliot reeled back as if struck. Klara gasped, then cursed.

"Ow!" Captain Lind cried out.

"I'll hit you again if you don't shut up. Your sister, Mom? Really? And you blackmailed Elliot into marrying me? You're disgusting."

I had never liked my cousin so much as I did in this moment. But then a sob broke through me, the enormity of it crashing down all over. I was wrung out. There was so much to do, but all I wanted to do was sleep. Or cry. Or both. Right now, being held was enough. Elliot pressed me tighter to him, and I gripped his now-damp suit jacket.

"All the more reason we must turn over the recording, so she's punished," he husked in my ear. "I don't care what happens to me, as long as you're safe." He planted a kiss on my temple. My chest swelled with warmth, and my stomach did a queasy flip. I couldn't lose Elliot again, not after all this. The best-case scenario was jail. The worst . . . I didn't want to think about it. My mind was skittering a million miles an hour, grasping for a solution, willing me to spring into action, but my body was spent.

"Can we deal with it in the morning?" I asked. "I need to sleep. After I get dry and warm."

"I can't get her down to the brig by myself," Klara said, mostly to Elliot. "But I do have bio-lock access, since I'm her apprentice. We can lock her up until tomorrow. Let her stew."

"When I get out of this, I will throw you out of a goddamn airlock," Captain Lind hissed. "All of you."

"What by the moon is going on here?"

Miranda Fairfax stormed in, my sister, Ben, Daniel, and Evgenia filing in behind her. My sister broke away toward me, click-clacking across the tile, her red gown billowing behind her like an old-fashioned movie star's.

"Leo, oh, my God, what happened? Are you all right?" Carina collapsed breathlessly beside me, pulling me into a crushing hug.

"It's a party, and everyone is here," I joked limply as Elliot retreated. I groaned into her shoulder as I realized I would have to tell her the truth about our mother and aunt. I couldn't bear to do it tonight, not now. "I'm fine," I said. "I'll be fine."

"I hope you have a good reason for having the captain tied up?" Miranda grilled Klara and Elliot, who had joined them. She seemed more perplexed than upset. Ben took over from Klara the task of holding Lind in place. I wanted to listen to their conversation, actively participate, but then I was swamped by Evgenia and Daniel, who joined Carina in her fussing. Evgenia instructed Daniel to pick me up off the ground and get me into a chair, stat. And she sent Carina flying to the back of the room to grab more towels.

"We have to get you dry," Evgenia said, attempting futilely to use the two soaked towels to dry me further. "You'll get sick. Should we take you to the med bay?"

I shook my head. "I'm shaken, but not ill."

Carina returned with more towels, which Evgenia swapped out. She had to use more than one, as Elliot had. The stock towels at the pool didn't even wrap around me.

"What happened?" Daniel asked, sitting down on the lounge chair across from me. Evgenia and Carina perked up at the question. They wanted to know too. The mere thought sent a wave of exhaustion through me. I gestured loosely in the direction of the crowd where Miranda was currently holding court.

"—stole Leo's invention. We have the patent, and her confession on audio," Elliot was just finishing saying. "She tried to drown Leo too." He darted a glance in our direction, eyes landing on my sister. "And there's more, but it's complicated. We can talk about it in full detail in the morning, if that's all right with you." Miranda pinched the bridge of her nose between her thumb and forefinger, giving an exasperated sigh. "Fine, we can reconvene in the morning to discuss business. Mr. Carmichael, Miss Lind, I will put you in charge of seeing Freja to and from the brig. Just have her on the bridge at nine a.m. sharp."

"Miranda, this is ridiculous, you can't possibly—" Captain Lind started, but Miranda cut her off with a sharp glare.

"You'll address me as Commander Fairfax and show me due respect. In fact, you know what? I am stripping you of your captain title, pending an investigation. Your daughter will serve as captain in the interim."

"But there's an election tomorrow—"

"You mean your play at fascism disguised as democracy?" Miranda snapped. "Postpone it. Klara can run for your seat; I don't care." With one last nod at Ben, Miranda left.

"Uh, wow, okay, I was not expecting that," Daniel said. I couldn't help but laugh, which turned to a cough as pain shot through my center. My lungs had not yet recovered enough to handle spontaneous spirited reactions.

"Come on, Mother, let's go." Klara tugged on her mother's still-tied arms. "And because I love you, we're going to leave you in that ball gown *alllll* night. I know how much you value appearances."

She and Ben frogmarched the captain toward the exit, onward to the brig. I didn't even know we had a jail on board, but Klara seemed confident in her direction as they went off. Then they paused at the entranceway, and my cousin threw one last, contemplative look over her shoulder at me. Sadness, apology, pity—any one of those could have described it, but I wasn't sure. In the end, she just nodded at me and moved on.

Elliot came over to the lounge chairs, and I budged over so he could sit next to me. He tucked a damp strand of loose hair behind my ear and threaded his fingers through mine.

"Can you walk down to the *Sofi*?"

"You definitely can't carry me," I quipped.

"Shush, I totally could. But I don't think you'd want me to."

"Oh," Daniel said softly from across the way. "Right. Okay."

Panic, then guilt sluiced through me. I hadn't wanted him to find out like this.

"Daniel, I—"

"No, no, it's okay. I understand." He moved to get up. "We'll talk tomorrow. Get some rest." Daniel didn't linger to deliver or receive any more platitudes. My stomach twisted with guilt.

"I'll go see that he's all right," Evgenia said, standing. "Even though I'm still not entirely sure what happened here. But I'll take the rescuing and the handholding as good news?"

Elliot put his arm around me, and I leaned my head against his shoulder. It was like coming home.

"Oh, yay!" Carina exclaimed with a clap. "You two stopped being stubborn idiots!"

"Hey, I had very good reasons to be a stubborn idiot," I defended lightly. Evgenia snorted a laugh before excusing herself again to catch up with Daniel.

I looked at my sister and sighed resignedly. She was going to learn some harsh truths in the next twenty-four hours, about Ben's business and our mom's death. "I will tell you all about it later," I said. "But right now, I really do need sleep."

Elliot on one side and Carina on the other kept me steady as we made our way slowly but surely down to the *Sofi*. At the bedrooms, I hesitated. Where was I going to sleep?

"Come on," Elliot said, taking me over from Carina and steering us toward my bedroom. Also now his bedroom. Our bedroom?

"I'll be downstairs if you need me," Carina said, stealing me away for one last hug. "Love you, Leo."

"Love you, too." I squeezed her tight. "Don't forget to hang up your dress so it doesn't wrinkle." I left her with one last bit of levity, a balm for the news to come.

The door to my bedroom closed behind Elliot and me, and the final *snick* of it closing popped something inside me, like a pin pricking a balloon. I deflated against the wall, sliding down until I was sitting, engulfed by damp fabric and the crushing weight of the last half-hour. Elliot moved in next to me, taking my hand again.

"Do you want to talk about it?"

"I don't know." I filled my aching lungs to the brim with air, then exhaled slowly. Just breathing, being alive, nearly made me cry.

"Elliot, I'm scared for you. Miranda's going to find out about your business when she listens to that recording tomorrow."

"She already knows," he said. "Ben told me. He explained it all to her. He knew about Lind's blackmail and thought if he was straight with Miranda, something could be worked out."

I groaned. "How could he be so stupid? Elliot, what are we going to do?"

"Miranda wants in, the same deal Lind wanted," he said quietly. "She wants the black-market operation running through the *Lady Liberty*. Ben said we'd talk about it tomorrow." Elliot focused intently on his fingers, which he was meticulously kneading together. "You were right," he said after a minute. "I can't control this. If someone as big as Miranda Fairfax wants a piece, after Lind was willing to blackmail me . . . I'm no Robin Hood. I should have listened to you sooner. I have to give up the business."

My heart thudded in my ears as I processed this new information. Elliot was safe. He wouldn't be arrested or killed. All because I was right about the inherent corruption in the thing he loved. It was a Catch-22. He was heartbroken, though he would be free. But could I really be happy with him, with myself, if he was miserable?

"Miranda seems all right to me," I said, turning it over in my mind as I spoke. "My mother adored her family. The *Lady Liberty* is a good ship, right? She spearheaded the usefulness measure, even though it worked against her own ship's interests. She has to be good. Maybe she's the best and only way to make the black market work?"

"Leo . . ."

"No, hear me out. I don't want you to have to give up what you love."

"I love *you*." He turned to me, took both my hands in his. "I nearly lost you tonight, Leo, and it made things crystal clear. Nothing is worth more than you. Miranda can have the business. I don't care."

"I love you, too," I said, my voice watery with the tears threatening up my throat. They were happy tears, at least. "Nothing has to be decided tonight." I pushed off the wall and stood, offering Elliot my hands and pulling him up as well. "Now, help me out of my ruined dress and lend me one of your shirts to sleep in."

"Aye, aye, Captain!" He laughed, working deft fingers across my back, unlacing the bodice. Then his fingers stilled against my bare skin. "Leo. Couldn't you be captain? There's a power vacuum now, and you could use political power to achieve a lot of the same goals."

"Uh, no. Klara can have it," I said. "Or anyone else who wants it, for that matter. This ship needs free elections, no royal titles required. I don't want to be the best of bad options, or a pawn for ambitious men to marry."

"Is that what it was with Daniel?"

I whipped around on him. Elliot paused with one button left to go on his shirt.

"No, it wasn't like that at all. Not completely, at least. He's really sweet. I consider him a friend." I chewed my bottom lip. "I'm not looking forward to that conversation tomorrow."

"Then forget about it, just for tonight." Elliot sidled close, dropped his shirt to the floor. He kissed me, soft and tentative. We nuzzled noses, then leaned our foreheads together.

"None of this seems real," I said, closing my eyes with a sigh.

"It is," he answered. I felt his lips graze my jaw, then my neck, then my exposed shoulder. I took a step back, grabbed his arms, and used them as leverage as I stepped out of my dress.

"Last time I saw you like this, circumstances were very different," Elliot joked. I flashed back to the night of the dance party, Elliot catching me changing. He'd teased me, and I'd pushed him away.

"I wish I'd told you everything about my feelings back then, but I was convinced you were just toying with me."

"Both of us were idiots. Too proud to be honest."

"I was scared," I said. "And angry. I wanted to punch you, more than once."

"And now?" Elliot drew close, a mischievous grin playing across his features. He fingered the elaborate boning of my bustier. My breath hitched.

"I don't want to hit you anymore."

"Progress."

He kissed me on the cheek. I grabbed him by the waistband of his shorts, yanking him in close and kissing him properly.

"I was serious about going to bed," I said. "To sleep. And I still need that shirt."

"Before or after?" He waggled his eyebrows, like a huge dork.

"Don't push your luck," I chided, barely suppressing my grin.

And then there was no before, or after, only now, and then the alluring pull of sleep.

I found comfort in the rhythm of Elliot's chest, rising and falling against my back, his soft exhales gently jostling the hair at the nape of my neck. I smiled at how he always fell asleep in record time, ages before my mind would let my body settle into slumber. Some things never changed. And I had missed this. I grabbed Elliot's arm, which was slung over my waist, and curled it under my chest. Three years ago, I'd let him go. Come through a night just like this one—well, okay, not half as dramatic as this one—and I'd let it all fall apart. This time, I wouldn't let go. This would be the first night of many to come with Elliot steadfast by my side, and I by his. And with that thought, I fell soundly asleep.

EPILOGUE

The stars sparkled above our heads, sprawling like diamonds against a deep and endless black sky.

"There's Leo." Elliot used his hand to guide mine in tracing the rough pattern of a crouching animal. "And Carina." We traced that, too.

"Those are nowhere near each other in the sky," I mused, leaning back into Elliot's chest, enjoying the way it expanded and contracted steadily. His breathing mirrored the gentle *whoosh* of the waves hitting the simulated beach, in and out.

"I made a special request," he said.

"Consider it my grand compromise, since you agreed to the beach," Klara threw in beside us. She was lounging to our right, decked out in a bikini and sunglasses, despite the lack of fake sun. She tilted her head back and relaxed into a sigh. "I love the beach."

"There's no water, and I get to be fully clothed, so I'm fine," I said. It was the magic of the digi-deck. It could be whatever we wanted it to be, in any combination, and my cousin could grant us access whenever we wanted. Sure, Elliot and I had had a more solitary and romantic idea in mind, but this was fine too. It had been two weeks since the Valg Ball with everything both falling spectacularly apart and miraculously coming together, and, dammit, we all deserved an evening out.

"I like that we're together, Leo," my sister chimed in. "Even if it's unnatural. Not like it matters anyway, since we'll never see a natural sky from Earth. Or visit a natural beach."

"How surprisingly deep of you, Carina," I kidded her. Ben was rubbing off on her in a good way. And I was learning to be fine with her and Ben. I'd be a hypocrite otherwise, being with Elliot. There was still the question of him and the black market, tabled for now. Miranda had her hand in it, and we had her protection. We were playing it by ear.

"I don't want to go back to Earth. It sounds awful," Asta sniffed. "It's cold and barren."

"You are a shame to all Norwegians, and this Russian, with your aversion to the cold. But don't worry, I'll warm you up!" Evgenia said, snuggling closer to her on their shared love seat. It wasn't a real beach, so our furniture was a mixed bag.

Asta and Evgenia were officially an item now, which meant she was part of our group. I'd had to spend more than one evening the past few weeks with Theo tagging along as well. He and Daniel argued a lot, about not only politics but music. Metal verses musicals. Fortunately Theo wasn't here tonight, so Daniel was his normal, charming self.

Well, nearly normal. Things were still strained between us,

and I didn't blame him one bit for it. The breakup conversation had been painful, and I was undoubtedly the villain for going back on my promise. But he'd stayed, our friendship genuine if in need of mending. I'd tempted him with a political opportunity—he could rebuild the *Scandinavian*'s fragile governmental ecosystem . . . alongside Klara. They bickered like crazy, but without her mom around and the pressure to marry for power, Klara was slowly mellowing to her old self. Oh, of course, she was still persnickety, often shallow, and infuriatingly snobbish, but she'd ceased being actively mean.

Aunt Freja was in prison awaiting trial. No one particularly cared that she'd been underhanded with my water-filtration system, but murder was frowned upon. Carina had taken the news well enough, but Father was a wreck. He was ridiculous on a good day, but he was my dad, and so I'd taken care to spend extra time with him lately. Double the reason that a night like this was needed. At least he was happy about my engagement this time. He'd always approved of Elliot, he pretended, scrupulously avoiding the topic of Elliot's newfound wealth as the real reason he found no complaint.

"Refill?" Ben appeared with a pitcher of sangria. I nodded at him to top us up.

The hours passed with more drinks, light conversation, and even karaoke—Daniel's suggestion, of course. As everyone else launched into a rowdy group number, Elliot and I stole away to take a walk down the "beach." It was easy to get away to our own relative privacy, since the digi-deck ran the width of the ship.

"I do kind of wish there was actually an ocean," I mused as we strolled. Klara had brought in sand, which crunched and gave satisfyingly under my feet.

"Really?"

"Yeah." I shrugged. "Seems romantic."

"And terrifying. Oceans are thousands of miles tall and wide and endless fathoms deep. And they can kill you easily. Like space, but wet."

I snorted. "Space but wet? Really?"

"I'm not articulating myself well." Elliot bristled, though I knew not seriously. He and I had slowly but surely reestablished some of our old rhythms, particularly the ability to be playful with each other. There were no longer unspoken feelings and misunderstandings keeping us guessing, assuming, and ultimately apart. We had space to breathe and grow. As much as some things were effortlessly easy between us, we had both changed in three years, so there was getting to know each other again too.

"I thought you were the one who plunged into ice-cold water just to make friends," I teased him. "I'm the scaredy-cat."

"In your defense, you have a very good reason to dislike swimming."

"And you, thankfully, have immensely good timing."

He squeezed my hand, and I squeezed back. It was the closest we got to talking about what happened. I was trying my best to forget.

It was really Klara I had to thank for fortuitous timing. As soon as Elliot had told her where I was and why, she'd sounded the alarm. She knew her mother better than I'd thought. And I knew she was wracked with guilt at her worst fears having been confirmed.

We walked a few more minutes, until we nearly reached the edge of the illusion. There were carefully hidden laser lights that sparked into view when we stepped too close.

"Let's not go back yet," Elliot said, orienting us parallel to the water so we could watch the waves roll in but never reach us. I hummed my assent, liking the way his fingers threaded through mine, our joined hands keeping me comfortably weighted in the moment. I tipped my head back to once again peer at the stars. I would never get enough of them from this Earth-bound angle, false though it was.

"Leo, will you marry me?"

My head snapped back down. "What? Wasn't that already agreed upon?"

"'Agreed upon,'" he repeated. "So romantic." He bumped my shoulder playfully.

"I don't require any sweeping gestures, El."

"Well, too bad." He raised our joined hands up to the sky, guiding them as he traced more stars. "Will. You. Marry. Me. Leo?" The last word was the actual constellation. The rest was bullshit. But it was beautiful bullshit. My cheeks started to hurt from smiling so wide.

"Fine, you huge sap. Yes." I hauled him in by the lapels and kissed him soundly and surely, as I fully intended to kiss him every day for the rest of my life. Elliot was my choice. And no one would ever persuade me otherwise.

ACKNOWLEDGMENTS

They say second books are the most difficult to write, and I am no exception. But here we are! I owe massive debt of gratitude to the entire team at HMH for working me from concept to final copies.

To Emilia Rhodes, my fearsome editor, who has the patience of a saint, and who delivers edit letters like warm hugs. I learned so much from this process and I hope I've come out the other end a better craftsman. To Cat Onder, my publisher, who championed this book from its inception, and leads the best publishing team a girl could ask for.

To Tara Shanahan, rockstar publicist, for juggling a million things and doing them all brilliantly—I know I will always be well taken care of. To Tara Sonin, wizard of social media and mastermind behind Jane Austen meets The Bachelor. To everyone in marketing, publicity, sales, and editorial: Amanda Acevedo, Veronica Wasserman, Lisa DiSarro, Alia Almeida, Emma Gordon, Elizabeth Agyemang. To Colin

Mercer for a stunning cover that took my breath away and inspired a gorgeous dress. To Alix Redmond, who makes copy edits a delight.

Elana Roth Parker, my agent and favorite human, I grow more and more thankful for your business partnership and guidance daily. You never fail to say precisely the right thing, and to fight for me, no matter what.

There are so many people without whom I could not have survived the process of writing, editing, and promoting this book, but in particular, I must thank: Rosiee Thor for appearing like magic to be the friend I didn't know I needed, and for always grumbling with me over stars titles. Emily Wibberley and Austin Siegemund-Broka for writing dates at Tiago (and other places with excellent cold brew), and for all the rides (and being awesome humans, generally). Emily Duncan for reading the messiest draft zero and capslocking at me that it gave you FEELS. Deeba Zargarpur, born editor, for reading multiple drafts and offering incisive commentary at every turn—I could not have finished this book without you. Natalie Simpson, still my fasted alpha reader, and a better friend than I deserve.

Emma Theriault, you were the one that got away (that sounds creepy but you know it's not), and I am so delighted that we are friends now. Your writing is goals and you are awesome. Heather Kaczynski and Elly Blake, still thrilled to be on this publishing journey with you, and know you are always there for me when I need you. You remain some of the best people and writers that I know.

The Cobbler Club, who supports me whenever I need (especially with writing dates and dinner at the Cheesecake Factory) and forgives me when I disappear for weeks (months?) at a time: Jessica Cluess, Gretchen Schreiber, Alyssa Colman, and Emily Skrutskie. Kat O'Keeffe and Lainey Kress—thank you for not being weird about it when I basically announced we were going to be friends. I am so glad we are now.

Every amazing human who read drafts of *The Stars We Steal*, or let me brainstorm at them, or who exchanged eyes emojis with me: Emmy Neal, Mary Elizabeth Summer, Emily Lloyd Jones, Rory Power, Christine Lynn Herman, June Tan, Victoria Lee, and so many more! My AMM Fam, especially Rosiee Thor (again!), Kevin Van Whye, Liz Parker, and Rebecca Barrow.

The Electric 18s, and especially my California Electrics: I am so thankful for your friendship and support, and for all the coffee writing dates and karaoke sessions you let me pull you into. Bree Barton, Britta Lundin, Lisa Super, Maura Milan, Farrah Penn, Marie Miranda Cruz, Dana Davis, Costa Singer, Aminah Mae Safi, Leslie and Ashley Saunders, and Emily & Austin (again!).

To my WriteGirls Taya Kendall, Miranda Rector, and Joy Gursky—thank you for thinking I'm cool (for some reason) and for serving as a constant reminder that teen girls are, indeed, superheroes who will change the world.

Thank you to every librarian, bookseller, teacher, reader, book festival, fan con etc. who graciously treated me like a Real

Author, and read my words and had pretty nice things to say about them. Every event I've attended is an honor, and every comment, review, recommendation is greatly appreciated. Particularly those Actual Teens who read, thank you!

Jane Austen, for balancing feminism, class, wit, and romantic angst like no other. Especially thank you for writing *Persuasion*, which I believe reaches each of us precisely when we need it, and accordingly found me at just the right time.

And to my mom, who is always far too gracious and understanding when I disappear into my writing cave, and who forgives me, mostly, for how messy my apartment becomes in the process. You've always supported my creative process with tireless enthusiasm and belief, and I carry that with me always.